D0093690

Then Everything Happens at Once

Also by M-E Girard

Girl Mans Up

Then Everything Happens at Once

M-E Girard

HARPER TEEN

An Imprint of HarperCollinsPublishers

HarperTeen is an imprint of HarperCollins Publishers.

Then Everything Happens at Once
Copyright © 2023 by M-E Girard
All rights reserved. Printed in the United States of America.
No part of this book may be used or reproduced in any manner whatsoever without
written permission except in the case of brief quotations embodied in critical articles
and reviews. For information address HarperCollins Children's Books, a division of
HarperCollins Publishers, 195 Broadway, New York, NY 10007.
www.epicreads.com

ISBN 978-0-06-320668-7
Typography by Kathy H. Lam
22 23 24 25 26 LBC 5 4 3 2 1
First Edition

This one is for all the girls, but most especially the girls like me and the ones like Miss Beckie. ♥

ONE

Sometimes, I can imagine exactly what it's like to be other girls—girls with sugary little souls tucked into sparkling bodies. I close my eyes, and I'm there, lit up from all angles. It makes every movement, from tucking a leg under me to raising an eyebrow, feel like some graceful motion worthy of the entire universe's attention. When I've got a proper hold on that feeling—that feeling of being 100 percent grounded in my body, in a moment—I'm so completely on board with the idea that my whole self is a work of art, and it seems inevitable that someone would be at my feet in complete awe and devotion. Maybe even multiple someones—I mean, why not, right?

It's never long before that feeling goes poof, and then I'm back in the real world and feeling supremely foolish for even thinking such shittery.

Freddie is three feet away from me, and even though my eyes

have blurred from staring at his whole self, triggering sparks and foolish thoughts within, he'd never look back at me. Not in a way that goes beyond eyeballs and sight, anyway.

Have I met a guy or girl—or *anyone*—in real life who would look at a fat girl like me and think she's worth looking at? Not yet. Not ever, maybe.

Freddie is no exception.

I am standing in his garage on a frigid February Friday night, helping him work on his car, because my plans with my best friend, Lara, fell through when she decided to ditch our movie night to spend the evening either fighting with Trey or making out with him—it could plausibly be either. Trey is Freddie's best friend and the rightful car-fixing wingperson who should be at Freddie's side right now, which means the Lara and Trey drama, once again, brought Freddie and me together.

Am I crushed that this is my Friday-night backup plan? I *should* be because, well, who likes to constantly get ditched by their best friend? But I'm here, alone with Freddie. So I guess I still win.

Is it ridiculous to *know* within yourself that you have zero chance of something happening, yet you still do everything you can in case there *is* a chance? Maybe a little, but my reality is ridiculous, I guess. I feel like I'm always positioned between two opposing forces—feelings, realities, qualities, circumstances— and I'm just living in that space of contradiction. To be honest, I'm totally at home in the awkwardness of it all.

This is my life, and nothing really happens in it. My life is about watching things happen to other people and daydreaming about what it would be like if I was the star—what it *will* be like, I should say. I'm not a total pessimist.

I'm just really, *really* tired of watching.

The small but mighty heater hums from the corner of the garage, but still, I keep my red peacoat on because it looks perfect with my shiny black leggings and the black suede ankle boots on my feet. Freddie's phone rests on the workbench behind his car, and we are both standing in front of it, watching a YouTube video on replacing the transmission of an older Mustang. There is nothing the guy in the video is saying that sounds like English to my ears, so it's back to staring at Freddie. I start with the thick dark locks of hair he combs in a subtle quiff style, to his torso, which is currently obscured by a sleeveless puffer jacket but that I know is lean and defined underneath from the weights he started lifting a few years ago, and also genetics. My eyes then move to his hands, to the one bringing his vape up to his lips, and I lick my own.

The details of Freddie are sometimes *this* close to throwing me over the edge.

"You got that?" he asks.

"Totally," I say. "I was paying full attention. I could probably do it by myself if you want to simply sit and watch."

"Just guide me, and I'll tell you what I need," Freddie says as he reaches for this flat thing with wheels he calls a "creeper."

"So, like, how sure are you that this car won't fall and crush you to death?"

"Bay, do you seriously think I'd be working under my car if it wasn't a hundred percent safe?" Freddie says matter-of-factly. "My dad and I were meticulous. The Shitbox is on four jack stands, *plus* the wheels are propped on wood blocks, and they're all chocked. It hasn't moved a hair in over six months."

"If you say so."

"Okay, so we're at the clutch cable part."

I watch that part of the video again.

"It looks like he puts the long thing through a hole, and then there's a clip that slides in there?" I say. Then I laugh, thinking about the words that just came out of my mouth.

"What?"

"Nothing."

Guess it makes sense I'm the only one whose mind is not on car stuff right now. The reality is this: there is more sexual tension between Freddie and a clutch cable than there is between him and me. Still, you have to be "primed and ready for life," according to my mother. She's always told me that you can't force things to happen in life, but you can put yourself in a position where they could.

She was talking about setting yourself up for success by being not only a hard worker but a smart worker too, the way she was about the piece of land she inherited when my grandpa died and the decision she made to put a drive-through coffee place on it. I choose to apply this advice differently. I put myself right there in Freddie's path in Grade Seven, literally, on the sidewalk.

The moment I saw him, I was hooked. His face, his body, his

mannerisms, his voice, his smile—I was thirteen years old, and I knew *exactly* what was going on. It was a full-on physical, magnet-type sensation.

At that point, one of the guys in his friend group had been asking me out every single morning, just so his friends could laugh. Every single day for all of Grade Seven, *Hey, Baylee, wanna go on a date?*

Freddie didn't laugh. He would just look away, act like it wasn't happening. Doesn't sound all that thoughtful and considerate, but back then, you were either the one laughing or you were the one disengaging, walking away. Not having to lock eyes with him while I got roasted by some of the idiots he hung out with was actually . . . kind of sweet.

So naturally, I liked Freddie even more. I started talking to him as we walked home from school, headed in the same direction. At first it was about homework. Then it was about books we were reading. Pretty soon, we were talking at school, too. So here I am, *such* good friends with a guy who makes me want to do things he's only interested in doing with other girls—any girl except for me, it seems like. Friendship-wise, though, no other girl has been where I am, so there *is* that.

[Rianne] Ditched AGAIN?! If I wasn't working right now, I'd totally crash your movie thing. I miss out on everything.
[Baylee] I have to get a job. My mom keeps talking about me starting a couple nights a week at her store.

[Rianne] So DO it! You'd be the girl whose mother is her boss. You'd get away with everything!

How do I tell Rianne I've been dodging my mother's offers to hire me as a part-time barista at her drive-through coffee shop because the uniform dress code requires you to *tuck in your shirt*? I have my own dress code, and it is forbidden to wear my clothes in a way that basically screams at people to look at how fat my stomach is. I don't think I'm capable of tucking in my shirt—my arms wouldn't even cooperate with the tuckage.

[Baylee] She'd probably make me do all the worst jobs. No thanks. But Bookworm Café might be a cool place to work.
[Rianne] Yes! You should totally apply. So what are you doing now, then?
[Baylee] I'm at Freddie's to help replace his transmission.
[Rianne] Since when do you know how to fix cars?!
[Baylee] Since never. I have no idea what's going on. He said all I had to do was hand him stuff and like, supervise.
[Rianne] That sounds SO boring.

Rianne is my second-closest friend. She's the type who's always invited me to the epic parties she throws, and she continues to offer to let me borrow anything of hers I compliment, whether it's a hot-pink matte lipstick or a shirt that's clearly about forty sizes too small for me. Not that any of Rianne's things would ever suit me anyway. It's hard to describe her style, but it's basically a cross between rocker and fairy. There was a time I thought my total appreciation for Rianne's edge was bordering on crush territory, but then I came to my senses when I realized the idea of our lips touching did not make me tingle.

[Baylee] So boring but it was that or sit at home by myself.

She does not know about my massive feelings for my third-closest friend.

Freddie lies on the creeper, about to slide under the Shitbox. I head over, Freddie's phone and the almighty YouTube video in my hand. I tighten the waist ties of my coat, leaning my butt against the stool set up by the car, anchoring a foot in a bar of the stool by the pointy heel of my shoe. It occurs to me that I'm being viewed from an angle that no doubt showcases my second chin, so I suck everything in as much as I can, barely breathing, smoothing out my chins by cocking my head to the side and bringing my thick brown waves over a shoulder. It feels like it's actually working, like clenching my abdominal muscles has made everything from head to toe tighter and super attractive. I am almost able to ignore the reminder that it's all an illusion, that there is no way both my butt cheeks would even *fit* on this stool if I tried sitting on it.

These are the details of being a fat girl that knock you back down when you think for a moment that you're rocking it.

"I know we can do this," Freddie says. "We just have to follow what the guy does."

"As long as I don't break a nail in the process." I wag my shiny red nails so I can admire my fresh shellac manicure.

"I'm not promising that, but I guess I could buy you a fake nail replacement if you break one?"

"That's supersweet but also not even acceptable," I say. "*These* are real. A fake one would be so obvious."

Freddie is nearly invisible as he rolls under the car, so I grab my phone. My latest text to Lara went unanswered. No surprise there, and I'm not even mad. Freddie's presence keeps me zen, I guess. Or maybe it's just a layer of zen over a mess of agony, but whatever. It works.

I scroll through videos of winged eyeliner techniques for hooded eyes on TikTok for a while, then switch to Instagram so I can play this game where I mindlessly flick my thumb against the screen, making my IG feed page go faster and faster. Then I leave a comment on whatever post it stops on. The first time I do it, it's an ad for cold medicine, but I don't scroll again. I leave a comment, because that's the rule of the game. Rules must be followed, even if they don't make sense. Even if they're stupid.

[Baylee] This looks great. I can't wait to have a cold again so I can try this! 🖤

I'm fairly certain my phone is spying on me, because just earlier, I was talking to Freddie about this news article my mother sent me about this new virus in China, and all of a sudden, there are ads for cold medicines coming up.

I play the game again, and this time, it's a bright photo of a new blended coffee drink at Bookworm Café. Now I'm sure my phone is spying. I love that place, not only because of the amazing drinks and delicious sweets, but also because it's nestled inside a huge bookstore. The colorful chalkboard sign behind the new drink reads, *How Oreo doin'?*

[Baylee] Whoever photographs your products is doing a stellar job. 📧

Freddie asks me for clarification on something, and I realize his phone's gone dark because I've been busy on mine.

"Oops," I say. "Can you unlock your phone?"

I hold it low to the ground, and he taps in his code to unlock it.

"Can you hold this?" Freddie asks, his hand coming out from under the car, some dirty metal thing in it.

"Um, hang on," I say, my eyes searching the garage and falling on a pair of men's gloves on the workbench. I slip a hand inside one of them and reach for the gross thing Freddie's handing over, then dump everything on the workbench, including the gloves.

An Instagram DM alert comes through minutes later from someone I don't know.

[Alex] Hey. I don't mean for this to come off as creepy, but I'm the Bookworm photographer. TY for the comment. It's going to make me look good to my bosses. 😎

Well, that's interesting and totally unexpected.

I click over to this Alex person's profile. *Loyal friend—romantic—hard worker—partial high school dropout—lover of vintage things.* Three hundred followers and fewer than twenty posts. His page is made up of shots of different angles of an old car, vinyl records, a beat-up old leather jacket. No face shown in any post. Just a few blurry, shadowy partial body shots of some skinny young guy angled away from the camera. There's a little spark in my belly, a tiny indicator that lets me know I will form a crush if I keep looking. At this point, I could probably form a crush on an inanimate object without trying.

"Are you going through my phone?"

"I wasn't going to," I say, but now it's the only thing I can think of doing, so I pull up his texts. "Who's Natasha?"

"Hey! My privacy," he says.

"You're the one who gave me the idea!" I say. My thumb settles on a name. "You're still talking to Jess?" It takes everything in me not to open the conversation and snoop more deeply. I highly dislike Jess—the older, supercool, most cliché-attractive girl ever. The whole time they dated last summer, I barely got to hang out with him. Her moving away in September was a precious gift from the universe.

"Sometimes," he says.

"Then who's Natasha?"

"Just a girl I also sometimes talk to."

Our text convo is near the top, but he's got me listed as Baylee Kunkel. The formality makes no sense to me until I get lower down the list and find another text convo with a Baylee.

"You're talking to some other girl named Baylee?"

"Am I?"

"Yes," I say. "Last thing you said to her was 'I don't know—depends on the day,' when she asked what you do for fun. Stellar conversation, by the way."

"Oh, *that* girl. She was from the mall. Kind of weird."

"So now she gets to be Baylee in your phone, and I'm Baylee Kunkel."

"Change yours to Bay, then, and delete her altogether."

I delete the fake Baylee and consider deleting Jess. But instead, I pick myself as contact and change my name to *Ms. Baylee Marie Kunkel, Friend & Classmate*.

Nothing more.

"And Alice—who's that?" I ask. "She sounds old."

"She's not," he says.

"You can talk to that many people at once?"

"Yeah. Why not?"

"But you're like, trying to hook up with all of them?"

"Not really. I'm just feeling them out, seeing who might be interesting. Different."

Different from what?

His arm comes out from under the car. "Here, take this, too."

I slip on the glove and offer my hand again.

"Those are my good leather gloves," Freddie says.

"Yes, well, these are my flawless, clean hands."

He reaches over with his grease-streaked hand and brushes a finger against my exposed ankle, leaving a grayish smudge.

I stare at my ankle with my mouth hanging open. I should be very irritated right now. This is disgusting car grease.

Freddie rolls partially out from under the car. "What? Are you seriously mad?"

"I need to go home now and shower."

"No, you *cannot*," Freddie says. "I need assistance. You are staying."

"Fine," I say. "But you need to clean this."

He reaches for a dirty rag and starts to wipe at my ankle, but it's not skin on skin, so it's not that exciting.

"Never mind," I say, and I head over to the couch to fetch a makeup wipe from my purse. When I right myself, one of my boobs wastes no time wedging itself under its underwire, and my underwear rolls down my belly. I've gotten skilled at dealing with my wardrobe malfunctions in a way that goes unnoticed, but I still live in perpetual fear of Freddie's face registering just how much of an awkward ogre I sometimes am when I get up. When I do anything, really. But knowing him, he'd just look away, pretend he hadn't noticed, preserving my dignity.

This is why I can never hold on to the feeling of being in my body, grounded in a moment. There's always a thing that knocks me right back to awkwardness.

At the car, I resume my leaning against the stool, going back to my phone, to the DM from a mystery guy named Alex.

[Baylee] You're welcome. 😊 Did you come up with that pun, too? Or was that your bosses? 😶

[Alex] 😄 That was all me. 😎 I know it's a little cheese, but what else could I do with Oreo?

[Baylee] True. Kind of random, but is there a dress code at Bookworm Café?

[Alex] Just that whatever we wear has to be black, that way the green vest pops.

[Baylee] I have always wanted to work there.

[Alex] Do you have experience?

[Baylee] Not really, but my mother owns a coffee place. A drive-thru by the highway.

[Alex] Ahhhh, so coffee is in your blood then. But aren't u breaking ur mom's 💜 fraternizing with the enemy?

[Baylee] I would be but black is my color whereas burgundy is not.

[Alex] Is burgundy anyone's color? 😵

[Baylee] 🙆

"Okay, can you show me the next part again?" Freddie asks.

"Shit—your phone's locked again."

"What are you doing?" Freddie calls. Then his head pops out from under the car, and it almost touches my ankle. "You're supposed to be assisting."

"Supervising," I say.

"Why would I need a supervisor? I need someone to *assist*."

"I felt I deserved a promotion. Anyway, as your assisting supervisor," I say, "I have to ask what would happen if we don't put everything back properly and your transmission falls out when you drive?"

"It won't. But let's say it does," he says. "We could just blame it on my dad."

My face twists in a sad pout, and we lock eyes together. "Yeah, we totally could. And if I break a nail, it'll be his fault, too."

Six months ago, Freddie's father up and left to move in with the woman he was seeing on the side—we found out one night when we overheard his mother on the phone. I promised I wouldn't tell anyone, and I didn't.

Except for Lara and my journal, but it's assumed that any new piece of information I'm given will be shared with them.

"I'm going to fix this car myself and he can just keep paying for the parts," Freddie says. "Sure, it's all his fault that I'm not driving my car yet, even though I've had my G2 license for over a month, but it's just a minor bummer. Isn't it pretty zen here now that he's gone?"

"It's like, next-level zen," I say.

There was definitely always tension between him and his dad, but they also spent a lot of time doing stuff on weekends together. This isn't the first car Freddie's given a makeover to.

"Is he visiting this weekend?" I ask.

Freddie shrugs. His dad comes for a few hours every other weekend, mostly to visit Freddie's two-year-old sister. Freddie's got an open invitation to spend weekends at his dad's new house, an hour away, but he's never been.

"Do you think Shaya can tell he's gone?"

"Doubt it. For a whole year before he left, he was supposedly '*working late*,' so it's not like he was around that much. She's just happy to be with my mom all the time," Freddie says. Then he rolls out from under the car. "Tonight would've been a lot more fun if the car was already running, though. We could've been taking a road trip right now."

"Yes! Where would we have gone?"

"Well, there's this food truck park like, thirty minutes north of here."

"Really?"

"Yeah, fifteen food trucks in a row," he says. "Mexican. Caribbean. Greek food. Fried mac and cheese, chicken and waffles."

That literally sounds like a dream, but as if I'd go stuff my face next to Freddie. Anytime we eat around each other, I try to have the appetite of a tiny little girl, and I save my real eating for home.

"What about going to Port Perry?" I say. "There are all these cute little shops, and it's by the water."

"Let me look it up," he says.

Freddie and I end up on the couch, and I look over as he scrolls through his phone.

Say he leaned over and kissed me right now. Is this what it would be like to be his girlfriend? Do I *want* to be his girlfriend? All I know is I want what's happening right now, *plus* I want to see him naked. I want whatever that is.

"Check this bookshop out," he says. "I bet they have old screen-writing books there."

"Probably," I say. "How's your script coming, anyway?"

He shrugs and plays me the meme of some sports guy sitting at a table for a press conference, and in a thick Greek accent, the guy goes, "Sometimes maybe *good*, sometimes maybe *shit*."

I laugh. "Oh, I'm sorry. Can I read it?"

"No way."

I might not be allowed to read his script, but I treat the fact that I know about it as sacred. "Why is it a secret, though?"

"It's like this thing I really want to be good at, except I don't really know what I'm doing," he says. "It makes me feel like some kind of loser who thinks he's something he's not, you know?"

Yes, I do know—not about writing, but definitely about other things. "Why would you feel that way?" I ask.

He shrugs and keeps scrolling while I watch the screen of his phone. Finally, he goes, "When I was like, eleven, I wrote a poem and my dad laughed."

"What a turd!"

"I mean, the poem was really bad, and I hate poetry, so I don't know why I decided to write this rhyming paragraph of shit, but still. You don't laugh when your kid shows you something they wrote, right?"

"Nope. That's next-level mean." I think for a minute. Then I say, "Maybe you should take a screenwriting class and make your dad pay for it."

"Maybe."

"Well, we should totally go to Port Perry. Then you can sit by the water and write your script, and I'll bring my journal so I can write down super-deep thoughts while the breeze flows through my hair."

Deep thoughts about how I can't handle how much I want him to touch my ankle again.

"Too bad it's February, or else I'd borrow my mom's car and we could go tomorrow," he says.

"Well, maybe we could still go?" Anticipation builds inside me, and it becomes full-on butterflies as Freddie turns his head to look at me. "I mean, it might be pretty in the winter, too."

He goes to answer, but suddenly the garage door starts to rise.

Lara stands a few feet behind Trey, and her arms are folded, a clear indicator that they've had yet another fight.

Freddie climbs to his feet and heads over to bump fists with Trey, and I deflate internally as the butterflies die.

TWO

I avoid making eye contact with Lara for the sixty seconds it takes to reset my expectations and shove down the disappointment of having been robbed of my private Freddie moment. I remind myself that nothing would've happened anyway, that I would've gone home in a few hours, totally turned on and next-level frustrated. The zen layer is safely restored.

Lara is stone-faced, but when we look at each other, she kind of shrugs like, *Well, this sucks.*

Trey is that guy who had a pretty face as a young boy and probably hated how it made people assume he'd be sweet and non-threatening, so he went the other way, bulking up, permanently squaring his shoulders, and always maintaining a serious, smoldering expression to prevent the dimpled, twinkly-eyed smile from poking through too often. He used to laugh along with the others when I'd get asked out every morning back in the day, but this is not something I hold against him. When we all started hanging out together, it's like all the stuff that happened before then got filed away somewhere and we moved on. Besides, if I were to avoid associating with anyone who made fun of me and/or laughed at my expense before we got to high school, I'd probably be an awkward loner.

Lara came later. First day of Grade Nine, having just moved to Castlehill, our Toronto suburb. If I had to describe her in two words, I'd pick fierce and sophisticated. She's Sri Lankan, as tall as me—five nine or so—with thick, silky dark hair that cascades down her back. She's also got near perfectly shaped eyebrows that accent her hot-girl resting bitch face. Near perfect because the perfect eyebrows belong to me. Another thing about Lara is that where Rianne has to shop very carefully for accessories that complement her style, and I basically just have *one* store I can shop at so I make do with what's there, Lara looks more put-together than all the other girls our age because every article of clothing in just about every store is *made* for her. Also, her parents have money.

Right now, she's wearing skintight black jeans ripped at the knees, a drop-shoulder oversized cream sweater, and a tan trench coat.

"It's about time," Freddie tells Trey. "This is getting old, bro. You could at least text me to let me know you're going MIA."

"Why didn't you ask Rav to come help until I got here?" Trey and his white teeth say.

"Because Baylee is a lot more help than Rav."

"True, true." Trey laughs, then unzips his jacket and heads over to the car. "Men, let's get to work! Girls, you can have a seat and watch."

"Oh my god—*so* fun!" Lara says, rolling her eyes so hard I worry they might not fall back into place.

"Most fun I'll have had all night!" Trey says, mimicking the same overly enthused tone.

"How sexist can you be?" Lara says, and he pretends to put his fingers in his ears. "And no one wants to watch you guys work on that piece-of-shit car."

"Come on," Freddie says. "Her name might be the Shitbox, but she is not a piece of shit."

"Well, it's broken and it's not a very nice-looking car," Lara says with a shrug. Freddie fixes her with a glare. "What? It's true."

"You're so *nice*, Lara," Freddie says. "Your honesty is *so* refreshing."

Trey laughs, and I cover my face with my hands.

Lara tips her head toward the door as she makes eye contact with me. I climb to my feet in the most graceful way I can manage.

"Time to go," I say to the room, then to Freddie, "Okay, well, bye."

"Port Perry," he says, with a thumbs-up, and I try not to smile too wide.

"Port Perry what?" Trey asks.

"Nothing," Freddie says.

Trey and Freddie become completely car focused as Lara and I slip out into the night. I punch in the garage code we all know, closing the door behind us. Our steps leave a trail of crunching sounds behind us as we make our way down Freddie's driveway, which is lined in a thin layer of icy snow.

I expect her to unload about Trey and what a piece of crap he is, but instead, she says, "I'm sorry about tonight. I really am."

Still, I'm not letting her off the hook that easily. "You know what? I've gotten used to this."

Lara groans. "I'm sorry."

"I mean, I thought we were going to have a stellar evening— you, me, my mom, and Rebecca, watching *Dirty Dancing* or *Mean Girls* in our pajamas. But it's fine. You know how much experience I have getting excited about things despite knowing they'll *never* happen. I've trained my whole life."

She lets out an exaggerated sigh.

My training has largely consisted of hundreds of elaborate scenarios I've created about myself and Freddie, mostly, but also the other seventy-five crushes I've had since Grade Six or Seven. My pastimes include manicures, reading, writing in my journal, and whipping myself up into a sparkly ball of excitement over stories that are totally imaginary.

Lara is the one person who knows this, who can watch me from her seat in English class and tell that I'm daydreaming about something that's most definitely boosting my heart rate.

We stroll down Freddie's street, soon passing the walkway that would lead to my house. I guess we're going to take the long way so we can talk.

"I know I've been kind of flaky, but Baylee—sometimes it's really hard to talk to you about what I'm going through with Trey because . . ."

"Because what?"

"Can I be totally honest?"

I shrug.

"Well, you're always so black and white about everything. You're kind of harsh. It just makes me feel like you don't understand where I'm coming from because . . . well, you can't relate."

Ugh.

I want to be the kind of friend who can have real discussions—discussions about uncomfortable things—and stay super collected and even-tempered. I think Lara is like that, and maybe I'm trying to be something I'm not. Because I just want to call her a bitch right now for saying what she said.

"Are you mad at me?" she asks. "You said I could be honest."

"I'll be honest, too, then." I glance over to gauge her reaction, and she looks all ready and willing to hear what I have to say. "It's pretty clear to me. I'm sitting here, watching it all go down, the same thing happening over and over. It's like you *want* the drama and the games. Why else are you still hanging around Trey? You two never get along for more than twenty minutes before it falls apart."

The truth is, I find it kind of exciting, being part of the Trey and Lara drama—the arguments, the tears, the storming off in the night, Freddie and I in frequent communication as we each handle our respective best friend through it all. It's literally the closest I get to experiencing anything real. The sweet agony of romance woes—I want that so bad. Even the woes part, although I've observed enough to know how to avoid making the same mistakes, not to end up in the same shitty situations everyone around me gets into. You see it all so clearly when you're on the sidelines, and I've been taking mental notes.

"Okay," she says. "Maybe that's how it looks from the outside, but trust me, no one goes into it *looking* for drama."

"How are you not mad at me for what I said?" I ask.

"You weren't mad at me for what *I* said."

Except I was—I am—I just spend a lot of time acting differently on the outside from what I feel on the inside.

"How come you're so calm and mature when you and I talk, but when it's Trey, you're just . . . ?"

"I'm what?"

Dramatic, petty, *annoying*. "Different."

"Trey and I are definitely not good for each other," she says. "I don't think he likes me, and I think I've been pretending I don't see it."

"Lara—do you actually like *him*? If your answer is yes, then please elaborate by telling me what you actually like about him," I say. Lara thinks it over, and when she goes to open her mouth, I hold up a finger at her. "Nothing about his looks."

"He has a really sexy voice—"

"Vocal cords are body tissues!"

"I know! I'm just kidding," she says, but I'm not convinced. She shrugs. "I don't know. I guess I was hoping there would be more in there. Like I'd be the first girl to get to know the real Trey."

"He used to eat worms when we were seven."

"Stop!" Lara says, then she frowns. "Well, what do you like about Freddie?"

"What does it matter? He's not my boyfriend."

"But you want him to be."

I shrug. "I'm not sure."

"You must," Lara says, stopping to meet my gaze. "Or else what would be the point of having such a big crush on him?"

"I guess there is no point."

Freddie is the ultimate thing I get excited about, despite knowing it'll never happen. That fact makes my insides hurt. No—more like burn with rage. Freddie and all the boys I've crushed on, they only date certain types of girls. Types that aren't me. The fat-positive girls I follow on Instagram and TikTok tell me there are people out there who are into girls like me, but out there is clearly not here. Half of Grade Eleven is already over, I'm going to be seventeen in less than two weeks, and I'm still just sitting here yearning. Yearning for very specific physical things to happen, and I want them to happen with Freddie.

Sometimes I wonder if Lara is acting on the outside as much as I am. "Maybe you think you like Trey but really, it's just that you want to mess around with him?"

Her eyes get wide. "No! I am not that kind of girl."

I *am* that kind of girl, I guess. Or I would be if I could. I'm like, the purest, virginal slutty girl there is.

"Okay, but would you enjoy his company enough to just be friends with him?"

"We used to be friends, before we started dating."

"No, you weren't. We just all hang out together—you, me, Freddie, Trey, Rav, Rianne, sometimes Matt and Steph—but we are not all *actually* friends. I would never call Rav my friend and hang out with him alone. He's just there. Same goes for Trey. He's really hot, but he's kind of blah as a person."

"He really is hot," she says with a heavy sigh. "Maybe we need new friends."

We resume walking, and the cold is threatening to make its way up my back. I am so regretting letting my legs agree to follow her on the long way home to my house.

"Anyway, the Trey stupidity is over. This is the last breakup."

"You break up every couple weeks."

"This one is real—I swear on my Jimmy J Smoky Glam Shadow Palette," she says, and my mouth forms into an O. "I know! This isn't a joke. You're my best friend and I want to apologize for deserting you over a guy. I just get caught up in the moment, and I don't think clearly. That's not a good excuse, though."

"Okay, but what makes this time different? He's still the same sexy sack of meat."

"The difference is me. I am not weak. I want to be like you," she says.

"What do you mean? What I am like?"

"You're comfortable by yourself. You can get in your own head, sure, but you're just you. You don't need someone else—you just said you're not even waiting around for Freddie to be your boyfriend. You're doing your own thing, and that's enough for you. I want to be like that."

"Wow," I say.

"What?"

"Nothing." I guess I'm really selling this version of myself I'm projecting.

We reach the stop sign and loop left, taking my street.

"So, what are you going to do about Trey?"

"I need to turn my focus to something that isn't him," she says. "So that's going to be . . . you! You're going to be my substitute boyfriend."

"Interesting," I say. "You are so not the kind of girl I'd date."

"That's slightly insulting," she says. "Are you trying to make me cry?"

"I'm just saying, you're not my type." I shrug. "Way too girly. Plus kind of clingy."

"Come on! You'll love the cling. It'll be the opposite of the ditching—think about it." She wags her eyebrows to entice me.

My mind flashes to all our makeover nights, Bookworm outings, movie dates, Music Discovery Events—which is something I invented where we each present five new songs to the other, lying down on Lara's bedroom floor with our eyes closed, patchouli incense burning, so we can fully absorb the lyrics and melodies. It would be nice to go back to hanging out all the time, the way we used to.

"We could have a Five-Minute-Crafts Sunday," she says.

"Ooh!" The excitement pulls my face in all directions, I'm sure. "Yes! I saw this one craft with cement and twine—it was such a *mess*, and it was so ugly!"

"I bet we can get Rianne to put it on TikTok," Lara says.

"Okay, I accept! I'll be your boyfriend," I say.

She smiles and sighs with what I assume is relief that all is forgiven, and we can start over.

My house comes into view. "Do you want to come over? I know we're already walking to my house, but do you want to come in to try and salvage our plans?"

"They're already salvaged," Lara says. "I texted your mom."

"You texted my mom? When?"

"Like, five minutes ago."

"What did she say?"

"She says she's pleased to know Movie Date is back on, and she's putting Bagel Bites in the oven as we speak."

"That's a little bold, inviting yourself over behind my back like that," I say.

"I know. So clingy."

As Lara and I continue down my street, I pull up a photo of the Alex Bookworm guy so she can see. "What do you think of him? Is it just me or is he, like, oozing with hotness?"

She brings my phone closer to her face. "You're basing this on what? He's all blurry. Is his face in any of these?"

"His right upper limb is very sexy."

Lara laughs and I loop my arm through hers.

"Who is he?" Lara says.

"Just someone who works at Bookworm," I say.

"Why are you stalking Bookworm employees?"

"I was bored because you ditched me, remember?"

"Oh, right."

We make our way up my driveway, and I unlock the front door. Lara goes in ahead of me, and I'm about to swipe my IG app closed, but in the spirit of being primed and ready for life, I send the Alex Bookworm guy another DM. Just in case.

THREE

The next morning, I stretch out on the couch, my mascara-gooped eyes prying themselves open long enough to catch a glimpse of Lara passed out on her sleeping bag, one leg up on the couch. This happens a lot at Movie Date nights, being too tired to make it up to my bedroom, so we crash in the living room. I take off my hoop earrings and massage my battered earlobes before mashing the side of my face against a throw pillow—which is precisely the moment my sister, Rebecca, decides to wake up and start having a tantrum. She's about ten feet away from the couch, in the space that would normally be a dining room. Her bed is modified for accessibility, so it looks kind of like a crib, but higher off the ground and with shorter rails. I pull myself up, leaning over the back of the couch to see what's up. From here, someone might assume my sister is two years old, because she's so small, but she's actually twelve. She holds her breath and waves her arms around in anger-infused panic. Mom is bent over the crib rail, pulling back the covers and giving my sister room to have her fit.

Most nights of the week, there is a nurse here to look after my sister, but not on Fridays, which is the reason for Mom's makeshift bed on the floor next to Rebecca's crib and also why Movie Dates are on Fridays. We make a thing of it.

Lara rolls over but keeps sleeping.

"Want me to get Tylenol?" I ask my mother.

"That might be a good idea," she says.

We don't always know why Rebecca gets upset, since she's non-verbal and has some pretty severe cognitive impairments, so Mom likes to cover her bases in case something hurts. Rebecca has cerebral palsy, among other conditions, and over time, her muscles have gotten short and stiff in places, which means when she's been lying in the same position awhile, like when she sleeps, she can wake up sore and next-level grumpy.

I roll off the couch and slip by my mother as she now rocks Rebecca. Mom's in the black silk robe I gave her for Christmas last year. She is the only person I know who I could technically swap clothes with, but this would never happen. My mother is a fat lady who thinks there is nothing wrong with this mandatory tuckage of shirts into pants at work—enough said.

In the kitchen, I pick up one of the clean plastic syringes propped up to dry on the rack. I measure exactly five milliliters of the thick pink Tylenol liquid. I fill another syringe with five milliliters of water from the bottle that's replaced daily with fresh boiled water. I can't really look after Rebecca on my own because there are a lot of complicated things to worry about, but I can help out in little ways like this.

My house is sort of like the kind of house I picture some recluse of a poet would live in, a drunk one with an aversion to sunlight. The furniture is old, dark wood or velour, lumpy and comfortable. The walls are warm autumn colors, with heavy drapes blocking the sun from coming in, but the lamps throw just the right amount of yellow light to create the best shadows. The decor is courtesy of my grandpa, who died when I was really little. Mom moved us into his house and left almost everything as is. Later, she realized the darkness helped with my sister's sleep, which is a constant battle with her, so everything just stayed the same.

The dining room is my sister's room because it's important to have everything accessible and close to the exit, should there ever be an emergency.

Mom continues cradling Rebecca, pulling my sister's shirt up to reveal the feeding tube that sticks out of her belly. I connect the syringe of medicine to the tube and push the liquid through, followed by the syringe of water. My mom taught me how to do this a few years ago—only under her supervision, though.

"I can hold her," Lara says, padding over from the living room.

"Good morning, Lara," Mom says as Lara takes a seat in the rocking chair by the window. Mom checks her watch. "Baylee, we better get a move on."

"What are you guys doing today?" Lara asks.

"We don't have a clue yet," Mom says. "Might have to just see where the day takes us. You want to come?"

One Saturday a month, we have an outing for Rebecca. Sometimes it's Bookworm, or the museum downtown, or the grocery store, or the lake in the summer. I could be sleeping in or hanging out with my own friends, but the outings are nonnegotiable. My mom's rules must be followed.

"I can't. My parents want me home for the afternoon. My uncle is coming from Toronto," Lara says, rolling her eyes to convey her excitement about the whole thing. Mom places Rebecca on Lara's lap. Lara holds her around the waist the way I taught her and bounces my sister on her lap a bit. Rebecca hangs forward, her head kind of lolling to the side, and soon, the first smile breaks through. "I can hang out with her while you guys go up to get ready, though."

"That's nice of you. You're doing a great job. Beck looks comfortable. I'll have the baby monitor on, so holler if you need anything," Mom says.

I reach for my phone just as it buzzes with a text.

[Freddie] Hey. You should come over later.
[Baylee] It's Beck Field Trip Day. Maybe after dinner?
[Freddie] OK. Well, text me when you're back.

"Mom," I say, "can we go to the mall?"
"Sure."

"Will we be back by five?"

"Of course we'll be back by five," Mom says. "We'll be back by four, max."

"You can come sleep over tonight, if you want," Lara says.

"Okay! I might swing by Freddie's later, though."

"Maybe I could come?"

"Oh. Okay," I say, my back to her. "I'll text you when we're back."

"I told you you'd love the cling!" Lara says as I head up the stairs to my room.

It's the only part of the house that doesn't have the same old-grandfather decor, because I painted it myself. Purple walls with big butterflies outlined in black. Lara and I did it all in one weekend.

"What's this cling thing about, Boss?" Mom asks, having followed me up the stairs.

Boss is my mother's nickname for me. Apparently, even when I was a baby, I was stubborn and would only ever do what I wanted, when I wanted, so she started calling me Boss. My sister is the exact same way. There are times she won't even wake up when Mom and the nurse are getting her dressed for school and settled in her wheelchair—she'll just keep on sleeping and let out these whines of annoyance when they bother her, trying to braid her hair. She'll sleep all through school, then she'll stay up all night, giggling and doing what she wants. Mom likes to blame this trait on our sperm donor, and she says that pigheadedness should've been listed in his donor profile. Better than being a pushover, I guess.

"She's breaking up with Trey," I say, stepping into my walk-in closet to flip through outfits. "For real this time. And I'm the thing she's going to focus on to keep from going back. She's going to pretend I'm her boyfriend and cling to me."

"Oh," Mom says, taking a seat on my bed. "Well, that sounds interesting. Except you don't seem to want her to come with you to Freddie's later."

"It's not that," I say.

"Oh, okay. I must be wrong, then."

Mom gets up, looking ready to bolt from my room. She's always got something to do, somewhere to go.

"Well, it's just . . . ," I say, coming out of my closet. "If Trey ends up at Freddie's tonight, too, it'll cause drama. And if it's just Freddie, well, he and Lara don't really like each other, so it'll be awkward. Either way, the fun gets sucked out of it."

Mom sits back down. "What about Rianne? Why doesn't she come, too?"

"It's Saturday, Mom. I told you she always closes at the ice cream shop on Saturdays."

"Well." Mom takes a breath, looking like she's giving some serious thought to my problem. "How about you spend the night at Lara's and you go see Freddie tomorrow? She needs her boyfriend, right?"

I shrug, laying a couple of outfit choices on my bed.

"So, what's our plan for the mall? Laser tag and food court?"

"I was kind of hoping to get a new shirt or something. There's a clearance sale."

"How about we do the laser tag place first, then we'll wander the mall for a bit?"

"Deal."

Mom nods as she gets up from my bed, glancing at the baby monitor to make sure all is well.

[Baylee] I'll come around 5.
[Freddie] 🖼

FOUR

A little while later, my mother drops Lara off at home on our way to the mall. Rebecca giggles with glee from her car seat at the back of our mom's minivan, and I turn up the volume of this irritating folk music my sister can't get enough of.

"My ears are bleeding!" I yell.

"Mine, too," Mom says, and we laugh.

At the mall, Mom and I unload Rebecca's custom wheelchair from the back. Mom scoops Rebecca up and straps her in, then zips the fleece liner that covers Rebecca's whole body so that only her head sticks out. This way we don't have to dress her in winter clothes, and it's easy to take off when we're inside so she doesn't overheat. It can still be a whole production, which might draw some stares, but getting stared at is nothing we're not all very used to in this family.

The laser tag place is attached to the mall, so we go in through the mall entrance. The guy at the counter recognizes my mother and waves us in. It's like Rebecca can already tell what's about to happen, because her arms start going, swatting at the air. We get ushered through an employee door off to the side, and suddenly everything is dark around us.

"They're a little rambunctious today, so I'll put the walls up," the guy says to my mother.

The arena appears before us, and even though I wouldn't be caught dead running around, chasing and getting chased for fun, my eyes just love the experience of being in here. It's pitch-dark, but there are lights everywhere that make it look like some kind of futuristic spot in space. Rebecca loves neon colors and lights—this is next-level magical for her, I'm sure. Years ago, my mother worked out this deal with the owner of the place that she gives him and his husband free coffee whenever they come by the store, and he lets us in to watch. Kids are chasing each other in the dark, yelling and laughing as they fake-shoot each other, which is another thing my sister loves—I mean the noise, not the shooting.

Mom parks the wheelchair against the wall, and the guy wheels over a couple of panels to put at our sides, just enough to keep anyone from slamming into us. We lay a vest across my sister's lap, the strips of pink lights across it glowing and flashing, and for the next thirty minutes, she is mesmerized. I put my phone brightness to the lowest setting, and I pass the time texting Rianne and Lara in our group chat, while Mom responds to work emails.

[Lara] Text me when you're done. Are you still going to Freddie's?

[Baylee] I'm not sure.

[Lara] Okay, well, if you need a ride to my house, my dad said we could come get you.

[Baylee] Ok. Thank you.

It's so nice of her father to offer that, but all I can think of is Freddie. My whole entire day will be about him now, even though I know I shouldn't let myself get swept up like this. What I should be doing is spending the night with Lara. This is literally day one of the substitute boyfriend plan—I can't already be feeling like I need my own space.

Once we're done with Rebecca's thing, I've come to the conclusion that I will do both things: see Freddie alone first, then head to Lara's a little later than usual. Pretty much having my cake and eating it, too. Or more like eating two pieces of cake in the same night as opposed to saving one for the next day. Everything all at once—that's totally me.

I power through the mall as fast as my heeled winter boots will allow, because I'm on a mission to find something cute to wear for tonight. Soon, we arrive at the one and only store in this town that carries stylish clothes in my size.

Mom pushes Rebecca along, several feet behind me. The fingers of my left hand are crossed with the hope that the decent stuff isn't already picked through. The reality is, the only way I'm able to shop here is if there's a killer sale going, or if I have cash coupons. I used to think that it only made sense for bigger clothes to cost more money, because there's a ton more fabric involved. But then I saw this TikTok by a seamster who basically was like, if that was the logic, then shirts that are XXS would cost way less than size large, but they don't. It's only fat people who pay more for clothes. Another rule that doesn't make sense, but you just live with it.

"Are we looking for anything in particular?" Mom asks, parking Rebecca in front of a couple of mannequins wearing neon-colored items, which grabs my sister's attention instantly.

"I'm basically open to anything that fits and, um, doesn't look like it's made for an old lady," I say. "No offense."

"I'm not old! Forty-five isn't old."

"Okay, well, that isn't made for a mom, then."

I flick through the racks fast, grabbing different sizes of the same tops because it's anyone's guess how any particular item will fit. I sometimes get lost in a 2XL, and other times my body might barely squeeze into a 4XL. I add a tunic top in the prettiest shade of cherry red I've ever seen to my modest pile of choices.

"Ooh, very nice," Mom says. "Show Beck."

I hold it in front of my sister, who immediately tries to swat at it. It totally clashes with the purple unicorn shirt she's got on.

The few minutes that I firmly believe each item in my hands will look amazing on me fill me with confidence and glee. In reality, I already know I won't get the red top because it's not black, and the eighties graphic tee is cute, but it's too short to cover my whole belly, and the silky-gold tank is made of a spandex-type fabric that is too thin, which means it'll snake over each curve and fat roll like a layer of plastic wrap.

There's a code I live by when it comes to the way I look, the way I present myself to the world. You just *do not* knowingly accessorize with something that'll accentuate your fat. Sure, a flowing black top will still allow outlines of fat to show through—I know I'm not fooling anyone—but that's not the same as knowingly contouring the fat with bright colors and clingy fabric. It's not the same as tucking your shirt into your pants.

"I have my own personal standards, Mother."

"Your standards are a little rigid, Boss."

It's worth noting that my standards and rules are only my own. Do I think it's the worst thing in the world when another fat girl tucks her shirt into her pants? No. Do I sometimes even think it looks cute? Yes. Will I do it? *Never.* It wasn't a decision I made to come up with these rules. They must've appeared at some point, but to me, it's like they've always been there.

On my way to the change room is my favorite section of the store, underwear and lingerie. Last year, I spent all my Christmas money on one of the fancy, push-up-plunge bras that are arranged high on the wall, prominently displaying their back-fat-smoothing design. It changed my life—no exaggeration. Wearing a bra is torture on account of the wire stabs and strangulation marks courtesy of the bands and straps, but with this design, it hurts like, 75 percent less.

"Stop it," Mom says from where she flips through the rack of clearance dress pants. "Keep moving."

Too late. I fall deeply in love with a hot-pink leopard-print set that comes with matching underwear. "Moooom!"

"No."

"Mother, *please*. This is life or death," I say, already reaching for the back of the rack, looking for my size. "I have a coupon for forty percent off a regular-priced item!"

Mom sighs. "Just go try things on, and we'll see."

In the change room, I waste no time slipping the most beautiful bra in the world over my D-cup boobs, and it looks as amazing as I knew it would, seeing as the other two bras I rotate through at home are the exact same design, just in simple black instead. I come out in the red tunic over the black leggings I came in with. "Mom?"

My mother steers Rebecca's chair between the racks of clothes, making her way into the change room hallway, blocking the way for the two other ladies who are trying to come try stuff on.

"I'm sorry. I just need a second," Mom says as she tries to maneuver around the boxes, empty racks, and clusters of plastic hangers. Rebecca's chair is lightweight and low-profile, but it's still a chore to get around the random crap store employees have piled against the wall. The women wait with polite smiles.

"Oh, Boss. " Mom grimaces. "That shirt is not appropriate at all."

"I know. It fits all stupid."

The neckline is hanging so low that my future bra is on display, clashing with the red of the shirt, while the waist sits too snug against me. Why do these designers assume being this fat means having a flat stomach while *also* having Triple Z boobs?

"Go try the other stuff," Mom says.

I come out in the eighties graphic top, super disappointed in the overly short sleeves.

"Now this I *like*," Mom says.

"I'd have to get something to wear over my arms," I say, pulling at the sleeves as I stand in front of the full-length mirrors at the end of the hallway. All I see is the squishiness that seems to hang down over my elbows. These are the arms of an old lady who bakes cookies for her grandchildren, and she hugs them too tight so they suffocate.

"The shirt looks great."

My mother is the type of lady who will wear anything without consideration as to how it might look on her. Whatever 3XL garment that is hanging on the thrift-store rack is worth getting, just because it's there and it's cheap. Right now, she's got on a sweater that's meant to be oversized, yet it barely goes past her belly, and her jeans are baggy in the butt and tight at the ankles.

"I don't really trust your opinion, Mom," I say.

"Why?"

"Well, you're my mother," I say.

"If you get the top, I'll get you the bra," Mom says, looking very proud of herself.

"Blackmail!"

"Not blackmail when I'm offering to buy you two things instead of one. Right, Beck?" Mom says, tapping my sister's foot.

I let out a sigh. "I accept."

I'd do anything for the bra and me to be together. Besides, I have a cropped denim jacket at home that I can pair with the tee.

I head back to the change room to slip back into my own clothes. I rip the tag off the bra, then slide back into the black baby-doll top I came in with, my favorite shirt design because the front fans out under the breast area, which means the boobs get to be on display while the belly can be free under the lovely, loose-fitting part. I stare at myself in the mirror, tousling my hair to add volume. I smile because the mirror usually reflects a flattering version of myself, the version I want to see. The mirror is kind; it's the camera that's a bitch and reflects all the shittery.

The salesperson reaches for my purchases over the counter. I pull away when she tries to reach for the folded black bra in my hand. "This is the one I came with. I'm wearing the one we're buying," I say, pulling the strap out from under my shirt so she can see. She takes the tag when I hand it to her and gives me a plastic bag for the bra I came in with.

While Mom pays, I take a moment to check my phone and see a few unread texts from Lara. But a new text from Freddie takes precedence.

[Freddie] You and I might be going for a ride later. Just saying.
[Baylee] Did you fix your car?!
[Freddie] Or maybe I'm just borrowing my mom's car. You'll have to come over and find out.

Finally having a friend who drives is the coolest thing ever, and the fact that it's Freddie—my stomach does little somersaults, thinking of the idea of riding next to him, the confidence of wearing a sexy new bra running through me.

I might have to be a little later getting to Lara's. Perhaps Freddie could even drop me off there.

"I guess I'm just the bank, huh, Boss?" Mom says, pulling me out of my daydream.

"Thank you, Mom," I say, and she nods. "Sorry."

We stop at a bench so Mom can check Rebecca's feeding tube to make sure it hasn't leaked all over the place, which is a thing that can happen because either the cap on the tube comes open by accident, or liquid manages to come out from around the tube. Mom usually puts a diaper against that part of my sister's belly when we're out and about, under her shirt, to absorb any potential mess. While Mom does that, I take a moment to redo my sister's ponytail, which looks horrid now that she's accidentally hooked her fingers through it while going wild with excitement earlier. She gives me a dirty look but doesn't fuss, probably because she knows I'd tell her to be quiet. Not, like, in an evil way, but in a stop-whining-I'm-trying-to-help kind of way.

"There," I say, patting the top of her head. "You no longer look like crap. You're welcome."

Rebecca cracks a grin, staring off at the tiled floor. People assume kids like my sister don't really know what's going on around them, but this kind of thing totally proves otherwise. She might not understand words, but she gets tone.

"Let's go," Mom says.

"Can we grab something at the food court, though?" I say. "I can't be this close to the smell of deep-fried stuff and not get anything. That would just be cruel."

"To go, though," Mom says.

A DM pops through.

[Alex] About 2 years.

His answer to my DM to him last night, asking him how long he's worked at Bookworm.

[Baylee] Can I ask you another question?
[Alex] Totally.
[Baylee] What does "partial high school dropout" mean?

[Alex] Well I sort of messed up some of Gr 10 and most of Gr 11. My attendance was minimal at best.

[Baylee] What grade are you in then?

[Alex] I'm working on credits now at Castlehill Alternative. Not exactly in a grade, but I guess I should technically be in Gr 12 now. What grade r u in?

[Baylee] 11. Were you at St. Peter's?

[Alex] No. C-High.

[Baylee] That's my school. Do we know each other?

[Alex] Maybe? You would've started Gr 9 and I would've been in Gr 10.

Grade Nine at Castlehill High was a blur of nerves and excitement of being at this big, new school full of older people. It would help if I knew what he looked like, but I feel weird about asking him to share a photo of himself. I bet if I described myself plus the way my hair was back then, he'd know exactly which of the awkward fourteen-year-olds I was—there weren't that many of us fat girls with dumb hair.

[Alex] Look at the yearbook. You'll see me.

Except I don't have the yearbook for Grade Nine. It's way too expensive. Lara has it, though.

[Baylee] Okay. I will. 😊

"Let's go, Boss," Mom says again.

I compose a response to the DM, allowing myself to become consumed by the swirl of glitter surrounding me, as I think about the fact that Freddie is waiting for me, I'm wearing the most attractive bra ever, and this Alex guy is messaging me again. A burst of butterflies erupts as I picture myself cruising down a country road with Freddie.

[Lara] What time can you come?
[Baylee] Maybe 7?

All I know is I'm going to Freddie's, alone.

FIVE

Freddie's street runs parallel to mine. From my mother's bedroom window, I can see his, which overlooks his backyard, just four houses to the right. There's a perfectly situated shortcut a little way down the road, a walkway that connects our streets. As usual, I'm in completely inappropriate footwear considering the weather, so I take careful, slow steps, aiming for the cleaner patches of pavement. It's worth it to have that sound in my ears, the pretty sound of heels clicking on the ground.

There's a tightness in my belly as the walkway comes up on my right, and I take a peek to see if anyone's there. There is nothing but an empty tiled path, so my confidence returns, and the clicking of my heels carries me all the way to Freddie's house.

His garage door is open as I come up to the house, and the

Shitbox idles in the driveway, dense exhaust smoke and rock beats escaping from the car. The sun is already going down, and it feels so much colder than it did earlier.

I tap on the passenger window. Freddie waves me in.

I open the door, leaning my head in through the escaping cloud of strawberry vape. "It works!"

"Get in!" he shouts, putting his vape on the dashboard.

I am about to be the girl Freddie takes for a ride, in this car, at last. We've driven around the neighborhood in his mother's SUV a couple of times, but this is us in his car. We can go wherever we want. Total freedom.

I tuck myself into the car, immediately realizing that I failed to consider this thoroughly. This car is *small*. I reach for the adjustment bar under the passenger seat to push the seat as far back as it'll go.

"Trey and I did most of it ourselves last night. We kept going until two a.m.," Freddie says as he turns the volume down. "But his brother came to help us finish."

"Oh," I say, totally distracted by the sensation of doom that moves through me as I realize the seat belt won't reach all the way around me to clip. Freddie is looking out his window, and I yank on the belt. He doesn't turn to look over, which tells me this is him being thoughtful and looking away from this awkwardness. "That's awesome. Uh . . . so it's safe to drive?"

"One hundred percent. His brother took it for a test drive," he says. "I told you Mark's a mechanic, remember? He helped us finish this morning, and he double-checked everything."

"Right," I say, wrapping the belt around me, trying again to bring the two pieces of stupid-ass metal together and failing. "Mark's a mechanic. Very cool."

I could just puff out a huge breath of annoyance at the awkwardness and effort it takes to get my big self into this tiny car, but instead, I take small breaths, sucking my belly in for dear life, still not able to make the stupid metal pieces come together.

"Where would you like to go?" Freddie asks. "You get to choose."

"Um, let me think." I take advantage of the moment he spends scrolling through his phone to place my purse against my left side, camouflaging the belt latch resting against me, coming at least five inches short of meeting the buckle.

This is a total nightmare, and I should've seen it coming.

The reality is: when you allow yourself to get too full of excitement and delight, thinking everything is just wonderful, the universe will intervene and put you back in your place.

Freddie starts reversing the car. His left hand is on the wheel, while the right is on the stick, which is like, *two* inches away from my thigh. The speakers are pumping out Freddie's rock tunes, and even though this isn't exactly my kind of music, when I'm with him, I can see how this stuff would have a spot on the playlist of my life. The nerves give way to a pink and glittery feeling. This is a whole vibe, me going for a ride with Freddie. It makes me wish his hand would find its way to my thigh.

The only way the moment could be better is if it was a summer night. *And* if the seat belt was longer.

We are quiet as Freddie drives us through the streets of our town, headed for the highway. I feel totally safe with him at the wheel, and that thought just adds a whole new layer to my crush.

"So do you think Trey knows he and Lara are actually done for good?" I ask once we're in the middle lane of the highway, cruising.

"Who knows?" he says. "But honestly, she deserves better, right?"

This comment pulls my gaze to his face. "Why do you say that?"

"Look, Trey's my best friend." He sighs. "But he's not trying to have a deep relationship. So if that's what she's trying to create with Trey, it's not going to happen. She could find someone decent, but she just doesn't."

I turn my head the other way, staring at the pavement blurring next to me. "That's true."

"She was out of his league," Freddie says.

My heart twitches with a flash of darkness. I would be lying if I said I've never worried about Freddie and Lara finding each other. I've thought a lot about this, and I've come to the conclusion that he could be complimenting his mother's Dyson vacuum and I'd still take it personally, like what he was actually doing was going on about all the things the vacuum has that I don't.

He continues, "But if anyone knows that, it's her, right?"

"Stop it," I say, yet all I feel is grateful for the addition to his comment. *This* is the reason I don't spend every moment riddled with fear that Freddie will go for my best friend.

"She's completely in love with herself," he says.

I let his words hang in the air. Is that a good thing? A bad thing?

It reminds me of this saying I've heard before: You can't love someone else until you love yourself. I'm kind of fuzzy on the actual wording. It might be: You have to love yourself before another can love you.

The heat coming through the vents starts to overwhelm, and Freddie reaches to turn the dial to the middle, red and blue on either side. "All right, now that I've got you cornered with no place to go," he says, "I gotta ask you for a favor."

"You're going to ask me to babysit your sister, aren't you," I say, and he flashes me a toothy grin before returning his gaze to the road ahead. I can't help but smile back. "When?"

"Monday night."

I fake a sound of annoyance, as if hanging out at Freddie's house to watch his two-year-old sister is the worst thing in the world.

"Come on, Bay. It's for a great cause."

"Fine, I'll do it."

"Yessssssssssssss," he says. "Thank you. I owe you."

"You should pay me."

"I am now broke," he says. "Any dollar in my possession from now on will go directly into this gas tank. I'll be broke forever."

"Not if your script ends up being a movie."

Freddie snorts. "It's a long way from that," he says. "Anyway, don't you want to know what I'm doing Monday?"

"Not really, but you seem very interested in telling me."

"Jess is in town," he says, wagging his eyebrows my way. My insides disintegrate with the venom coursing through me.

Jess, the girl who is supposed to be living three hours away, too far to still be so present.

"Wonderful," I say. "I'm really sad to see how hard it is for her to find someone in her new town."

"But Bay, *why* would she need to find some moron over there when she can come home and hit this"—those eyebrows again—"whenever she wants?"

With that, I roll my eyes and stare forward. His words knock me off-balance. Sometimes, it's like he thinks I'm a guy, the way he talks to me. Maybe I should fist-bump him, but all I want to do is claw Jess's eyes out.

"I'm kidding," he says. "We're just going to the coffeehouse. Who knows where things will end up?"

"Sounds lovely."

Up ahead, cars begin to light up red, and just like that, we're in some random bout of sudden traffic. We go from zooming in the fast lane to crawling. The seat belt I was holding around me seems useless now that we're not moving, so I loosen my grip on it and breathe a little.

I focus on my phone, grateful for the distraction of Rianne's latest DMs. Lara sends me a photo of herself with her cousins, along with a reminder to get my butt over there.

Another DM waits to be read.

[Alex] So r u an actual bookworm, then?

[Baylee] I like to read, but I'm not always the best at getting all the way to the end. So much homework and stuff to read for school. It gets in the way. By the time I get back to the book, I forget what it was about, so I have to start over.

[Alex] I know what u mean.

[Baylee] I kind of just love Bookworm in general. I 🖤 all the journals and stationery. And the cafe, of course. I go there a lot with my friend Lara.

[Alex] Weird that I don't remember seeing u there.

[Baylee] Weird that you went to my school.

[Alex] Weird that we've frequented the same spaces and never met.

[Baylee] So weird.

[Alex] 😆

"Anyway," Freddie says. "Wanna hear how expensive car insurance is?"

"*So* much."

It goes in one ear and out the other, but I do enjoy the feeling I get texting Bookworm Alex while Freddie's voice swirls around me.

I tap my name on the screen, which takes me to my Instagram profile. I try to view my profile the way I imagine Bookworm Alex might. Photos of fresh manicures I give myself, books I say I'm reading but that I don't finish, my friends while hanging out at Freddie's or one of Rianne's parties. And many face shots, either showing off when I nailed my winged liner, or when my shadow was blended expertly. When there are body shots of me, it's usually just the upper body, and although I clearly look like a *significantly* fat girl, I'm also super aware that only my best angles are on display here.

The point is, Bookworm Alex has to know I'm fat.

"Come on, Bay. Put the phone away and enjoy the scenery."

"What scenery? Dirty snow . . . and more dirty snow. Oh, look—a bunch of other cars. Look there—a big warehouse." I give him a wide smile full of sass.

The car gains momentum, then stops abruptly.

"Why is every moment of the day rush hour around here?" Freddie says, huffing a breath.

"Says the guy who's been driving one day," I say. "You sound like someone's dad. Not mine, because I don't have one, but, maybe Rianne's dad or—"

Freddie opens his mouth to interrupt me, but then we get hit from behind and I jerk forward, my face connecting with the dashboard.

Six

This is the first time I've had a nosebleed, and that part is making me cry more than the actual pain. Drops of red land on my lap, and I've got nothing but my hands to hold against my face. At least my coat is red. I hold my head back, trying not to mess up Freddie's car.

"Oh, shit," Freddie says. "Your face. Are you okay? Oh, damn, Bay. Squeeze the bridge of your nose."

The idea of pinching anything on my face right now makes my eyes water even more than they already are. I breathe through my mouth and try to focus on swallowing the blood before it chokes me.

Freddie reaches into the back seat and hands me a sweater to hold up to my face. He whips his head to look behind us, fury in his eyes.

I cough a thin spray of fresh blood into my hands and the dash-board. It makes me gag.

"Damn," he says. "I can't believe this."

"Oh *no*! Your car!" My words are muffled behind my hands and my obstructed nasal passages. "Is my nose smushed?"

"I'm sure it's fine," he says. "Keep pinching it."

Someone appears at Freddie's window, and icy wind enters the car as the window goes down. "Are you guys all right?"

Freddie unbuckles his seat belt, then slips out of the car. "Did you just rear-end me?"

"Yeah, I did, but because someone rear-ended me first," I can hear the man say, and he sounds calm considering Freddie's accusatory tone. "It started a couple cars back. Not much of an impact, though, thank god. Hopefully the first guy has a rear dash cam."

"My friend's nose is messed up," Freddie says, and the man leans over to take a peek at me. "Did someone call 911?"

"My wife's on the phone with them now."

There's a knock on my door. I roll the window down a crack to an older lady. "Sweetie, are you okay?" she asks, and I nod from behind Freddie's bundled-up sweater.

Sirens get louder, and with that a wave of embarrassment washes over me. I wish I could just grab my purse and walk home. I should've just gone to Lara's. The most ridiculous thing is knowing that if I was anywhere else right now, I'd probably be spacing, my warped mind making up a dramatic scenario just like this, except with Freddie giving me mouth-to-mouth in some "Sleeping Beauty"–type romantic moment with no real consequences.

I cry all over again, thinking about the idea of my face being messed up permanently.

Freddie opens my car door and starts swiping at my arms with baby wipes someone must've given him. He's being so sweet, and I can't even enjoy it because I feel the intense urge to puke. My phone is somewhere at my feet. So many eyes are on me. I keep my own aimed low.

A paramedic comes to my side and asks me what's going on, what hurts. When I'm coaxed into pulling the sweater away from my face, it looks like the bleeding has mostly stopped. The whole area throbs and feels three times its size as he presses against different areas of my face. He asks if I'm on blood thinners, and I shake my head no. I keep my nose purposely plugged, afraid of breathing through it. I bring my focus strictly to the questions I'm being asked, not wanting to think about everyone looking, about Freddie's car being messed up, about the blood that is now stiff on my face with the cold having invaded this cursed car.

Today is not a good day.

Traffic begins to move, and all the cars are being funneled over to the right lane. Those of us involved in the pileup stay put, waiting for the police to deal with the scene, I guess. I see a man rubbing his neck, pain evident on his face, while another paramedic tries to lead him over to the ambulance. I see a mother cradling a toddler who looks riveted by all the people hanging around. Everyone's breath comes out in clouds of vapor. Freddie keeps circling around to check on me, then he goes back to chat with the other people hanging out against the highway median.

The paramedic from earlier comes with a basin, telling me to aim my head down a little and continue pressing my nose without letting go for at least ten minutes. She has a kind face, and she doesn't seem to be mad at me, which makes me like her even more. "We're going to bring you in to get looked at, okay? Can you call a parent to come meet you?"

"Can't I just go home and ice it?"

The paramedic offers me a sympathetic smile. "Look, it would be pretty foolish not to go get checked out. We don't know how hard you hit your head."

"I didn't really hit my head," I say. "Is everyone laughing at me?"

She tips her head to the side. "Why would anyone be laughing?"

"I don't know."

"Do you want to call someone now?"

I shake my head. "I don't think I can. Can you ask him?" I point to Freddie.

The paramedic smiles, then pushes herself up. "I'll get your boyfriend."

Behind my hands, I grin so wide and resist the urge to wrap this lady up with the lasso of love shooting out of my eyes. The fact that she believes Freddie could be mine makes her my favorite person in the world right now.

Freddie comes over a moment later.

"Can you call my mother? I feel like I'm going to say something stupid if I do it." Mostly I'm afraid I'll start bawling if I hear her voice right now.

He nods and pulls his phone out of his pocket. The paramedic explains to him what she told me. I don't hear what he says to my mother because he wanders away while he talks.

"Do I have to pay for this?" I ask.

"Pay for what?"

"The ambulance ride."

She laughs a little. "I think someone watches a little too much American TV."

A police officer appears next to me. He crouches next to the car.

"Hey there," he says, and even though he sounds nice enough, I feel as if he's going to cuff me and drag me away for being a dramatic loser. "How are you doing? Can you tell me what happened?"

"I'm not sure. We got hit and I went forward."

"The airbags didn't go off, huh?" the officer says.

"I wouldn't say we got hit, really. More like bumped," Freddie says, pointing to his chest, then pressing a hand against it. "My seat belt didn't even squeeze, and I barely hit the guy in front of me."

"Well, your friend sure went flying, didn't she," the officer says. "You were wearing your seat belt, too?"

Cold fear spreads through me, and for a moment I think I'm

about to pass out. Because no, I *wasn't* wearing one. In this moment, I regret and despise every single thing that's made me fat. I curse pizza, and whipped-cream drinks, and cheese, and my stupid genes, and the fact that I dislike exercise. How the hell—when I'm not even able to bend over fully because my big squishy stomach is in the way—did I manage to fold over and hit the dash? Why couldn't my fat be used for good, for once?

"I would've, but I . . . couldn't." My voice is thin and low. Freddie is on his phone, and I steal glances at him to make sure he doesn't listen.

The officer reaches for the belt hanging to my right. "What do you mean? It's not working?"

"It doesn't reach all the way around."

The officer pulls on the seat belt until it locks up. "It does seem a little short."

"I'm sure it fits a regular person," I mutter.

Freddie stands next to me, staring at the ground. He heard that part, and his face makes it clear just how uncomfortable the whole thing is making him.

This right here is the worst thing I've experienced. This is worse than all the times I've been made fun of by complete strangers or evil little fools at school growing up. It's worse than the combined looks of people who watch me as I approach their personal space—on a bus, in a restaurant, on a plane, in a movie theater—like I'm about to flatten them from not knowing how to handle my own body.

Is this the worst day of my life? Probably not, but I'm sure it'll make the Top Five.

"You can arrest me," I tell the cop. "Take me away now."

The officer laughs. "How about you get a ride with the medics? Make sure everything's okay."

"Sure, okay. Let's go."

"Bay," Freddie says. "Want me to meet you there?"

"No. It's fine." I keep my head down as paramedics walk me over to the ambulance.

SEVEN

The hospital is a lot of waiting. There are people scattered about the waiting room, which is made up of rows of blue chairs against floor-to-ceiling windows that look into the lot where the ambulances arrive. A few look dead in their seats. Some are coughing up bits of invisible germs all over their neighbors, which is something that would drive my mother up the wall, and it's why I always go right for a mask whenever I enter a hospital. A lady is picking her arm so savagely that her fingernails are bloody. There's a near-naked guy being dragged to the ground by three security people as he shouts about the power of the Lord flowing through his veins. I keep the thin yellow mask over my nose and mouth, and I bathe my hands in sanitizer whenever I touch any surfaces.

The triage nurse I saw a few minutes ago told me to get comfortable, because the wait will be long. It goes by priority, and busted noses with controlled bleeding are far down the list compared to heart attacks and strokes. She gave me a small plastic bag full of tiny ice cubes to put against my nose, at least.

"Saturday night in the ER—this isn't your day, huh, honey?" this old lady in front of me says. She has kind eyes, thick black hairs sprouting from her chin, and a massive butt squished into the tiny seat of her walker.

"I guess it's no one's day in here," I say.

"I'm just here 'cause I got bad kidneys and none of my doctors wanna do anything about it. But I've got to keep pushing, because I'm trying to get ahead of this virus, you know? No one believes the few cases we have will lead to a pandemic, but mark my words, coronavirus is coming. It's already here."

I nod, averting my gaze because I really don't want to be talking right now. Is *pandemic* even a word? Maybe it's like *pandemonium* and *epidemic* put together?

"You've got the right idea, wearing that mask," she says, tapping a finger against the side of her mouth. "Maybe you're smarter than the rest of us."

"I just don't want to get my sister sick," I say. "She gets sick easily."

"Oh, that's honorable, honey."

My phone buzzes with a call from my mother, and I pick up right away.

"Baylee—what is happening? I've been trying to reach you, but it kept going to voice mail. Where are you? Are you okay?" she says.

"Phone signal is kind of weird in here," I say. "I'm fine. Just broke my nose, maybe?"

"Oh my god," Mom says, and I am glad I'm talking to her now and not earlier. I can resist the urge to start crying now that I'm composed. "What happened?"

"Someone rear-ended Freddie's car a little. I just bumped my nose. It wasn't Freddie's fault."

"You're at . . . did . . . to take . . . now?" Mom's voice cuts in and out.

"I can't really hear you."

The call gets dropped, so I begin a text letting her know what's going on.

[Mom] Juliana is heading over, so I can come get you. I want to speak to the doctor.

My mom's best friend, Juliana, is the only non-nurse person with enough training to stay alone with Rebecca. While I wait, holding the makeshift ice pack against my face, I think about this hospital, and the fact that she won't dare bring my sister to this place unless it's an absolute emergency. My mother always says these kinds of smaller hospitals have no idea what to do with kids like my sister, so whenever possible, we drive out to Toronto, to the specialized children's hospital, for all of Rebecca's appointments.

Still, any hospital equals bad vibes.

I take the mask off my face when I feel some wetness coming through from the slight ooze of blood from my nose.

"What the hell happened to you?" a man whose breath smells like beer says to me. There's dried food or vomit on his shirt. He gestures with a thick index finger to my torso, then up to my face. That's when I remember what I must look like.

"I was dead, but then I came back to life," I say.

It takes him a minute to process. Then he laughs.

My compact mirror reveals smudged makeup because of the crying and rubbing of my face. There is redness over the bridge of my nose, and my nostrils are crusted red. There are still streaks of old blood running down my chin. My hair looks like it belongs on a dug-up body, or like I suffer from uncombable hair syndrome, which is a thing that I have googled before. There are dried blood droplets sprinkled over my jeans, and a few even soaked into my brand-new bra, totally clashing with the hot pink. I groan and google how to remove blood from fabric.

The bra thing is bad, but not as bad as the fact that Freddie knows I'm legally too fat to be in his car.

My phone regains a bar of reception and a slew of texts pop through.

[Freddie] Is everything OK? How's your nose?
[Freddie] Let me know how it goes.
[Freddie] I'm taking my car to get shampooed—no big deal. ^^

[Freddie] Know what? I think I'm going to work this little mess into my screenplay—it'll add a lot of action.

[Freddie] So basically it's actually a good thing this happened.

[Freddie] Except for your nose, though.

[Freddie] But really—I hope you're okay.

[Freddie] ???

His concern makes it even worse. He's such a decent guy. But I can't ever see him again, not after this.

I sign into the spotty hospital Wi-Fi, and soon my phone buzzes. A conversation has been unfolding in the group message window, too extensive for me to be able to scroll up and find its beginning. I flick my thumb down once and start reading wherever it settles.

[Lara] Did you even clear it with your parents first?

[Rianne] It'll be fine! I've already invited EVERYONE.

[Lara] How have you invited everyone already?

[Rianne] I sent texts and DMs to the usual people and it might already be spreading like wildfire.

[Lara] Did you invite a bunch of people we don't know again?

[Rianne] I can't control in which direction the fire burns.

[Lara] 😑

[Rianne] Relax. It's not like I put it on TikTok. Anyway. BAYLEE!!!!!!!!!!!!!!! WHERE ARE YOU????????

Lara is typing her response, but I insert myself into the conversation before she can finish.

[Baylee] I'm not sure if I can come on Saturday.
[Rianne] BAYLEE!! This is for your birthday!
[Baylee] My birthday is not next Saturday. It's the week after, and it's on a Friday???
[Rianne] That's what I was saying earlier! I'm on the schedule to work on your birthday! 😟
[Baylee] Oh.
[Rianne] Plus they have me opening the next morning because of stupid March break! So we're having your birthday next weekend instead! I switched with the other closer for Saturday night.
[Baylee] I actually have a good excuse why I might not be able to come. Trust me.

A separate text from Lara comes through.

[Lara] What's your excuse? Mine is Trey, but Rianne said she'd make sure he's barred from her house.
[Baylee] Well that's nice of her. I would be OK with Trey and Freddie not being there.
[Lara] ???
[Baylee] . . .
[Lara] Where are you? Are you on your way yet?
[Baylee] I'm sort of unavailable at the moment.

[Lara] ???
[Baylee] I'm in the emergency room. I might've broken my nose.
[Lara] WHAT??????????? HOW????????? ARE YOU OKAY???????

It's not that I have a problem with my best friend knowing what happened, but it's just really difficult to feel like some kind of victim who deserves concern when it's more that I'm a complete fool who suffered a ridiculous freak accident on account of my abdominal girth.

[Baylee] I'm OK. It's a bit of a ridiculous story.
[Lara] Wanna video-chat?
[Baylee] I can't. There are people everywhere, and I didn't bring my earphones.

Finally, I'm called away from the waiting room, into an actual small room with a stretcher where I see the doctor for maybe five minutes. She seems pretty confident that whatever I smooshed is minor, and my nose doesn't need realignment or anything like that. A nurse swoops over, handing me some Advil and a cup with barely an ounce of water.

"Go back to the waiting room, and we'll call you back in to be reassessed in a bit," the nurse says. "Do you have a parent coming?"

"Yes."

I go back to sit in the waiting room, grabbing another face mask on my way.

I'm about to respond to Rianne's four messages demanding what my excuse is for ditching my sure-to-be-epic birthday party, but a more important message comes through.

[Alex]   Ur latest post.
[Alex] U have really pretty eyes.

With that, my hold on bad feelings loosens. Earlier I posted a close-up of my face to show off my new brow filler. My makeup is now a mess of abstract-painting-looking smears, but at least I have the evidence that it did look stellar today.

[Baylee] That kind of just made my day. And if you knew what kind of day I'm having, you'd know how difficult it was to salvage it.
[Alex] Why? What's going on?
[Baylee] Well . . . . currently I'm covered in my own blood.
[Alex] Um what? What happened?

I DM him lies. Lies I'm surprised I can come up with on the spot, a story about helping my good friend Freddie work on his car, and then one of the doors accidentally gets pushed open into my face. All the essential details and players are present, just rearranged a little. I've only been trading messages with this person for twenty-four hours, so I get to make myself up, and he doesn't know any different.

[Rianne] WHY ARE YOU LEAVING ME HANGING?
[Rianne] I'm texting you from the bathroom at work.
[Rianne] I've been sitting here so long, waiting for you to answer, that my supervisor probably thinks I'm having a huge poop.
[Baylee] EW
[Rianne] Uh, HELLO? The party?
[Baylee] It's just that. . . I kind of smushed my nose. It's not broken, but I'm at the hospital right now.
[Rianne] OMG??????????? You're not dead, right?
[Baylee] No. This is me alive-texting you.
[Rianne] Shit. I have to go back to work. OK text me what happened, and I'll pretend I have to poop again in a bit so I can come read your messages.

It feels like I've been here for hours. Luckily, there are charging stations, so I plug my phone into one. I stare at my DMs with Alex for a while, hoping I'll be there to see him start typing a message to me. I overthink what I could type to him to the point that everything sounds completely ridiculous.

Someone sits next to me, their leg touching my thigh, which makes me pull away. It takes me a moment to realize who it is.

EIGHT

Lara shakes her head dramatically as she takes in my appearance. Her thick black hair is pulled into a large bun on top of her head. She unzips her white winter jacket, revealing this black romper thing I would love to be able to get away with wearing, except rompers are next-level tuckage of shirt into pants and therefore forbidden.

"What are you doing here?" I ask.

"I made Kavith drive me over."

Lara's got three superhot cousins who are always around because they live in the house next door to hers. "He's waiting outside?"

She shrugs. "He's doing a TikTok live with his dumb friends, straight from the hospital parking lot. He's fine." She takes a closer look at me and makes a sour face. "You look like an extra from a cheap zombie movie."

"I've literally never felt more beautiful."

She keeps shaking her head, and I pretend to try and fix my hair before giving her a wide smile, painfully aware of the weird feeling of crusts and chunks deep in my nose.

"Freddie told me what happened," she says.

"What did he say?" Now I'm wondering who else he might've felt the need to tell the story to, like Natasha or *Jess*. I bet they'd really get a kick out of the seat belt thing.

"Just that there was some super-low-key rear-ending situation and your nose got most of the action."

"Well, what he said is pretty much accurate. Except for the part about me being too fat to buckle up."

"Shut up," she says. "You're not serious."

"I am."

"Well, that makes no sense. Please, you're not that fat." When she says it, I almost believe her. "His car is a piece of shit. It's not you."

I shrug, hoping she senses that I'm done talking about it.

"What are you waiting for now?" she asks.

"I have to see the doctor again to make sure the bleeding has stopped. I should be able to go home after that."

"Did you hit your head?"

"No. I just basically went forward and bonked my nose on the dash. It wasn't even that hard."

She nods, then makes herself more comfortable, crossing her

legs in a way I cannot possibly comprehend, tucking her right foot behind her left calf so that her legs look twisted. "Want me to stay and keep you company? I could distract you."

"Sure."

I wait for her to take my mind off things, but all she does is get distracted by her phone, texting furiously one minute, then smiling the next.

"Who are you talking to?" I ask, trying to lean over and catch a glimpse of her screen.

She pulls her phone away, then throws me a guilty expression.

My body moves to better see her. "What?"

"So I started talking to this guy."

"How?! I thought I was your boyfriend for a while." I roll my eyes, a flash of annoyance erupting within. Looks like we were *both* busy hanging out with different boys instead of clinging to each other. "Where did this new guy come from?"

"You don't know him. I met him at Bookworm."

The hint of panic makes me blurt out, "Is it Alex?"

"No, why? You know a guy named Alex from Bookworm?"

"Just that guy I was DMing."

"Oh right—are you still talking to him?" She raises her eyebrows and puts on a curious face. I sense the interest in my thing is a little fake, that she's dying to bring the spotlight back to her. I'm the built-in audience, a fact I've always been okay with because I love listening, learning, and mostly, I love judging.

"Kind of," I say. "Anyway, go on."

"Well, my guy is *not* the Bookworm guy you're talking to. My guy . . . well, he seems pretty sweet, and it's like he's trying to earn my attention, but not in a creepy way."

"So all this has been going on while you were with Trey?" I ask.

She frowns. "I was just randomly DMing with this guy here and there. Nothing inappropriate. Totally platonic. It's just now that it's taking a flirty turn. Like, today."

I ask her some general questions, like how old he is (seventeen), what school he goes to (St. Peter's), and what he looks like (hot). "So what's the problem?"

"The problem is . . ." She takes a dramatic breath. "He's good friends with Taylor."

"Ew. Gross."

Taylor is Lara's pre-best-friend—as in *pre* me. There was a time when Taylor and I were competing for Lara's friendship. Taylor was Lara's first friend when they moved to Castlehill, their houses conveniently located next to each other. But then Lara and I started talking in class, and then things just grew from there while Taylor shrank into the background. There's also the fact that Taylor is next-level shallow and fake. She's the one who started the nickname Kunkel's Cankles, something that follows me to this day. Lara was the one who told me where the insult came from, which led to the final fight between the two of them last year. They're still civil toward one another, seeing as we're forced to cross paths at school, but the friendship that once was died for good.

I don't even *have* cankles. Face, boobs, hair, hands, and

ankles—those are the five things I appreciate about myself, in order.

"I thought you met him at Bookworm," I say.

"Well . . . I *saw* him at Taylor's when they were hanging out on her porch, like last year or something, but I ran into him at Bookworm recently, and that's when I started messaging with him on a very occasional basis."

"So they're friends?"

"They hang out a lot."

"Do you think she has a thing for him?"

"Yes. I'm like, one hundred percent sure she does."

I ask her to elaborate a little, then I let her vent about her feelings. It's pretty clear she's looking for permission—I've gotten used to figuring out what she needs from me early on in the conversation. Still, I like to hear her describe what it's like, this whole dating/drama thing. It all plays in my mind like a movie. A movie I have a tiny part in.

"I think I should stay away, right? I don't want to do that to her."

"Why? She literally has no soul, and she would do that to you in a heartbeat."

"Well," Lara says, looking thoughtful and torn.

"She totally would. Come on, Lara," I say. "How many times has she stood there, flirting with Trey at his locker, knowing you can see everything?"

Lara shrugs. "What if she and I were really good friends— would you be saying the same thing?"

"If you two were good friends, I'd have nothing to say because I'd be best friends with Rianne, and we'd be far away from you and Taylor."

"Come on! Be serious, Baylee."

"Okay, fine. Honestly, Lara," I start, but there's a long pause, because sometimes telling the truth feels like I'm doing something wrong. "It's kind of like you only broke up with Trey this time because you already had someone else lined up."

"I didn't! I swear. It's just today we DMed a lot and I can feel a little something, like it *could* end up there if I wanted it to," she says. I wonder what it must be like, to talk to people and just know that something could happen as opposed to knowing the total opposite. "The situation is a little complicated, so I'm trying to think ahead and prepare."

"I guess *I* better prepare for you falling off the face of the earth again and start interviewing for the position of best friend." I avoid her gaze. "Sorry."

Lara and I are quiet, and the awkwardness makes me reach for words that'll make things right again. "I guess if it was me, I would go for it because I don't care about Taylor's feelings. If she and I were close, though, I guess I'd try and have a conversation about it before things started for real with the guy. She can't be mad at you when nothing's happening between her and that guy, right? It would suck, but it's not like it's your fault."

Lara makes this face like she has no idea if I'm right, but she likes my argument.

"Although . . ." I give her a sour look. "I just want to say that the fact he's friends with a brainless, shallow idiot like Taylor is a bit of a red flag."

"Stop!" She fake-slaps my arm.

My name is called overhead.

"Want me to wait for you?" Lara asks. "I can tell Kavith to come get me later."

"They want me to go home with a parent, and you don't look old enough."

Lara laughs, and off in the distance, I notice my mother walking through the emergency doors, a mask over her face. She scans the waiting room, and her eyes settle on me. She frowns and heads over. I'm reminded of the extra mask I picked up but forgot to put on.

"Okay, I guess I'll go," Lara says. "Text me later!"

Mom nods at Lara as they breeze by each other.

"Sorry, Mom. I had a mask almost the whole time. It just got a little wet, so I took it off, but then Lara showed up and I forgot."

"Never mind that," Mom says. "Let me see."

"They called my name," I say. "I have to go up there."

Mom follows me to the counter with plexiglass. A nurse opens the door to let me back into the actual emergency department, directing me to a room. The same doctor from earlier asks me about the pain and other symptoms I don't have.

"Now I'm going to have a look to see what we're dealing with," the doctor says.

She comes at me with an otoscope that has a light on the end, carefully putting it into each of my nostrils, not touching each side of my nose much. Still, it's enough to tickle, and I explode in a sneeze that brings with it a trail of mucus and a slug of blood, which makes me squeal. "Oh no! That's disgusting."

"Don't worry. That's to be expected. It's the old, clotted blood. I want to see if the bleeding is controlled," the doctor says. "Yeah, I think I see the cause. You must've had a scab there that got torn. That's my guess, anyway."

"My nose gets really dry in the winter," I say.

While we all wait to see what my nose does, Mom talks about the humidifier she bought me years ago that sits in my closet collecting dust, then she asks the doctor questions about how to deal with any further bleeding. I'm praying I won't need tampons up there or something. Five minutes pass. I breathe carefully through my nose and there doesn't seem to be any trickling of blood down my throat.

She tells me to come back to the ER if the bleeding gets worse, or if I start feeling more serious symptoms, like a persistent headache or vision issues.

"And do not blow your nose very hard, okay? Nothing more than a soft, heavy exhale through your nose," the doctor says. "All right. You're good to go. Take it easy. And wear your seat belt next time, okay?"

The doctor slips out before seeing the shocked expression on my mother's face.

"What's that, Baylee Kunkel?"

"Nothing, Mother. Let's just go."

A nurse pokes her head in. "You're free to go, ladies. I have to prep this room for the next patient."

"Yes, well, that'll have to wait because I just found out my daughter *was not wearing a seat belt* while riding in a car." Mom motions for me to take a seat on the stretcher again. The nurse makes a face and closes the door behind her.

"It's not like I was trying to *not* wear a seat belt. I'm not stupid, Mom," I say. "We were stopped in traffic, and I unbuckled to take off my coat. Bad timing, I guess."

Mom narrows her eyes at me, trying to determine if the truth is what she's just been served or otherwise. Sometimes it's not only easier to lie, but it just feels better.

If I told my mother what really happened, she might have a second of feeling bad for me or even having empathy, but then she'd just get next-level mad at me for even going along with being a passenger in a car without a proper seat belt. I should've known better, but I still did the dumb thing because I wanted to be the girl in Freddie's car more than I wanted to be safe and follow the rules. She will not understand that part.

Mom sighs. "Let's go."

She points to the hand sanitizer as we pass by it, and both of us slather our hands with it.

"You better keep away from Beck for a couple days," she says. "Just in case. For all we know, the coronavirus could be in this very hospital."

"I was very careful, Mom. I swear."

In the car, Mom lets a heavy sigh escape her lips. It's not a reproach, exactly. It's her usual reaction to a stressful situation that finally settles, like she acknowledges that it could've been worse and that another disaster might just as easily follow it up.

"How's your nose?" Mom asks.

"Okay as long as I don't touch my face. The pill they gave me helped with the throbbing," I say.

"Well, I suggest you call it a day and go to bed," she says.

"There's blood on my new bra. I have to clean it."

"We'll figure it out, Boss."

The intense urge to doze hits me as we drive, and I lay my head against the window. As we turn and head down our street, I spot Freddie seated on the front steps of my house.

"Wait—Mom, keep driving!" I say.

"Why?"

"Just go. Please. Can we go to your drive-through for something warm? Please?" I suggest, knowing the night nurse will arrive any minute to look after my sister. "The nurse might already be there, so Juliana will be able to leave. Please?"

"You couldn't have told me that ten minutes ago, when we were driving right by the store?" Mom keeps her foot on the gas, and I know she's going to keep driving, so I take a deep breath. But then she slows down. "Look who's here."

"No, Mom. Please. Let's just go," I say. "I don't want to talk to him."

Mom drives past our house, and I turn my head to avoid making eye contact with Freddie. Mom calls Juliana on speaker. "Jules, everything okay?"

"She's still asleep."

"Good," Mom says. "Her nurse will be there by eleven—can you let her know I'm running a little late, but I'll be back very soon?"

"Sure thing," Juliana says. "Is Baylee doing okay?"

"It was a nasty nosebleed, but she's fine."

Mom ends the call and taps my leg. "What's going on with Freddie? Did something happen? Sheila told me the accident wasn't his fault."

She sounds a little too concerned and on alert, like maybe Freddie's mother didn't tell her the truth. "He didn't do anything. It's me who ruined his car on the day he got to finally drive it."

"You're not the one who caused the accident, Boss. They'll work it out with the insurance company. The car who started it will have to pay for damages."

"You didn't see the inside of the car, Mother. There was blood everywhere."

"He wouldn't hold that against you."

Mom shakes her head and brushes a hand against the side of my head. My phone buzzes with what I know is a text from Freddie, but I ignore it.

Nine

The next day, I wake up with hazy memories of what happened, assuming they're echoes of another one of my elaborate fantasy scenarios. But then pain spreads through my face when I go to rub the sleep out of my eyes. My bedroom door is still open from my mother's checks on me through the night, to make sure I didn't have some head injury that put me in a coma.

[Rianne] Still alive, right?
[Baylee] Totally.

She sends me a thumbs-up, and I open another text conversation.

[Lara] How are you? Want me to come over?

I respond, telling her I'm just tired and I might be up for hanging out later.

[Freddie] You drove right past me last night. What's going on? Are you ignoring me?

With that, I'm taken right back to feeling so very stupid and ashamed, but with an added layer of cringe because I did zoom on by him last night like a coward.

[Baylee] It was an accident. Just forget about it.
[Freddie] Okay. But what's up with the awkwardness?
[Baylee] I can pay you back for the cleaning.
[Freddie] Don't worry about that.

I roll out of bed and head across the hall for a shower. When I get back to my room, I find my brand-new bra drying on my bed, no sign of the blood. It helps my mood. Lara and I text for a while, mostly about this new crush of hers.

[Lara] He says he sees something different in me.
[Baylee] Different from what?
[Lara] Just . . . different.

Lara is typing some more, taking forever, so I switch over to a more stimulating conversation, pulling up my DMs with Alex.

[Baylee] Can I ask you a very serious question?

[Alex] Always.

[Baylee] Do you DM other Bookworm customers like you DM me?

[Alex] No way.

[Baylee] Interesting.

[Alex] I didn't think we'd keep talking after I thanked u for commenting on my post, TBH.

I go to his IG profile and notice a new post from this morning. An overexposed angled shot of a skinny upper body in a black polo shirt and white button-down over that, arm wrapped around a biology textbook. I can see the bottom of his face, including a cheek piercing. The caption reads: *Sundays are for homework.*

I save the photo to my phone.

[Baylee] What is that green thing behind you in the photo you posted earlier?

[Alex] One of my prized possessions. It's my velvet beast.

Another photo comes through of a large, avocado-colored couch.

[Baylee] Wow! I've never seen a couch like that.

[Alex] I really like old things. My great-uncle died about three years back. He was like my grandpa, and he left me all his stuff. My whole basement is full of it.

[Baylee] What else did you inherit?

[Alex] My record collection is very sacred.

We chat for a while, moving on to our favorite TV shows, books, and music. When Alex has to leave for work, I realize my room only felt so cozy and lovely because of him. Boredom hits, and Lara's latest text telling me to come over is suddenly very appealing.

Downstairs, Mom is scooping Rebecca up from the floor to put her back in her bed. I watch my mother tuck Rebecca's arms under her weighted blanket and turn on the colorful bedside lamp. Soon Rebecca settles into staring at the colors as they dance around the room.

"I'm thinking of going to Lara's for a bit," I say. "Can I go?"

"Don't you think you should take it easy, Boss?"

"I did. I've been taking it easy for hours. Now I'm bored, and it's barely three in the afternoon," I say. "It's just Lara's. Her dad's a neurologist. It's literally the best place for me to be."

It doesn't take much convincing, and she even allows me to call an Uber on account of the shittery that landed all over me yesterday.

Lara lives in a big house on a cul-de-sac that is about a fifteen-minute drive from my house, where shiny cars that are mostly BMWs and Mercedes are parked in large driveways. Taylor's house is to my right, and I always take a glance at it with the dirtiest look ever, just in case she happens to be looking out a window. I knock and Lara's uncle lets me in. Kavith acknowledges my arrival from the living room where he and Nimal are settled around a gaming console. Nimal winks at me the way he always does, and something inside me swells. An aunt nods a smile from the laundry room. Some man I don't know says hello as he struggles with two cases of water bottles, likely taking them to the extra fridge in the garage.

"Are you all better now?" Lara asks from her spot in the sitting room, which is this fancy living room without a TV.

"I feel like my nose will never be the same."

"The most important thing is that it doesn't even look that bad."

"But it hurts!"

"But your face still looks nice, right?" she says.

Lara is an only child, which means she's her parents' princess. She gets everything she wants, and since money never seems to be a problem in their household, whatever she gets is top-of-the-line, including the newest iPhone, a MacBook that's not even a year old, and a bedroom that's more than twice the size of my own.

"What do you feel like doing?" Lara asks.

"I don't know. What do *you* feel like doing?"

"You're usually the one who comes up with ideas, and then I pick the best one!"

"I'm just not at my best today."

Something is on the stove, and the spicy, pungent scents of onions, oil, and so many spices and ingredients we never use at home radiate through the whole house.

"Wait—is that what I think it is?" I ask.

Lara nods, and seeing the glee that's no doubt all over my face, she adds, "That's obviously the real reason I invited you."

"Your father's biryani is sixty percent of the reasons I'm friends with you."

As though conjured by my thought, Lara's father comes in from the garage. "Baylee! Lara told me the story of your unfortunate little mishap."

"Yes, well, it was next-level unfortunate."

"I trust your nasal trauma is minor?"

"I think so."

"Good, good. Well, to help you feel better, my dear, I decided to make you your favorite."

"Really? You're making it because of me?"

"In your honor," he says. "And we've got some pakodas left over from a few nights ago, as long as you don't mind them reheated."

"Not at all. That is so thoughtful. Thank you, Mr. Kariyawasam," I say.

Lara's father checks the pot resting on the stovetop, releasing a wave of smell that makes my stomach growl, then he disappears back into the garage.

"Your dad is such a decent person," I tell Lara.

"Hey! Give me some credit," she says. "I'm the one who told him biryani would cheer you up."

"You are the best," I say, and she smiles wide.

"Freddie says you wouldn't let him come to the hospital, and you drove right by him last night. Maybe we should talk about that?"

"You and Freddie are still talking about me?"

"He messaged me, asking if you're mad at him."

"I'm *not*. It's not like I was trying to cut him out deliberately."

"I get that," Lara says, scrolling through her phone, typing. "I guess he just feels bad that this whole thing happened."

"Who are you texting?"

She gives me a coy smile, but just then, her mother breezes by the living room. Lara gives me a sharp glare, but I already know I need to drop it. It's not that Lara's forbidden to date, but her parents are under the impression that she goes on the occasional innocent, respectful date. They don't know of the Trey and Lara drama, or of all the boys who came before. *Definitely* not of the boy who comes after.

"Oh, hello, Baylee," Mrs. Kariyawasam says. She comes over to cup my face very gently. "It is good to see you're okay."

"Thanks," I say.

She moves to the kitchen. "I am making a little snack for the boys. Do you ladies want some?"

"No, thanks," Lara says, then to me, "Let's go upstairs."

"Baylee? Would you like a little snack?"

"Yes, I would. Thank you," I say.

"Fine, but we'll take it upstairs," Lara says.

A minute later, Mrs. Kariyawasam presents me with a small plate with cherry tomatoes and vegetable sticks arranged around a couple of fish patties.

"This is so pretty," I say, because it is *not* a box of stale crackers or a Pizza Pop thrown in the microwave. "Thank you."

Lara's mother smiles at me as she continues preparing snacks for the cousins.

Lara is standing with one hand on the banister. "Let's go up to my parents' bathroom and I'll curl your hair."

My mouth widens. She knows how much I love that bathroom, because it looks like a spa, huge and all white tiles, large mirrors, with his-and-hers sinks.

"Hey," I say as we head up the stairs, being super careful with my little snack plate. "Is this you being nice to me because of my freak accident? The food, the bathroom, the hair thing."

"That's kind of what this is," she says. "But mostly, this is me finding a place where we can talk about stuff without my parents hearing."

"Can you do my eyebrows, too?"

"Fine."

Lara puts on our usual playlist of favorite songs, and the music that comes from her portable speaker fills the magical bathroom.

"Bend your head into the sink," Lara says. I hold a towel over my face while her fingers lather my scalp, washing the mousse and hair spray out of my hair.

"You know how people go for massages or to the spa?" I ask, and Lara makes a sound of acknowledgment. "Do you think you can pay someone to scratch and rub your head? Is that a thing?"

"I have no idea."

"I would ask for that for my birthday."

Lara indulges me and keeps lathering my hair longer than necessary. Then she starts pouring hot water over my head. She finishes rinsing my hair, then I settle on a suede bench in front of the vanity. She starts untangling my hair with a wide-toothed comb.

"So when's your first date with this new guy?" I ask.

"There is no date! Baylee, I keep telling you—I literally exchanged a few random texts with him in the past few months, and he was actually kind of annoying. But yesterday—I don't know why, but he seemed a little more interesting. We're not even talking about dating or anything. It's . . . different."

Different but the exact same, I bet.

"What do you think Trey would do if he found out you're already interested in some new guy?"

"No one is going to tell him that, right?" Lara says. "Everyone involved is very discreet. The new guy—*if* he becomes a thing— well, he might just have to stay a secret."

"Secrets are fun," I say. "As long as *I'm* included."

My phone vibrates.

[Alex] U look awesome in that photo.

Earlier today, I posted a photo of myself at Rianne's house. It's from months ago, but due to some sort of sorcery, the angle and my posture made my whole self look inoffensive to my eyes, which is a super-rare occasion. There are usually at least seven things about myself that make me gag—whether it's my second chin, my shirt sitting awkwardly against my stomach, or my hair being too flat on one side—but this time, there was nothing for me to pick apart. The girl in that photo is who I wish I looked like in real life. It's me, but it's not *really* me.

[Baylee] 😶
[Alex] 😄
[Baylee] Can I tell you something?
[Alex] Totally.
[Baylee] I think your cheek piercings are really cool.
[Alex] Thanks! Those r only temporary.
[Baylee] Temporary?
[Alex] Just keeping them in for about a year total. That way u get clean scars that mimic real dimples.
[Baylee] Oh, interesting. I didn't know that.
[Alex] What r u up to today?
[Baylee] I'm hanging out with Lara. At her house. (She's the tall brown girl in the other photo I posted.)
[Alex] Which means Rianne is the little edgy one.
[Baylee] Correct.
[Alex] That sounds like fun.

[Baylee] What about you? Do you have a best friend?

[Alex] I do. Her name is Pen, and she's kind of a ballbuster.

[Baylee] So then your best friend is a girl.

[Alex] She is.

"Who are you typing to?" Lara asks. My head is yanked all over the place as she blow-dries chunks of my hair with a large, round brush.

"The Bookworm guy," I say.

"Can I read what you're saying?"

"No!"

"Why? Are you guys being gross?"

"You're so nosy," I say. "We're just talking. He's telling me about his friends right now."

"Oh, boring."

[Baylee] That's super interesting.

[Alex] Is it?

[Baylee] Well, it has the potential to be. Like are you two friends because when the time is right, you're going to hook up? Or did you used to date and you're still in each other's lives, maybe waiting to hook up again? There is a story there. I feel it. 🫤

[Alex] Ha. Well, 1: there is nothing like that between Pen and me. It's kind of funny to think about, actually. 2: Why does having a girl as a best friend mean there would have to be some kind of romantic or sexual thing between us?

[Baylee] There wouldn't have to be. It just happens a lot. I know it's narrow-minded to think girls and guys can't be friends, but honestly, I just see it play out that way too often to ignore it. My friend Freddie has dated nearly every girl who hangs around us. My friend Lara is almost the same when it comes to guys.

[Alex] . . .

I put my phone down, and heat settles in my cheeks.

"What's wrong? It's already over?" Lara asks.

"I said something stupid," I say.

"You rambled again, didn't you," Lara says, shaking her head. "What did you say?" she asks, but I stare at the floor. "Come on, tell me. I can fix it. This is my area of expertise."

"Is it weird that his best friend is a girl?" I ask. "No, it shouldn't be weird. That's just really ignorant of me."

"A little ignorant, but it makes sense. I think if the best friend is his ex-girlfriend, then it will definitely be weird and it's a legit concern."

"Maybe . . ."

Lara stands in front of me, pulling my hair down with the brush while she runs the dryer against it. "I got it! Just tell him the last guy you dated was friends with his ex and you got burned. Blame it on baggage!"

"There is no last guy I dated."

"Well," she says, eyeing me through the mirror, "he doesn't need to know he's the first guy you're dating."

"He's not going to date me."

"Why not?" she asks. "Candace has a boyfriend."

I know Candace, the Other Fat Girl in my class, has a boyfriend. I've spent enough time comparing myself to the other fat girls in my school, analyzing how many pounds might make up the difference between them and me, striving to be just a little more put-together, a little more polished than them because I'm always the fattest one.

I personally think I am better-looking than Candace, but she's the one with the boyfriend. If this was a competition, she already won.

"Is it weird that I don't have any friends who aren't . . . thin?" I ask, not really having intended to say this out loud.

"Well, Candace is kind of a bitch, so that's probably why we're not friends with her."

[Baylee] I'm sorry. That sounded super ignorant. I guess this topic is a lot bigger than I thought it would be.

[Alex] R u saying u have automatic romantic or sexual feelings for that Freddie guy?

[Baylee] Not at all. Ew. That's just wrong.

[Alex] Well, how about Lara, then?

[Baylee] Me and Lara?! Wow. I've never even thought of that. That's definitely the ew-est of all.

[Alex] Exactly. That's how it is with me and Pen. But I mean, what makes u and Lara not have romantic or sexual tension? Just because ur 2 girls?

[Baylee] No. Because it's just *so* not like that between us.

A cry of desperation escapes my lips. "I'm making it worse! I am such a stupid loser."

"What did you say?" Lara puts the dryer down and extends a hand. "Give me. I'll fix it."

"No! *I'll* fix it. I'll just be honest."

She rolls her eyes. "I don't think some rando DM guy is owed such deep honesty, and it might actually make things awkward, but . . . you do you, I guess."

"Okay, fine. I'll tell him your thing," I say. "You know more about this kind of stuff than I do. Guess I need to learn to play games."

She makes a face, and I know my comment hit her the way I meant it to. "I'm not saying it's cool to be shady and a liar," she says, taking hold of the dryer again, "but when you're just newly talking to someone—especially someone you don't know yet—you have to like, be careful how much drama you lay on such a fragile connection, you know?"

I nod, rereading the last few messages between Alex and me, trying to decide how I should approach things.

[Baylee] This is not coming out the way I mean it to. I know it seems like I'm being stupid about gender stuff right now. This conversation just ended up going totally wrong.
[Alex] How were u wanting it to go?
[Baylee] . . .

[Alex] U keep typing then stopping. Just say what u want to say. It's OK. I'm not scary. 😊

[Baylee] Okay, the truth is . . . I guess I was mostly fishing for information using really stupid stereotypes and ignorant words.

[Alex] U wanted to know if u should be jealous of my best friend?

[Baylee] Um, kind of.

[Alex] I think u and I have some things to discuss.

[Baylee] OK?

[Alex] Go hang out with ur friend. We'll talk later, OK?

"So?" Lara says. "Did I fix it?"

"Yeah," I say. "It's all better now."

I throw my phone on the counter.

TEN

Downstairs, the weekday-morning routine is in full swing. Mom is fixing her own hair and applying lipstick all while packing Rebecca's stuff for school. The nurse who takes my sister to school and spends the day there with her is getting Rebecca dressed, who is clearly still asleep. My sister and I are on the same page right now. I am tired, my face hurts, and I have a headache. The idea of a Monday morning at school is making me wish I could just keep on sleeping and ignore everyone.

"Mom," I say, "I feel worse today than yesterday."

She puts down the jug of formula she just mixed and comes over to check my face. "What's the matter?"

"I'm just sore and tired," I say.

"Fine, you can stay home. But please text me every hour to let me know how you're doing," Mom says. Rebecca whines as she's placed in her wheelchair. Mom and the nurse start strapping her in and zipping her into her coat cover. "I mean it, Boss—every hour."

I nod and head back upstairs, setting an hourly alarm on my phone before I curl up into a ball under my duvet, thinking about the pain in my face and not about Freddie. Definitely not about the very real possibility that the brief thing I had with Alex might be over now.

My late-afternoon lunch is almost a whole box of Cheez-It crackers. I left ten at the bottom, which means I did *not* eat the entire box. Mom won't be home from work for an hour or so, which means the afternoon worker she hired for Rebecca is here. She's a physiotherapy student who comes after classes to take over for the school nurse until Mom gets home. Sometimes she also comes on weekends so Mom can pop in at work to take care of things.

[Freddie] You didn't come today. Are you OK?
[Baylee] I'm fine. Just tired.
[Freddie] Do you want to come over?
[Baylee] Now?
[Freddie] Whenever.

Then it dawns on me that I completely forgot about his Monday-night plans.

[Baylee] Sorry, I totally forgot about babysitting Shaya.

[Freddie] Don't worry about that. Anyway, I'm not seeing Jess anymore. We can just hang out. If you want.

Did he cancel his date because of me? That possibility is enough to lead to my first smile of the day.

[Baylee] Who else is there?

[Freddie] No one.

Just me and Freddie.

[Baylee] OK.

[Freddie] Cool

[Baylee] I'm not trying to ignore you.

[Freddie] That's how it seems, though.

[Baylee] I ruined your car.

[Freddie] It just needed to be shampooed. I got it detailed, which I already planned on doing. It looks fine now.

[Baylee] You can drive it still?

[Freddie] Yeah. It's just cosmetic stuff on the bumper and fender. Not a big deal.

Maybe I can just go and feel the vibe.

I spend an hour getting ready, blasting a pop-hits playlist. I settle on a pair of tight black jeans, one of the several black baby-doll tops I own, and a khaki-green cropped jacket over that. I add lots of gold bangle bracelets and gold hoop earrings. When I make it downstairs, Mom is rocking Rebecca, who is clearly in a terrible mood, judging by the way she's trying her best to whack herself in the face, self-soothing having turned into self-harm.

I head for my sister's small dresser and grab a pair of her thick fuzzy socks.

"How's your face feeling now?" Mom asks.

"A little sore, but I feel a lot better. My headache's gone," I say, handing my mother the socks, and she slips them over Rebecca's hands. "Can I go to Freddie's for a bit?"

"I guess we're no longer avoiding him?"

"Well, he's being nice."

"That's great, Boss," Mom says. She gives me a funny look. "You and Freddie are still just friends, right?"

"Um, obviously. What else would we be?"

"A lot of big events and emotions in your world over the last few days. I just like to know what's going on." Mom fakes an innocent expression. "That's all."

"Well, everything is still unchanged, Mom. There is nothing happening," I say. "I don't want to date anyone or . . . any of that stuff anyway."

It's like, literally, all I want to be doing—all the stuff.

"Well, I have to admit: it's nice that I haven't had to worry about you getting wrapped up in boys." I let her words slide off my back, but there's more: "I feel like I've been lucky with you. You've got a good head on your shoulders."

"My head is just a big stupid ball, Mom," I say. A big ball crammed with thoughts and obsessions.

"Come on, Boss," she says. "You actually remind me of me when I was your age."

"Because you *also* never had a boyfriend in high school?"

"Not just that."

Mom gets distracted, repositioning Rebecca, who went quiet when Mom and I started talking.

"How come you've never dated anyone?" I ask.

"What do you mean?"

"You never wanted a boyfriend? Or a girlfriend, even?"

Mom shrugs. "Maybe when I was a lot younger. I had a couple dates, and it was fine. But then I got older, I got busy, and then I realized I like nonromantic relationships a lot better."

"Oh."

"Maybe you're feeling like that, too, huh? It's not easy when you're surrounded by people who want other things. The world is still so focused on everyone partnering off, getting married, having babies—that's not the only way, right, Boss?" she says. "I wish someone had told me that when I was young."

I think this is supposed to be a nice, uplifting mother-daughter talk, where she's telling me she understands me, that I can continue being the way I am because even though it's a different path, it's still a super-legit one.

I've let her believe I'm completely unconcerned with the fact that there's nothing going on in my life when it comes to romance, love, and sex. That I'm completely uninterested. I wonder what she would think, knowing that even when I'm focused on something else, my ridiculous yearning is always right there below the surface.

Mom places Rebecca into her bed and brings out the compressor for my sister's breathing treatment. The machine starts rumbling loudly, and Mom attaches the already-prepared little cup of breathable liquid medications to the tubing, and mist starts flowing out of the mask Mom holds against my sister's face.

"Right?" Mom says again, turning to make eye contact with me.

"Right, yes, Mom," I say. "Anyway, I'm just walking over to Freddie's place. We're not going for a ride or anything."

"Well, good," Mom says. "I know that accident wasn't his fault, but it still makes me feel better that you're not getting into the car again today."

On the walkway that connects my street to Freddie's, my stomach clenches. It's dark at this hour, but the walkway is well lit, and I spot Garrett, the jerk from down the street, kicking empty bottles around and flicking cigarettes in every direction. He's tall and a little heavyset, but I guess he's more accurately described by the word solid than fat. His hair is always unbrushed, a mess of thick dirty-blond waves, with ears that stick out too far, and a round nose over pouty lips. His only decent features, in my opinion, are his eyes and his height. I've known him for years, but he doesn't go to my school.

He's just one of the guys in my neighborhood who would make fun of me. He and his friends picked this walkway as their hangout spot, which means I was often within view or earshot.

It used to be direct comments when we were little, calling me fat, acting like my walking by was causing an earthquake, but the last few years, it's changed to looks or the sound of hushed, gritty little laughs that my whole body feels as an attack. I guess they don't have to be outwardly vicious when they know I'm completely aware of what's going on, so the tiniest action will totally lead to the reaction they want.

If I really loved myself, would I just strut past Garrett, totally untouchable?

"Hey, look!" Garrett says as I approach. "It's B."

One could think he's saying B for Baylee, but that's not what I hear when he says it. When we were twelve, he told me he was going to start calling me B for Bertha because it suited me better.

I roll my eyes as acknowledgment and keep walking.

Sometimes I wonder about those big girls on Instagram, the ones who build their whole online personas around being confidently fat. Would they walk by in crop tops, strutting their stuff right past those who cringe or laugh at them, if they were alone like I am now? Because I feel like maybe it's easier to act like you're totally worthy of worship when there are four hundred thousand people commenting below with daily encouragement and envy. I've got no followers, no entourage—I don't even have any fat friends to talk about this with. The only one telling me to keep my head up is me, and the reality is, I can't even hear me. The voice of my judgy self is always so loud. She instructs me to suck it in, but simultaneously, she reminds me that sucking in is a waste of time because everything is bulging and hanging regardless.

I'm not turning around, though, because I'm not a pushover. I want to go see Freddie, and he's only a little farther away.

"Hey," Garrett says. "Hold up! Stay and chat. I just wanna ask you a question."

"Um, no thanks?"

"Come on. It's just one tiny question."

I'm older now, and I talk back instead of pretending I don't hear. "You must be next-level bored now that you have no friends, huh?"

"Yeah, well . . . they're all a bunch of dicks. Most of 'em, anyway."

Something must've happened last summer, because the three or four guys he used to hang out with went away. Only Garrett walks up and down the street by himself now.

He takes a few steps toward the middle of the path, like he's hoping to intercept me when I reach that point.

"Winter sucks, am I right?" he asks.

"Yeah, it sucks."

Garrett pulls a pack of cigarettes out of his pocket. "You want a smoke?"

"No." My nose throbs, probably on account of my heart rate doubling in beats and force since I noticed Garrett's presence. He's not even that scary anymore, but I can't get rid of that leftover physical reaction. "What do you want?"

"I'm just saying hi."

I stop, tipping my head to the side. "You're not trying to say hi to me. You're trying to find a new way to call me ugly and fat just so you can laugh, right?"

"You're not ugly," he says matter-of-factly, and it stops me for a second. "Your face is nice."

My face is nice—those are the words I hold on to. It's so pathetic that I manage to extract a compliment out of that whole interaction. The confusion is heavy right now.

"Okay, well," I say. "Thanks."

A furrowed brow is the response he gives me.

I continue walking, hugging the fence to my right, putting as much distance between myself and Garrett as I can.

"I'm just trying to have a conversation with you," Garrett says from behind me. "I'm not *always* an asshole, ya know."

"I feel like your whole purpose here on earth is to be a nuisance."

"It's just jokes!" Garrett says. "Everyone gets so offended over the littlest things, am I right?"

"Hey, Baylee," Freddie says from the end of the walkway. Sometimes Freddie walks over to meet me, which usually fills me with glitter, but today I wish he'd stayed home.

I glance back to see Garrett give Freddie the middle finger. Freddie returns the gesture, then hitches his chin up at me to carry on walking over.

"Okay, fine. But I got a question for you, Freddie, since B here doesn't seem to wanna talk to me," Garrett says. "I'm asking for a friend, all right? Is B your main chick? Or maybe your side chick?"

"Whatever, Garrett," Freddie says, not even looking his way. "Keep talking. No one is listening."

"I'm getting some secret side-piece vibes, am I right?" Garrett says.

"You couldn't be more full of shit if you tried, Garrett," Freddie says.

"Hey, man, some guys are into that," Garrett says, and when I glance over at him, he gives me a wide grin. "Some guys are like, 'Damn, I want me *all* of that!'"

"Oh my god, shut *up*!" I yell. "Seriously!" This isn't about Garrett actually thinking Freddie and I could be a thing. This is him making fun of Freddie and using *me* to do it.

Freddie stares at the ground, and Garrett is quiet behind me.

"Can we just go?" I tell Freddie, who seems to snap out of it and spins on his heel, me following close behind.

I already know this whole scene will forever be etched in my mind. Later, I will replay this, coming up with better dialogue. I might even picture myself smacking Garrett right across the face. It's not that this kind of trash crushes my soul or anything. It just has a way of lingering as this icky, heavy feeling of wrong. Rewriting it makes it less icky.

I hate Garrett. I have always hated him, and it just makes me so mad that I'm still thinking about the fact that he said I'm not ugly, which might mean that he thinks I'm the opposite and . . . what would that mean?

ELEVEN

Freddie leaves the garage door up a couple of feet and takes a seat on one side of the couch. I stand by the other end. The heater blows heat all around us. Freddie's car is parked in the garage, the bumper cracked and scuffed in a couple of places.

"Garrett is a tool," Freddie says, pulling his vape out. "No use wasting any mental energy on him, right?"

"It's not an intentional thing that I'm doing, Freddie."

"Are you just going to stand there?" he asks, blowing thick, strawberry-scented vapor my way. "Sit. Stay awhile."

So I do, my back straight, purse on my knees, legs crossed at the ankles. When I'm uncomfortable and hyperaware of my size, my purse becomes my shield. I'm not exactly sure what the act of holding up a small object in front of my huge self does to reassure me, but it works.

"Want me to beat Garrett up for you?" He taps my knee, trying to get me to return his smile.

It works, because the idea of him defending my honor makes me tingle all over.

"You can't beat anyone up, can you?"

"I bet I could. Look at this," he says, then he's unzipping his jacket, slipping an arm out, and flexing his bicep, which is definitely *there*. "Bench-pressing a hundred pounds is paying off. Touch it."

"No way!" But my hand is already in the air, not ready to pass up an opportunity to touch him. I squeeze, keeping my touch as light as possible, and my shiny red nails against his brown skin is making me forget who I am. "That's pretty . . . firm."

He nods in satisfaction, putting his jacket back on. "How's your nose?"

"If I take Tylenol, it's fine. If I don't take Tylenol, then I feel my heartbeat in my face."

"That's a really cool description," he says. "I am going to write this down real quick, in case I can use it in my script."

"You would have to credit me, then," I say. "Or pay me for my clever—cleverity."

He laughs. "Cleverness, Bay. What the hell is cleverity?"

"I make up words, too. If you like them, you can also credit me, and/or pay me."

He laughs. "How much is cleverity worth?"

"I charge like, thirty dollars a word."

"That's a lot. I'm broke, remember?"

This conversation is like totally ridiculous improv, and the bad vibes from earlier fade away.

"Look, I feel really bad about what happened," Freddie says, dragging the vibe right back. "I didn't realize the seat belt—"

"Can we not? Honestly, it's totally fine. I don't want to talk about this."

"I know, but if I'd known—"

"Okay, thanks. Thanks for the apology. Anyway, this coronavirus stuff is kind of weird, right?"

He shakes his head while I flash a fake, innocent smile. The reality is, if he'd taken a regular girl out for a ride, there would've been no seat-belt catastrophe. It was *me* who was the problem, not the seat belt.

"Yeah," he says, typing into his phone. "It's definitely weird."

"Who are you texting?" I ask him.

"Jess," he says.

Oh, to be able to go back in time and *not* ask a question. "Rescheduling, I guess?"

He shakes his head. "Not even a little. It is now officially over."

"How come? What happened?"

"It wasn't supposed to be serious with her. But she's looking for a boyfriend, and now that I have a car, she thought I'd be driving up to see her on weekends."

"So it's done?"

He nods. "I told her I'm not looking for that."

"What are you looking for, then?"

"I don't know." He sighs. "Maybe that's why I keep feeling people out. No one's really been it, you know?"

I nod, but no. Not at all, actually.

"I think I'm just looking in the wrong place, or at the wrong people," he says.

My feelings for him swell.

"Do you talk like this to your friends?" I ask. "To Trey or Rav?"

He snorts. "No. I talk like this with *you*."

"Well, I think that's super mature, what you said."

We settle into a new kind of silence, and I let myself relax into the couch.

"So, I gotta be honest," Freddie says. "I'm kind of having some thoughts about someone else. Someone different."

There's anxiety in the air now, and not all of it is mine. "Okay . . ."

He nods while his hand moves to the back of his neck. "The thing is . . . ," he starts. "You know how you and I are pretty tight, right?"

Wait—what? Waves of electricity move through me. I sit up straight again.

He's clearing his throat, fidgeting with the way the hem of his jeans falls over his scuffed, weather-beaten high-tops.

He drops his vape, then accidentally kicks it while trying to pick it up.

Oh. My. God.

"I feel like we're usually on the same page, but I'm sort of nervous about bringing this up, because for some reason I'm kind of thinking your reaction to this might be . . . intimidating. And now there's this vibe."

My mind starts chanting an irritating chorus of *I can't love Freddie until I love myself. I have to love myself before Freddie can love me.* Unless . . .

Could this really be happening? How am I able to go from knowing something is impossible, to rearranging my entire outlook and suddenly becoming convinced something impossible is not only *possible*, but that it's happening right freaking now? It's like I'm a pessimist with sudden-onset bouts of unrealistic optimism.

It takes all my strength to murmur my next words: "What are you trying to say right now, Freddie?"

"Okay, so, I've just been thinking that . . ." He trails off when the garage door starts opening as headlights appear at the bottom of the driveway.

Mrs. Morales's SUV pulls up on the driveway, and she pops out of the driver's door, waving at us as she moves to the back seat to unbuckle his sister, Shaya.

"Mom, what are you doing here? I thought you were going to baby swimming, then for dinner."

"Well, swimming was canceled because a kiddo pooped in the pool just before we got there, and by the time they get that cleaned up, it would be time for the next class," Mrs. Morales says.

"Poor little guy. His mother was dead of embarrassment. Anyway, I rescheduled dinner and swimming for next week, and I just stopped for some groceries instead."

"That's gross," Freddie says.

She leans into the car. "You can either carry the groceries inside, or," she tells Freddie, holding a snowsuit-bundled Shaya out to us, "you can carry this sack of potatoes. You pick."

"Hi," Shaya says. "I poop."

Freddie laughs, ruffling Shaya's shaggy brown hair. "I pick the groceries."

"How could you give away the surprise like that, Boo?" Mrs. Morales says to Shaya.

"Nice try pawning her loaded diaper off on me."

Mrs. Morales comes over to me, Shaya on her right hip and a purse hanging from her left shoulder. Shaya struggles to get down, so Mrs. Morales lowers her to the ground, keeping hold of one of her hands as Shaya pulls to go in the opposite direction.

"Hello, Baylee! I'm glad to see you're all right."

"Yes, I'm fine."

"We're all relieved it wasn't worse. How's your nose?"

"It's still here."

"I'm glad. I don't even notice anything."

"It's the cover-up. I'm pretty good with makeup."

"Very nice," she says. "Well, I'm making sure Freddie refreshes himself on defensive driving."

"I know how to drive, Mom," Freddie says.

"I know you do." Then to me, she says, "Anyway, say hi to your mother for me."

"Hi, Bayee," Shaya says, holding a grasping hand out at me like she thinks I'll come pick her up the way I normally would. "I poop!"

I wave, managing a half-assed polite smile and a weak response wave to Shaya's excitement at seeing me. Mrs. Morales picks up Shaya, tucking her horizontally under an arm, and the two of them disappear inside.

I was in a moment just then. A moment that I hadn't fashioned in my own mind. This was happening for real and it just freaking went poof.

"I guess I should get going," Freddie says, a thumb gesturing to the SUV, where the groceries wait.

"Okay?"

"There was more I was going to say, but it doesn't really feel like the right time now. Maybe I'll text you?"

I stand and wander out of the garage, watching Freddie looping too many plastic bags over his fingers. "I don't understand."

"Don't worry about it. It's my fault," he says, seeming uncomfortable. "I'll text you later."

I shuffle down the sidewalk.

"Hey," he calls, and I turn. "You want a ride to school tomorrow?"

"No." The word just shot out of my mouth. "I mean, no, thank you."

Freddie looks down, and I continue putting more distance between us, leaving a trail of heel clicks behind me. When I get home, Mom looks surprised to see me back so early.

"I'm making spaghetti," she says. "It's almost ready."

"Okay," I say. "But I'm not very hungry right now. I'll come down later."

Mom looks at me with suspicion, because I am usually always hungry. My mood doesn't affect my appetite, but it affects my ability to sit on the couch next to my mother, slurping spaghetti while obsessing over Freddie and what just happened. I take the stairs up to my room.

[Freddie] I know I was being a little cryptic and weird.
[Baylee] Try a lot. And leaving me hanging, all confused, is not OK.

It takes an incomprehensible amount of time, like at least ten minutes of me sitting on my bed, staring out the window, but his response comes.

It's not a text, though. It's a voice note.

"Let's say there's a group of friends—like at school—and maybe two of those friends are curious about each other. Maybe one of them just realized that there's more to the other than they originally thought. But if they try it out, it'll create a lot of awkwardness and general bullshit with the others. Should they still go for it?"

I start typing a response, but another voice note comes through.

"I'm being cryptic again, but just think about it. Don't react too quickly. Just really think about it, okay?"

I'm not thinking about it. I'm feeling it all over my body.

This is it. I'm done waiting for things to happen.

They're happening now.

TWELVE

The next day, I get a ride to school with my mother on her way to work at her drive-through coffee store, except I'm now a good thirty minutes early and the school is deserted. After I hang the faux-leather messenger bag I use as a backpack in my locker, I settle on the ground against my closed locker, purse in my lap. My fingers scroll through photos of arm tattoos that resulted from a Google search. I'm pretty much decided on the fact that I will start tattooing my upper arms as soon as I have access to thousands of dollars. I could do with a little extra edge, and my gross, doughy arms covered in black-shaded flowers, hearts, or music notes would definitely make me hate them less.

[Alex] Hey. Maybe if ur not busy tonight, we could DM for a bit?

[Baylee] OK.

[Alex] I have something to do after school, but I can message u when I'm home later.

[Baylee] OK.

[Alex] How r u?

[Baylee] OK.

[Alex] Everything is just very OK with u then? 😏

[Baylee] It's all very swell, actually.

[Alex] Swell. I like that word.

[Baylee] It's a good word.

[Alex] I'm sorry I went MIA for a bit there. I realize I came off like a bit of a jerk.

[Baylee] I came off like a jerk first.

[Alex] I have more to say but I gotta get to school. Talk later?

[Baylee] Um. OK. 😊

The first few students start shambling down the hallway, and I go back to scoping out the arm-tattoo situation, feeling warmth inside from Alex's reappearance. I never thought some rando DM guy suddenly dropping off the face of the earth for a couple of days would feel like such a major loss, but now that he's back, I feel a whole lot more settled and ready to deal with anything today might bring. Even Freddie and that whole awkwardness.

"*Baylee!* I feel like I haven't seen you in forty-seven years," Rianne shouts from the other end of the hall. She stops at her locker, then heads over and takes a seat on the floor next to me. "Saturday—you're sleeping over, too, right?"

"Of course!"

Rianne runs her fingers through her purple hair, then fluffs her razor-slashed black bangs. "I went with a very vintage raccoon-eyes look today—what do you think?"

"I like it," I say. "Makes you kind of look like you had a wild time last night and you passed out on a stranger's couch for a few hours."

Rianne nods in satisfaction. "I love that. In reality, I video-chatted with my grandpa and folded laundry, but I would much rather people think I slept in an alley behind some club."

As bodies begin to crowd around us, Rianne and I climb to our feet and rummage through our lockers to get our first-period things. The guys are visible now, coming down the hall together, likely because Freddie picked Trey and Rav up. I'm all twisted inside, thinking back to Freddie's voice note. I can't tell if he's avoiding me, because I'm too busy doing everything I can not to look at him.

"Hey," I say, nudging Rianne with my elbow. "I totally forgot to ask Lara how it went yesterday with Trey and all that."

I kind of forgot about Lara altogether yesterday.

Rianne shrugs. "It was all right. I mean, we just steered clear of the guys all day. But we can't do that forever. We need to talk about our end-of-year trip. Trey's already convinced too many people that canoeing up north and sleeping in tents is the way to go."

"He must be stopped."

"He must. I'm not sleeping in a tent and acting like that's a good time."

"Neither am I." I fake a gag. "Mosquitoes, poop holes in the ground for toilets, canoes." Canoes that I definitely *won't* fit into.

The end-of-year trip is an idea a couple of guys on the hockey team threw out there months ago, then suddenly our whole grade decided to get in on it. Only trouble is, no one could agree on what to do, so we're all planning separate trips, and in our group, Rianne's the organizer.

Lara arrives, heading straight for Rianne and me. She looks especially nice today, with heavier makeup and her hair twisted into a high messy bun and oversized gold hoop earrings. She must be hoping Trey will notice and . . . do what? Maybe she just wants him to look and wish. Just being looked at that way must be such a thrill.

"Where do you stand on the trip?" Rianne asks Lara as we walk together.

Lara shrugs, keeping an eye on the guys, and we all note them coming over at the same time.

"Well, for the record, I vote against the wilderness thing," she states, having now decided to have an opinion, when Trey's within earshot.

"Of course you would," Trey says, from his spot between Freddie and Rav. "Luckily, no one gives a flying fudge what you think."

"Trey, come on," Freddie says at the same time as I open my mouth to tell Trey off.

"Yeah" is the only thing I can think of saying in the moment, and I glance at Lara, who sends hate rays to the floor with her eyes. Usually it's my job to stand up for my best friend, and Freddie does the same for Trey. I'm confused. I don't want to look at Freddie directly, but it kind of feels like he might be staring at me.

"Guys, I'm really getting sick of this drama constantly interfering with the group," Rianne says. "Can you two just make up your minds and move on?"

"My mind is made up, and I've moved on," Lara says.

"I don't really care where you've moved on to, but don't act like you weren't just baiting me with your comment about the trip," Trey says.

"I wasn't baiting you," Lara says. "I'm not the *only* one who doesn't want anything to do with camping."

"Here's an idea," Trey says, laying on the fake enthusiasm thick. "You girls do your own thing! We'll bring different girls. *Better* girls." When Freddie lifts a hand to smack his shoulder, Trey looks at Rianne and me. "You two can still come."

"Come *on!*" Rianne cries, throwing her hands up in the air. "You and Lara are constantly ruining everything."

Rianne is always somehow able to state the harsh, impartial truth and get away with it. If I said that, Lara would see it as a personal betrayal. But because it's Rianne, Lara lets the comment hang in the air, shakes her head, then makes eye contact with me for support.

That's when I notice Taylor at her locker to my right, so obviously eavesdropping.

"I am so down with camping," she says as she slams her locker door shut. Then she gestures to the small group forming around her, the other guys on the basketball team Freddie and Trey are friendly with and the girls Lara would probably be hanging out with if it wasn't for Rianne and me. "We all are. Just saying."

"Literally no one asked you," I tell Taylor.

She ignores me and starts whispering with the girl next to her.

"Let's just agree on something we all want to do," I say to my own friends. "We can each come up with an idea, then we'll vote."

"I vote for Lara not coming," Trey says.

"I think that's a great idea," she says. "I've decided to no longer spend my free time around you anyway. Butthurt Trey is even worse than regular Trey."

"I'm not butthurt," Trey says, and I see Rav roll his eyes. "You're not that great to be around, Lara. Trust me."

"Trey, let it go," Freddie says. "Let's just let things cool down awhile. We'll talk about this next week or something."

"I don't know why you're trying to protect her feelings all of a sudden, bro," Trey says. "You can't stand her either."

"What?" Lara flashes Freddie a look of shock. "Wow—that's really great."

"That's not—" Freddie starts, then he smacks Trey's shoulder again. "Nice, Trey. Real nice."

"Whatever, bro. Just keep her away from me," Trey says, before heading in the opposite direction.

"Hey, Freddie," Taylor says, coming too close to him. "How's your car? I heard it was like a crime scene in there."

"Keep on walking, Taylor," Freddie snaps, then walks off after Trey, Rav following.

Taylor doesn't even make eye contact with me, but she knows I heard. I let it go, even though I'm furious enough to want to rip a chunk of hair from her head, because if I let it go, she's less likely to drop the name Kunkel's Cankles out there for my friends to hear.

"Way to go, everyone," Rianne says. "The splitting of our group is in effect. Girls on one side, boys on the other."

"It'll calm down soon," I say.

"Can you two just get back together already?" Rianne asks.

"We are *not* getting back together," Lara says.

Rianne's eyebrow goes up. "Yeah, I'm sure."

"I'm one hundred percent not getting back together with him—trust me. He'll just have to grow up and stop being a jerk."

"I kind of believe you," Rianne says, looking suspicious. She turns to me. "What do you think?"

"I think she's serious. It's done for good," I say, which makes Lara smile with vindication.

"Interesting. Well, I'm warning you: this better be smoothed over by Saturday. If it's not, then the guys aren't coming. I'm not having this ruin Baylee's party," Rianne says.

"But how can we not have guys there?" I ask.

"Oh, we'll have plenty of guys there, just not *these* ones. They want better girls? Well, we can get better guys," Rianne says, then she seems to lose interest. "Do we *have* to go to class? Can we get out of this somehow?"

"We could just walk right out," I say.

She wags her eyebrows at me, and then I'm doing it, too.

"We are *going* to class," Lara says.

"Let's go for ice cream," I say.

"Ugh, I'm not going to work on my day off! Let's go to the mall for fries with vinegar and ketchup," Rianne says.

"Bye," Lara says, heading off to her first class.

"Farewell, my fellow wannabe-delinquent friend," I tell Rianne.

"Farewell. I shall miss you," she says. "See you at lunch."

I head over to my social sciences class, which I dislike because none of my actual friends are in this class with me. I take my usual seat at the back, where there are long tables instead of individual desks.

When this unfamiliar-yet-familiar guy walks in after everyone else, I have this moment of sheer confusion, knowing this person isn't a stranger, but they don't belong in this setting.

THIRTEEN

Garrett shambles toward the back, throwing superior, dirtbag expressions over the students already seated, like he's assessing what spot would benefit him best in the long run. I allow the disgust to reconfigure my features, knowing it's a matter of milliseconds before he notices me.

And then he does. And his grin turns into an open-mouthed, almost-gleeful expression of recognition.

"Mr. Ronson," the teacher calls, "why don't you take a seat up here?"

"Well, sir, I'd much rather sit back there with my friend B," Garrett says. "We go way back!"

I lose all feeling from the neck down. Heads twist to see who B is, and it feels like they all know he's calling me Bertha. Garrett heads over and takes a seat next to me, going as far as dragging his chair a few inches closer.

"Why are you here?" I hear myself saying.

He laughs. "I couldn't stand to be away from you, B."

"Whatever you're thinking, I'm telling you that you are not going to invade my school life," I say. "There's no way I'm letting you do this here."

Garrett lets out this good-natured laugh. "Do what? I'm not doing anything. I seriously think it's cool that I'm in your class. It's cool, am I right? What are the chances."

Mr. What's-His-Face goes through roll call.

I lean away from Garrett. "Do not speak to me."

Garrett snorts in response, then pretends to zip his lips shut.

I keep my eyes aimed at the front, while Garrett's whistly, exaggerated nasal breathing continually reminds me of his presence.

Lara sends me a text that I'm able to read on account of being all the way at the back.

[Lara] Bookworm later?
[Baylee] OK.

Alex can't talk until later tonight, which means there's a good chance he's working after school. I feel a pang of excitement at the thought of seeing Alex for real, finally finding out what he looks like.

Maybe he's afraid I'll think he's ugly?

What if he *is* ugly?

No. There's no way. Last year I had a crush on Brian, a guy

Rianne and Lara rated as the ugliest guy in our grade, but we were paired up for a project and he would tell me all kinds of random stories instead of actually working, which was how I realized his voice is really attractive, and his smile gave me chills. At least for a couple of weeks. I know Freddie is like, typical hot, but my eyes also appreciate a lot more than that.

Unless Alex is gross. What if he doesn't brush his teeth?

"Tsk-tsk," Garrett whispers, nodding at my phone. "I won't tell on you, though."

"Don't talk to me!" My words are a hissed whisper. "I'm trying to pretend you're not here."

"Why? I'm not even doing anything."

I ignore him, trying to pay attention to the teacher, but my body vibes in a bad way. I spend the rest of class trying to come up with believable ways to be let out of class early, never settling on a plan. When class ends and everyone goes stampeding out, Garrett takes his sweet time.

"Why are you here? Who changes schools in March?" I ask him.

"It's a really simple story. I got expelled from St. Peter's before Christmas," he says. "Well, not exactly expelled. But it was strongly suggested that I get the hell out. So now I got three Grade Eleven credits to finish by June, then I'm supposed to redo all of Grade Twelve next year."

His candidness has me pause, but only for a moment. "But how are you in an advanced class if you're such an idiot?"

"I didn't say I got expelled because I'm an idiot," he says. "Well,

I *am* an idiot, but not in the intellectual sense. But no worries and shit, B, because I got a backup plan if my brain cells fail me: I'm gonna cheat on you for tests."

I roll my eyes and push to my feet.

"And we'll be partners for group stuff, but you'll do all the work, obviously," he adds.

"I will drop this class."

"No, you won't. I think we're gonna have a great year together, B," he says. "Well, half a year. But hey! We'll be together next year, too. You're the only friend I've got." His mouth twists with a grin full of mischief and turdiness, then he points at the chair I was sitting in just a moment ago. "Is that butt sweat?"

Of course, I look, and there's nothing there, because I make a point to get up in a way that would wipe the chair, but the fact that he just mentioned that butt sweat on a chair is a thing—I run my hand along my backside.

"Nah, I'm just messing with you," he says. "You're good."

I walk away convinced I am not returning to this school.

Fourteen

Bookworm Café makes the best whipped cream drinks, like this strawberry shortcake cream-blended drink I'm addicted to, and they're never stingy on the crumbly topping. As Lara and I walk in through the main bookstore entrance, I scan the coffee shop area to the right: three girls, no boys. The door that leads to the office or staff room behind the counter is open, but there's no guy back there that I can see. Something that was clenched inside me releases.

I'm now full of a mixture of relief and disappointment, feelings that are quite familiar to me and that always seem to go together.

"I've got to tinkle," Lara says.

"I'll wander."

I pull my shoulders back, adjust my shirt, fluff my hair, and add a layer of neutral-pink gloss to my lips. While Lara pees, I head for the stationery section, where I browse the journals, my eyes widening at the price tags. I am physically unable to stop checking my phone. I can't decide who I'd most like to hear from: Freddie or Alex.

Fifteen minutes later, I take a seat on one of the chairs scattered through the bookstore and send Lara a text.

[Baylee] Did you fall in the toilet? Do you have diarrhea?

She doesn't respond. I continue sitting here, thinking about Freddie's voice notes and the things he asked me to think about.

[Baylee] Are we avoiding each other now?
[Freddie] No. Sorry. I just needed some time to figure stuff out.

Figure what out exactly? I thought *I* was the one who was supposed to be thinking.

Am I stupid? Am I not seeing something super obvious, right in front of my face? I want to believe that Freddie wants what I want, and I even send a wish into the universe that he becomes my secret—but I know better.

[Baylee] Look, whatever it is, I'm fine with it.
[Freddie] Maybe I shouldn't have said anything. It's way more complicated than I thought.
[Baylee] You can't take it back now.
[Freddie] I know. I should've spent more time thinking it over.

[Baylee] I mean, why can't the two friends just be a secret? Then other people's feelings wouldn't get in the way.

[Freddie] You think that would be better than honesty?

[Baylee] Honesty is for the two people involved. Everyone else can just mind their own business. Just please stop being weird with me.

In my fantasies, it's a given that Freddie wouldn't want his friends to know of his interest in me. It's better this way, because then I can daydream about us tucked away somewhere private, and my mind can't intrude with ridiculous, soul-crushing scenarios of Garrett or Trey laughing at Freddie for walking away from a girl like Jess in favor of a girl like me.

I assumed I'd be a secret. I'm okay with it.

He starts to type a few times, but nothing pops through.

There's a skinny white guy with fluffy blond curls sitting almost directly across from me. Well, he's not exactly sitting, more like sprawled over the chair. He looks about my age. He sighs loudly, letting his head fall back into the void behind the back of the chair.

"I hate reading. I hate books. I hate *you*, Mom." He says the last part louder. There's a lady browsing the self-help books one aisle over, but she doesn't flinch at this guy's whining.

Now he plays with an eyelid, trying to fold it over. It's disgusting, but once he has one flipped and staying in place, he starts with the other. I stare at him, thinking about how I would *never* consider letting someone like him kiss me.

I don't think I would.

Well . . .

Am I even allowed to have super-rigid standards? What would it say about me if I acted all shallow and picky? Shouldn't an inexperienced fat girl like me be empathetic when it comes to other people's shitty qualities? But would the version of me who loves herself make a list of "must-haves" and "must-not-haves," turning people away until that perfect person showed up? Is that what loving myself should look like—not settling? Simply knowing that I'm worth it and deserve nothing but the best? What if the best is a loser who flips his eyelids over?

God—I hope this isn't Alex.

No, it could never be him, because an employee behaving this way at their place of work wouldn't have a job for as long as Alex has worked here.

"What is the look on your face about?" Lara says, patting my shoulder as she arrives at my side. I nudge my chin up toward the guy and his creepy eyelids. He's now chanting the word *mom* and moaning in annoyance, gazing around him to creep people out, I suppose.

"I'm trying to determine if that turd over there could be my new crush," I say.

"Ew," she says. "Please."

"But what if I love him?" I say. "Look at those skills."

"Oh right—he should put that on his résumé." Lara and I stare at him another minute, then she calls out to him. "Hey!" He raises his head slightly, blinking his gross lids at her. "That is offensive, and you're going to get pink eye. But can I take a photo?"

He shrugs, readjusting one of the lids as it threatens to unfold. "Whatever."

Lara takes the shot, shaking her head as she inspects it. "Rianne needs to see this."

"She does," I say. "But tell her he's mine and she can't have him."

We laugh, listening to Rianne's voice note response as we head to the café. Lara orders a huge herbal tea, while I go for the strawberry shortcake drink.

"Are you drinking tea because your stomach hurts? Is that why you were in the bathroom for fifteen minutes?" I ask as we wait for our order at the other end of the counter.

"Stop!" She swats my arm. "I kind of lost track of time texting the guy."

"I should have figured."

Lara's plain, hot-water drink is ready to be picked up within seconds. My drink is a little more elaborate, and I watch as one of the girls behind the counter pours ingredients into a blender.

"Did Freddie tell you about his car?" she asks, not waiting for me to chime in. "He got it detailed at that place over on Thorne yesterday—"

"Yes, I know that."

"Did he tell you that when they heard what happened, they gave him an excellent discount?" Lara asks.

"No, he didn't. That's nice of them," I say.

She shrugs. "I thought that would make you feel better, because you were so worried about the mess."

"Well, thanks."

My drink appears on the counter, looking like twelve hundred calories of deliciousness. Lara and I head to our usual spot, which is taken, so we choose the table next to it, figuring that when the laptop guy packs up, we can hop over and reclaim our rightful place.

For a moment, I consider laying all the Freddie stuff out on the table, feeling so desperate to have a levelheaded outsider's opinion on the situation.

"Isn't Trey such a jerk?" Lara says.

"Yes, but are we surprised?"

"He could really cause problems for me, if he doesn't get over it."

"It's literally been four days since you guys broke up—maybe some time just needs to pass? You guys have broken up for weeks before. Maybe he thinks this is that again."

"Yes, but I was still texting him when we were broken up those times. This is different. I haven't talked to him at all, except for this morning."

"Has he been texting you?"

She tips her head back in exaggerated exhaustion. "All the time!"

"Maybe *he* just needs to find a new girl to text with."

Lara shrugs. "Maybe he does. Maybe I should throw Taylor his way."

"Ew, no. You can't do that. Then she'd be hanging around with us," I say.

Just then a guy comes out of the back room. A tall white guy with short dark hair. He's thin, but his arms are ripped with muscles. We're close enough to the counter to hear him speak with one of the girls behind the counter, something about next week's schedule and how he can't close on Thursday.

It could be Alex, if he suddenly decided to change his hair color from blond to black-brown.

"Why are you drooling over that guy and being so obvious about it?" Lara whispers, then her mouth falls open. "Oh. My. God. Is this him? Is this the guy?"

"Stop it," I say, turning my head. "Let's go."

When I imagined sneaking a look at Alex, it wasn't with Lara questioning me about it at the same time. It was supposed to be private and safe.

She holds her hands out, like *What the hell?* but she gets up to follow. I grab my drink and my jacket, then I motion for Lara to hurry up and do the same. She stares at me like I'm being super pathetic, but she slips her coat on anyway. We head off and I am almost safe.

"Excuse me?" Lara says, making me stop and turn around. She's moved to the counter, where the possibly-Alex guy is jotting things down on a piece of paper.

"Oh, sorry, I'm not working right now," he says.

"That's okay. I'm actually just wondering if you know my friend," Lara says, pointing at me.

Right at me. I die a little inside. Actually, I die a lot.

FIFTEEN

I just booked it, said nothing, and ran toward the exit as fast as my heels would allow. Now I step outside, unsure where Lara is, but 100 percent set on running away without her. This is so typical of her, totally bold and spontaneous with absolutely zero consideration for the fact that we are not part of the same world. She cannot do that to me. This might've ruined everything.

I press my back against the cold brick and pull my phone out.

[Baylee] I'm sorry for taking off, but this is too awkward.

Alex's response comes almost right away.

[Alex] What do u mean? What's going on?
[Baylee] I didn't want it to happen this way, if we were ever going to meet, that is. But Lara just doesn't think.

It takes a minute before his response comes.

[Alex] Don't worry. It's not me.

Huh?

[Baylee] ???
[Alex] The guy ur friend Lara is talking to right now. It's not me.
That's Andre. I was actually in the back room, stocking.

I shove my phone into my pocket, staring around me in a panic. Occasional shoppers rush back and forth from their cars and Bookworm's main entrance. Lara is still in there, and I'm out here alone, standing a little farther down the strip mall.

[Alex] I'd actually been thinking about us meeting. That's what I wanted to talk to u about tonight, except . . .

Except I'm the fat loser who took off, while my super-pretty, charismatic friend stayed behind.

[Baylee] Except you didn't realize this is who I'd be in real life?
[Alex] Except I sort of realized a little while ago that u assumed I'm a guy and I never corrected u.

What? I read the text five times.

[Baylee] You're a girl?
[Alex] Yes.

The despair and total embarrassment I was feeling disappear in an instant.

Alex is not a guy.

I pull up the photo I'd saved, the one where he—*she* is holding the textbook. I guess I totally assumed she was a guy.

But this doesn't have to be a big deal. That photo plus the other ones on her Instagram are of someone hot.

All the girls at my school are so typical with their girliness, but I've seen the type of girl who makes me tingle the same way Freddie does. I follow some of them on Instagram, and although I haven't seen all of Alex, it feels like she could be like that. It feels like maybe nothing has changed?

Unless her photos are deceiving.

What if she's not boyish at all? What if she's super girly, smells like pretty perfume, and isn't even into girls—let alone fat ones?

I'm so confused, and the hope is slowly evaporating.

[Alex] This isn't the way I wanted things to go, but it just got harder and harder to tell u.
[Alex] R u still there . . . ?
[Alex] I just thought u were a really cool person. I don't want u getting the wrong idea.

There's the confirmation that I was *totally* getting the wrong idea.

Getting the wrong idea is what I do best.

I was so busy turning Alex—a faceless internet font, a rando DM presence—into some version of Freddie who would actually see me and want me, that I didn't even stop to consider the fact that this person might just be looking to make a friend. After all, I'm the quirky fat girl who has no trouble making friends. Wasn't that always the more likely scenario?

Now I'm replaying all the conversations we had, all the comments she made. It all feels very different now. Everything that sparked butterflies in me now seems so innocent.

All that cryptic shittery I laid on her about her best friend and the sexual tension stuff—that's why she got weird with me. That's when she realized I had a crush and that I'd blown an innocent interaction up to be some romantic thing.

How could I seriously think this person would be into me?

[Alex] Can I come out and talk to u?
[Baylee] No! Don't. Please don't.
[Alex] . . .

I thought I was finally meeting someone whose attention was on me for something more than friendship, only to find out that, once again, I just made it all up. It's always one-sided.

[Alex] Lara is on her way out now, BTW.

Nothing was happening before, and nothing is happening now. I am used to this. There is huge disappointment, but the relief is not far behind. Relief that I won't be thrust into some brand-new situation I wouldn't know how to handle anyway.

I tuck my phone into my coat pocket, take a cleansing breath, and wait for Lara to appear.

I can't believe I've been talking to a girl this whole time.

"You loser!" Lara cries when she sees me. "That wasn't even him."

"Thank god."

"That guy's name is Andre, and he's kind of cute," she says. "And super chatty."

"I can't believe you would do that to me," I say.

Lara looks taken aback by my tone. "What do you mean?"

"It could have been Alex!"

"That's the guy's name? I was trying to ask Andre about the other guys he works with, but he had no idea what I was talking about. He kept saying there's only this old guy named Charles who works on Thursday mornings."

"Can you stop?" I say. "You totally put me on the spot."

"I was just trying to help," she says. "Nudge you along a little."

"I didn't ask you to. I asked you to follow me out the door."

"You're being kind of dramatic, Baylee," she says. "It wasn't even him. Nothing happened."

"What if it *had* been him? What were you trying to do?"

"A nudge—I told you."

Or was she trying to make sure all Alex would see was her?

I need to drop this, because none of it matters now. "Can we just go? It's freezing out here."

We head for the bus stop in more silence than usual.

"Can you bring your Grade Nine yearbook tomorrow?" I ask her.

"Why?"

"Can you just please bring it?"

"Fine."

Lara's ride arrives, and although her uncle offers to drop me off at home, I say no.

On the bus, I lean my forehead against the cold window.

I can't believe I thought Alex might've liked me.

SIXTEEN

The next day, my mother drives me to school again.

"I wanted to talk to you about what's going on with the coronavirus," Mom says.

"What do you mean?"

"You've been reading the news articles I've been sending you, right?"

"Of course."

I read a couple of them, but they're so long and I haven't really been all that interested in what's happening, because it's all happening elsewhere.

"I just want us to keep the dialogue open," Mom says. "It looks like people are catching it here. It's not just a travel thing anymore."

"Oh, okay."

"Do you know what this means?"

"I'm already always making sure I don't bring things home to Rebecca. I'll just stay away from anyone who seems sick."

"That's a start." There's a look on her face as she turns on the news on the radio. All the way to school, we listen to the newspeople talk about the number of cases in Canada, and a man who caught it from his wife.

"Well, maybe people will actually get flu shots now," I say.

"This isn't the regular flus we've got vaccines for, Boss," Mom says. "This is new, and we're going to make sure we don't bring that crap home to Beck, okay?"

I nod as we pull into the school. "Okay."

I hop out of the van and make my way through the main doors. As soon as she arrives, Lara comes straight to find me at my locker.

"Are you still mad at me?"

"The whole thing was awkward," I say.

"I shouldn't have gone up to that guy."

"It's fine. It's over now."

"I formally apologize."

We lock eyes, and I can tell it's difficult for her to be the one who says sorry first. "I formally accept."

"Here," she says, then hands me her yearbook.

"Thanks."

"See you at lunch," she says as Rianne comes up behind her.

In class, Garrett insists on sitting next to me. I pretend to ignore him, but he keeps asking me questions about the chapters he should've read already.

As soon as the lesson starts, I pull out Lara's yearbook. I go through the Grade Ten students, and there are no students named Alex. But then I find her: Alessandra Leone. So pretty but with an edge, the right side of her head shaved. Her hair is long and black, her makeup on point, thick cat-eye liner.

This is not the kind of girl I have any tingles for.

I deflate with the confirmation that for an entire week, I actually made one of my elaborate scenarios merge with reality. My imagination is next-level sophisticated.

"Why are you looking at that?" Garrett says.

"No reason."

I'm on edge, waiting for Garrett to say something to crush my soul, waiting for him to make others laugh at my expense, but he doesn't.

"What chapter should I pretend I read up to?" he asks.

"I don't really know how they expect you to catch up when you've missed so many weeks of classes," I say. "But it's not my job to hold your hand."

"I didn't realize you were this mean, B," he says. "See, I'd usually make some time-of-the-month joke right now, but I won't."

"How can you seriously think that everything you've done in the past doesn't matter in the present?" I say, then I make a show of moving to the edge of my side of the table and angling my body away from him. "You're trying to be nice to me, and it makes no sense. It's all fake."

"Come on, B. You can't seriously think I'm that bad."

"Yes, I do."

He shrugs and lets out a deep sigh. "Fine. I won't ask you for help anymore. Happy?"

"Not really."

"Okay, I lied anyway." He puts his textbook down between us and points to a page. "It's just a quick question, B. Can you just explain the whole anthropology thing to me? Because I thought it was all about digs and using those little paintbrushes to get sand off old artifacts, am I right?"

When I look at his face, he's got this dumb grin like he's waiting for me to laugh.

"You're very . . . confusing," I say.

He shrugs and takes his book back.

The more he talks to me, the more he asks me questions about our schoolwork, the less I find myself tensing up and wanting to lash out or run away. It's like he's becoming some annoying, harmless guy in my class—a guy I don't really have to spend much energy on. It's a little like what happened with Trey once we all started hanging out, like there was this understanding that things changed, we're different people, and we've just moved on. I just tucked away that old version of Trey in my mind—the one who laughed at me and sometimes made fat jokes—and he became a different Trey that I don't have any particular problem with. But with Garrett—it's on a different scale.

I just feel like the twelve-year-old I used to be would be so mad at me right now, like I'd be betraying myself by not actively wishing him harm, for allowing myself to have an almost conversation with him.

At lunch, while I'm putting my things away in my locker, Alex texts me.

[Alex] R u OK?

It's not a conversation I want to have during a chaotic cafeteria lunch, so I slip away into the small corridor between the two sets of doors that lead into the gym.

[Baylee] Totally. I was just a little shocked, but it's OK now. I've had time to process.
[Alex] I really feel like a jerk for not coming clean sooner.
[Baylee] I should've asked you your pronouns when we started talking. I shouldn't have assumed.
[Alex] No, it's my fault.
[Baylee] Well it's all swell now. Everything makes sense.
[Alex] OK but nothing's changed on my end.

Of course nothing's changed on her end—she knew what was going on the whole time. It's on my end that wires got crossed.

[Alex] Can we meet? Like, officially?
[Baylee] OK, sure. Why not, right? ☺

[Alex] Saturday?

[Baylee] I've got my birthday party that night, but maybe earlier in the day?

[Alex] It's your birthday?

[Baylee] Not technically. It's the week after, on the 13th. This is just the party Rianne is throwing for me, at her house.

We make plans to meet one town over, at Crestonvale Square. I push through the door, a smile on my face, until I smack straight into Taylor and her two friends.

"Watch where you're going," Taylor says. "You almost slammed me across the hallway."

Her two friends continue on, both looking at their phones, but Taylor stays behind, waiting for me to react while she makes a show of fixing her clothes and adjusting her purse, like I tackled her or something.

"Too bad that didn't work out, I guess," I say.

"You might be seven times my size, but I'd still kick your ass," she says.

Attitude and annoyance grow in me, and I allow them to because none of my friends are around to hear her call me names. These are the perfect moments to lay into her. "First of all, you forgot to blend your foundation toward your neck, as usual. Second of all, you only curled the sides of your head, and none of your friends told you the back is all flat, so you just keep walking around like that. You're welcome."

She lifts her phone to record me. "I don't even understand why you're saying these things to me."

I stare at her.

"Every year, I try and be nice to you, but you're just such a big angry person," she says.

"Don't record me, Taylor," I say. "You better not post that anywhere."

She flips her hair over her shoulder—including the unraveled, weak waves at the back—then speaks to the camera. "I'm not sure why I have this reputation for being a massive bitch. Here I was, just walking along, minding my business, and I nearly get knocked to the ground, and then *I'm* the one getting insulted for it. There are two sides to every story, and now you've just witnessed the truth."

"I doubt your seven followers care," I say. "Anyone who knows you is painfully aware that you're just an empty corpse that was granted the ability to walk, and your only skill is frying your hair with bleach and a flat iron."

"See? Do I deserve this?" she says to her phone, then she slips it into her purse and faces me. "Don't worry, Kunkel's Cankles, I'll blur your face when I post it."

"I think it would be a much better video if you were to blur your *own* face."

A dry laugh I know so well rings out from somewhere to my right, and that's when I notice Garrett sitting on the ground, in the little alcove that leads to the science labs. There's a sandwich in one of his hands, while the other one holds our social studies textbook open in his lap.

"Mind your business, Ugly New Guy," Taylor says to Garrett.

"Oh, so if I want in on your business, I gotta go follow your pathetic Instagram, then?" Garrett says. "No, thanks."

"I don't have time to be talking to losers," she says. "Bye."

Taylor walks on and rejoins her friends.

"Don't you dare start calling me Kunkel's Cankles instead of Bertha," I tell Garrett, a finger aimed at him in warning.

"Bertha?" he says, with a look I could almost believe was genuine confusion. Then he laughs. "Oh, right. You've got a good memory, huh, B?"

"Whatever, Garrett."

"You can't honestly think I'm like her. Maybe a little before, but not now. That girl is a *witch*. She probably eats babies for breakfast, am I right?"

I almost let out a laugh. Almost.

Instead, I turn around and walk away.

It would be so much easier if Garrett would just go back to being evil, because this current version of him is unsettling. He's got me wondering if he was ever as awful as I remember him being. I don't know how to be around a deactivated bully.

SEVENTEEN

Saturday comes quickly, and I'm nervous, as though this were a blind date. It doesn't matter how many times I tell myself this is nothing to get so wound up over, I still feel the somersaults of anticipation and excitement deep in my belly. To be honest, I'm still holding on to the idea that the Alex I envisioned will be the one standing in Crestonvale Square when I get there.

I can't figure out why I'm still running straight for disappointment, but here we are.

Crestonvale Square is a place where restaurants and entertainment spots are arranged around a large movie theater, the kind with dozens of rooms and with big recliner seats. There are walkways that connect each spot to the next, neon light shows on the sidewalk, and music that plays over speakers erected along the paths. Everyone comes here, even in the dead of winter, when the huge fountain in the middle of the square turns into a skating rink.

I stand by the metal fence that surrounds the dessert place's patio. It's four in the afternoon, which means I've got three hours before having to be at Rianne's. My phone shows no alerts. The anxiety is like a little ball of nausea swinging up and down from my heart to my belly. I become convinced that if I try to talk, I'll be out of breath. I'll be the fat girl who's gasping for air while standing perfectly still.

A cautious gaze around me reveals the sprinkling of people walking in groups, alone, or hand in hand. The rink is mostly children skating with their parents, and beyond it are the steps to the majestic theater entrance. I've always dreamed of coming here for a date.

"Think it's weird we never talked on the phone first?" a voice says from beside me.

It's her, leaned up casually against the same barrier my butt's touching.

"Oh my god," I say, taking her in, and then I have to look away. "What?"

"I looked at the yearbook."

"Oh." She lets out a little laugh. "Yeah, that would be the old me."

No one who looks like Alex has ever been right here, in front of me, in real life. They've only ever been on TV, on Instagram or TikTok.

Alex is almost as tall as I am—or she would be if I wasn't wearing my heeled ankle boots. She's thin, wearing ripped jeans and a white button-down shirt that peeks out from underneath a dark gray winter trench coat. Her short hair is dyed blond, but the black roots are very noticeable, in a stylish way. It's brushed in all directions, looking perfectly tousled. Her eyes and her piercings are stunning. There's silver everywhere, but no makeup in sight.

"Your voice . . . ," I hear myself say.

"My voice what?"

"It's exactly the way I imagined it."

She tips her head to the side, looking at me with curiosity. "How so?"

"Well, I mean, obviously I had given you a guy's voice, on account of the misgendering mishap, so I spent all week making it less masculine in my head, but I just couldn't make it super high-pitched either. I had to work within this narrow framework or else the vision of you I'd created would've crumbled. And then I saw the yearbook today, and it crumbled. But now . . . it's uncrumbling." I am rambling and my cheeks are burning. I hold my hand out. "Hello, I'm Baylee and I overthink everything."

She takes my hand and shakes it slowly. "Sounds like you've had a rough week, reinventing me and all."

I shrug. "It gave me something to do."

She continues holding my hand, slowing the shake down. Then she looks down at my feet. "Those are some serious shoes."

"Thank you," I say, letting go of her hand. "Wait—was that a compliment? Are they ridiculous?"

"They're very much *not* ridiculous."

I look at her feet, at the beat-up, lace-up suede boots that kind of look like winter sneakers. She notices and goes, "No, don't look at my footwear! There's probably dog shit on them, but I had no choice but to wear 'em."

"Why?"

"They're the only pair I have at the moment. I have to go shopping, which is a thing I dislike doing so much." Alex nods, and then her face changes to reveal confusion. "Did I just tell you there's shit on my shoes?"

"You did."

"Wow. All right." She extends her hand again and I take it. "Hi, I'm Alex, and I ramble when I'm nervous."

"Me too!"

She laughs, but all I do is smile. The kind of smile that pulls my ears back and makes my eyes water a little. She's still holding my hand, and oh god—here I go. If I had any doubts before, they're gone.

This crush has smacked me right in the face, and I don't feel steady on these heels right now.

Out of nowhere, two strangers walk over like they know us.

"Hi, people," a girl says, smiling wide.

She's a curvy blonde who instantly makes me remember who I am. Anytime I sense that I've finally gotten a hold on myself and that I feel completely okay with the fact that it's me who is standing in a moment, starring in my own life and totally deserving of the spotlight, some other girl who is amazing in all the ways I am not, who looks the way I wish I could, has to walk over and remind me that the feeling I have doesn't belong to me.

Just like that, I lose the glittery vibe and take a step away from Alex.

"Hello," I manage, assessing this girl's outfit. The jacket made of leather or faux equivalent, slashed with silver zippers, is something they'd never make in my size. It's totally not appropriate for this weather, but I appreciate the choosing of fashion over comfort, as my feet freeze in these heeled boots. Her hair is wild, her makeup heavy, and on her feet are studded pointy suede boots. She has the edge I've been wanting to add to my look, except it's effortless on her. More importantly, it's available to her.

Next to her is someone with a masculine look that I refuse to assign a gender to on account of how much doing that very thing screwed things up between Alex and me. They're in baggy jeans and a puffy black winter jacket, and their only accessory that I can see is a chunky silver chain.

"How's everything going?" the blonde says to no one in particular.

Alex sighs. "Baylee, these are my friends. This is Blake, and that's Pen."

"Hi," I say to the short-haired person, and even though I'm pretty sure she's a girl, because Alex told me her best friend Pen is a girl, I'm still scared to come off like an ignorant turd, so I say, "Alex told me about you. She, her?"

Pen stares at me with a dead look. "She-her what?"

"Stop it," Alex says, smacking Pen's arm. "She's asking your pronouns. Don't be an ass-bag."

"She, her, but hold the bows and high heels," Pen says.

"It's a long story," Blake says to me, flashing me a friendly smile. "It could maybe be a book, even. Anyway, it's righteous to meet you, Baylee. Alex has told us all about you."

"Really?" I resist taking a glance at Alex, but inside I'm butter-flies. "You're really pretty. Your whole look is so on point."

"Oh wow—thanks so much. Well, your shoes win everything, by the way. And I totally love your eyebrows. What do you use?" She inspects my face closer. "I've been dying to ask since Alex showed me your picture. They even look really good up close."

I reach into my purse, grab hold of the cream filler and micro-felted-tip brow pen, and hand them to her. "I fill my brows in, then I define them and add hair with the pen. Oh—then I brush them in place with a clear gel. It's a little pricey, but it's so worth it."

She pulls her phone out to take a photo of the products. "Drug-store? Sephora?"

"Either," I say.

Blake turns to Pen and says, "Can we go real quick? There's a Shoppers two blocks away!"

"No way. The movie starts in like, ten minutes," Pen says.

"Previews start then, not the movie."

"But I love the previews, babe."

I wasn't sure they were a couple because of the space between them and the initial platonic vibe, but now I can see it, and I'm both jealous of what they have and relieved that the blond babe is already taken.

"Thank you so much for invading our space at the most inappropriate time," Alex says. "Can you guys possibly, um, get the hell out of here now? You were supposed to be incognito."

"Dude, we *were* incognito, right on the other side of the fountain, but then Blake's all, 'The eyebrows! The eyebrows!'" Pen pulls up a wrist to check her watch. "All right, I'm outta here. Previews are vital, dudes. Later."

"Pen and I came here for our first date," Blake says to me.

"Let's go!" Pen says before taking off.

Blake offers Alex and me a wave, then scurries after Pen.

"Okay, well . . . ," Alex says, coming up next to me as we both watch her friends walk away. "I think the ice is broken, right? We shattered that ice. We beat it back into being water. We can handle anything now, right?"

I turn to respond, but all I've got is a smile and a little shrug.

Alex hitches her chin at the restaurant entrance to my left. "Let's get some dessert, shall we?"

Eighteen

Inside Sweet Little Things, we head for the counter, and I scan the overhead menu. At this point, I could order something ridiculous, which is what I really want because I don't come here often, but I don't want to be the fat girl with the big bowl of calories in front her. I settle on a slice of New York cheesecake, because it looks plain yet the slice is large, so it feels like a fair trade-off. I skipped eating today to dedicate myself to my makeup and outfit choices. I'd like to blame the fact that there just wasn't enough time to eat, but in all honesty, I was afraid I'd give myself nervous diarrhea if I ate.

I don't *feel* like I'm starving right now, but my fool of a stomach keeps growling. Deep twisting cramps right below my sternum lead to loud gurgles that kind of sound like thunder. Thankfully this place has a steady supply of music and loud voices, otherwise I'd have to fake some emergency to leave.

Is my stomach this angry that I'm not feeding it? Is it in withdrawal?

"I've got this," Alex says when I reach into my purse to pay.

"You're buying me dessert?"

"Indeed I am."

"Wow—that's really . . . sweet."

Alex looks impressed. "That pun was aces."

My cleverity was totally unintentional, but I flash Alex a coy grin.

While she pays, I take a sideways look at her, my attention moving to her hands, to the way she stands, to the way she looks down when she grins and chuckles a little at something the cashier says. I feel like I'm glowing pink right now and everyone could see it if they looked hard enough.

Once Alex holds both of our desserts, I lead the way by veering left, away from the booths I might not fit into, and choosing the tables with stiff but sturdy-looking chairs. My phone buzzes with what I assume are texts from Rianne and Lara about tonight, but I ignore them. Alex sits across from me and runs a hand through her hair, then does this quick nose-rubbing thing with thumb and index finger, a gesture Freddie does that usually makes me bite my bottom lip, which I realize I'm doing now.

Alex works on a mouthful of banana split.

"I've never seen anyone order one of those in real life," I say.

"Really?"

Thunder erupts from my stomach, and I swear Alex makes

a face like she heard it but doesn't know where the sound came from.

"I am going to go use the loo." My face heats up because I'm not British. "The facilities. Be right back."

In the bathroom, I stand in a stall, trying to will my stomach to go ahead and burp or eat itself or freaking die already. Now it's completely silent, even when I press hard into the spot where the growls are coming from.

I google "embarrassing loud stomach growls while on a date."

Not that this is a date, but it's what I imagine a date might be like.

I scroll through the populated results, skimming all about loud grumbling stomachs getting in the way during exams, first kisses, even funeral masses. High-anxiety situations, basically. And here I thought I was the fat girl who hadn't fed in a few hours and was suddenly feeling the wrath of her empty stomach.

It's not a hunger thing. I'm not sure if that makes me feel better.

When I get back to the table, I start eating my piece of cake because according to one of the Google articles, feeding the anxiety is the only way to quiet things down.

"So tell me about Pen and Blake," I say. "You seem pretty close."

"Pen switched over to Castlehill Alternative from St. Peter's halfway through last year. Blake is still at St. Peter's." Alex does that low chuckle, her dimple piercings pulling in as she smiles. "The first day Pen showed up at my school, she walked right up to me and went, 'Dude! Finally someone who looks like me!' Then she started asking me if I was into video games or Ninja Turtles, which I am very much *not* into, but we became best buds anyway. Blake just came along as a package deal, but it's cool because she's pretty great."

"She's magnetic," I say, forcing myself to push Blake out of my mind to avoid falling back into my insecurities again. "That's a really nice story."

"How about you? How did you and your friends come together?"

"Just . . . school."

"That's it?"

"Well, Rianne and I met a long time ago, like Grade Five. We sat next to each other and always got paired off for group assignments. I met Lara when we got to high school. She was best friends with this evil girl named Taylor," I say. "But Lara and I started talking about makeup in French class, and even though she seemed super snobbish and above everyone else, we just clicked. We used to hit all the cosmetics stores on a weekly basis, and we were like, barely fifteen. I didn't have money to be buying anything, so she'd let me take what I wanted from her older stash."

"That's nice of her."

"She can be pretty thoughtful."

"What happened to the Taylor girl?"

"She sort of faded away when Lara and I started spending our whole weekends together. Hanging out with me is a lot more fun than sitting around with Taylor doing Instagram Lives to attract a bunch of guys."

Alex scoops bites of her banana split, looking totally riveted by my ramblings. "What do you and Lara like doing, then?"

"Usually I make up ridiculous activities that are so much fun. Like I came up with this Five-Minute-Crafts Sunday thing where we pick one of those disgusting crafts—you know the kind of IG pages I'm talking about, with those stupid crafts that are either so ugly or they take, like, two weeks and a table saw to accomplish?" I say, and Alex nods. "So we'd pick an idea to reproduce, like maybe a melted-crayon thing, or painting over a set of thrift-store heels, and we'd post about it on Instagram."

"You guys were meant to be."

"That's what you'd think," I say.

"What do you mean?"

"It's just—no, never mind. I'm just rambling."

"You can tell me, though. I'm curious."

"Okay, well," I start, exhaling while the words arrange themselves in my mind, "it's like she thinks I don't know why she ultimately chose me over Taylor, but I know why." Then I add, "Or maybe she's not even, like, consciously aware of it herself, but I am."

"So what is it? What are you aware of?"

"I don't even know why I'm talking like this," I say. "I'm kind of embarrassed."

"Don't be," Alex says. "I guess I can be kind of pushy sometimes, but that's because I've got therapy every other week, and I'm just used to having to grasp a thought and run with it to figure out where it leads. We can talk about something else, if you'd rather."

"You go to therapy?"

"Yeah, for the last year."

Therapy is like a banana split: it's this thing that I know *of*, but it's not real. It's on TV.

"How does that work?" I ask. "I mean, I just write in my journal to figure things out for myself."

"It's cool that you do that. Writing is a great way to get feelings out and gain perspective," Alex says. "So for me, a year or so ago, I decide to change how I looked—obviously. You saw the yearbook."

"I wouldn't even figure the two versions of you as siblings, you look so different," I say. "Your makeup was fire, though!"

She laughs. "Makeup was kind of my thing then."

"Can you please teach me that liner application?"

"Anytime. Although I'm kind of rusty now."

"So, what happened? How come you changed?"

"You know when you try on an outfit, and you're like, 'Oh, this is nice,' and you wear it awhile but then you're like, 'This is nice, but not for me'?" Alex says. "I was never really girly as a kid, but I loved makeup. I was fiercely dedicated to that girl's gender expression for a solid year. I had like, forty-five hundred Instagram followers for my makeup looks and ideas at one point."

"And no more makeup, just like that?" I ask.

"Sometimes I still think about the makeup artist thing, but not as much as I did before. I'm still trying to figure things out."

"Me too," I say. "So, then you started therapy?"

"Well, my dad was like, 'Hey, kid, I've got psychotherapy covered under my work benefits. You wanna go talk to someone about stuff?' And I was like, 'Okay?'" Alex says. "So I met with Kristy to see what the vibe was like, and here we are. Honestly, I don't understand how everyone *doesn't* see a therapist. Talking to someone else who is trained to help you dig and understand yourself is a game changer."

"I kind of want to see one now. I didn't realize that's what it was like." I don't want to admit that I thought you'd have to be rich and next-level messed up for therapy to be an option.

"Maybe your mom's work benefits are like my dad's?"

I shake my head. "Doubt it. And even if they are, whatever stuff she gets through them would go to my sister."

"Oh, well, maybe you could ask your mom?" Alex offers. "Do you mind if I ask why your sister would be the one to get any support stuff?"

"My sister has special needs," I say.

"Oh, okay. That makes sense, then." Alex smiles. "Maybe you could tell me about her sometime?"

I nod, and Alex goes back to the rest of her banana split. We talk about school awhile, which brings us back to friends.

"Your friend Pen seems kind of . . . generally annoyed," I say.

Alex laughs. "She's a little rough around the edges. Like, to Pen, everything is either black or white, but she's clearly neither, and life is clearly neither, so she's just constantly in this state of being ready for a fight. My theory is that she thinks that if she doesn't keep putting her foot down on everything, then someone or something will come along and like, mow her down."

I can't speak for a moment, because it's like I've been presented with a person who is just so much more than I thought people could be. It makes me feel like a really immature, shallow turd.

"Well, my theory on Lara is that . . . ," I start, staring at the wood pattern of the table, thinking about some of the things I've never said out loud before. "She needs someone who can't outshine her. Someone she'll always be better than, you know? Someone safe who will never compete with her," I say, stabbing my fork into my cheesecake and letting it stand there. "That definitely wasn't going to be Taylor, so . . ."

Alex's gaze pierces through me, and maybe this explains why I'm rambling about things I've only ever hinted at in my journal.

"I feel like maybe that's *one* perspective," Alex says, "but there's no way you don't outshine her. I've known you thirty-nine minutes and I can already tell that much. Trust me."

We have this moment of smiling and locking eyes, and I start thinking that maybe this is a real moment. But then my stomach starts to twist, the precursor to the thunder, so I shove a chunk of cheesecake into my mouth and crunch myself down in an effort to squish the noise or strangle it. "Yum, I mean, wow. Cake is so . . . cakey. I love it."

"Cakey, huh?" Alex reclines against the back of her chair, shuffling her feet. "Mine's banana-splitty."

"That's perfect. That's how it should be, right?"

NINETEEN

On the bus back toward Castlehill, I stare out the window, replaying my meeting with Alex. In an alternate universe, I might've thrown her an invite to Rianne's. But in this universe, I am not bringing a brand-new crush—a girl I *just* met—to meet my friends. If I can barely keep my awkwardness at bay when it's just Alex and me, how paralyzing would it be to have Lara, and Freddie, and Trey around me at the same time?

There's also a fear I don't want to spend too much time acknowledging: the fear that with Rianne and Lara next to me, Alex might come to her senses and realize that I—and all my awkwardness and newbieness—am not worth it.

A shudder moves through me at the thought.

I obsessively check my phone, hoping for a text from Alex that hasn't come yet, but the possibility of it keeps me giddy.

[Rianne] I'm SO sorry, Baylee. I think the party's off.

[Baylee] What do you mean?

[Rianne] The power's out in my entire neighborhood!

[Baylee] No way! What is happening?

[Rianne] A generator blew or something. It's been out a whole hour. I was hoping it would be back on soon, but my dad called the power company and there's an automated message estimating 2 to 3 hours!!! Everyone's supposed to be getting here in an hour. WTF!

[Baylee] Oh no!!!

[Rianne] It's already FREEZING! Is the power out at your house?

[Baylee] I'm not sure.

[Rianne] Where r u?

[Baylee] I was in Crestonvale. Going home now.

If the power was out at my house, chances are it will be back on by now, since my mom had us put on priority power restoration due to my sister. Outages in my area are usually over quickly.

[Rianne] Ok, well, LMK! Text me later. This SUCKS!!!!!

When I get back to my fully powered house, my mother and sister are in the living room, my sister curled up with her pillow and a rolled blanket keeping her from accidentally falling off the couch. The TV is on, and judging by the lack of reaction my entrance causes, I'm guessing Mom's dozing. When I get to my room, the relief of not having to go out and hang with a ton of people really hits me. I need time to process today.

My phone buzzes, and it's Lara's house line.

"Hello, Baylee. This is Mr. Kariyawasam. Could you be so kind as to ask Lara when we are to come get her? I have to send Kavith for her. I must head back to the hospital, and she is not responding to my messages."

"Um . . ." But Lara isn't here. We were supposed to be headed to Rianne's right about now. My mind goes wild, trying to come up with an explanation. "I'm sorry, Mr. Kariyawasam. I'll just ask—"

"Oh, I'm so sorry! One moment," he says. I hear muffled voices, then he comes back. "So sorry. I thought she was at your home, but her mother says she is with Rianne. My apologies, Baylee! Thank you!"

"Oh," I say. "That's okay. No problem."

I wander the top floor of my house, firing off a series of texts to Lara that go unanswered. Then I text Rianne.

[Baylee] Lara's still en route to your place?
[Rianne] No. I texted her at the same time I texted you about the party being off.
[Baylee] Her dad just called thinking she was here, but she told him she was going over to your house.
[Rianne] ???????? Guess they'll be calling HERE next.
[Baylee] She's not responding to my texts.

[Rianne] WHAT?! I'm not about to get in trouble because
of her!

Some time passes while I stand at my bedroom window, scoping out Lara's social media to see when she last posted, looking for clues. No reply comes from her.

[Baylee] Did you get ahold of her yet?
[Rianne] Yeah. She's calling her parents.
[Baylee] She's not responding to my texts. Is she mad at me?
[Rianne] 🙍 She didn't seem too thrilled when I called her
four times in a row until she answered. That's what you get for
being a scheming little LIAR!

Walking through the upstairs hallway, I send a bunch of question marks to Lara's phone.

While I pad around my mother's dark bedroom, I peer out the window at Freddie's house. His bedroom light is on, and he moves through his room. I'm being a total creeper, spying on him in his room, but I can't help it.

I decide to send him a text.

[Baylee] Hey. Can we maybe talk about all of this weirdness?

I keep thinking I'll see him pick up his phone to text me back, so I continue staring.

Then I see another figure in Freddie's bedroom. The figure wanders closer to the window and there's a flash of dark hair. There is no response to my text.

I fire off another set of texts, this time to Lara.

First my heart slows down, and then it pounds each beat as it accelerates.

Please don't let it be her.

I can't see that well from all the way across four backyards, and my texts go unanswered. Still, I know it's her.

Lara is in Freddie's room.

TWENTY

There is literally no way this can be happening right now.

How *dare* she?

How dare *he*?

The rage creeps up my throat, forcing some kind of growl out of me.

I stalk across the hall, then down the stairs, and slip on the same boots I had on earlier.

"Where are you going, Boss?" Mom asks.

"Out," I say, then I'm outside.

All I can think is that Lara's guy—the guy Taylor supposedly has a huge crush on—was Freddie, and *I'm* the one with the huge crush who's in the way.

Outside, I take each step carefully, putting my weight on the fronts of my feet to ensure that I'm properly anchored to the ground, and make it down the street without falling on my ass.

Garrett isn't on the walkway when I get there, and I guess that's good for him because I might've just tackled him for the hell of it. When I near Freddie's house, I dial his cell.

He picks up.

"Can you come outside and talk for a minute?" I say.

"You're here?"

"Yes."

There are muffled voices, then he comes back. "Okay."

The call ends. I wait on the sidewalk until the garage door starts to rise. Freddie's in his unlaced high-tops, staring at me with total confusion as he slips on his jacket. "What happened?"

"So you and Lara, huh? That's like, a *thing* now?"

He turns his head away, the look on his face making it clear this is not a conversation he wants to be having. Along with the dread, there's this expression of regret, like he's mentally cursing all the things that led to him standing here, right now, in front of me.

Good—*feel* bad, Freddie. I like it.

"Okay, so you're just not going to say anything, then?"

"I tried telling you about it, Bay," he says. "I tried telling you a few times, actually, and then it seemed like you sort of knew what I was talking about but that you didn't want to actually *know*."

"You launched into some stupid, vague hypothetical. You could've been a little clearer. You could've been like, 'Hey, Baylee, by the way, Lara and I are *doing* it.'"

"We're not." He shakes his head. "And you told me to keep it a secret, remember? I thought I was doing what you asked."

"Oh god," I say, clawing at the side of my head. "How did this even happen?"

He stares off into the night.

"No, I mean actually," I say. "How did this start? She was your best friend's girlfriend until, like, a week ago."

"It hasn't even started," he says. "We were just hanging out for a bit before going to Rianne's for your party. Nothing happened."

"So you were just going to meet up with Trey at Rianne's, with his ex-girlfriend as your date? That makes no sense."

"I wasn't going to do that. I would've dropped her off down the street—never mind. Doesn't matter."

Freddie stares at his phone in a way that draws my attention. I point to it. "Is she listening right now?"

Neighbors might be outside at this point. I'm not sure how loud I'm being. But the only thing I care about right now are my shoes and how fierce they look. They are elevating me, literally and also figuratively.

"So you're going to be pissed at Lara for this?" Freddie says.

"Yes!" I throw my hands up. "Oh, *and* you. I'm going to be pissed at *both* of you."

"Why, though?"

"Both of you set up these elaborate mind games. I've been an ignorant idiot this whole time, and I thought you . . ." I stare at him like he's something that tastes sour. "You're just an asshole, Freddie."

He holds his hands out. "Why are you like this? You're impossible to talk to."

"I know I am."

"Well? What is it?"

"I'm *profoundly* unhappy, okay? I am sick of everything. I'm sick of feeling like I'm the last to get picked in my own life."

Freddie looks down at the ground and his arms fall to his sides. He seems awkward, intentionally avoiding looking up at me. And I get it. What could he possibly say? This is so much bigger than him.

It's never me—why is it never me? What is wrong with me? I try so hard, and it doesn't matter. I don't want to feel like this anymore.

I take a deep breath. "Can you please do me a favor and tell Lara not to text me for a while?"

"Come on, Bay."

"She should've known better. And you know what? You should have known better, too. On some level, you should have *known* this would be different." I stare at the sky for a moment or two, long enough to let the truth come out to my lips. "You—you're an asshole because your stupid vague words led me down a sparkly road. And her—well, she's an asshole because she knew what this meant."

Lara can come to school in a messy bun, mascara, a white tank top and sweats, and it's fine. She can still draw them all in, including Freddie, apparently, without even trying. I could never pull that off because minimal effort means being a frumpy slob who needs a shower and is drawing attention to her fat rolls.

The unfairness of it all just kills me.

"Don't text me for a while," I say.

"Come on, Baylee. I knew it would be awkward, but is it this big of a deal?"

"Of course it is! How can you act like she hasn't told you exactly why this is a *huge* deal?"

He waits, looking helpless, looking like he's waiting for me to spell it out.

But why would I do that when my magnet feelings for him have just been flipped around, and all I feel is completely repelled?

"Don't tell Trey," he says. "Okay? Please?"

I walk down the sidewalk toward the walkway. He doesn't follow me.

Sometimes I wonder if the way I feel about Freddie has more to do with me than it does with him. Were we ever really friends? My whole friendship with Freddie has been about me yearning for him to finally wake up and want me the way I want him. I just want his attention. Does he even know me if I'm never myself around him?

I just wanted him to want me back, and he fucking doesn't.

He wants my best friend.

TWENTY-ONE

I wake up and open my eyes, and for a split second, I firmly believe that the wild images in my mind and the intense sensations in the pit of my stomach are just part of a particularly vivid scenario I made up before going to sleep last night, contaminating my dreams. Was I really screaming precious, mortifying secrets at Freddie in the street? Did I really watch Lara having private time with him in his room? It all has to be make-believe.

[Rianne] What happened last night?
[Baylee] What do you mean? What did you hear?
[Rianne] Well, I had no power for almost 4 hours and you were supposed to text me back. . . remember??????
[Baylee] Oh, crap. I totally forgot. Last night ended up next-level sucking.
[Rianne] ????? What happened?

[Baylee] . . .

[Rianne] WAIT. Let's go for pizza at JJ's and you can tell me then!

[Baylee] I don't know.

[Rianne] Come on. Let's just go! Plus we can talk about how to fix your birthday party. I might just call in sick for you so we can celebrate it on March 13.

[Baylee] You'd do that?

[Rianne] Totally. Now let's go to JJ's!

[Baylee] OK fine. I'll meet you there in an hour?

[Rianne] Yes! Did you text Lara? Is she coming?

[Baylee] DO NOT TEXT LARA.

[Rianne] 🎧 Wait wait wait! WHAT HAPPENED?!?!?!?!?!? 🎧

[Baylee] I'll see you at JJ's in an hour.

[Rianne] 🐱 OK fine. Hurry.

In my closet, I mentally try on several outfit combinations until I narrow it down to three that I will actually try on once I've showered and washed the film of anger off my body.

Mom's knock disturbs my quiet. She opens the door before I acknowledge her but doesn't come farther than just inside the doorframe. The staticky sounds of my sister's babbles can be heard through the baby monitor clipped to the waistband of my mother's pants.

"Boss," she says. "Can I come in?"

I poke my head out of my closet, hoping the expression on my face will convey how much I do not want to mention my chaotically leaving the house last night and returning fifteen minutes later with my makeup all smudged.

"What happened last night?" she asks.

I shrug. "Nothing important. Anyway—I'm going to meet Rianne at JJ's, okay?"

"Baylee," Mom says. "What's going on?"

"Well, Mom, it looks like Lara and Freddie were going to start dating behind my back." I drop the chosen shirts and pants on the end of my bed.

"Oh." She nods. "That's a little awkward, isn't it?"

"It's awkward and also many other things."

Mom takes a seat on my bed, letting the silence hang. I head over to the jewelry tote that sits in my bookshelf, nestled between my shellac nail supplies and a stack of books, and I rummage for earrings and my silver bracelet. Rebecca launches into loud, repetitive moaning sounds, a signal that her falling asleep is a definite possibility. Mom lowers the monitor volume.

"Having your two friends suddenly spend all this private time together would make anyone feel left out, maybe even a little jealous, huh?" Mom says.

How wrong she is just triggers me. "It actually makes me super mad, Mom. Mad enough that I'm not talking to either of them, ever again."

"Okay, Boss. You're allowed to be mad," she says. "Take some time to process."

"I'm going to be processing at JJ's with Rianne, okay?"

"Sure."

Mom gets up and heads for the door, grabbing a couple of dirty socks off the ground and dropping them in my hamper.

I wait for Rianne between Zippy Mart and JJ's, staring at the overpass that hangs over the creek beyond the parking lot, in the field that runs next to this mini strip mall.

[Alex] Hey, u. 😎

[Baylee] Hi. 😊

[Alex] Full disclosure: I wanted to text u right after u left last night.

[Baylee] 😊😊😊

Rianne steps onto the curb at the other end of the strip mall, waving when she sees me. She's still rocking the raccoon look, and her purple hair peeks out from under the hood of her black winter cape, which makes her look like some kind of goth winter pixie. Her boots even have chunky heels and big silver buckles.

"It took everything I had not to text Lara," she says. "Tell me now!"

"Okay, but can we at least get some food first?"

We head inside and grab one of the last two free tables by the window. Rianne goes up to order for both of us, and she comes back with two slices of gooey cheese pizza. Yellowish grease circles are already forming on the white paper plates.

"I have like, three hours before I have to go to work." She groans.

"I'm going to try not to eat three slices of this pizza, but it's going to be hard," I say, sinking my teeth into the hot cheese layer.

"I know! So good," Rianne says. "But get to it! You two got into a fight?"

"Not exactly."

"Are you mad that she ignored your texts last night but responded to me?"

"Not quite."

Rianne frowns. "Oh no—are she and Trey back together?"

"She and Freddie are together, actually."

Rianne's jaw hangs. "Whoa."

"Yes."

"How did you find out?"

"I saw her at his place."

Rianne starts on her slice, shaking her head. "We really need to start making new friends. Everyone's dated everyone else in this group. That's kind of messed up."

"Not me," I say. "I haven't dated anyone."

She shrugs. "You're still pure. While I literally went out with Freddie in Grade Seven, Trey in Grade Eight, and Matt last year—ew. Lara's dated Trey and now Freddie. I guess there's always Rav, Baylee, if you're desperate." She laughs, expecting me to join in. "What? What did I say?"

"Nothing."

"Do you think Trey knows?"

"No—no one knows except me. And now you."

"Really?"

I nod. "They're saying they just started '*talking*,' and they're not officially dating yet."

"They'll never be official—unless Freddie is trying to start a huge thing with Trey. Our group is literally about to implode," she says. "I'm done trying to figure out this stupid end-of-year trip. There's no point."

"We could do our own thing," I say.

"Yeah, okay." She folds the rest of her slice in half, picking at the cheese that sticks out the sides. "Just the girls, then."

"Maybe you and me could tag along with Candace and Steph's group. They're renting a cottage by the lake," I say. "Plus, it's a guarantee that Taylor won't be anywhere near."

"Okay, but you mean Lara, too, right?"

Disgust twists my features before I have a chance to reel in my reaction.

"Spill it. Tell me why you're so mad at Lara."

I take a breath, unsure how I'm going to flip my thoughts and the truth around to minimize what's really going on.

"I might've had a tiny crush on . . ."

Rianne's eyes widen. "On Lara?!"

"No!"

"I'm just kidding. On Freddie," she says. "Obviously."

"You knew?"

"Well, I wasn't sure, but you and he have your own thing, and it kind of makes sense that maybe there was something more there, right?"

There's nothing actually there. That's the problem.

"Anyway," Rianne continues, "this whole Lara and Freddie thing definitely sucks, but we can't just cut her out. It's not her fault."

All I want is to cut Lara out forever. Right now, this is the only thing I want.

I search for a way to reply to Rianne, but then a shadow falls over us as a body comes to the window from outside.

"Look who it is," Rianne says. *"Awkward!"*

Freddie's hands cup the sides of his face against the glass as he cuts the glare to be able to see inside JJ's, and his eyes lock with mine.

"How did he know I was here?" I say, breaking eye contact. "If my mom told him, I'm going to—"

"I posted about it on Instagram," Rianne says, showing me a photo of her reflection in her bedroom floor-length mirror, with a caption that reads: *Check out the fit—headed to JJ's for pizza with @BayleeKokBYEeee!!!*

He cocks his head to the side, asking me to come out.

"Nice one, Rianne."

She makes a face. "Did *I* know all this drama happened? No. How was I supposed to know tagging our location would be a problem?"

"Okay, fine. You're right."

Freddie taps on the window. I stare at the crust that remains on my paper plate, and Rianne's shoulders rise in a shrug as she looks over at Freddie. He keeps tapping, and now other people are looking over at our table.

I sigh. "I'll be back in a minute."

I head for the door, tying my red peacoat and sweeping my hair to the side. Freddie meets me outside the door.

"Are you calm today?" He holds two fingers in the shape of a cross aimed at me, like I'm some vampire he's trying to keep away. I don't laugh, so he sighs. "I just wanted to talk to you quickly."

"And I said I need a breather from you and Lara."

"You make it sound like we personally attacked you or something," he says.

I don't respond, because a personal attack is exactly what this feels like. It feels very intentional.

"I'm sorry, Bay. I don't really know how to fix things."

Freddie has no idea what his body being so close does to mine. Sometimes inside my head it's me screaming at him to just kiss me, to just come closer and touch me.

I walk along to the right, past the convenience store, the last store in the strip mall, and pick a spot of icy grass to stand on. Freddie follows.

I watch him kick a piece of ice around.

"This silence is awkward," he says.

"You're the one who said you wanted to talk. I said I didn't."

"What a mess. This is so not what I was looking for," he says, his tone betraying a hint of frustration.

"It's really irritating the way you act like you're the one getting pulled into drama, like you're *not* the one who created it in the first place," I say. "You get that *you're* the one who started dating your best friend's ex a couple days after they broke up, right? You made that decision."

"We're not dating!"

"What are you doing, then?"

"We're just talking. I just wanted to get to know her differently and see."

"See what? See if this girl you can't stand—who you say is annoying and 'completely in love with herself'—is hot enough for you to consider blowing everything up around you?"

"No!" He shakes his head. "I feel like you're someone else right now, Baylee. You're not usually this . . . I don't know."

"Maybe that's because when we're together, I become this pathetic version of myself who tries to be supercool, who tries to make herself small just so she can make you feel important," I say. "Maybe it's because everything's been about you. Until now."

"Why—why would you have to do that? Why would you make everything about me?"

"I have to be better than all the rest, so you'll want to hang out with me as much as you do. If not, then how else would I get to be around you? How else would I get to sit there, smelling your cologne, drooling over your perfect fucking face and body?"

There. I said it.

He palms his chin while he stares at me, eyes narrowed, face unreadable.

"Stop acting like you don't already know!" I snap. There's no one around, but even if there was, the words are already there, ready to escape my mouth. "I wasted too many years obsessed with the idea of being around you. You smell good, and you make me feel things, and I just wish you— *Ugh*. I don't know. Forget it."

What I want to scream at him is that it's still not fucking fair that yet again, I get overlooked in favor of my excellent-looking, thin friend. I've known Freddie for years—he should've been able to overlook my size and see the stupid fucking beauty within, right? That's my first thought, but then I change my mind, because I am angry and sick of these stupid self-loathing thoughts I'm always having. Why can't Freddie think I'm just as hot as my thin friends? Why couldn't that have been a possibility?

"Just forget it," I repeat.

"No," he says, but I don't know how to interpret his response. No, what?

"I don't want to see you anymore," I say. "Being around you makes me feel like shit in all the ways—like, next-level shit. I'm tired of it."

"Wait . . ." He's dazed, his voice trailing off.

He's so beautiful, he makes me want to cry.

"You and Lara can just go off together to frolic in the fucking meadow and leave me out of it."

I turn back toward JJ's, passing by the convenience store. There are hushed voices to my right, and I turn to see two guys standing beside a truck I saw pull in earlier. It takes a moment for me to clue in that one of them, some skinny guy with emo-style sideswept bangs, looks familiar. The other one has his back to me.

The emo guy locks eyes with me and recognition passes over his features. "I know you."

I nod.

"Well, I guess we all know each other, then," Pen says, turning around.

"Oh, hi," I say, not having realized she was there. Awkwardness settles over us, and the silence is broken by Freddie dropping an F bomb on his way past, headed for his car. I point to the skinny guy, desperate to pull the focus away from Freddie. "You're Tristan, right? You're friends with Garrett."

"Shizz, man. Not anymore!" Tristan says.

"You know Garrett?" Pen says to me.

I nod, then I point to JJ's behind me. "I have to go. My friend's in there."

"Thought *that* was your friend," Pen says, pointing to Freddie's car as it pulls out of the lot. "The dude frolicking through the parking lot."

"He's not my friend now."

"Sounded like more than a friend thing, though."

"Well, it wasn't. Not even a little bit."

I shrug and head inside to fill Rianne in on some of the details. Most of what was said—like the part where I, once again, threw my feelings at Freddie—I keep to myself.

Late that night, I get a text from Lara.

[Lara] I know you hate me now, but please don't tell Trey.

Telling Trey is the scenario I will play out in my mind before I go to sleep, enjoying the destruction it would cause. Loving the way it would instantly make Freddie and Lara regret having gone there. Relishing the idea of the two of them losing their closest friends, too.

[Baylee] I won't. But please stop talking to me.

I haven't decided if I'm mean enough to tell Trey, but what I do know is that telling him would make it real. I don't want that.

TWENTY-TWO

The week unfolds in a not-entirely-awful way. Rianne and I spend our lunch periods working on a group assignment for English class. Lara manages to avoid everyone by blending in with Taylor's crew, which is the most predictable thing ever. The only reason I'm able to keep coming here, day after day, is Trey. His presence means Lara and Freddie cannot come near each other at school, which means I'm not subjected to witnessing their usual flirty, sexy expressions being aimed at each other. It's like it's not even happening.

All anyone is talking about in the hallways is the coronavirus.

"Why do you look so sad today?" Rianne asks me on Thursday, bumping her shoulder against mine in English class.

"Just kind of realizing my birthday is tomorrow, and I'm going to spend it sitting at home, staring at the wall."

"I told you—I can call in sick!"

"Don't bother. You could get in trouble if your parents find out," I say. "We can just hang out Saturday after you get off work."

"I'll bake you a cake!"

"Can you do red velvet?"

She considers this for a moment. "I can add red food coloring to vanilla cake?"

"That'll work."

Class breaks for lunch, and I head for the bathroom, mostly to check my latest DMs from Alex in total privacy.

[Alex] So ur bday is tomorrow. U prob have plans already but I thought . . . would u maybe want to come out with me, Pen, and Blake?

[Baylee] YES!

[Alex] OK, awesome. 😄

[Baylee] Where?

[Alex] I was thinking Toronto. If u feel like going to the Village, that is.

[Baylee] Which village?

[Alex] THE Village, with a capital V. The queer area, downtown.

My eyes widen with the realization that these are real plans. This is me heading downtown with older, cooler people.

[Baylee] I would love that. How do we get there? GO train?

[Alex] Not at all. I drove my dad to the airport yesterday, so I've got his car.

[Baylee] What kind of car is it?

[Alex] A big, black SUV. We'll be riding in style. 😎

I breathe a sigh of seat-belt-related relief and float out of the bathroom with my head deep in the envisioning of this very legit birthday outing. Then the universe decides to put Freddie right in my path.

"Hey," he says, stepping closer.

"Okay," I say.

We stand there, me trying to seem nonchalant to the point of having zero reaction, him staring at me like I'm being next-level immature.

"You know what?" he says. "Forget it."

"Okay, sure."

None of it will ever be forgotten.

I ride the city bus home and arrive to find my mother instead of the worker who does late afternoons with Rebecca. Mom has the news on loud enough so she can still hear it from anywhere on the main floor of the house, which is typical these days. There are grocery bags on the floor by the entrance, waiting to be carried to the kitchen, but she's just standing in front of the TV like something major distracted her. I'm about to ask her what's up when my phone starts buzzing.

[Rianne] OMG did you hear? MEGA LONG MARCH BREAK!!!!!!
[Baylee] What do you mean?
[Rianne] Check out the news. NOW.

"Mom?" I call, grabbing a couple of heavy plastic bags. "How come you're home so early?"

"Juliana let me know stores are crazy busy all of a sudden, so I left early to stock up on a few things."

"What's the March break thing about? Rianne texted me."

"They've just announced that schools will be closed for two weeks after March break."

Inside, I'm swelling with excitement, but I keep my voice level when I ask, "So no school from, like, March sixteenth to . . . sometime in April? How come?"

"This is not good," Mom says, looking like she's talking to the TV more than she's talking to me. "There's a press conference, and the premier and government people are assuring everyone that we can all still go on vacation and have a great time, but now they've realized young people are catching corona, so schools are going to shut down to try and stop the spread. Seems a little ridiculous to tell people to go on with their travel plans, if things are progressing to the point of closing schools."

"How young?"

"What?" Mom turns to face me. "Oh, healthy young people—children. Which means it could spread in schools and day cares."

"So we're off for three weeks?"

No school means these people—Lara, Freddie, Garrett, Taylor—they no longer exist. Not for a long while, anyway. This is perfect timing, and I just feel so zen about things now. I understand this is the wrong thing to be feeling, so I make sure to keep my face very neutral.

"What do they expect parents to do with day cares and schools closed?" Mom says.

"I wonder what Freddie's mom is going to do."

Talking about him makes me check my phone, like I'm expecting him to have texted, even though I don't want him to.

[Baylee] Did you hear about school being closed?
[Alex] Yeah. My boss called to see if I can give him more availability. They're super short-staffed all of a sudden.
[Baylee] We can still go out tomorrow, right?
[Alex] I guess? I mean, it's just schools and day cares that are closing.

"Mom?" She heads over to meet me in the kitchen, carrying the last of the grocery bags. "I can go out tomorrow, right?"

"Go out where?"

"Just . . . here," I say, figuring my mother would be a hard sell on a Friday night in downtown Toronto during regular times. "Bookworm or Hot Mugs for karaoke night."

"No. Absolutely not. I'm sorry, but if they're closing schools to prevent people your age from spreading the virus, I'm not letting you go hang out in a crowded coffee bar."

"Okay, but what if it's not a crowded place?"

"I would prefer not, Boss," Mom says, distracted with the stacking of canned goods in the annoying corner cupboard we can barely reach.

"But, Mom, it's my birthday."

"I thought you were getting together with Rianne on Saturday," she says. "I got a cake for tomorrow. I thought we would spend it together, safe at home, watching a movie."

"Well, Rianne got the night off," I say. "It's my birthday, Mom."

"Just Rianne?"

"Yes."

"Bookworm or her house—that's it," Mom says. "I mean it."

I nod, then fire off a text to Rianne as I shove boxes of pasta and crackers into the appropriate cupboard.

[Baylee] Can you cover for me tomorrow?

[Rianne] Why, what's up?

[Baylee] I'm sort of going out for my birthday. Downtown.

[Rianne] With who?! Why can't I come?

[Baylee] Because you're working!

[Rianne] Fine. But with WHO?!

[Baylee] If I tell you the story, will you pretend you're with me tomorrow night?

[Rianne] If you tell me ALL the details, I'll even make a fake IG post about you being at my house.

[Baylee] Deal!

[Rianne] Video-chat me.

After the groceries are put away, I run upstairs and into my walk-in closet. I close the door and sit cross-legged on the floor. I slip my earphones in, then video-chat Rianne.

"Tell me!" Rianne says, her voice too loud in my ears, so I lower my headset volume.

"So I kind of met this person—this girl—from Bookworm."

Rianne's mouth opens wide. "Yes! This is juicy. What happened? Oh my god! Wait—where does Freddie fit into all this?"

"Nowhere. He's nothing," I say. "So anyway—we hung out once."

"Where? What did you do? What does she look like?" Rianne's face comes close to the screen. "I need the details."

So I tell the story of meeting Alex at Crestonvale Square. There are different kinds of butterflies within as I realize I'm the one with the juicy story to share. I can almost see myself sitting next to Rianne, listening to me talk, completely riveted.

"Baylee! You went on a date with her!"

"No, I didn't," I say. "It was literally our first time hanging out."

"That was a date!" She laughs. "Do you not know what a date is?"

I shrug because no. I don't.

"And tomorrow is date number two!"

"No, I don't think so. We're going out for my birthday, and her friends are coming."

"Uh, Baylee—ever heard of a double date?"

I make a face, and Rianne waves it off. She starts asking me about cheek piercings, and I answer as best I can, feeling myself distracted by the idea of dating Alex. Wouldn't I be aware of the dating if that's what we were doing?

TWENTY-THREE

The next day, most of our time at school consists of talking about our superlong March break, and most of the teachers don't seem to be in the mood for serious learning. Our math teacher even pulls out the trivia game she usually saves for the end of the year. My mind and belly are full of butterflies in anticipation of my after-school plans.

I get home with enough time to freshen my makeup, brush my teeth, and throw on the outfit I picked out last night. Alex pulls into my driveway in a shiny black SUV, with Pen and Blake in the back seat. Alex assured me she'd pick me up before five, which means Mom isn't here to see me *not* going out with Rianne. I fluff my hair one last time, rubbing my lips together to even out the gloss. I take the passenger seat, afraid to look at Alex and reveal how giddy I am about tonight.

"Hi," Alex says.

"Hi."

"Happy birthday!" Blake yells, arms up.

"Yeah, happy birthday, Baylee," Alex says.

"Thank you," I say.

"Did you know you live super close to Pen's parents' house? They're just a few streets over," Blake says.

"Really?" I ask, twisting my head to look at Blake. "Well, I guess that kind of makes sense."

"She's friends with Garrett," Pen says.

"What?!" Blake says.

"No, I'm not. He just goes to my school now," I say. "He and his evil friends have been guarding the walkway by my house for years."

"Tristan's not evil," Pen says.

"No," I say. Whenever Tristan was among Garrett's group of turds, he was quiet and definitely seemed out of place. "How come I've never seen you hanging out with them there?"

"I stayed away from that group when they got together," Pen says. "I had better shit to do."

"Yeah, like play *Smash Bros.* or whatever," Alex says.

"It's Smash *Brothers*," Pen shoots back.

"It's spelled B-R-O-S."

"It's still Brothers. You don't say Mario *Bros.*, you say Mario Brothers," Pen says. "Forget it, dude. I don't need to be arguing with you about something you know nothing about."

Next to me, Alex laughs as she steers the car down my street.

My phone buzzes, the way it's been buzzing all day with

notifications for birthday messages from people from school, from the uncle and cousins I never see, from Juliana.

[Lara] Happy birthday, Baylee. 🍲 My dad and I are going to drop by later to bring you a batch of biryani.

I roll my eyes at how thoughtful she can sometimes be, even though she's probably just going to swing by my house on her way to Freddie's.

[Baylee] That's OK. I'd rather you didn't.
[Lara] . . .
[Baylee] I'm just not home right now, and I don't want you coming to drop something off to blow my cover with my mother. She doesn't know where I am.
[Lara] Where are you?
[Baylee] Out.
[Lara] Fine.

Delicious food isn't going to make me suddenly forget what happened.

[Baylee] Can you please thank your father for me, though? That's really nice of him.
[Lara] Fine.

I stare at Alex while she drives, and when she notices, she gives me a shy smile. I can't believe I'm here right now, headed downtown on a Friday night. It's exhilarating, this feeling of being out there, having a life. Is this what a date feels like?

Downtown, we head to the Village. After finding an underground public lot with a flat rate, we set out walking down Church Street. I try not to seem like such a newb about it, but I've never been to the queer area of Toronto, certainly not with friends, just to hang out. We might've driven through at some point, trying to avoid downtown traffic on the way to SickKids Hospital, but that's about it.

Pen and Blake walk a little ahead of Alex and me, and they move closer together as Pen hooks her pinkie around Blake's.

"Where are we going, exactly?" I ask Alex.

"This trashy restaurant that does drag shows. The menu is pretty great."

I gaze around, taking in the different shops and eating spots. There are a few people scattered about. "It's a little quiet around here. Is it because it's winter?"

"No. I guess it's still early for the dinner rush?" Blake says. "I mean, we don't come often, but it does seem a little dead tonight."

"It's gotta be the virus-pandemic stuff," Alex says, looking around. "Maybe we shouldn't have come out."

"Too late, we're already here," Pen says.

We veer left to a one-story building that sits a little farther in, with a large empty patio out front that lines the sidewalk. We pile into the small foyer and wait by the hostess podium. A young-looking guy with perfectly tweezed eyebrows comes to us right away. Inside are several tables, a wall of booths, and a long bar counter. The person behind the bar is wearing hospital gloves, pouring drinks. A couple of booths and tables are taken, and three or four people sit at the counter.

"Welcome to Raunchy Chauncey's, kids," the hostess says. "Where would you like to sit? It's a little more pathetic than usual in here tonight, so you get your choice."

A quick glance at the booths tells me that even if I manage fitting in, I won't be able to slide out, so I point to the tables by the window facade that looks out to the patio. "Can we sit by the windows? It would be cool to see outside."

We sit, Alex and I on one side, Pen and Blake on the other.

Little droplets of rain start randomly sprinkling the window. Pen looks at her phone, then holds her fist up in victory.

"What?" Alex asks.

"Mild weather and rain means no snow tomorrow," Pen says. "I hate plowing and shoveling. Who the hell likes getting up at four a.m. for that kind of shit? I'd rather still be doing fall cleanups. And I *hate* fall cleanups."

"What's fall cleanups?" I ask.

"We clean up . . . in the fall," Pen says, and Blake smacks her forearm, flashing a warning glare. Pen shrugs innocently, then says, "My brother has a landscaping and yard-work company. I work with him when I'm not at school. Since landscaping business is nonexistent in the winter, you switch to snow removal stuff."

Alex's phone must vibrate, because she fishes it out of her breast pocket. "It's my dad. I'll be right back."

As she walks away, my eyes are drawn to the way her crisp black polo shirt folds against her, the way her jeans hang just a little too low on her hips, the way the veins on her forearms seem to pop.

"All right, let me ask you this," Pen says, leaning forward. "Are you into Alex? Like, not just as a friend?"

"Pen! None of your business," Blake says. "I told you to keep that to yourself."

Pen is still focused on me. This is about the weird conversation she overheard between Freddie and me. My cheeks get hot, and my head fills with potential explanations of what happened, and what's going on right now.

None of it is adequate. It's too big to explain.

"Alex is my bud, you know? She's had enough confused girls messing with her. She might not wanna say anything, but I got her back, you know? I'm being honest with you."

"Um, okay?"

"I'm just saying," Pen says, looking at Blake now. "No need to lead anyone on, right? If you've already got some stuff going on with someone else, then—"

"Ignore her. She can be kind of a douche," Blake says to me.

"Yeah, but what I'm saying is still the truth. Me and Tristan overheard enough to know that—"

"So? Let them figure their own stuff out. Please!"

"I have nothing going on with anybody. Nothing at all. But say I did, I would never be messing things up like this. I would be smart," I say, shuffling my feet, pulling at my top so that it doesn't cling too much.

"Dude, I saw what I saw and I heard what I heard. It wasn't nothing."

"You like to make up your mind about stuff before you've got all the facts," Blake says. "You become convinced about something, and then you get all wound up about it, Pen. Can you stop making everything awkward? Alex will be back any second."

"Fine!" Pen says. "I'll keep my mouth shut."

Blake smiles at me, her black-smudged eyes twinkling in the light in a way that makes me wish, for the hundredth time, that I was her, except for the dating Pen part. "I feel like we should go to the bathroom, right?"

She pops up from her seat, and I follow, glad to put some distance between myself and Pen.

In the bathroom, Blake fluffs her hair, sending her blond locks flying about. I wish I could feel the way I imagine Blake feeling. She is one of those people who walks around like the skin they're in fits them in every way, like no one else's attention or approval matters, like no makeover could ever improve them because they are already their best selves. She is living that feeling I only ever get tiny glimpses of.

There is a clear line between girls like me and girls like Blake, even though we're probably both considered fat by the world's standards. Girls like me are not just a little bit chunky. Girls like me are a lot of everything. Girls like me worry about fitting into the booth at the restaurant, we worry about rickety folding chairs giving out on us, we worry about being wider and taller than all the boys—than all the people, really. Some of us can't even fit a car seat belt all the way around ourselves.

I've never wished to be skinny, but I wish so bad that I wasn't *this* fat. That I was closer to Blake, curvy with squish in all the right places, and moving through the world would be easier.

"I think Pen is getting the wrong idea about everything," I say. "She really doesn't like me, but it's for things that aren't actually reality-based."

"Pen seems harsh, but it has to do with the way she says things," Blake says. "Ignore her. She's got a thing with loyalty, and Alex's ex was a terrible person, so Pen has decided she's going to be Alex's shield."

"Okay, but I don't think Pen has anything to worry about. It's not like that between me and Alex." I grab locks of my hair, freeing my hoop earrings. The angle I see in the mirror right now has no double chin, and I like it. "It's not like that."

"But you get that it could be, right?" she says, locking eyes with me through the mirror.

That makes me laugh, but under the laughter is me wishing with all my might that it could be like that between Alex and me.

"Do you like Alex?" Blake asks.

I nod. "But—I mean . . ."

"But what?"

I shrug because it's too much to lay out there, on this person I don't really know.

TWENTY-FOUR

An hour or so later, we walk out of the restaurant to a darkened sky. The drag show that was set to begin at seven was canceled when a couple of the performers had to bail.

"This wasn't as exciting as I thought it would be," Blake says.

"I thought it was great," I say.

"Your birthday could've been a lot more fun," she says. "Last time we came, the show was amazing and the vibe was just magical."

I'm not going to admit that it all feels very magical to me, making the one-year difference in age between us obvious, so I shrug in response.

The four of us stand on the sidewalk, gazing up and down the street.

"What are we doing? It's cold, and the sky might start leaking again," Pen says.

"Where can we go?" Blake asks.

We stand there a few more minutes, and it becomes pretty clear that our options are slim.

"I guess we can just drive back," Blake says. "Maybe we can grab a coffee or something on the way?"

I'm about to agree when some guy runs over to us.

"The coronavirus isn't real! It's a government conspiracy," he yells at us. "Don't be sheep!"

"Go home!" Blake yells back.

"Babe," Pen says, her voice sharp. "This is Toronto. You're gonna get us murdered."

While we power-walk our way back to the car, I pull my phone out to check in with my mom, who made me promise I would.

"Oh, look at those earrings!" Blake says, pointing to the front window display of a boutique. "Can we please stop quickly?"

"Aw, babe. Let's just go!" Pen whines.

"I would, um, kind of like to go in," I say, pointing to the purse I would love to see up close.

"It's your birthday, so you get to pick what we do," Alex says.

Pen says, "I'll remember that when it's my birthday. It's going to be *Mario Party* for an entire day, and you won't be able to bail."

We head inside the little shop, where everything seems handmade and features a lot of leather, stones, and metal. My eyes move across the jewelry, belts, and bags. Blake holds a pair of rustic copper hoops up to her ears, checking herself out in the mirror. I head for the studded red leather satchel that caught my eye.

206

"Three hundred!" I say.

"Yikes," Alex says. "It's nice, though. It suits you."

I put the bag back, pouting. Alex wanders deeper into the store when Pen asks her to come look at something. On the other end of the counter is a tray of wallets. I waste no time locating the matching red leather wallet, silver studs lining the front of it.

"Oh my god," Blake says, coming up next to me. "That wallet is *righteous*. How much?"

"Ninety-nine dollars," I say. "I wanted the purse, but it's way too much."

"The wallet totally goes with the purse you have already, though." Blake picks up the matching black wallet. "Let's get them!"

"You can afford this?"

"I've been putting in too many hours at the Gamer Depot since Christmas. Time to buy myself a present!" Blake nods. "I'll get black, you get red."

These people all have jobs. I should have a job, and I am suddenly feeling really opposite of legit for not having one. The little bit of money I came here with was spent on dinner. I suppose there's always the emergency credit card my mother gave me years ago. I do have a little backup money in my piggybank, plus it's my birthday, so I could put the money I'm sure to get toward the cost of the wallet. I think it'll be fine as long as I tell my mom about it before the bill comes in.

"I would love to change up my style a little," I say. "Or more like, add to it."

I was going to elaborate, but I don't want to come off like a young weirdo, trying to copy the older, cooler girl next to me.

The feel of the heavy red wallet in my hand is lovely. How could I put it back now, when it already feels like it's mine?

"Okay," I say. "Let's do it."

"We're twinning now," Blake says.

We head for the counter, and I swipe my credit card. The clerk takes such care wrapping the wallet in tissue.

Out on the street, the four of us pass a hot dog cart, and Blake goes, "Wait—can we get a hot dog?"

"We just ate, Babe," Pen says.

"So? I'm hungry again," Blake says. "And I *never* pass up an opportunity for street meat. Come on!"

Pen and Alex shake their heads no, and although I could totally eat a hot dog, I decline the invite. Blake is just laying her hunger out there, totally not ashamed about being able to eat more than everyone else she's with, but I can't be that girl. Not tonight.

"Whatever," Blake says. She turns to Pen. "I'm getting a hot dog with *lots* of onions, so I guess you and me are not making out later."

"Oh, we're still making out," Pen says. "You'll just have to chew a whole pack of gum first."

Alex laughs and pulls out her keys. "Why don't Baylee and I go get the car, and we'll pick you up here?"

"Sure," Blake says, then she's pulling Pen by the sleeve.

Saying no to the hot dog thing was the right decision, because now I get to walk alone with Alex. We cross the street and make our way to the ramp for the underground lot. At the SUV, we stand next to it. A little red car comes down the ramp and parks next to us. Three people exit, laughing, and their voices echo.

"So, I've been thinking," Alex says. "We should hang out more."

"Really?" I say. "I think so, too. We have a really long March break now, so I've got nothing but time."

"I took a ton of shifts, but I think it would be really nice to spend the time I have between them with you."

"Next-level nice."

Before I have a second to consider what's about to happen, Alex steps over to me and grabs the fingers of my left hand with her right one. It's the lightest touch, and I feel it resonate as goose bumps in the small of my back. It's like I'd been waiting for her to touch me like this my whole life.

She raises my hand, like she's some noble sir and I'm a delicate beauty, and she brushes her lips against my knuckles.

I literally die right there, in this underground lot. A death of a thousand butterflies.

TWENTY-FIVE

On Saturday evening, Alex and I are texting, discussing possible plans during March break. Neither of us mentions last night. I want to so badly, but no matter how I picture myself bringing it up, it feels awkward or cheesy. A glance at my hand sends shivers through my back with the memory. When I seek Google's advice, it says, *Hand kissing is a gesture indicating courtesy, politeness, respect, admiration, or even devotion by one person toward another.* Which qualifier did Alex have in mind? How do I know what's going on without being told?

[Baylee] The phone? Really? You want to speak to me live?
[Alex] I do. I want to hear ur voice.
[Baylee] Well . . . . OK!

My phone rings about three seconds later, so I put down the piece of leftover chocolate birthday cake I was working on. I answer it, saying "hi" and "hello" together, which turns into this weird combo thing.

"High-low to you, too," Alex says.

"Of course, the first thing I say ends up super dumb."

"It's all right. I think it's cute," Alex says. "What are you up to tonight?"

"Probably nothing exciting. Possibly painting my toes red. You?"

"Possibly talking to you," she says. "Although I've been thinking I might go grab a coffee at Hot Mugs."

I feel tiny fireworks in my belly, anticipating that she might ask me to hang out.

"Really?" I say, trying my best to seem nonchalant. "I think that sounds like a really good time."

My mom's voice rings out over Rebecca's cries, yelling my name repeatedly in a way that makes it clear she's probably been calling me for a while. I cut my Spotify playlist.

"Can I call you right back? My mom needs me."

"Sure."

I yell, "What?" into the hallway.

"Door's for you, Boss. I've been calling ten minutes," Mom yells back.

A glance out my window reveals Freddie's car on the street out front. Now that my music is off, I can hear his voice downstairs. I spin around my room to find my new push-up bra and change out of my ugly T-shirt and shorts. The possibility of this occurrence is exactly why I make sure my hair and makeup are always done.

In the living room, Mom is sitting on the couch while Rebecca is on her play mat, rolling around happily with Freddie crouched next to her. The news headlines roll on the TV screen.

"This is going to get out of hand real fast," Mom says.

"Yeah," Freddie says as he holds one of my sister's light-up toys above her head, and she tries swatting at it. "There are over a hundred cases in Ontario now."

My sister, oblivious, smiles to herself as she wiggles around on her mat.

"What are you doing here?" I ask from where I stand on the bottom step of the stairs.

"I was hoping to talk to you," he says. "Please."

Mom gives me a look of curiosity, like she can sense something serious is going on by the way Freddie's last word was spoken.

This is stupid. Alex is waiting for me to call her back.

Yet here I am, slipping on my boots and coat, throwing a couple of pieces of gum into my mouth and following him outside.

Freddie stops by his car, rolling on the balls of his feet, fists in the pockets of his jeans. For some reason, I find myself wondering what it would be like to have the ability to walk over and have him wrap his arms around me. Why am I thinking this? Why did I come out here? I shouldn't even be in this place with him, physically or mentally.

But he came after *me*. I wasn't the one running after him this time. This feeling could be addictive.

"What are you doing here?" I ask.

"Happy birthday, one day late."

I cross my arms. "Okay?"

"Can we hang out for a bit?"

"Not really." I run my hand through my hair, tipping my head to the side, extending my neck in a way that I hope flattens my chins—because I can't help myself.

I throw him what I hope is a fierce glare.

He sighs. "Just come with me. Let's go for a ride. I'll take you to Port Perry."

"Now?"

"Sure," he says. "Anywhere."

As if I'd get into his car again. I study his face, wondering what kind of mood he's in. Nothing explains what he's doing here.

"I fixed the seat belt, Bay."

"Oh, well, in that case, I guess everything is just perfect. Your car's seat belt was the root cause of all the shittery that's happened in the last few weeks."

He snorts at my sarcasm.

"I would like to talk to you about some stuff," he says. "Can you just come?"

He came for *me* this time. This must be what it's like to be Lara. To be busy elsewhere and have a guy coming after you, not giving up. This isn't right, but I like it.

"Fine."

We get into the car. I don't say anything, and neither does he.

I send my mother a text: Just outside with Freddie for a while.

Soon, it's obvious we're headed to the empty lot of the factory his grandfather worked at. He brings the car to a stop in the middle of the lot, and his fingers drum against the steering wheel. I can't look at him. All this weirdness is like a pair of jeans one size too small.

"Let's get some air," he says, pulling the keys out of the ignition.

We both lean against the back of the car, a couple of feet separating us. The night is mild again, and the sound of melting snow and ice trickling down a sewer grate to our left can be heard. Freddie pulls out his vape, and the smell of grapes surrounds us. He hops onto the trunk, and the car bounces against my butt.

"What do you want?" I ask.

He gives me a sharp glance, clearly not impressed with my tone. Time passes, then he goes, "I'm thinking of applying for university in Vancouver. They have a pretty solid screenwriting and story design program."

It's like my lungs lose air. "Why? I thought you wanted to go somewhere in Toronto."

We were all planning to stay close by for college. We were all still going to hang out together. He wasn't supposed to be far away.

"I can change my mind about stuff," he says.

"Well, I think you're just trying to make me mad," I say.

"Why would you be mad?"

"People always think moving far away is going to make things better. That's so unoriginal." Silence. I take a breath, letting the annoyance growing inside me take the wheel. "So you're just going to like, run away to a part of Canada that's going to end up lost under the ocean soon? Solid plan."

He snorts. "You make it sound like it's sinking."

"It kind of is!" I cross my arms, looking out at the vacant field past the paved lot. "Super slowly, but still."

"I'll get a houseboat. How's that?"

"That's a dumb idea."

I find myself getting more and more irritated with the way my earrings and wavy locks can't ever play nicely together.

"You could come with me," he says.

My fingers freeze around the left earring, head hanging to the side. His hand reaches over to pull my earring free from the tangles. Fingertips touching my cheek, making my jaw slack.

"Oh, please." My voice is some pathetic whisper. "And do what?"

He jumps off the trunk, exhaling, and the vapor calls my attention. Freddie kicks at a discarded piece of wood, moving in front of me.

He turns away from me. "Lots of stuff."

"Like what?"

His back is to me now. His hand moves up to his neck, massaging it, then he vapes a little more. It's dark out here. I look around, a chill creeping up my back. What if this is the kind of place where lowlifes come settle drug debts or something? They'd find us and they'd have to kill us. They'd shoot us dead right before I can find out what kind of stuff Freddie wants us to do on his houseboat.

Freddie turns to me, and there are three feet between us. "As if I'd buy a houseboat."

I don't want to be talking about houseboats. I don't know what I want, but it's not this.

He offers me his vape, and I take it because that's the closest we ever come to his mouth being on mine. A puff later, I give it back to him.

"Why aren't you out here with Lara?"

"I felt like being out here with you," he says. "Although, this vibe is really making me regret it. I wish you'd just get over whatever it is you're worried about."

"I'm not worried about anything."

"Why do you care so much about who I'm with all of a sudden?" He doesn't look at me. "You never cared before."

"I did, though. I'm just a phenomenal actress."

The weirdness is out here with us. It makes my head light, but it's like my heart beats too hard from within it. Maybe this is what happens before one passes out. Or maybe this is a stroke.

Freddie's next to me now. We lean against his car, side by side, when I feel the warmth of his hand against mine. Accidental skin brushes that send me over the edge. Will I be forty-five and still feel like this around him?

He takes a step forward, almost like he's about to walk away, but instead, he turns and he's nearly in front of me. My eyes trace him from the bottom up. I'm so obvious about it, too.

I want to touch him so badly right now.

He stares at me, and I can't stop looking at his lips. The weirdness is still smothering me. His lips—I am internally shouting at them to come closer. I can't even think properly.

"You know I'm not actually getting a houseboat in Vancouver, right?" he says.

"You were just trying to make me mad."

"Maybe."

Freddie's fists close around the front of my coat, pulling me closer. We're almost at eye level.

What is this? Is this magic? I want it all to stop.

No, I don't.

He grabs for the middle button of my coat, undoing it.

There are only four buttons on this coat, and the two top ones were already undone. Freddie reaches for the last one. It's so quiet that I can hear the sound of cars zooming on the highway in the distance. His hands slide over my hips. I don't like it. It's too close to the squish above it. He watches me. My chest goes up and down all exaggerated. My fingers tremble, lose sensation. I am so terrified that he'll move his hands up and recoil from the shock of me not feeling like the kind of girls he's used to.

Panic starts collecting on my skin, in my stomach.

My gaze travels up. Almost meets his. I want to tell him to keep going, and that I'm sorry for being so awkward all the time, and to please not think I'm gross.

I look away, pulling my coat tight around me.

He sighs and backs away. "Sorry. It's okay if you're not into it."

What am I doing? What's my problem? This is what I want! I don't care who I have to push out of the way to get to it—even if it's myself.

"I am," I say. "Obviously, I am."

He turns, shoves his hands deep into his pockets. I take a step closer. I'm going to die right here.

Finally, we're looking at each other.

That look—his eyes narrowed, too dark—it's a look I've never seen aimed at me before. His lips are shiny. Did he lick them? Mine are covered in strawberry balm.

"Bay," he says. I've never heard him say my name from this close before. It sounds different. "Are you good?"

I'm not that girl. I'm not that girl who can't deal and wants to run away.

Who would I be if I wasn't wearing this body?

I wouldn't be me. I wouldn't be here right now.

And here is exactly where I want to be.

My hands curl around his wrists. Then I guide his hands to me, against my chest. He makes a noise then, like a sigh that sounds angry, and I feel it in places I had no idea noise could have an effect on. He presses against me, but the car is there to keep me steady. Now that his hands are on me, and his face dips into the crook of my neck, it's better. I can release some of the breath I've been holding.

I don't even know what's happening. Or what I'm supposed to do. My hands hang loose at my sides now.

It's so stupid that I might spontaneously combust. That my whole body is one massive shiver. Just because a guy's touching my boobs through layers of clothes.

Freddie. Is. Touching. Me.

Buttons. More buttons. This time, it's my shirt, and it's my own fingers moving up, undoing the first two. Because I'm okay with what's underneath. The hot-pink bra I bought specifically for this possibility is there, and I know it looks good because I spent time in front of the mirror before I left, checking out my cleavage from different angles.

"Bay, are you—"

"Yeah, yeah. I'm good." I'm all breathy. I don't recognize myself, and it's the most freeing thing ever.

We're looking at each other again, so long that I feel anxiety build within at the realization that he's seeing me.

He kisses me. Not like a feather brush of the lips. It's like he wants to leave with my bottom lip. I taste him. My body is on fire, and inside my head, all is quiet.

TWENTY-SIX

I wake up on Sunday morning and it's still dark out. Rain whips against my window, and my phone tells me it's late morning despite the sky's appearance. I sit up and perch cross-legged on my bed, replaying last night in my mind, alternating between hyperventilation and smiling like a maniac into my pillow. Right now, in this moment, I feel like everything in my life has led me to this moment. Everything seems so important.

My phone has zero texts from Freddie, but it has a couple from Lara and from Alex, and—

Oh no—I said I'd call Alex right back last night, then I disappeared.

[Alex] I don't want to come right out and tell u I'm bummed u never called me back last night so I won't. ☺
[Alex] Is everything OK?

While a playlist that matches my weird mood fills my bedroom, I stare at the ceiling and reflect on the last couple of days. It feels wrong to text Alex back when I'm lost in Freddie Land, but the more minutes go by—minutes where Freddie isn't texting me—the more I'm wondering how his presence last night so easily swayed me away from Alex.

It's like my brain rewired itself, and now I'm no longer in Freddie mode.

I'm thinking more clearly.

[Baylee] I'm so sorry! Everything is fine.

I'm obviously going to lie, but only because the truth is super awkward and not really appropriate. It was just a kiss, right?

That's a lie. Not *just* a kiss—not for me, at least.

One thing's for sure: the likelihood that it's only me pacing around my house, blowing up a kiss to mean everything, is very high. So I'm going to leave the earth-shattering feelings about kissing Freddie buried deep inside, next to the other big, pathetic feelings I'm always juggling, and on the outside, I'm going to act the way I should be acting. Chill.

[Baylee] Rianne stayed over. Something happened at home, and she needed to talk. We went to bed so late. I was going to send you a text. I had it all typed out. But I didn't even press send.

Soon it's like the lie spreads itself out through my mind, anchoring to reality, and it starts to feel legit enough that I almost send Rianne a text to check on her.

[Alex] Well, what r u up to today? Feel like a Bookworm donut?
[Baylee] I always feel like a donut.

I press send before giving enough consideration to that statement.

[Alex] I work until 4 but come by. We can hang out afterward. If u want. 😊
[Baylee] I do. I'll see you in a bit then.
[Alex] 😄

I stay holed up in my room, catching up on homework and connecting to the C-High Portal to review my social sciences assignment instructions. What should've only taken me an hour or so ends up taking me almost three because my mind wanders back to last night, and I end up furiously scribbling in my journal about the thought that is really consuming me right now. It's more than a thought—it's a full-on fact: Freddie is home, totally embarrassed and wishing he could go back in time and not come over last night.

The texts from Lara are still there, unread. I move to swipe left with the intent of sending them to the garbage bin, but instead, I'm tapping on her name.

[Lara] I know you asked me to leave you alone but I need to talk.
[Lara] Can we please talk?

I need to talk, too, so badly. But I don't have anyone to talk to about the things that matter.

[Baylee] Why do you want to talk?
[Lara] I don't want us to keep being mad at each other.
[Baylee] Well, I'm kind of busy. Sorry.
[Lara] What do you mean?
[Baylee] I have stuff to do today.
[Lara] What stuff?
[Baylee] I've got plans. I need to go get ready.
[Lara] You're busy all day?
[Baylee] Maybe. I'm not sure yet.
[Lara] Doing what? 🤔

It must be odd for her to have to be fit into my life, to be confronted with a Baylee who is out doing other things. I'm always available, always dependable, always ready and willing. I thought these were qualities of mine, but maybe I was just like that by default, because I had nothing else going on.

It would be nice for people to feel like time with me—like my attention—is special, not just a given.

[Lara] Can you not find an hour today to talk to me?
[Baylee] I don't want to talk about you and Freddie.
[Lara] I know. But you're my best friend.
[Baylee] I bet Taylor would love to hear all about Freddie.
[Lara] She's driving me up the wall. 😑 Besides, there isn't much going on with Freddie . . .
[Baylee] What do you mean?

Now she's the one taking forever to reply, forcing me to think about the fact that if I hadn't been with Freddie last night, then maybe he would've been with her. Maybe *I* got in Lara's way. Do I feel bad about it?

What I feel are residual tingles in every place Freddie's touch landed. What I feel has nothing to do with Lara. Shouldn't I feel bad?

[Lara] He's been ignoring me.
[Baylee] Oh.
[Lara] I sent him four texts and he hasn't bothered to respond.

There's a difference between Lara and me. I refuse to be *that* girl, the girl firing off desperate texts, begging for attention. I might feel like that girl on the inside, but I won't let myself become her on the outside. She can text-bomb Freddie, but I won't be doing that. I'm going to hold out and see if he comes to me. It's so much better if he comes to me.

[Lara] I'm not sure how to feel about any of this.
[Baylee] I'm not sure either. I haven't talked to him. Maybe he feels bad going behind his best friend's back.

The three dots appear, letting me know she's responding to me. I fire off a quick text before she finishes.

[Baylee] Sorry it's complicated. But I guess you would've known complicated is exactly what you were signing up for, right?

The dots disappear.

TWENTY-SEVEN

Before stepping into Bookworm, I pause out front of the Burger King next door to catch my breath. An incoming video call through messenger flashes through my screen. It's Lara. I debate whether to pick up long enough for the call to go unanswered. But then she calls again, so I fish my earphones out of my purse and plug them in.

"Hi," Lara says.

"What's up?"

"Where are you?"

"Just, out." All she can see behind me is the brick wall of the passageway between Bookworm and the rest of the stores in the strip mall, which leads to the bus stop.

"Are you with someone?"

"Not right now," I say.

"I'm surprised your mom is letting you go out. My parents

forbid me to leave the house until this virus stuff gets figured out," Lara says.

I shrug, but the truth is, my mother thinks I'm in Freddie's garage. I didn't tell her I'd be taking the bus to hang out at Bookworm, because it would've likely taken me thirty minutes to convince her to let me go. She was busy with my sister and the million phone calls with her shift supervisor about the upcoming work schedule, anyway, and barely noticed me leave.

"Okay, well, can we talk?" Lara asks.

"I already said I don't want to talk about Freddie," I say.

"Well, can we talk about us not being friends right now?"

"That would require us talking about Freddie."

"But Freddie and I haven't even *done* anything yet," she says. "We were just—"

"Yes, I know. 'Feeling' each other out."

"You talked to Freddie?"

"Yes," I say.

"When—today?"

"No. Just . . . before."

"What did you guys talk about?"

Is she using me to try and get close to Freddie?

"I thought you and I were supposed to be talking about our friendship."

"Okay, fine," she says. "You're right—we can't talk about one without the other. I'm just really confused about this. I don't understand where his head is at."

She thought she'd be different. She thought she was special, but she's realizing she's not. So she's looking for me to do what I usually do when this kind of thing happens—make her feel better. I always told myself it was because I was skilled at choosing my words, at being a good friend, but I've always known it's more that my sheer presence, seated right across from her, reminds her that no matter how shitty she feels about herself, at least she's not a desperate fat girl with zero prospects.

"What's the point of this, Lara? What are you trying to talk to me about?"

"Well, I've decided to *stop* talking to Freddie," she says.

"Oh."

"I thought you'd be glad," Lara says.

"Lara, the damage is done. You knew what Freddie meant to me, and you still went behind my back to try and take him," I say. "Do you get that?"

"I do, and I'm sorry for that. I really am, but at the same time . . . he wasn't yours. I know you wanted that more than anything, but it wasn't going to happen. That's not my fault."

The nerve. The *nerve*! I wrestle for a moment with the idea of letting her know exactly how wrong she is. Just for a moment.

I'm about to answer, but then she adds, "You even told me, when you thought we were talking about Taylor, that she couldn't get mad at me because it's not my fault."

"Okay, fine," I say. "Well, I guess I'm mad for no reason, then."

"I didn't say that," she says. "I get that it sucks. I wish I hadn't started thinking of him that way. It was a surprise. I'm sorry, Baylee."

"Okay, then."

"Sometimes you get caught up in the moment, in the feelings, and you have to follow them. I know it probably doesn't make sense to you, but even though I *knew* better, I just . . . got caught up." She looks for me to understand, but I keep my face blank. "I was thinking about what you said before, about the boyfriend-relationship stuff. I guess I *have* been acting like always having a guy is the most important thing in the world."

"And now you don't think so?"

"Now I realize it might be a bad pattern," she says. "It's definitely not worth all this. So, I've decided to stop talking to him."

"Wow—well, thank you, Lara. That's really mature of you."

"Are you making fun of me?"

"I'm not stupid, Lara," I say. When she flashes me a look of confusion, I add, "You're not having this new realization. You didn't stop talking to him—you just told me *he* stopped talking to *you*. You're just trying to save face."

She narrows her eyes, just enough to make her disagreement evident. Lara sighs dramatically, then rakes at her hair until she's pulled it into a lovely messy bun on top of her head.

"I should go," I say.

Her face changes, and she picks up the phone, her attention fully on me again. "Wait. So that's it?"

"I don't want to argue with you," I say. "I'm late—I have to go."

"Are you at Bookworm?"

"Yes."

"Who are you meeting at Bookworm? The Alex guy?"

"No," I say. "The Alex girl."

Lara looks surprised, but then her face changes like something clicks. "No wonder that Andre guy didn't know what I was talking about! Why didn't you tell me she was a girl?"

I shrug.

"You're embarrassed about it?"

"No, I'm not. I told Rianne about Alex."

"You told Rianne, but not me?"

"You and I are not exactly talking right now," I say while Lara is unable to wipe the fact that she's offended off her face. "At least, we weren't."

"So, what's going on with that? Are you . . . is this a crush-type situation?" Lara asks. "Are you two dating?"

"I think we are somewhere between feeling each other out and whatever comes after that," I say. "Maybe."

It feels weird talking to Lara about it, not at all like what I was hoping it would feel like. I don't feel superior. I still don't even feel equal.

"Hang on," Lara says. I can tell by her face that she's working on choosing her words. "So you're telling me that you've moved on to someone else, yet you're still going to sit there and hate me for talking to Freddie?"

The look on her face brings heat to my cheeks.

"Do you realize Freddie basically stopped talking to me because of you and your over-the-top meltdown, and this whole time, you're talking to someone else?

"I can't believe this!" is the last thing I hear her say, then I cut the call.

Inside Bookworm, I feel a pang of guilt. Or maybe it's shame. Shame that I got called out by Lara for something I hadn't even considered. I had the upper hand, and I just gave her what she needed to climb back up her tower. Now I'm back to being the petty, dramatic one.

It's nothing I'm not used to living with, so I push it all aside and veer right, toward the café.

There are definitely not as many people in here as there usually are for this time of day. The barista behind the counter is wearing latex-looking gloves, like at the restaurant in Toronto.

Alex is there, putting the finishing touches on the blackboard covered in colorful chalk calligraphy, announcing featured products. I watch as she pulls her phone out of her back pocket, frames the shot, and then spends a minute with her nose aimed at her phone screen, no doubt posting on the café's IG account. The baristas cross back and forth behind her, sometimes throwing questions at her, which she answers in a way that makes it clear she's in charge. A smile spreads on my lips.

What was I thinking? This is so much better than my hot and cold feelings for Freddie.

Alex is one of those people who is full of energy. I watch her bounce behind the counter, grabbing things, stocking things. At one point she hops right up on the counter to change a lightbulb, and afterward, she wipes up her footprints with spray and a large white cloth.

She sees me now.

The smile she gives makes my mouth want to crack open with glee, and if it did, a thousand pink butterflies would escape.

She waves me over.

"Sorry I'm a little later than I said I'd be," I say.

"It's okay. I'm just finishing up, then we can go." She waves an arm over to the glass display of all the things I shouldn't eat. "What would you like? My treat."

"I'm actually not hungry," I say. "Can I have a drink, though?"

"Absolutely. Anything you want, I'll make it," she says.

"Is it a thing now, that employees wear gloves?" I ask.

"I suggested it, after seeing what they were doing at Raunchy Chauncey's. My boss thought it was a good idea," Alex says. "So what do you feel like having?"

For a moment, I consider ordering tea. "I would like to try the Oreo drink."

"All right. Let me whip that up for you."

I wait by the other end of the counter for my free drink, enjoying the special feeling that comes from knowing someone who can offer me something on the house. The drink Alex hands me looks like it should be photographed for the product ad. The symmetry of perfect swirly mounds of whipped cream, crunchy cookie sprinkles, and chocolate drizzled over it all is striking.

"Wow," I say. "This is going up on my Instagram in about seven seconds."

"Tag the store!" she says. "All right—I'm going to grab my things. I'll be back."

I take a seat at my usual table, the one Lara and I always try to get when we come here. I take a pic of the drink, then I try and take a decent shot of myself taking the first sip. Some man a couple of tables away makes super-dry eye contact with me, making me feel like a total fool for posing with my beverage. But I do it anyway.

"Ready?" Alex says as she materializes next to me.

"Totally."

"I'm kind of thinking of inviting you to my place," she says.

She stares at me to gauge my reaction, eyes squinted with this playful, hopeful expression. When I nod my approval, she does this little victory fist pump.

TWENTY-EIGHT

We walk through the lot, headed to Alex's dad's car. The whole time I walk next to her, there's an internal battle between my overseeing judgy self and the me that wants to just be here, next to her, not worrying about anything else. The overseeing version of me keeps intruding, reminding me to suck it in, to jut my chin out so the one below it flattens out a bit, to ensure there's a bit of swing in my hips and absolutely no waddling. I just can't shut myself up.

We drive to the east side of Castlehill, to a subdivision of small town houses laid out in seemingly identical rows. I've never been friends with anyone who lives in this area. It feels like a whole different town.

"This is really nice," I say. "It's very . . . symmetrical."

"It's not bad," Alex says as we walk up her driveway.

"How long have you lived here?"

"My whole life."

I start worrying that I might sound out of breath, talking while walking, which is driving my focus right on my breathing, creating the very problem I'm trying to avoid.

Inside, Alex kicks off her shoes, so I step out of mine. The house is tidy and simple, with thin carpet that seems to have no color, like beige overkill. The walls are white, and the windows have basic plastic white blinds. It smells like fresh laundry, and it feels bright and airy.

"So your dad is away right now?" I ask.

"A couple of US flights. He's a flight attendant," she says. "I kind of wish he'd just come home."

"I hope he's safe."

"He's making sure to be extra careful," Alex says.

"So, you've grown up with a dad who was always up in the air somewhere?"

Alex curls her index finger around mine to lead me through the hallway. I can't help but look down at our hands. "Not really. He just started doing that about five years ago. Most of my life I guess my dad was in school and working shit jobs."

"Oh."

"My parents had me at seventeen, and it took my dad forever to finish high school and then be able to get through college with everything that happened with my mother."

"Wow," I say, which is when my eyes find photos in the living room to our right. There are school photos of Alex looking like a girly girl. There's a man I take to be Alex's father, and I can see where Alex gets her looks. "So, um, what exactly happened with your mother? Is it okay that I ask that?"

Alex nods. "She's the kind of person who never should've had kids, although I'm glad she did, because, well, I'm here." She smiles all goofy. "She made our lives hell for a while—although I don't really remember it. My dad has basically been my dad *and* my mom."

"My mom's also my mom and my dad. I get it."

Alex opens a door and leads me down the carpeted stairs. The basement has a couple of slivers of natural light from the thin windows on the back wall. Otherwise it's dim yellow lighting from a few lamps she's just turned on. Everything down here looks like it's from a different decade, one I wasn't alive in. The wooden furniture pieces are arranged around the massive avocado-colored velvet couch.

"Welcome to my happy place," Alex says, waving an arm around.

"When you said you got all your great-uncle's stuff, I pictured a ton of boxes of things piled high against a wall. Not an actual living room," I say, then I point to this big dark-wood cabinet. "This is so cool! That's your record player?"

"Yeah." Alex lifts the flap on the top to reveal it, and she opens the cupboard below it to show off a thick row of records. "It's the very definition of vintage. Totally unspoiled, right from the hands that purchased it all originally."

"This is literally pure gold," I say. I think the best part about it is how proud Alex seems of it all. You can tell just how special these possessions are to her by the way she touches them.

"Right?" She pats the velvet beast. "Give it a try. It's the best thing your butt will ever experience. Trust me."

That makes me laugh.

Alex says, "That sounded a little . . . wrong, I guess."

I take a seat, realizing I can't sit at the very back without my feet hanging off the ground. For a moment I wonder how my shirt looks right now, if it's tucked in places it shouldn't be, if the roll of fat underneath my boobs is sticking out farther than my boobs are. My purse goes on my knees, and all is instantly almost well.

"I'm gonna play you something," Alex says.

She crouches at the cabinet, talking to herself as she flips through records. "This? No—maybe this. No—wait."

Out of habit, I light up my phone screen to see who might've texted me. It's like I forget that the only person whose texts I would truly be interested in getting right now is in front of me.

[Freddie] Hey. How are you?

How am I? I am . . . not interested.

"What do you think?" Alex asks, which is when I notice there's music.

I stuff my phone deep into my purse, then ditch it on the floor and grab one of the square throw pillows to use as my fat shield instead. My eyes close as I try to make a show of taking in the music.

"Interesting. I like it," I say. "What is it?"

"It's Pat Benatar," Alex says.

"I like the way the record sounds."

"This was a pretty sweet system back in 1977," Alex says. "My uncle said it was like, five hundred, which would be—I don't know—twenty thousand dollars nowadays?"

She keeps making me smile, smiles that she returns every time. She sits cross-legged on the wide couch, facing me. We listen to the record for a bit, and I find myself really loving the crackly breaks between songs, like it's part of the music. It's definitely a lot smoother transition than just straight-up silence for a couple of seconds.

"She's pretty good," I say. "Is she still alive?"

Alex laughs. "Of course she's still alive. She's like sixty-something and she's still touring and making music."

A softer, slower song comes on and we listen. Alex mouths the words and closes her eyes.

"I feel like Rebecca would totally be into this Pat lady," I say.

I relax into the couch, letting my head fall against the cushy high back.

"So I've been wanting to ask you about your sister." There's caution in Alex's words. "You said she has special needs, but I wondered what that means. Is it okay that I ask?"

"Of course," I say, so I start with the medical details, because what most people want to know is what's "wrong" with her. I can tell Alex doesn't mean it that way, but people are usually curious, and I get it. "She has severe cerebral palsy, which causes a bunch of different issues. She gets looked after the way a baby would, I guess, because she can't talk or walk or even eat the way people typically would. Plus, she's medically fragile, so when she gets sick, it's always a huge deal. It's never just a cold, you know? It's pneumonia and dehydration and issues getting her to put on weight."

"Sounds like a lot," Alex says. "Can I ask, um, is she *there*? Like, does she interact at all?"

"Oh, she's *definitely* there. Her moods are very obvious. So when she's mad, you can tell. When she's bored, you can tell. When she likes something, there's no mistaking it. Same for stuff she doesn't like."

"So, you would totally be able to tell if she liked Pat Benatar, then."

"One hundred percent. If she doesn't like something, you get the dirtiest look ever or whining. If she likes something, then you get the massive smiles and the big waves."

"That's really cool."

I pull out my phone again and open the media folder I have of my sister, full of photos and videos I've taken, and I hand it to Alex.

"You did *not* give her perfect spiral curls," Alex says, zooming in.

"Of course I did! It was picture day at school!" I say. "It was such a pain, but her hair is so thick, and it looked really good."

Alex scrolls through the photos and short videos.

"Do you ever wonder what she's thinking?"

"All the time. And like, what do her dreams look like? What does she think about before she falls asleep?" I say. "I have no idea."

Alex's gaze finds mine. "I don't know how to feel about that. It's kind of sad."

What's sad is that my mother has made sure to tell me, since I was very little, that Rebecca probably wouldn't be hanging around as long as other people's siblings normally do. But I don't tell Alex that.

"It's just how it is," I say, with a shrug.

"Kind of scary, with this virus stuff."

"I try to be very careful with germs."

This is the moment Alex picks to reach for my whole hand.

Next thing I know, she is leaning toward me.

"Is this okay?" she asks.

"Yes."

My mind is almost quiet as her lips come closer to mine.

It's not my first kiss, but that's what it feels like. I close my eyes, and my chest moves up and down with slow, deep breaths. I decide that I could probably be kissed like this, by her, forever and it would be awesome. Except my projected self is there, ordering me to suck it in, to fix my shirt so it doesn't cling too much, to extend my neck.

Alex's hand comes up near my side, and I shift away from it.

"What's wrong?" she says.

"I'm just . . ." I pull myself up, straightening against the back of the couch. "Can you maybe . . . avoid certain areas? I'm just—sorry."

"Don't be," she says. "I'll avoid whatever you want. But you should know that nothing about you should be avoided."

I give Alex a half smile, staring at her lips, at the silver in her cheeks. She's so thin, and I just can't comprehend the fact that a thin person like her would be okay feeling a body like mine. Does she understand that things are not just bigger on me, they're also like, shaped differently?

She kisses me again, keeping her hands to herself. For a while, at least. But then they find themselves on me. I want to touch her, too, but my arms are frozen at my sides. The internal cringe is in and out as my focus shifts between the things that are happening and the way my mind wants to judge and interpret those things.

The chanting in my head gets too loud, and I push her away.

"I'm sorry," I say.

"What's wrong?"

"I just . . . I'm not really used to this."

She nods. "It's okay. We can just hang out. We don't have to do anything."

For the next hour, we are together, but I am in my head trying to come up with a way to build a wall around that voice in my mind. Trying to recapture the feelings and confidence I felt with Freddie. Here I am with Alex, in a scenario of my dreams, and I can't shut the hell up and just go with it.

TWENTY-NINE

March break was going to be amazing, despite all this coronavirus stuff. It was going to be me and Alex hanging out, maybe getting over the weirdness of the other night and making up for it. But then someone died of the virus in Ontario, and now no one knows what's going on. Things pile on quick over the next few days. My mother is constantly on the phone, untangling messes and coming up with solutions when some of her employees start calling in sick out of fear. The worker who was supposed to be here all week to look after Rebecca during March break canceled on Thursday and Friday, so Mom's been home, making the occasional quick trip to her store when her best friend, Juliana, can come over to be there for Rebecca.

[Freddie] Did I do something?
[Freddie] Hey?
[Freddie] We can just forget the whole thing then.

[Freddie] Hello?
[Freddie] . . .

Freddie is in the background, sending exactly one text a day, but I don't respond. I simply enjoy the fact that he's trying to get to me, and I'm too busy with other things to give him my time.

I am busy constantly messaging with Alex.

[Alex] Can I ask u something?
[Baylee] Of course.
[Alex] Am I the first girl you've dated?
[Baylee] Yes.
[Alex] So this is like, super new to u.

All people are new to me, but I want her to know this less than I want her possibly thinking I'm newly discovering I might be attracted to girls. Better her think that than me having to awkwardly explain all the ways I suck.

[Baylee] It's new, but it's not like it's freaking me out.
[Alex] R u sure?

It's not touching other people that's freaking me out—it's other people touching *me*.

[Baylee] Yes. I swear.

I wish I wasn't so awkward. I wish I could explain the reason I'm like this, the things that scare me, but it would make me look like some inexperienced newbie, like some self-conscious fat girl. How would any of this be attractive? How would Alex want to make out with someone like that? Telling the truth is for when you have nothing to lose.

Before I know it, it's the following Sunday, exactly a week since I've seen her. A whole week, and life is all different. A state of emergency is declared, which sounds serious, but I don't really know what that means. What happens after you declare that? Who comes running?

Mom prepared grilled cheese and tomato soup for us, and now we settle in front of the TV to watch the news, of course, because that's all that's allowed on the living room TV these days. We see numbers and statistics from other countries, and we hear scary stories about other places. While I eat, I google the coronavirus. There are articles claiming to predict what it will look like when it really hits this continent full force. It sounds super dramatic, and I don't really understand how it can just spread like that, especially when you see it coming.

I remember how weird the word *pandemic* sounded when it was first being used, weeks ago, and now it's like *the* word. It's everywhere.

[Baylee] Is your dad home yet? The news is kind of scary.
[Alex] Got back this morning. 🙏

[Baylee] That's great. I'm glad.

[Alex] Me too. But he's in quarantine at my house, just in case.

[Baylee] Where are you then?

[Alex] My aunt's, 2 doors down. For 2 whole weeks. 🙁 They're telling anyone who's out of the country to get their asses back home ASAP. These r weird times.

[Baylee] And Bookworm is really closed for a while?

[Alex] Yeah. My boss had a video meeting with everyone. Still waiting to see what's going to happen, but for now closed.

"It's so weird that places are actually closing," I say. "How long is it going to last?"

Mom shakes her head, not paying attention to me. Her store is still open, but they're down to drive-through only because sit-down service is now forbidden.

"Closing the border is a big deal," Mom tells the TV. "This is going to be bad."

"Like, how bad?" I ask. "Are we all going to die?"

I was exaggerating, being dramatic, but saying the words out loud . . . Could we seriously all be dying? Is this going to be the apocalypse? The hairs on my arms stand up and shivers run up my back.

"I don't want you to be scared," Mom says. "But at the same time, Boss, it's normal to be scared. Not knowing is scary. But we're going to make sure we keep ourselves safe. We have to limit our contact with other people. It's meant to slow down the spread, but in our case, we can't afford to let it in here, okay?"

"Okay."

"So you are going to have to limit yourself, too. That means staying home. You understand that, right?"

"Inside the house?"

"I mean no going out anywhere."

"Oh, well, yes, I figured things being closed meant we weren't going to be able to go places," I say. "So, are you going to work still?"

"I have to." Mom stares off into the distance. "But I have to come up with a plan," she says, mostly to herself. Then she turns to me. "You get that this means no going over to Freddie's house, no going to Lara's or Rianne's, right?"

I stare at the floor, letting this part of our weird new reality settle over me. My mother keeps talking, stuff about the spread of germs, about limiting contact with other people.

What about Alex?

Well, this will not work. This will not work at all.

[Baylee] Wait does this mean we don't get to hang out anymore?
[Alex] ☹

For how long?

I was so awkward last time we saw each other. This can't be the way we leave it now, for who knows how long.

My mother's phone rings. While she talks to whoever is on the other end, I take the rest of my soup to the kitchen and pour it down the drain, scraping at the skin of congealed tomato soup that sticks to the bottom of the sink.

"I don't know, Sheila," I hear my mother say, and my ears perk up. Sheila is Freddie's mother. "How long?"

I wait in the doorway between the kitchen and Rebecca's room.

"Okay, fine," Mom says. "I'll ask her, then we'll get back to you. Yes, right away. Give me ten minutes."

When the phone call ends, my mother turns, presumably looking for me.

"Sheila's a little desperate," my mother says, shaking her head like she's unsure about something. "They're pulling her mother out of the seniors building she's in, and they're taking her to Sheila's brother's in Kingston."

"How come?"

"I think they're panicking a little," Mom says. "Sheila's brother has the four-year-old twins, and their mother will look after them with day care being closed. They both work at the hospital, so they're in a real jam."

"Oh."

"Sheila asked if you could come stay with Shaya."

"Why can't Freddie do it?"

"He's helping and running some errands."

"You're letting me go over there?"

"This is a one-time exception," my mother says.

I tell myself that I agreed to this because I want to help out, not because I'm hoping to run into Freddie.

I head upstairs to take the shower I've been putting off taking, scrunch some mousse in my hair, and blow-dry it quick. Halfway down the stairs, I hear Mom on the phone. Rebecca babbles in the background, and it sounds like she's on the floor, rolling around.

"Yes, I understand what you're saying, but with everything going on, I just feel that my child's well-being is at risk—" She pauses, presumably to listen to the person on the other end. "I understand that . . . *yes,* I'm aware that's how things work." Another pause. "So, you think it's fair to put my child at risk while you wait to see what happens?" More pausing, frustrated sounds from my mom. I sit on the stairs, listening, making sure to stay out of sight. "I would appreciate that. Yes, I will. Sure—go ahead and cancel. Fine." A brief pause, then: "What a bitch that woman is."

I settle at the kitchen table to start in on my quickest makeup look, winged black liner, mascara, pink gloss, and a touch of highlight powder. "What's going on?"

"You know how they are," Mom says, as she picks my sister up from the floor, and I know she means the nursing agency. "They tried to send a couple of brand-new nurses tonight to train. We're supposed to be staying home and limiting our contact with other people, and this dingbat scheduler tries to send a couple of strangers to come wing it with Beck. I don't think so."

"So there's no nurse tonight?"

Mom shakes her head, and I can tell she's already planning for tomorrow's exhaustion from having to be the one to look after my sister all night. She sits with Rebecca in her lap and does that little tapping motion on Beckie's back, like she's trying to burp her. Rebecca smiles and waves a little fist around.

"Well, maybe I can sleep here with her tonight, and I'll just call you down if anything happens?"

"I might take you up on that, Boss."

Mom rearranges the long feeding tube by pulling at it like it's a vacuum cord getting in the way. It makes me remember the time Beckie got her fist hooked around it and pulled the whole thing right out of her stomach, which is basically like poking a hole in a water balloon—a mess of formula and stomach liquids. I was, like, twelve, and I panicked, trying to apply pressure to the little hole like it was a bleeding wound while my sister rolled around like nothing was happening.

"Wake me up if I'm asleep when you get home, okay?" Mom says.

I nod.

THIRTY

When I get to Freddie's, his mother lets me in. She rushes around the foyer, dragging empty suitcases to the door, her cell phone tucked between ear and shoulder.

"Tell your mother I appreciate this so much," she says. "So much."

"You and Freddie are both going to Kingston?"

"Just me. Freddie is at the pharmacy, filling some prescriptions, and he's trying to stock up on some things. Then we're headed over to pack my mother up. Freddie should be back in a couple hours, tops," she says.

"Oh, okay."

Shaya is in bed, as promised, although I wouldn't have minded hanging out with a baby tonight. She loves when I read to her, changing my voice for different characters. Right now, she sleeps diagonally in her crib, her faint breathing coming through clearly from the baby camera I carry with me. I sit in Freddie's living room, scrolling through the TV apps, trying to decide on a movie.

[Alex] My dad sneezed twice. Not me sitting here convinced he's got rona.
[Baylee] ☹ He doesn't. He won't.
[Alex] ☹
[Baylee] I'm sorry. I wish I could be there to cheer you up.
[Alex] Me 2. What r u up to?
[Baylee] Babysitting my friend's sister. They're driving up to Kingston to bring his grandmother to an uncle's house.
[Alex] How wild do we think this is going to get before everything goes back to normal?
[Baylee] Realistically, it's not like this could become an apocalypse, right?

Alex doesn't respond.

I settle on *Dirty Dancing* so I can skip to all the good parts, where you just know Baby is feeling the butterflies that always live inside me. Each time I throw my phone across the couch, I am convinced I won't pick it up again for a while. Eight seconds later, I'm reaching over to grab it and check again. Just in case.

[Mom] Beck fell asleep! I'm going to bed, too, okay? Just nudge me when you get home.

I pad upstairs and peek in on Shaya. I tell myself this is necessary, to make sure that what I'm seeing through the camera is what's actually happening for real. I'm not up here because Freddie's bedroom door is at the end of the hallway, closed but unlocked.

His bedroom is dark wood furniture, gray carpeting, a skinny shelving unit of Blu-rays, and screenwriting books neatly arranged on a simple work desk. I flip through one of his books, tracing the notes he scribbled in the margins, stuff about character arcs and beats, whatever those are. When I open the left wardrobe door, his cologne is sitting on the shelf in front of his folded sweaters, just like I knew it would be.

I sit on the edge of the bed, and I bring the bottle up to my nose.

My judgy self assures me that I look like some desperate junkie huffing glue.

Alex hasn't responded to my text, and now I'm thinking about Freddie. Is this still about wanting what I can't have? Is that why I'm sitting here, on Freddie's bed, wondering what it would be like if he showed up to find me here? I just want that feeling of him looking at me.

How can it be that Alex and all the butterflies she gives me don't stop me from wanting Freddie to be here right now, from wanting to smell this cologne on him?

What is it that I need to do to unhook from him?

This is so like me, though, wanting absolutely everything, having no idea how to set limits. I literally never just grab a bowl of chips—I take the whole bag and I *have* to eat the whole bag.

Leaving crumbs at the bottom doesn't mean there's anything left. Why am I like this?

I need to be smart.

The sound of the garage door opening sparks fear, and the cologne nearly falls out of my hands.

I rush to place the bottle back in its spot. Then I turn off his bedroom light before leaving Freddie's room. When I'm halfway down the stairs, the door to the garage opens. Freddie ditches his shoes by the door, pulling off his light sweater, which leaves him in a white tee.

"Hi," I say.

"Hey."

I make my way to the front door, holding on to the baby monitor until I can hand it to him.

"She's still sleeping," I tell him.

"Good," he says.

"Okay, well . . ."

"Stay."

"I can't."

"You've been ignoring me," he says.

"You ignored me first."

"When?"

"After . . . that night."

"I wasn't ignoring you," he says. "You made me think I did something wrong, Bay. That you're pissed at me."

"Well, it's neither. Sorry. I've just been busy."

He doesn't look impressed by my answer. "Too busy to send me a text?"

I shrug, and he heads for the living room. He collapses into the corner of the couch, closing his eyes with his face aimed up at the ceiling.

"I can't stay. I have to go," I say, taking a few steps back.

"Why? Why are you trying to run away from me?" he says, leaning forward, elbows on his knees. "I knew this was going to happen."

"What?"

"You—being weird because of last week."

"I'm not being weird because of that." I pause. "I'm sort of, um, having a thing with someone right now, and I shouldn't be here."

The internal cringe at telling Freddie that someone else is interested in me that way—it's intense, and I stare at the floor.

"Oh," he says.

"Yes."

"What kind of thing? An exclusive-dating thing?"

"No." At least, I don't *think* so.

"So you need to leave because you have a thing?" Freddie says.

I meet his gaze. "Yes."

"Why?"

"Because . . . you are distracting."

"How do I distract?"

"Because every time I see you—" I break eye contact with him now. "No, never mind."

"Tell me."

The baby monitor crackles away as I take a couple of slow breaths, wondering if he really does want to go down this path. I do. I want to so bad.

"I can't think properly when you're around."

I wait, but Freddie doesn't respond. He gets up to find the baby monitor, where Shaya's rhythmic breathing continues. I watch as he hooks his Spotify playlist to the Bluetooth speaker on the fireplace mantel. What I've said replays in my mind.

Freddie presses the light switch, plunging the room into near darkness. With that small gesture, so much of my anxiety flies out the window. He comes to sit directly next to me.

"How come you turned the light off?" I ask.

"You like the dark," he says. "You're always more chill when the lights are off."

A thoughtful gesture that makes me smile. His cologne is everywhere.

"Would you ever tell anyone about this?" I ask. "About us?"

"No."

"Because you're embarrassed?"

"No," he says.

"Really?"

"Really," he says. "I wouldn't tell anyone because it's not a thing to be telling people about."

"Okay. Yeah," I say. "That's how I feel, too."

I want this to be private. Separate.

"Bay?" His head comes up right next to mine. I'm staring ahead, deeply focused on the fireplace. "You being around makes me feel things, too."

I let go of the breath I've been holding.

When he kisses me, I feel it everywhere. His body exerts this pressure against mine, making me recline on the couch. I wish I could stop visualizing myself standing next to the two of us sandwiched on the couch, seeing all of me squished unattractively under his amazing body, but I can't. The judgy projection is standing there, making sure I know just how wrong this is, how much I don't belong in this scene.

This is the other night, with Alex.

"Freddie, I'm kind of nervous."

He holds himself up over me, his face lined in shadow. "Why? Don't be."

"I just . . . don't understand why I'm here right now, when you could be with someone else."

"What someone else?"

"Lara."

I shouldn't have said her name. Why would I do this now?

He sits up with a deep sigh. "Why do you always wonder why it's you and not someone else? It's like you don't want to be here."

"They never look like me, though, the girls you're into," I say, because once I started telling him the truth, the pressure just flew away. I want him to know what it's like. "Since when are you into—what did Garrett say again? Oh yeah, *all* of this?"

"Maybe since I realized all of this was into me?" he says, then he's shaking his head. "Bringing up Lara and Garrett in the span of a minute—you really know how to kill the mood, Bay."

We sit there, in silence, while everything we've said hangs in the air. My eyes are aimed at the dark spot where the floor at my feet would be. Where do we go from here? I guess . . . home.

I push to my feet and reach for my purse.

His hand stops me, grabbing for mine.

"You're not seriously leaving," he says.

"I, um, killed the mood?"

"Maybe for, like, three minutes," he says, pulling at my arm. "It's not hard to get it back."

"Really?"

"Just don't bring anyone else up," he says. "It's just me and you, okay?"

Freddie takes his place back on top of me, and I'm scared to reach for his arms, even though I'm dying to run my fingers over his biceps. I want to touch him, but I feel like I don't have the right to.

"Wait," I say, pulling my mouth off his. "When is your mom coming back?"

"Come on! My mom? You're bringing up my *mom* right now?"

"I'm sorry! I'm just worried she'll walk in."

"Kingston is a four-hour round trip, minimum. The way she drives, it'll be more like six."

An hour later, Freddie's lips are against my ear, and he says,

"I could make out with you forever, but I kind of want to do more."

"Me too."

So I take his hand.

Upstairs, in his room, he sets up the same playlist on his room speaker.

"Can you do me a favor?" I ask.

"Sure."

"Can you, um, play the soundtrack to *Dirty Dancing*?"

He lets out a little laugh, then starts scrolling.

We don't go all the way, but we get pretty far into it. Sometimes it's overwhelming—so much stuff going on at once. Other times it's flashes of feeling totally self-conscious, worrying about how parts of me are situated at any given time, about the sounds I'm making. But those flashes don't last, because mostly, it's the best thing ever.

THIRTY-ONE

The next morning, Mom is asleep on the floor next to Rebecca, who snores in her crib. I tiptoe to the kitchen in an oversized T-shirt. The shirt hangs loose over a shoulder, revealing my hot-pink bra strap. There's a huge cartoon chicken on my shirt, but I feel . . . nice. My makeup is smudged, and my hair is wild, but through the reflection of my front-facing phone camera, I am not hating what I see. This feeling wrapped itself around me last night, like a pair of sparkly wings, and it's still here this morning. It's as though I am aware of every inch of my skin.

I walk around the kitchen, peek out the window, put the kettle on the stove, but it feels like I'm in a movie, like I'm the main character.

Today is Monday, the day we should've been headed back to school after March break, except this break will be a long one. It's not exactly clear when schools will open up again.

At the table, I scan for an Instagram DM from Alex. There's a message request from Garrett: Hey, B. What's up?

I don't approve it, but I don't delete it, either.

Nothing from Alex. I want to know what's going on, but the last message in the chat is mine, and it's on read. This is right about when Lara would be firing off the desperate messages if a guy went MIA on her, demanding a response, which means this is where I hold out and hold on to my self-respect. I'm holding out.

The group chat flashes.

[Rianne] This is so weird, guys!
[Lara] My parents are really losing their minds over my grandparents and my mom's family in Sri Lanka even though they're doing way better with the rona than we are on this continent.
[Rianne] I'm not allowed to leave the house EVER AGAIN!
[Lara] None of us can. That's the point.
[Baylee] Are all your parents all being next-level strict about it?
[Rianne] My parents won't even let me go outside unless I'm shoveling, except it hasn't snowed so I guess I can't go out until it's time to mow the lawn.

Down the hall, my mother stirs.

"Morning, Boss," she says. "You didn't wake me up last night."

"I tried, but you were out cold."

"What time did you come home?"

"Late," I say. "Freddie was gone a while. I slept on their couch for a bit."

"How is everyone over at the Morales house?"

"Not sick."

"Good."

I head for the living room and let myself fall into the couch. Mom checks on Rebecca, then grabs the house phone. She settles next to me, so I move my legs over. The text I'd been waiting for finally comes through.

[Freddie] Bay, we should have started doing this months ago.
[Baylee] !!!
[Freddie] I can't stop thinking about you.

I flatten my phone against my belly, trying to wipe the exaggerated smile off my face. When I look at my phone again, Freddie's sent me more words—words about my face, my lips, other things I can't believe I'm reading next to my mother.

Mom is on the phone with my sister's case manager, the person who is ultimately in charge of my sister's care and the resources she's given by the government. I eavesdrop, scrolling through BuzzFeed for the perfect fun list to turn my attention to.

"Frances, how long have we known each other? Have I ever been unreasonable?" Mom says, then she goes on, asking my sister's case manager about the possibility of converting the day nursing hours for school to home hours. "I don't understand. If

I'm entitled to those hours during the day, why can't the nurse just come *here* instead of the school? That way I can still go to work." Silence as she listens. "Well, that makes no sense. Those rules are stupid."

I reread Freddie's texts about ten times, feeling sparks in my belly every time.

[Freddie] I plan on doing things with you. To you.
[Baylee] Stop! 😳
[Freddie] 😏

"I gotta get to the store," Mom says, suddenly frantic. "Doris is on her way over."

Doris is one of the nurses who used to look after my sister years ago. She retired when I was in Grade Six or so, but she lives nearby and my mom kept in touch, so she visits us from time to time.

"There's no more toilet paper in this town," Mom says. "I have to get out there and stock up."

"Why isn't there toilet paper?"

"Everyone has lost their minds, that's why."

[Alex] . . .

I suppose that's an appropriate response to my last message about the likelihood of this pandemic turning into an apocalypse, but still, I sent that fifteen hours ago.

[Baylee]
📱 . .

A voice note comes through. "Realistically, it better not. What are you doing for the rest of the night? I was thinking we could maybe video-chat? It would be nice to see you."

[Baylee] Tonight?
[Alex] Tonight, what?
[Baylee] Your voice note—you asked about video-chatting.
[Alex] Yeah, *last* night.
[Baylee] The voice note just came through now . . . ?
[Alex] Stupid phone! I was wondering why you never responded. 🤦
[Baylee] I was wondering why *you* never responded! 📱
[Alex] I feel better now. So happy to know u weren't avoiding me.
[Baylee] 😶
[Baylee] It's the apocalypse and people are desperate for toilet paper?
[Alex] That's what my aunt said. She's out right now shopping for us. No toilet paper, but also no wipes or disinfectant spray. And shelves are kind of empty in general. It's chaos!

"It's not just toilet paper, Mom. My friend says it's just some kind of pandemic pandemonium."

"Shit on a stick with a brick!" Mom yells, rushing up the stairs. "Watch your sister. Doris is on her way."

I head over to Rebecca's room and notice that her formula is running low, so I grab the pitcher in the fridge to add some. I scoop her out of her crib and put her in my lap. I press play on her folk CD, singing along because I've heard this song about teddy bears going out for a picnic four hundred times.

This CD player is so old, and so is this stack of CDs. Maybe old enough to be considered vintage at this point.

I take several photos of myself with Rebecca in my arms. She never looks at the camera, but that's because her eyes never seem to focus on anything. In most of the shots I take, she's smiling or laughing from my tickling her. I send a photo to Alex.

[Alex]   She's so sweet.

Next, I take a twenty-second video of us to send to Alex. Freddie texts at the same time, but I swipe the notification away.

The doorbell rings. I prop my sister up against my shoulder, my arm under her butt, and she holds her head up a bit, looking around. I head for the door and pull it open wide. Doris stands on the other side of the screen door, supporting herself by holding on to the handles of her wheeled walker. She sneezes twice and pulls out a tissue from her pocket. There are droplets of spit on the windowpane.

"Hi, Baylee," Doris says, then her eyes settle on Rebecca in my arms. "Look at my little Miss Beckie."

She was always Rebecca's favorite. I bet my sister would love to get cuddled in Doris's squishy body. But it's not going to happen.

"Hi, Doris," I say. The door stays closed, and my eyes stay on the spray of spit that's on the window. "My mom doesn't have to go out anymore. We were going to call you and let you know."

"Oh, that's okay, honey." Doris goes for the screen-door handle, and before I have a moment to think, I flick the lock up.

"I'm sorry," I say. "But you're sneezing. You could be sick."

"Oh, that's just allergies," Doris says. "Remember I always had allergies when I worked here? I'm up to a double dose of Reactine every day and still . . . sneezing all day."

"Oh, okay. Well, better safe than sorry, right?"

"Baylee?" Mom calls from the stairs. "Is that Doris?"

Mom arrives next to me, and Doris's hand is still on the door handle.

"What's the matter with you, Boss? Let her in," Mom says.

"No, she's sick," I say.

"I'm not sick! Michelle, I was just telling her about my allergies," Doris says to my mother. "Remember my allergies?"

"Mom," I say, then I turn to face her so Doris can't read my lips when I whisper. "I'll go to the store. I'll find toilet paper, okay? I told Doris we didn't need her to come anymore. Can you just tell her to leave?"

"Baylee," Mom says, throwing a polite smile over at Doris, who is settling on the seat of her walker. "She was a nurse for forty years—she wouldn't—"

"She sneezed up goo all over the door, okay? If she comes in here, I'm going up to my room with Beck, and I'm locking the door."

Rebecca starts giggling, which I take as a sign of agreement. I walk over to the stairs, then I throw a look at my mother, letting her know I am not kidding.

"I'm so sorry I called you all the way over here," Mom tells Doris. "I really feel terrible, Doris. I'm just all over the place these days. Everything is so wild."

"Don't you worry," Doris says. "I think it's good your kid is taking this pandemic thing seriously."

"I'm just so sorry, Doris. How can I ever thank you for dropping everything and walking over on such short notice?"

"No worries, Michelle," Doris says, and when I peek over from behind my mother, I see Doris wheel herself around. She throws a hand up in a wave and goes, "It's just allergies, though."

"Thank you, Doris," Mom says. "Stay safe!"

I head over to Rebecca's crib and lay her down. Mom closes the door and comes over.

"We can take Rebecca for a ride and hit all the stores, and I'll go in until I find toilet paper," I offer. "I can be fast. I'll put flats on."

Mom lets out a sigh and rubs her fingers through Rebecca's thick brown locks. "I might just swipe a box from the store, if it gets down to it."

"You're going to steal from your own store?"

"If we get desperate enough. It's not like I've nearly as much staff or customers using the bathrooms now."

Doris is probably going to dislike me now, and when I think of the way I locked her out, it feels like I overreacted. It just didn't feel worth it, letting her in.

THIRTY-TWO

A few days later, Alex invites me to a video chat with Blake and Pen. I sit cross-legged on my bed, waiting for the call. Mom works from home most of the time, but she goes in a few hours three times a week to oversee things. She has medical masks, some of those nursing caps, and this super-involved disinfecting routine that includes taking off all her clothes as soon as she comes into the house and hopping into the shower immediately. It's so much work that she's stopped wearing any makeup and jewelry. She doesn't even style her hair anymore.

My phone goes off with a video-chat alert.

First I see Alex, seated on the green beast. The way she smiles at me makes fireworks go off in my belly.

"I wish I could see you for real," she says.

"Me too," I say. "I know I've asked this like, forty times already but how long do you think this is going to last?"

"It can't last that long, can it? Imagine not being able to see anyone for like, years? That doesn't even make sense."

"It makes no sense at all."

"Your makeup is on point today," Alex says, leaning in closer to inspect it. "I love classic black winged liner."

I make a show of looking downward so she can see how straight my lines are today.

"Ooh, look at that technique," Alex says.

We both stare at each other, and I wonder if this is the moment she would kiss me, if I was actually in front of her. I wonder if I would be able to let things go further than that. The me that I am right now firmly believes I would be different—I would *feel* different. But there's nothing to do about it. Everything is virtual these days. A virtual thing is better than no thing at all. Not so long ago, a virtual Alex would've meant everything and more to me. It would've been more than enough.

How can things just not happen again? How can I just go back to daydreams and late-night fantasy scenarios?

At this point, I figure all Alex would have to do to get me to break the rules is ask. I've looked online, and although *social distancing* are the only words on everyone's lips these days, keeping two meters between yourself and anyone who doesn't live with you, and the guy running the province is telling everyone to stay home and only go out for essential trips like the grocery store or the hospital, it's not like we're on actual house arrest. I think my mother is the only one whose rules I'd truly be breaking, and an angry mother feels like a worthy price to pay for seeing Alex again. If Alex asked, I'd sneak out to see her.

But she doesn't ask.

We hint at it, joke about it, but Alex follows the rules. So I follow the rules, but I also wonder if maybe she just doesn't want to see me that badly.

Blake and Pen arrive, and I'm a little surprised to see them together, on the same screen.

"What's up, dudes?" Pen says, and Blake waves.

"Your parents are okay with you two seeing each other? Because my mom is making a very big deal about this distancing thing," I say. "Two meters isn't enough. I have to be a kilometer from anyone."

Anyone except the people my mother allows in the house, like the nurses, Juliana, the afternoon worker, and very nearly Doris and her allergies. Then there are all the people Mom comes across while at work. Seems like a lot of people. Seems like the virus could easily get to us, if it wanted.

"Well, Pen lives with her brother," Blake says. "I live with my parents, but when it meant I was going to have to stay there and not see Pen—"

"She moved in here," Pen says. "At least until this shit gets sorted out."

"Wow," I say. "Your parents must be really, really cool."

"They're righteous," Blake says. "But Pen and I have been together over a year, and I'm always here anyway, so it just made sense. Although Pen and her brother eat Kraft Dinner like, four times a week. I don't know if I'll survive."

"That's not such a bad thing. I think I could eat it every day," I say.

"Do you put ketchup in it?" Pen asks. "I like it with lots of black pepper, too."

"I like making it with tuna and a bit of cream instead of milk," I say.

Pen nods in approval. "That's some gourmet shit."

For the next hour, we chat through this app that also allows us to play games. It's 100 percent nothing like hanging out for real, but it's also 100 percent better than not hanging out at all. When we play trivia games, Alex's success has us all suspecting she's got Google assisting her.

"Come on, people. I just have a lot of random facts inside this head," she says.

I stand at my window, cracking it open to let some cool air in. Garrett has just come out of the walkway, and he wanders down the sidewalk.

I point my camera his way. "I think that's Garrett."

"He's probably hoping he'll run into you," Pen says.

"Me?" I turn the camera back my way. "What are you talking about?"

"I talked to him the other day, and he told me he's been talking to you," Pen says. "You better watch out, Alex. Garrett's got his eye on your girl."

"Should I be worried?" Alex says. The way she cocks her head to the side and her hair hangs over her eyes is making me wish she was here. But she can't be here.

"I haven't been chatting with him. He DMed me, but I didn't respond."

"Why are you talking to Garrett so much these days?" Blake says to Pen. "That's a little . . . concerning."

"I know, but he keeps messaging me," Pen says. "The whole thing is weird, but it's hard to tell him to eat shit now."

"Why? It's *Garrett*," Blake says. "You just say, 'Fuck off and die,' then you block him."

"Yeah, yeah," Pen says. "Anyway. What were we talking about?"

I wish I could switch to a private chat with Pen right now to ask her about Garrett. Something about her words and her tone—I think I know the position she's in when it comes to Garrett.

Blake is shoving her hand into a bag of chips, then she reaches for some portable game system. Pen looks offended. "Don't touch the Game Boy with dirty chip hands. Come on, babe."

Blake bats her eyelashes and holds a hand up for Pen to see. "I licked them clean."

"Oh, man!" Pen grabs the system and goes off-screen. "Now I'm gonna have to disinfect that shit. It's not like there's any Lysol to waste!"

Blake laughs and leans in toward the screen. "I love driving her crazy. I made these cute little paper dresses and put them on her Ninja Turtle figurines, and she lost her shit on me!"

"This is how bored we've become," Alex says.

The conversation continues about things I'm not a part of, but I lie on my bed and listen, flipping through view options so Alex is the only one on my screen. Does this count as friends hanging out? It kind of just feels like watching someone's live on Instagram or TikTok.

Alex raises a piece of paper to the screen, the words *I miss you* handwritten. Just for a second, but it's long enough.

"I saw that, Alex!" Blake says. "What did it say?"

"None of your business," Alex says.

I want her to ask me to come see her. I want the feeling of her standing in front of me, seeing me. It's stupid, but part of me feels like maybe I'm just not pretty enough. Maybe I'm too awkward.

An hour or so later, we decide to end the chat. It's dark out, and a new nurse is downstairs with Rebecca. She seems young, barely older than I am—not that it's easy to tell, because she's wearing a blue medical mask and a colorful fabric cap over her hair. Her current mission is to stop Rebecca from crying, bent over the railing of the crib and alternating between patting her butt and rubbing her back. My sister doesn't like that kind of touch. It's like it makes her even more angry, which makes sense, because if I was pissed off, some stranger awkwardly rubbing my back would not translate to comfort. She's probably like, *Who are you? Why are you touching me?*

I tiptoe on through to the kitchen, keeping an eye on things. I down a glass of orange juice, watching as a look of desperation settles on the nurse's face, making her eyebrows scrunch in the middle. She tries suctioning Rebecca's mouth every couple of minutes, which just makes Rebecca try to hit herself in the face in frustration. I used to just walk on by and not pay attention when I was little, because they're the experts and I was supposed to be in bed.

I head over and grab the air compressor, the small machine that pushes air out of a thin tube for Rebecca's breathing treatments. When I flip the switch, the loud rumbling instantly startles her into quieting, and her interest is piqued.

"If she cries a lot like that, just turn this thing on and put it close," I say, placing the compressor into her crib. "We hook the tubing into her hand like this. She likes to play with it."

"It's so loud," the nurse says.

"I know, but she likes it," I say. "And we're so used to the noise, so it's not like turning it on at four a.m. would even bother me or my mom. The crying, though—that's hard to ignore."

Rebecca is quiet, holding still as she listens to the rumbling. Seconds later, a smile appears, and she starts smacking her hand on the pillow while holding the plastic tubing.

"Thank you," the nurse says. "What a great tip."

"You're new."

"The agency wasn't able to set me up with another nurse to give me proper orientation to work here," the nurse says. "I don't really know much about your sister beyond the medical details."

"The main things to know are that she can be really moody, and there are things she just hates. When she cries too much, she starts choking on her saliva and then everything goes to hell from there."

I launch into a spiel about Rebecca's likes and dislikes, sharing tips, and the nurse actually takes notes with a pen and notepad. Rebecca is now having a total giggling fit.

"And sometimes you just have to leave her alone," I say. "Trying to help just makes it worse. You can try Tylenol, too, if nothing else works. Especially if she makes this face—" I make a grimace, scrunching up my nose and squinting my eyes. "That usually means she's uncomfortable. The nose crinkling is how you know something hurts."

The nurse writes down these final details, then she watches Rebecca.

"I can't believe that worked so well, with the compressor," the nurse says. "I think I'll go get her formula ready now, since she's okay."

I make my way up the stairs, noticing my mother sitting on the top step, clearly eavesdropping on the new nurse. When I reach her, she scoots over so I can get by, grabbing my arm as I go.

"You're a very good daughter," Mom says.

"I have my moments," I say. "Are you going to keep spying?"

"For a little while longer," she says. "I come and go, just to check."

"How come you're letting new people in here all of a sudden?"

Mom sighs. "I have no choice. They approved the school hours to become day hours at home, but now they've got to get a whole bunch of new nurses trained. It was either that or have no nurse at all."

"Do I have to wear a mask in the house?"

"Don't even get me started on that. I was texting with Dawn," Mom says, referring to my sister's main nurse, who's been coming here a long time, "and she says the ones who make decisions about how things are handled can't even agree on how you catch it. Is it in the air? Is it in snot and saliva?"

"In the air? Like, we'd have to wear hazmat suits, like apocalypse, zombie, CDC suits?"

"Boss, at this point, who knows?" she says. "The second you feel a scratchy throat or a runny nose, then you'll want to wear a mask so you can keep those germs to yourself."

I'm about to keep going up to my room, but then I add, "We really should be writing something up with all this information about Beck. We know every little thing about her, but they don't."

"You're right," Mom says. "You want to write it? I'll pay you if you make it look nice on the computer."

I nod, considering. "I guess I could do that."

When I get to my room, Alex has DMed me some sweet words.

[Baylee] I wish we could see each other.

[Alex] Me 2. U have no idea.

[Baylee] Well, why can't we?

[Alex] . . .

[Baylee] We could stand six feet apart.

[Alex] U really think that would work? U think I wouldn't be marching right up 2 u? I've just been thinking about kissing u since the last time it happened.

Butterflies. A thousand butterflies.

[Baylee] Me too. Would it really be such a big deal? Pen and Blake are together.
[Alex] Trust me, I want to so bad. But ur sister could really get sick, right? Why would u want to take a chance like that?

She's right, but it's not what I wanted to hear. I feel foolish for suggesting it in the first place, now that she's pointed out how dumb I am, so I don't respond for a while.

Garrett's DM request is still sitting there, waiting to be acknowledged or deleted. He's added another message.

[Garrett] Come on, B. Don't leave me hanging!

My mind shifts into focus, retrieving Pen's words. The curiosity leads my fingers to the virtual keyboard.

[Baylee] Hi.
[Garrett] Hey hey
[Baylee] I saw you outside earlier. Were you meeting friends? Are you allowed?

[Garrett] Nah. I was getting out of the house for a bit. Although if I felt like seeing friends, I would.

[Baylee] Oh.

[Garrett] Were you gonna call the cops on me?

[Baylee] I might do that next time.

[Garrett] Next time, you should come hang out. I'll give you a smoke.

It's not my imagination, the thrilling sensation building within, thinking about the possibility of Garrett hoping to see me. It's shameful, nothing to ever be admitted out loud, but that feeling I have inside—it's very *there*.

What's that about? What's wrong with me?

Now I wish he would talk to me, but he's gone quiet, and I have nothing to say to him.

[Baylee] R u up?

[Freddie] Always.

[Baylee] How are you?

[Freddie] I am wondering why you're not over at my house right now.

[Baylee] Well, what would we be doing right now . . . if I was at your house?

[Freddie] You want me to go into details?

[Baylee] Yes. I mean, if you want.

[Freddie] I definitely want.

There are so many things I'd never admit to out loud. I thought I was a pretty decent person, but I'm starting to think that maybe I'm not.

I'm addicted to all the things that are happening.

Were happening.

Nothing is happening now. Just talking to people online, looking at them through a screen, typing about all the things I wish I could be doing.

[Freddie] Come over.
[Baylee] I want to.

But I can't. I shouldn't. Or maybe I could?

THIRTY-THREE

April starts with a lot of sunshine and warmer weather, and the news keeps repeating the same things, at least for where I live: people must be two meters apart from everyone except those they live with. Going outside seems to be bordering on illegal. All public outdoor areas are closed. Only essential outings are permitted. Exercise means going for a quick walk alone—no friends, no stopping to say hi to your neighbor, no hanging outside a coffee shop. Basically just walking your dog super quickly is the only outdoor activity that's sure to look appropriate. If I had a dog, I'd walk it all the way over to Freddie's.

Our houses are prisons with unlocked doors.

It's early afternoon and I'm DMing with Alex.

[Alex] Tonight is my first virtual therapy session. Seems super weird that I'll be sitting in my aunt's garage, talking at my phone.

[Baylee] How long is the session?

[Alex] 60 minutes.

[Baylee] Do you know what you're going to be talking about?
How does that work?

[Alex] I can come in with topics I want to discuss, but a lot
of the time, Kristy will start with the gist of what we were
going over the previous session, and she'll ask me how
that's going now.

I wonder if Alex ever talks about me to her therapist.

[Alex] You want to hear something that's kind of weird?

[Baylee] ???

[Alex] We're sort of in a long-distance relationship, u and me.

[Baylee] You're so close, though.

[Alex] I know. I hate this.

[Baylee] I hate it, too. I wish I could just sit across from u, even
with 2 meters apart.

[Alex] Two meters would still feel too far, though.

[Baylee] I don't really want to just be seeing you through a
screen.

[Alex] Maybe things will get better in a couple weeks. We can
wait, right?

Someone different could wait. The old me could wait forever. I
haven't seen Alex in more than two weeks. It's not that much time,

but it feels like forever. What if two more weeks just keep getting added on and it never ends?

I send my mother a text.

[Baylee] Can I do therapy?
[Mom] What are you talking about?
[Baylee] My friend sees a therapist because her dad's work benefits cover it.

A couple of minutes later, Mom knocks on my door and opens it when I say, "Yeah?"

"What's this therapy thing, Boss?"

"Why do you look all worried?" I say.

"Therapy is serious. I think I should know what's making you suddenly ask for that. What's going on?"

"It's not even serious, Mom." I am cross-legged on my bed in pajamas, hugging my pillow, while Mom takes a seat at my desk. "It's not like I'm having a breakdown or something. I just have a friend who sees a therapist, and she says it's a really good thing."

"Who is this friend?"

"Just this girl I met."

"Met where? School?"

"No. Bookworm," I say. "Anyway, she was telling me about it, and I thought it sounded cool. Plus . . . it's not like there's anything else to do."

Mom studies me for a minute. "You would tell me if anything was going on, right?"

I roll my eyes. "Just forget it, then."

I focus on my phone, scrolling through my Instagram feed but not taking in any of the posts. Mom pushes to her feet.

"I'll look into it," she says.

"Hey, Mom?" I say, and she nods. "What happens to people who still hang out?"

"What do you mean?"

"I mean, say Lara and Trey were still dating, and they went to each other's houses?"

"Well, they would be careless idiots."

I sigh. "I mean, like . . . would they get arrested?"

"Well, no," Mom says. "But they could be fined, maybe."

"Really?"

"I don't know all the bylaws, Boss," Mom says, a little annoyance creeping into her tone. "It doesn't matter, does it? You should all be staying home, regardless of whether there's a fine involved or not. The whole country is being told to stay home and stay away from others to help flatten the curve, so that's what we should do. Tell Lara it's not worth it."

"Yeah, okay."

Mom leaves, and I head for my nail supplies. While a playlist of cheeseball songs I used to love when I was like, fourteen fills my room, I give myself a fresh manicure. My hands are so steady that the end result almost looks professional. I pull out my journal, feeling a sense of excitement at the thought of pouring my feelings out onto the page, knowing I'll have the added bonus of being able to admire my shiny red nails as I write. Most of what I write is about wishing I could somehow experience looking at myself through Alex's eyes, through Freddie's eyes, through Garrett's eyes, even. Just for a minute. Just enough for it to click inside. It's like if I could see myself from other perspectives—all three of them mashed together—then maybe I'd feel steadier in my own shoes.

[Freddie] Come meet me.

Freddie wants to see me badly enough to break the rules. Knowing that makes my stomach somersault. It makes me reach for pink, shiny gloss so I can raise an eyebrow and pout at myself in the mirror while rereading his text.

[Baylee] I so wish I could.
[Freddie] Why can't you?

He wants me enough to risk it all, but there's a little fear and resistance inside me suddenly. There was no hint of this when I was silently begging for Alex to demand to see me, but then again, she wasn't asking, so it wasn't real.

[Baylee] What if I got my sister sick?

[Freddie] You can't get her sick through me.

[Baylee] How do you know?

[Freddie] I've been at home with my mom and sister since
Kingston. My mom works from home now and Shaya's out of
day care. No one's been here.

[Baylee] Well, what if I gave you the virus?

[Freddie] You're not gonna get me sick. You're home all the
time, too.

[Baylee] . . .

[Freddie] Do you know what Matt and the rest of the hockey
team have been up to?

Of course I know. The rules are more like guidelines, and
people are finding all kinds of ways around them. I see the posts
online—I know some of the other people in my class have gotten
away with a lot. Strictness looks different depending on which
parents you ended up with. My mother's gotten in my head, the
whole "keep two meters apart" thing starting to feel like a law.

[Baylee] How are you going to leave your house?

[Freddie] What do you mean? I'm going to take my keys and go.

[Baylee] 😶

[Freddie] I told my mom I'm going for a drive. You can say you're
going out for a walk. No one needs to know we're going together.

[Baylee] I don't know...

[Freddie] It feels like I haven't seen you in years, Bay.

Part of me has already jumped out the window to go to him. I just have to get my feet to move.

[Baylee] Where are we supposed to go?

[Freddie] Let's go to the bridge. No one will see us there.

[Baylee] . . .

[Freddie] OK. Forget it. I won't keep pressuring you. I'm here if you change your mind.

[Baylee] Wait! Don't go.

[Freddie] I didn't go anywhere.

[Baylee] You're not sick, right?

[Freddie] I have zero symptoms. I've seen no one. We get our groceries delivered and my mom makes me wipe the rona off everything with Lysol.

[Baylee] OK.

[Freddie] OK?

[Baylee] Yes. Give me an hour.

Under an hour later, just before four, I've inched my way down the stairs, carefully timing my steps for whenever it was my mother's turn to talk so her voice would camouflage any sound I made. I flatten myself against the wall at the bottom of the stairs while I wait for her to find somewhere to settle. She's whipping from living room to kitchen, putting things away, checking on Beck, and making tea, judging by the sound of the kettle's hiss. Before the kettle is quieted, I rush to the front entrance and scoop up a pair of suede boots with a thick heel.

Upstairs, I left a big lump under my covers made with an old comforter that's usually tucked away on the top shelf of my closet. It's probably a dumb idea, but it works in movies.

Outside, Freddie is idling at the curb in front of my neighbor's. I slip into my boots and make my escape.

"Hurry, the neighbors will call the cops if they see!" Freddie calls from the driver's seat.

"Oh, shut up."

Freddie hits the gas, although not as much as he normally would. We drive in silence, his rock tunes flowing out of the speakers. We drive, and I steal glances at his hand, his arm, his face.

I pull my eyes away long enough to send my mother a text.

[Baylee] I'm going to take a nap. I'm kind of tired.
[Mom] Want me to wake you for dinner?
[Baylee] No. I'll come down when I wake up.

Freddie is next to me, and his cologne is everywhere. Even if this is illegal, it's worth it. I just don't care about anything else right now. The glances I steal at him lead to the kind of thoughts girls are supposed to be ashamed of. All I want is to take things from him that I'm supposed to pretend I don't want or need.

We park the car behind Zippy Mart and JJ Pizza so it won't be seen from the road. The lot is empty, but both stores are open because food is essential. We make our way through the tall dead grass, following the creek to where it passes underneath the bridge.

"I give the universe a bucket of gratitude for the fact that this place is deserted," Freddie says.

There's fresh garbage around the makeshift bonfire site in the shadows, so people have definitely been here, which means they could come back.

"Let's walk farther down," Freddie says.

Stones and broken glass feel sharp against the soles of my suede boots, throwing me off-balance. Freddie comes up next to me, giving me his hand for support. The physical connection between us eases some of the antsy sensations I was struggling with.

Just as quickly, I wish he'd touch me again.

The other side of the bridge is mainly a forest. To the left, through the trees, is a newer subdivision, and to our right the path breaks through to a field that eventually becomes the grounds of an elementary school. Ahead of us, the creek keeps going through the trees. It's kind of pretty with those old trees creating a canopy above us. We've never gone out this far.

"You know what we never talked about?" I ask.

"What's that?"

"Lara."

He shrugs. "What is there to say?"

"Are you still talking to her?"

"No."

"Not at all?"

"Not since before school ended for March break," he says. "You?"

"No. She's mad at me."

"Why?"

"It's complicated."

Freddie taps on his phone, and soon a song starts through his speaker. He puts the phone back in his pocket, the music trailing behind us.

"Where are you taking me?" I ask.

"I don't really know, actually. I've always wanted to explore the area."

"I'm not much of an explorer."

He makes a face. "I'm actually looking for a spot for us to . . . you know."

I haven't decided how I feel about this when voices start coming from ahead. A group of people our age is becoming visible through the trees. Fear erupts within me, and I search for an escape with my eyes, but there's nothing except for an empty space with a bunch of trees I'm too fat to hide behind. This whole idea was very much idiotic.

Even though no one is near me, I pull out the medical mask I have in my purse and throw it on.

"You planning on making out with these people?" Freddie jokes.

"No, but what if they cough or sneeze? It could shoot through the air and land directly in my mouth."

I pull the mask off again, keeping it in my hand, and I move back to stand against a large rock. The group gets closer to us, three guys and two girls weaving their way through the trees until they finally notice us. Freddie quiets his music, looking totally at ease. Their eyes settle on us, but they maintain a good ten feet of distance from us.

"I wouldn't go that way," one of the guys tells Freddie. "There's a guy raging in his yard, threatening to call the cops."

"Thanks for the tip," Freddie says.

One of the girls stares at him, and I can tell what she might be thinking and feeling. I watch her smile at him, and I know that what I'm suspecting is happening.

The group starts heading toward us, aiming for the path we took to get here. Freddie grabs my hand and pulls us away, like he's protecting our personal space, our social distancing. The group passes by. The girl looks at my hand in Freddie's, and it's subtle, but I'm trained to notice the look that's barely there. A momentary *What the hell is this?* expression, followed by a shrug.

In this moment, this girl is a stand-in for Lara, and I feel my face let go of the awkwardness I was feeling, my eyebrow pulling up high while I aim my best dirty look right at the back of her head as she walks away. Why *can't* I be here with Freddie?

He comes to rest against the rock with me, leaning in close. "You know what sucks?"

"What?"

"There is no way we can go to Port Perry now. Everything is closed."

"Maybe later, in the summer? Things are going to have to reopen, right?"

"Maybe."

Then he starts telling me about his screenplay. Without friends and school monopolizing his time, solid effort was put in, and he says he's headed into act three, which I guess is supposed to be impressive.

"I'm kind of wondering if you'd want to read part of it," he says.

"Really?"

"I want your opinion. Maybe just on the first act."

He comes to stand in front of me, so close that I'm staring at his lips again. He steals a glance down the front of my shirt, giving an exaggerated nod of approval, which makes me laugh. My eyes blur on his lips, my head getting hazy. Then we're kissing.

"Freddie?"

He locks eyes with me when his lips are still on mine.

"What if they saw us, those people? What if that brunette girl who was clearly into you just now came back and saw this?"

"I guess I'd tell her to stop being creepy and go home."

"That's it?"

"That's it." He nods, playing with the hem of my shirt. But still I can't help but wonder if this is only happening because life is interrupted. All the things that mattered so much—like school, the people in it, their judgment—are on hold. It's restrictions and house arrest on one hand, but it's total freedom from the usual bullshit on the other. Maybe in this world, we're different people, playing by different rules.

"You should come over later," he says.

"I'm not even supposed to be out *now*!"

"Tonight, when everyone's asleep. Sneak out," he says. "Come to the garage."

He wags his eyebrows, which makes me smile. "Maybe."

I already know I'm going to make it happen.

We walk back to the bridge. The group of people must've found somewhere else to go, because under the bridge is still deserted. I check my phone, finding texts from my mother.

My phone rings, and it's my house number.

"Shit," I say, glancing at the texts. "My mom knows I left."

"Uh-oh."

[Baylee] I just went to see Freddie. I'm on his lawn and he's in his garage. We're just talking.
[Mom] Get back here. NOW.

We make our way through the rocky layer under the bridge, to see a couple of police officers standing in the parking lot where Freddie is parked.

THIRTY-FOUR

I don't know how Freddie manages to be cool and calm in all situations that give me internal anxiety meltdowns, but he walks over to his car like we're not about to get arrested and thrown in jail.

"What's going on here?" the woman officer says.

"Not much. Just came for a walk," Freddie says.

I want to roll my eyes, because I look like the last person who would ever break the rules just to go for a walk.

"Come on," the male officer says, clearly not in the mood to play this game. "You guys know what's going on, right?"

"We've gotten a couple calls about groups of kids coming out here," the first officer says.

"Maybe you two somehow missed the news? Missed the word about all nonessential outings being out of the question?" the male officer says. He's lecturing us about our bad decision to disregard some of the rules meant to keep us safe, but at the same time, he's standing too close to us. I take several steps back until I'm sure the two meters that's supposed to keep germs away is between us.

He carries on with "Maybe you don't take this seriously, huh? People getting sick and dying isn't enough of a reason for you to follow the rules."

"All right," Freddie says. "We get it. We messed up."

I've only spoken to a police officer one other time in my life, and that was on the day of the seat-belt fiasco. That one was kind, but this one looks ready to hand me a very expensive ticket.

I finally find my voice. "Are we going to get fined?"

The male officer lets his gaze bore into me first, then Freddie. "Not this time. Smarten up and tell your friends to do the same."

"Okay," I say as Freddie nods.

Freddie pulls out his keys, and we get into the car.

As we drive away, Freddie says, "Damn. There's a possibility that this was *not* worth it."

"My mother is going to kill me."

Freddie doesn't say anything. The silence gives me mental space to try and come up with a way to explain this.

When I get home, my mother makes me disinfect my hands with sanitizer before going to the bathroom to wash up to my elbows thoroughly. She watches with her arms folded, her angry eyes on me.

"You snuck out?"

"No. I mean, I woke up and I guess you didn't see me come down. I decided to go outside. And Freddie was outside, too."

"Baylee, I saw the blanket in your bed. Was I supposed to think that was you rolled up under there?"

"No. That's stupid. I was just cold last night, so I got my other blanket out."

Mom's angry eyes fade a little when she lets out a sigh. "It is *very* important that you take this seriously, Baylee."

"I am."

Sort of.

Not really.

"I'll have to speak with Sheila. You both know better."

I know better, but I can't bring myself to be better.

"But he's five minutes away from here. Can't we keep two meters apart?"

"It's too soon to be taking risks."

"Okay, fine."

The rest of the evening I spend in my room, messaging with Rianne on and off while I eat the overbaked fish sticks and cold, dry fries Mom had made for dinner while I was out. On IG, I see that Lara's latest post was twenty minutes ago, and it's of her outside on her balcony while Taylor is far off in the background, standing on her own balcony next door, her fingers in a cliché peace sign. Lara's IG stories are full of little clips of the two of them that I don't want to watch.

Dawn, my sister's main nurse, is downstairs, going through Rebecca's nighttime routine of medications, bath, skin care, breathing treatments, and chest physiotherapy, which helps her move what's in her chest so she can cough it out. It's midnight, but Rebecca's sleep is always a mess anyway, and Dawn is the one my mother trusts the most, so if my sister's awake and in a good mood, they take advantage of the time.

Mom is in bed. I know this because I've been peeking into the hallway every half hour since nine.

[Freddie] I really wish you could come over tonight.
[Baylee] Me too. But it's too risky.

For the next little while, Freddie and I text about things I would like to be doing in real life. Heat moves to my face, and a funny feeling makes my head feel hazy. He's right there, across the street. So close.

[Baylee] I'm going to try to get past the nurse.
[Freddie] Really?

I've never asked Dawn if legally, she's obligated to tell on me. It's not like this kind of thing has ever come up before. Technically, Dawn is here only for Rebecca. She's not responsible for anything else that goes on in the house, which is why my mother always insisted on going over all the safety rules with me: fire safety, not answering the door to strangers, and keeping doors locked at all times—all while there was always an adult in the house with me. But still—she's known my mom for years. I think she'd tell.

Whether I take the front door or the door to the garage, I'll have to go down the stairs next to Rebecca's room.

[Freddie] Don't get in trouble because of me again, Bay.
[Freddie] But if you come, I will be fucking ecstatic.

I smile to myself at the top of the stairs and wrap my bathrobe around the off-shoulder top I've got on over black leggings. Not just any black leggings, but the ones with a crisscross pattern that goes from my ankles up the back of my legs to my butt. I've placed my pointy red pumps and my purse in a mesh bag.

I try to be quiet going down, but not overly so. If Dawn catches me, I'll just act as though I've come down to grab something before bed.

I have decided that if the universe wants me to see Freddie, I'll be able to get through the door, and if I'm meant to stay home and rot alone in my room, the universe will make Dawn turn around and catch me in the act.

Dawn flips on the mixer, which means she's making formula. The mixer is loud, and she'll be standing there blending it for a good two minutes.

I've left it up to fate, and fate says to go see Freddie.

I let myself out, rushing into the night in my pink bathrobe with feathery trim on the sleeves. The fuzzy black slippers on my feet have a surprisingly good grip.

In the walkway, I slip on the shoes, ball up the robe around the slippers, and place them into the bag.

Freddie's garage door is only up by a couple of feet. My heels echo into the night as I make my way up the driveway. He pulls the door up above his head, vapes, and lets out a huge cloud of vapor with his breath. He puts a finger in front of his lips, and I understand we are meant to be very quiet. It's unlikely his mom would hear us out here, but all precautions must be taken when you're trying not to get caught.

We stare at each other for a moment. I have this thought that maybe there will never be a time where looking at him gets boring. My whole body is on fire, and I'm still ten feet away from him.

"Well . . . um, hello," he says.

I smile, then rush inside so he can close the door on our illegal behavior.

"You know I wouldn't like, put you in danger, right?" Freddie whispers. "I mean, with Rebecca and everything. If I thought that—"

"I know."

My eyes take in the garage, the pullout couch dressed as a bed, the Christmas lights strung across the wall above the couch, and the music that plays through a speaker on the workbench.

"This is very nice," I say.

"I tried to make it a little less *garagey*."

"Hang on," I say, hesitating. "Is this thing going to bend if I sit on it? Is it sturdy?"

One of my internal, fat-girl considerations just fell out of me, right there, into the air around us. This is another way the mood gets killed by me.

"It's fine. Watch." Freddie bounces around on the mattress part. He looks ridiculous, which makes me laugh. I take a seat at the top end of the couch, by the back of it, because I figure that part is less likely to collapse or flip over. Freddie comes over to me, and I can already sense things are different tonight, more intense.

He listens to me and takes his time. He says, "Is this okay?" And of course, it is. It's next-level okay.

"Wait," I say, putting a hand on his chest at the moment I feel things amp up in a way that makes it clear hitting pause on things will soon be difficult. Last time, we got pretty far, but not as far as we are now.

"What's up?"

"Don't think I'm weird." I reach for my purse and pull out a little bottle of clear lubricant, which I offer to him.

"Wow—so you came here prepared," he says, then laughs as he waves a shiny condom. "Me too."

I pretend to go for a fist bump, which makes him laugh again.

The truth is, I've spent so long researching things about sex—all the kinds of sex—online that I was kind of ready for it to actually happen. Someone on YouTube made this video about lubricant, and the way they talked about it, it just stayed with me, the idea that this is a vital accessory. So I bought a little bottle of it like a year ago, and I've just hidden it in the little zippered pocket at the back of my purse, where it could remain a secret but also be there in case my fantasies were to come true.

I can't believe this is real.

Freddie keeps the lights off completely, doesn't even ask to turn them on. It's a small gift I didn't have to ask for.

When Freddie and I get to the part we're all taught to expect will hurt, it doesn't, and I know it's because of the contents of that little bottle I brought. It's the exact opposite of hurt. It's a rush, and every inch of me glows in the dark.

THIRTY-FIVE

The following evening, I join my mother on the couch as she watches a news reports on some little town I've never heard of until now. I zone out, staring at the TV, my eyes registering nothing that flashes before them. I am too busy deciding what I'm feeling today, other than the total giddiness that makes my head swim. This is a serious thing that happened last night. Not serious because a particular body part went into another. It's serious and important because I can let my mind take me back there without cringing at the mental images. I can conjure Freddie and me up in my mind, and all it does is make me want to do it again.

I hope Freddie wants to do it again, too.

"This is an abomination," my mother says, her words clashing with where my mind is. "Over twenty dead in one small nursing home."

"What happened?"

"There's been an outbreak at a nursing home. The residents didn't even stand a chance." Mom says. "Staff are sick, but they still have to go to work because there's no one else to look after these people."

"Why?"

"It's a small town."

[Rianne] OMG GUYS! Guess where I am??????
[Lara] ???
[Rianne] I'm in the car with my parents. We're on our way to Cedar Valley to break my grandma and grandpa out of there.
[Baylee] OMG, yes. They'll be safe at your house. The stuff on the news is so sad.
[Rianne] I know. My dad lost it when he saw that. My mom's making me move to the basement so they can have my room.
[Lara] Are you okay with that?
[Rianne] TOTALLY! I don't want them dying. Plus the basement has its own bathroom and my dad is going to finish the rec room so there's a door and everything.

"Rianne's parents are on their way right now to take her grandparents out of Cedar Valley," I tell my mom. Cedar Valley is about thirty minutes from here.

"That's smart. That place is half retirement, half nursing home. If it gets in there, it'll spread like fire," Mom says. "Good for them."

[Freddie] Come over tonight.

[Baylee] I'm not sure if I can.

[Freddie] Try. I'll be out there waiting for you.

I head back to my room to get away from the death stuff, and to start preparing for my possible escape tonight. I draw myself a bath, dropping a bath bomb in, and it fizzes pink. In the water, I spend some time writing in my journal, and the paper ends up sprinkled with bathwater.

I think of Alex, about what it would feel like to be at her house again, sitting on the green couch, just talking and watching her lips while records spin songs I've never heard before. But my mind takes me back to last night, to Freddie.

In my room, I lie like a naked starfish on my bed, letting myself air-dry before I apply coconut oil to my skin. There's a message request in my DMs that I hadn't noticed.

[Pen] So how come ur chatting up Garrett even after I told you he's interested in you?

She sent that hours ago.

[Baylee] I don't know. He confuses me.

[Pen] Huh?

[Baylee] What did you mean when you told Blake it's hard to tell him off now?

[Pen] What does it matter? You wouldn't really understand.

[Baylee] I might. Him and his friends . . . they used to make fun of me all the time.

[Pen] Yeah well, that's Garrett. He used to call me Steve.

[Baylee] Why is he different now?

[Pen] I don't know. I'm not sure I buy it.

[Baylee] He says it was all just jokes.

[Pen] Well I wasn't laughing. I used to wish he'd get hit by a car and bust both his legs.

[Baylee] I used to daydream about him becoming an orphan and having to move in with a really evil aunt.

[Pen] That's pretty creative, dude.

[Baylee] Thanks.

Pen doesn't respond.

[Baylee] I can tell you don't like me.

[Pen] I'm just watching out for my friend. You get that, right?

[Baylee] Yes.

I go through my moisturizing routine while thinking about Alex. I don't know how to fix things to make it so Pen isn't right about me, right about needing to look out for Alex. Am I doing something wrong? Am I breaking any rules?

Rianne sends Lara and me a photo of her grandparents in her living room, which is the most wholesome thing ever.

I kill the next few hours creating an elaborate scenario where I run into Garrett on the walkway, and we get into some kind of conversation where truths are revealed. No matter how much I try to control it, the scenario always ends with him giving me a look, and me knowing exactly what that look means. That feeling I get is why I replay the moment a few times. Then I move the scenario along, Freddie appearing at the end of the path to take me away, leaving Garrett feeling like he totally missed out. I just keep rewinding to the intense parts and replaying them.

I know there are some iffy elements about this particular scenario, some things that aren't exactly healthy, but I'm too addicted to feeling like this. And if it's all in my head, then it's safe.

[Alex] Hey. 😊
[Alex] I didn't, um, freak u out with the whole long-distance relationship thing yesterday, did I? I don't know why, but I've had this feeling like maybe we should talk about stuff.
[Baylee] I'm not freaked out. 😊
[Alex] OK because to be honest I've been kind of thinking about the relationship stuff.
[Baylee] Really?
[Alex] Yeah. Have u been thinking about that?
[Baylee] Um. I don't know how to answer that question.
[Alex] U and me. Do u think about where it could go?
[Baylee] Yes.

[Alex] What if I wanted u to be my gf?

[Baylee] !!!

Oh. My. God.

[Alex] NO WAIT. Don't answer. This was so wrong of me. Can we video chat later so I can do this properly, like a gentleman?

[Baylee] Yes!

This is the most important, most precious question I've ever been asked—or will be asked.

THIRTY-SIX

Missing Alex's video-chat call was an honest mistake—I was in the shower. Not calling back, though—that was intentional. Because I couldn't stop thinking about the reality of seeing Freddie again, doing what we did last night, feeling the sensations I felt. Having this call with Alex will make it official. I would officially be doing something really wrong.

So I'm dodging important conversations and I'm sneaking out again just so I can have sex.

How is it that I can simultaneously think it's the most amazing thing ever while knowing full well that it's wrong? Totally wrong.

Later that night, while I'm secretly tucked away in Freddie's garage again, he grabs my hand and pulls me to him. I hold myself up, flashing on that one episode of a crime show I saw as a kid where this very fat girl smothered a guy to death by lying on top of him. "I'm going to crush you."

"You're not gonna crush me. Stop it."

I let him kiss me, let the feelings and sensations wash over me. This right here is why I'm a terrible person. I'd rather have this than be a noble, law-abiding person.

I am sex-crazed and I literally don't even feel bad about it.

What is wrong with me?

I just need time.

Even if it's not really a perfect, sexy situation from start to finish. Even if it's downright awkward at times because of the way I internally cringe at my own behavior, at the way I must look to anyone looking in. Even if sometimes we get tangled up in each other, or someone makes a weird noise, or one of us bumps our head—it's still amazing. It makes me feel like I own every part of me. There are vibrations running through my body for hours after I leave Freddie, and for those few hours, I know I deserve to feel like this. I'm allowed.

On the bed next to me, Freddie's phone lights up with a text. A text from Lara.

"Oh, wow. Awkward," I say, pushing him away from me.

"What?" he says, then he notices his phone. "No, this is not what you think it is."

"You're not still . . . feeling Lara out, are you?"

"No. You are the only one I'm feeling out."

"Well, what's that about, then?"

He lies next to me, holding his phone up above him, and swipes the text away. "She won't stop texting me."

"Yes, well, that would be Lara's MO."

"Is she going to stop?"

"Not if I'm not there to take the phone away."

"Ah, so this is your fault, then," he says.

"It's actually all *your* fault."

"I don't think so. If you'd been a little more obvious about things, well, we wouldn't be in this mess, would we? We could've been doing this, and I wouldn't have been leading anyone on."

His words hit something in me.

"I think I might be leading someone on," I say finally.

He flips onto his stomach. "Really? You're seeing someone still?"

"It became strictly virtual when all this rona stuff got bad," I say. "It's just hard because, well, she's not *here*, you know?"

"Um, hold up," he says. "You're seeing a girl? Do I know her?"

"No, you do not."

He stares at me like he's seeing someone different in front of him, like he's searching for answers in my face to the new questions my revelation sparked.

"Did you promise her anything?" he asks.

"Not yet."

He nods. "Are you trying to tell me we're done?"

"What if I was?"

He sighs and rolls over, sits up on the side of the bed. "Well, this sucks."

Being with Freddie used to be so uncomfortable. It was all

performance, lies, and restrictions. I was so angry all the time, trying to balance this huge ball of feelings and desires. So much desire that I didn't know what to do with. And now everything is different.

He's the only one I tell the truth to. He's the only one I'm real with. Or rather, the person I become when I'm with him feels like a closer match to who I am on the inside. It feels like when I'm with him, I turn into the version of myself in photos taken at the perfect angle.

"Why? Why does it suck?" I ask. "That's not supposed to be, like, accusatory. I just want to know. Truly."

"This—me and you—I like it." He sighs again. "I know you. I like hanging out with you, and I really like doing this with you."

"What if we go back to school next week?" I ask.

"Doesn't change anything."

"It would be a big secret at school, then I'd come over at night?"

"It wouldn't have to be a secret," he says.

My breath catches, and I let the silence hang for a moment.

"What do you mean?"

"I just mean," he starts, "you and me . . . we could just be you and me."

"At school?" I say. "Around other people?"

"Bay," he says, looking back at me. "I know what you're getting at. I don't give a shit what other people think of me and what I like. *Who* I like."

I pause, mouth open slightly, letting his words settle around me. In the next thirty seconds of silence, I picture it all: him driving me to school, walking in the halls hand in hand, going to the movies together or to Hot Mugs.

It leaves me feeling overwhelmed. It's too big, too much. This garage, this private thing—that's what I want. I'm not sure about anything else.

"I guess you're into someone else," Freddie says, watching me not say anything back to him. "That sucks . . . for me."

"Freddie?" I ask.

"Yeah."

"I just want to hang out like this," I say. "With you. That's it."

I don't want to think about later, about the idea of being someone's girlfriend, about what's going to happen tomorrow when I have to deal with this mess I made.

So I kiss Freddie, and the talking stops, the words getting lost in the background.

Later, after Freddie runs inside very carefully to grab us some water, I watch him vape next to me.

"Freddie?" I ask, and he looks over at me. "When did you start thinking about this—me and you?"

"A while ago," he says, and he must see by the look on my face that I'm not ready to have him leave it at that. "I thought about it through the years, but honestly, I kind of felt like you didn't even see me like that. I was not catching any vibe from you at all."

"I really *am* a phenomenal actress," I say. "You seriously thought about me before?"

He nods. "But then that day you flipped out on me outside JJ's—that was like . . ." He lets out a grape-scented breath. "Yeah, then I was really thinking about it."

"Do you want to know when I started thinking about you that way?" I ask, and he hitches his chin up at me to go on. "First week of Grade Seven."

He laughs. "Seriously?"

"Maybe."

"You were thinking about this kind of thing in Grade Seven?"

"Sort of. Well, not *all* this stuff." I gesture to the messy sheets. "But some age-appropriate stuff."

"Why didn't you tell me?"

"So you could laugh at me?"

"I wouldn't have laughed, Bay," he says. "I would have been very shocked, though."

I shrug in a way that I hope makes me seem cute.

It's almost five a.m. by the time I decide I'd better get going. Freddie's nearly asleep next to me. I shake him awake by pushing on his bare bicep, taking my time, letting the touch linger. He makes some kind of moaning sound and yawns.

"I'm going to go."

"No. Just stay."

"Come on, Freddie. We'll get killed by our mothers."

"No, we won't." His voice is all slurred, laced with sleep. "Stay and I'll make you breakfast in the morning."

"Freddie," I whisper, tapping him on the shoulder to wake him again. "This romantic crap is killing the mood."

He starts laughing into the pillow, pushing himself up. "Shut up. I would've poured you cereal. It wouldn't have been all that romantic."

I slip into my shoes, feeling a little wobbly on my feet. Freddie lifts the garage door carefully, and I step out into the night.

"I'll walk you home," he says.

"It's like, five minutes away. It's pretty much daylight. It's fine."

I start walking, trying to minimize the clicking of my heels so as not to disturb the silence. Freddie walks with me to the path. The sky is a very dark blue with the five a.m. light.

"Okay, go home," I whisper when we get to the walkway. "We could get caught."

He holds his hands up in surrender. "Text me when you're home, okay?"

This time I do something different: I'm the one who leans in for a kiss instead of waiting for him to do it. It lingers on until I start thinking he'll ask me back to the garage, so I pull away.

"I have to get home before my mom wakes up to let out the night nurse."

We go our separate ways, and I come out of the walkway onto my street, a wide smile on my face. I pull the robe and slippers out, ready to throw on my disguise.

Just as Garrett steps out of the shadows.

THIRTY-SEVEN

He was standing next to the big tree at the end of the path. I walked right by him without noticing. He's smoking a joint, staring at me with a funny look on his face. There are more than two meters between us, but still, I take a few steps back.

"Hi, Garrett," I say.

"What's up, B?"

"Just on my way home." I feel weird throwing on a bathrobe, so I stop after slipping one arm through. "What are you doing out this early?"

"I haven't gone to bed yet. This is my middle-of-the-night smoke spot. My mom won't let me smoke weed on the property anymore, so I take a walk. The quiet is nice, am I right?"

"I guess." I feel for my house key, avoiding his gaze. "Okay, well . . . bye."

"Hey—wait!"

There's weirdness in the air. This whole scene looks bad, feels bad.

"See? I called it, didn't I?" he says.

"Called what?"

"You're his side chick. Or maybe his main chick?"

I meet his gaze, not sure what I see reflected in his. There's nothing I can think of to say. I feel shame creep up from my feet. Garrett's face is blank. My heart skips a beat as anxiety spreads through me. He reaches for his phone, and I'm convinced he's about to message Pen about this.

Alex will find out.

"Garrett, please don't say anything."

"Say anything to who?"

"Nothing. No one."

"Oh, to Pen, you mean?"

"Don't. Please."

"It's a big secret, then, huh?" he says, puffing away. "So you're the side chick. Or wait—wait a minute. You *have* a side chick, am I right?"

I hop out of my shoes and scoop them up with two fingers. I run barefoot all the way home.

When I reach for the door handle, it opens without my having anything to do with it.

Dawn stands there, mask over the bottom half of her face. Still, the shock of being confronted by me on the other side of the door is in her eyes, and she lets out a little yell.

"Oh my god," she says, trying to catch her breath.

Mom appears behind her, looking half-asleep. As she notices it's me, the drowsiness vanishes from her face. "Where were *you*?"

I have no shoes on, my bathrobe is only on half my body, my hair probably looks like I've been doing exactly what I've been doing. My mother keeps asking me where I was, and I can't seem to get myself to step inside the house, so Dawn stands awkwardly between us.

"Baylee," Dawn whispers, grabbing my arm. "Just be honest."

Mom's eyes drill through me, but she backs up to sit on the stairs. I let Dawn pass, and she squeezes my arm before leaving. I step inside, closing the door behind me.

"I was with Freddie."

"You were with Freddie? What does that mean? You've been there since when?"

"Since . . . a while."

"Were you two out? What were you doing? Who were you with?" Mom's tone rises, but she reels it in. "Did you go to a party? Please explain it to me."

"I was in his garage. It was just him. No one else."

"So you've been sneaking out to go see him?" she says. "You're lying and sneaking off into the night? Why would you do that?"

"Because I'm not just standing on his lawn, two meters apart, when I go see him."

Her eyes roll up to the ceiling when the understanding settles over her. She rubs her face, taking a couple of deep breaths. "So you and Freddie—you've been lying to me about that?"

I don't know how to respond.

"Freddie and Lara were supposedly in love a few weeks ago. Was that a lie, too?"

"They weren't in love. They were just . . . talking. It ended up being nothing—"

Mom holds a hand up to silence me. "Baylee, you know how vital it is that we follow the rules. You said you understood, so how come you're sneaking out in the middle of the night to do god-knows-what with a guy? How stupid can you be?"

"I'm sorry."

Even *I* can hear how weak that apology was.

"Baylee Kunkel."

"Yes."

I worry there's some of Garrett's weed scent on me. His face pops into my mind. He's going to tell Pen, and she'll tell Alex. And now I can never see Freddie again.

I might possibly be losing everything right now, all in one go.

"Are you listening to me?" Mom asks, pushing to her feet.

"I'm trying to."

"Do you understand that people are dying? Your sister could *die* because of you."

"She's not going to die," I say. "No one's going to die. Stop it!"

I kick off my shoes, pretty much deciding that I will not be listening to the things my mother wants to hurl at me. This is the wrong time. My head is already full of other considerations.

"Don't you dare walk away," Mom says as I try to get past her on the stairs.

"What? What do you *want*, Mom?"

"Do you understand what you've done?"

"Yes, I do."

"Do you see how careful I am when I come home after being around other people? Do you see how long it takes for me to disinfect everything?" She's gesturing to the makeshift sanitizing station she's set up by the door. The one I walked right past without using, because I forgot. "Then I run up to take a shower—every time. Do you even care?"

"Yes! I care. But he's *one* person, Mother. I haven't seen anyone else, and he hasn't either."

"I'm going to be calling Sheila, and we're going to have a long discussion about this. You and Freddie won't be the ones paying the price for your stupid decisions—we will. Your sister will. His sister could, too."

"So you're saying that if we somehow get the coronavirus, it will have been *my* fault."

"Yes!"

"It'll be *my* fault for seeing one person who stays in his house all the time, and his mom works from home, and his sister is always home, and they don't even go to the store to shop—they do delivery. And—"

"Stop arguing with me."

"No, Mom. It's going to be *my* fault if we get sick because of Freddie. But all the nurses who come here—there are seven of them, I counted—and then there's Juliana, and the worker, and almost Doris with her stupid allergies if I hadn't stopped it, and everyone you see at work, and the people you walk by at the store, and—"

"Shut your mouth, Baylee."

"How is that fair? I am always so careful. Freddie and I have been *so* careful," I shout, and my voice breaks. "This isn't fair!"

"It's not fair? You're going to talk about things not being fair as thousands of people are dying? As so many people never get to come home at all?" The look in Mom's eyes right now. It's like she doesn't recognize me at all. "We don't even know where this is headed. We have no idea if life will ever be normal again, and you just want to risk it all to go out there and mess around with a boy?"

"Okay! Okay," I say. "I'm sorry. Can I just go now?"

This is torture. I want to scream, throw my phone at the tiled floor, slam the door, and never come back.

"Go to your room. Do not touch anything, and do not come out," Mom says, moving to the side to let me through. "You're officially on quarantine in your room. I don't want to see you for fourteen days."

Upstairs, I turn my phone off, then curl up in a ball under my duvet. The things I don't understand, things that don't make sense, things I need explained to me—it all feels too heavy. I cry, and the tears leave black-streaked wet stains on my pillow.

THIRTY-EIGHT

I don't wake up until past dinnertime, my phone blowing up with messages and texts once I turn it back on. Mom has informed me, through text, that I am not to come out of my room except to use the bathroom. My meals will be left outside the door, and I have zero say about what I get. She has left a couple of surgical masks outside my bedroom door, and I am to wear a mask when I leave my room to use the bathroom.

[Mom] Put your mask in the ziplock bag when you're not using it to keep it clean. These are the only ones you get, because everywhere is sold out, so keep them safe.

I tiptoe to the bathroom as silently as I can, wearing my mask. Upon my return, I grab the two grocery bags resting on the floor near the stairs. Peanut butter, a loaf of bread, bags of chips, a box of Ritz crackers, granola bars, water bottles, sugar-free fruity water flavoring, a couple of protein bars, and plastic cutlery.

I wish, more than anything right now, that I'd suddenly woken up tonight and felt the error of my ways. There are so many versions of me, and sure, one of them is yelling at me to stop being so reckless and follow the rules, but the bossier, angry version of me is in disagreement. She says that what I did wasn't the worst thing in the world. She says I'm totally not going to be able to handle going back to . . . nothing.

[Freddie] Are you home yet?
[Freddie] Are you OK?
[Freddie] ????
[Freddie] I just ran over there and everything looks normal at your house.
[Freddie] I just called your house phone and your mom unleashed on me. I get why you couldn't text me back now.
[Freddie] Are you OK? Did she take your phone away?

I settle cross-legged on my bed, rereading the texts before I send my reply.

[Baylee] I just had my phone turned off.

He doesn't wait for a response. My phone rings.

"What happened?" he asks.

"My mom caught me when I got home. I'm locked in my room for fourteen days."

"Shit. For real? Quarantine?"

"Yes," I say.

We're both silent a little while, and I listen to his breathing.

"You went back to look for me?" I ask.

"Well, you just disappeared. I couldn't sleep, so I just went to take a look. I don't know what I thought I would find—bloodstains and tire marks from a getaway car? Anyways," he says. "I called your house, and wow—that was *not* a good time."

"What did my mom say?"

"Just . . . stuff," he says. "Then she called my mom."

"Oh no. I'm sorry," I say. "Did you get in trouble?"

"Yeah."

"What happened?"

"No car and no garage."

"Are you serious?" I say.

"That's nothing," he says. "She said if I don't respect your mom's wishes, then she'll be forced to send me to my dad's."

"She wouldn't do that, would she? You've never even been there."

"Doubt it, but I guess she wants me to know she's serious. I think your mom is pretty pissed."

"I'm not going to see you for a very long time, am I?"

He sighs on the other end. "This sucks."

There's nothing else to say, so we hang up. It's one thing if it's just me getting in trouble, but I cannot be the reason Freddie's life gets messed up.

On TikTok, Rianne has posted a video of her making this ridiculous vegetable-fruit-salad concoction with the help of her grandfather, and he actually agrees to taste it, and the whole time, her grandmother looks on in total revulsion. It already has three hundred likes and five hundred views. I watch it six times.

For a while, I sit on my bedroom floor, looking around at the purple walls, the window, the closed door of my walk-in closet, and I try to picture myself sitting in here for fourteen days straight. If this was before, I think it would've been doable. I think I might've even liked it, two weeks of lounging around, binge-watching shows, and writing pages and pages in my journal about all the things I was missing out on, all the things I couldn't have. Writing the same things over and over, trying to find the reason for it, the meaning behind it. It would've been this super-angsty, almost painfully romantic experience, staring at my phone until a text from Freddie came to save me from my loneliness, giving me just enough to create a vivid and totally unrealistic scenario.

But this is now, and scenarios were reality. Did everything really just go poof?

Later that night is when I muster up the courage to take a hard look at the messy Alex stuff. My mother hasn't texted me again. Below me, I can hear the rumbling of my sister's compressor. She's quiet tonight, almost like she gets that there's been enough yelling for one day.

I thumb through my journal, skimming the things I've written about in the last weeks. Sometimes I'm convinced I'm totally figuring myself out, then I wonder if all I'm discovering is that I'm a fucking idiot.

I feel like I am two people who are going in different directions.

This will be the last time I lie to Alex. I'm taking it as a sign that the universe took Freddie away.

[Baylee] I got in a major fight with my mother last night. She took my phone away, and now I'm grounded for 2 weeks.

I just have to focus on staying home for now, until things settle.

[Baylee] I'm sorry. I have my phone back now.
[Alex] Do u want to video-chat?
[Baylee] Yes! But in like, an hour? I am not camera ready at all yet.
[Alex] OK. Message me when ur ready.

There's something about the tone of her messages, like she's not impressed or she's guarded. But I'll make it up to her. I'll fix it.

Before I set out to get ready, I pull up my DMs with Garrett.

[Baylee] You haven't told Pen about this morning, have you?

I'm already typing my next message because I didn't expect him to be there, ready to talk back.

[Garrett] Lucky for you, I'm just getting up now. Sleeping the day away is a good time, am I right?

[Baylee] Can you please let me know me if you plan on telling?

[Garrett] I hadn't thought about it, B. Let's weigh the pros and cons, shall we?

[Baylee] The only pro for you is the ability to hurt me again.

[Garrett] Whoa, B. You're being way too deep and shit. 💀💀💀

[Baylee] You owe me, Garrett. If you're no longer an evil monster, then you know that you owe me for everything you did.

[Garrett] Why don't you just tell them both that you have a side piece? Honesty is the best policy, am I right?

[Baylee] It's not a side piece kind of thing. It's complicated. Can you just please keep it to yourself?

[Garrett] Relax, B. I got better shit to do than to fucking gossip about you being a little hussy.

[Baylee] A hussy?

[Garrett] I used the thesaurus on my phone to come up with a nicer-sounding word for slut.

[Baylee] Fuck you.

[Garrett] What! That was me being considerate!

[Baylee] 🖕

[Garrett] Nah but for real, B. I won't say nothing.

I swipe the conversation away and put my phone down.

When Alex appears on-screen, she looks better than I remember. Memories of the parking garage and of being at her house enter my mind, bringing with them the scent of her cologne. Male cologne might actually be the root of all this, because I seem to lose control every time that stuff wafts up my nose.

I was so awkward when we last hung out. It wasn't that long ago, but enough has happened for me to feel like a different Baylee. For me to wonder who I'd be if I was on the green couch with her again.

"Hey, you," Alex says, bringing her face up to the screen, pretending to try to get a closer look at me.

"I thought I'd dress up for you a little," I say, which is ridiculous, because I'm actually wearing my robe, but I wanted to feel pretty. I wanted to feel other things.

"I approve."

"Where are you?"

She pans the camera around. "My aunt's garage. It's the only place for privacy."

"You must be so excited to go home soon."

"Couple more days. I'm so tired of seeing my dad through the screen door," she says. "Can you believe the world is so broken?"

"No, I can't."

"I was thinking about how, if this was before, I would invite you over, and I would make you dinner or something. I had it all planned out."

"Really?"

She nods. "We were going to spend the evening lying down,

staring at the ceiling, and I would've told you all kinds of stories about myself, and you would've told me stories about you. Then we would've listened to some sweet tunes on my velvet beast. And . . ."

She does this little shrug that makes it clear where her mind is headed.

"And then what?" I ask.

"Hey—you look a little sad?" she asks, and for a moment, I think she can see through me, that she's figured something out. But then she says, "Are you going to tell me what the fight was about, with your mom?"

This doesn't count as new lies. It's just a continuation of the final lie. Just a little elaboration.

"Just . . . stuff that had been building, I guess." She wants me to go on. I like that about Alex, the way she listens. She's interested, and she wants me to run with the thought and lay out the real story. Except it's made up. "I guess I'm not really ready to talk about it."

Alex nods. "That's okay."

We don't say anything for a while, then she says something about school, so we go on asking the same questions in different ways: When will this pandemic end? When are we going back to school? When are we going to be able to go outside again?

They are questions with no answers.

We talk a while, and never does she ask me to be her girlfriend. I guess I wouldn't ask me either if I was her. The moment passed, and something is different.

THIRTY-NINE

I'm in my room for days, alone. Days of sitting on my bed, working through the e-learning classes Castlehill High put together. They've decided we're probably not going back to school for a long while, but that doesn't mean we can't continue learning. The learning is all just mindless clicking through screens of course material, assignments to be completed, instructions, prerecorded classes, due dates. Emails—so many emails keep coming while they figure out the details. I have three assignments in progress that I'm still waiting to learn more about, while trying to read about other things and taking notes. It's chaos.

I'm uncomfortable after fifteen minutes or so, no matter where I sit, ready to just pass out and nap at any given moment. There is nothing to break up the time. No point in focusing and working hard for thirty minutes, knowing we'll be piled in the halls soon, going for lunch, or huddled in the bathroom to talk shit about the guys or about all the girls who suddenly showed up to school with fake freckles.

So many people are dying of the virus now.

I don't personally know anyone who's got it, but what does that mean? Is it on its way? Is it going to show up all of a sudden and just wipe us all out? Sometimes I feel like we're all going to die. Other times, I feel normal, like some teenager grounded in her room, and I want to go out. I want to tell my mother that she's overreacting.

But my mother's not even talking to me.

[Rianne] This is so BAD. The virus got into my grandparents' building.
[Baylee] Oh no.
[Rianne] My grandma found out the lady down the hall that she goes to the grocery store with is sick. Like really sick.
[Baylee] ☹
[Rianne] My grandpa is SO smart. He just basically wrote my English essay for me. Well, I wrote it but he helped. He knows what a thesis statement is. It made so much sense when he explained it to me.
[Baylee] I'm so jealous.
[Rianne] I bet he can help you TOO!!! We should video-chat later. I'll make him teach class!!!

I talk to Rianne in sprinkles throughout the day. Sometimes Lara is in the group chat, but we just talk around each other.

My problems are small, but they feel heavy. I'm not a better person just because I'm locked at home, unable to do anything but homework.

I flip through my phone, going through all my photos. Shots of Rianne's parties, us in the halls at school, our trips to the mall, makeup selfies with Lara, photos taken solely based on Freddie's presence in them, just so I could stare at him when I got home.

I am next-level bored. I can't concentrate on anything.

I have never been this disinterested in learning in my life.

Nothing is happening anymore.

I'm alone in my room with my homework, and my hatred for math persists. Actually, it's grown, because now I don't even see the point in learning about it.

FORTY

Everything is late—my bedtime, my waking-up time, my email response time. All my music is trash, my favorite songs have been played so often that I can't even recall why I liked them so much in the first place. I stream TV shows for a change from streaming movies. I have a list on my phone of all the shows and movies I've watched, to keep track.

I watch *Dirty Dancing*, and it makes me think of that night in Freddie's room.

This bedroom quarantine is the worst punishment I've ever received. Every single day feels as long as four.

[Mom] Do you need anything today?
[Baylee] Stuff to drink. Maybe more chips.
[Mom] Is chips all you're eating?
[Baylee] No.

Eating sour cream and onion chips is the highlight of my day, so maybe I'm overdoing it a little.

I lie on my bed, staring at the ceiling, remembering being with Freddie. This is all there is left. The scenarios I make up in my head are so real that I can manufacture stomach flips and chills just by remembering Freddie's touch. It's not cutting it.

I feel lonelier now than I did when I had no one.

Is everyone else going crazy like this? What's wrong with me?

[Alex] What's going on? R u OK?

[Baylee] I'm swell.

[Alex] You've been quiet lately. Is it me? Am I boring?

[Baylee] It's so not you. I feel like I'm tired all the time. Maybe I'm just watching too much TV.

[Alex] It's frying your brain. 😵

[Baylee] What did you do today?

[Alex] Did some homework. Went for a walk and I happened to "walk by" Pen and Blake real quick.

That's not allowed. The premier of the province said so. My mother said so. Even Alex said so, when I asked her about seeing each other, two meters apart.

Seeing me wasn't worth the risk.

I tell her it's great, that she's so lucky to be able to go outside to break the rules. She gives me a sad face in response. Then I let the conversation die.

I sit cross-legged on the floor, my bookshelf in front of me. I pull out my old diaries, the little pink books I used to write in when I was in Grade Eight. It's words about Freddie everywhere. I think about my younger self, and I want to tell her, *Don't worry, you'll end up getting him. Not for long, though, because of a viral apocalypse, but you'll get what you want.*

It doesn't make me feel better.

Alex comes back, having changed the subject.

[Alex] My dad and I stained the basement furniture. So much work, but so worth it. It looks totally restored.
[Baylee] 👍
[Alex] I can't wait for u to see it for real, but would u like to see photos?
[Baylee] Sure.
[Alex] R u OK?
[Baylee] Totally! Send me photos!!!

Exclamation marks make me sound all better.

Later, I leave my bedroom door open and sit in the doorway, wearing a mask. I listen to my family downstairs, to the news coming from the television, and to my sister whining or giggling. I discover that the banister is a little crooked, and the baseboards up here don't exactly match. Sometimes I leave my room to run around the upstairs hallway, hoping my mother will catch me and yell at me. Because then I'd at least be talking to somebody. Maybe she thinks I'm having a great time up here.

I wave to Dawn when she comes at night, and she asks me how I'm doing. I don't tell the truth.

The amount of shittery currently existing in my life is pretty spectacular. It's past next-level. It's whatever level there is after that.

There is nothing to do, and there is no end in sight.

On TikTok, people are trying to sew their own masks because suddenly masks are the latest craze and shelves are empty.

We don't really know what's going on, so we wait. People are getting sick, so we have to stay home.

Staying home like this is its own sickness.

I can't even hang out with my sister. Does she notice she hasn't seen me in days? I'm always around and suddenly I'm gone—she must realize, right?

"Mom?" I call from my doorway.

"What?" she says.

"Can I come say hi to Beck?"

"After fourteen days," she says. "And it's barely been four."

"Please?"

"You should've thought about that before you put us all in this situation."

In my room, I cry while enjoying the last of my sour cream and onion chips.

Soon, my phone rings with a video chat from my mother. I wipe my face clean and answer. Rebecca's face appears.

"Ew, Beck," I say. "Your hair looks like crap."

She goes still, and although her eyes don't focus on the phone, she's quiet and definitely listening.

"What are you doing? What music are you listening to? Probably something super shitty, right?"

Her eyes move to the side, a serious look on her face as she seems to consider what I've said. Then she smiles wide, reaching with her good hand to swat at the phone.

"Your music is the *worst*," I say. "I hate it! Ewwwwwww!"

The screen shakes with my sister's whacks to our mom's phone. For the next twenty minutes, I read a chapter of my English book out loud to her, which is the longest I've been able to read something and pay attention. This quarantine, house-arrest thing might be a little less miserable if I could at least hang out around my sister.

Late that night, my phone buzzes. At first I think it's past midnight, but my eyes focus and it's actually past two in the morning. I wonder if this is what time is like for my sister, having no real concern for what happens when, time having no meaning, and just going with the flow.

[Freddie] Are we just not talking anymore?
[Baylee] It wasn't intentional.
[Freddie] I got my car and the garage back.
[Baylee] Don't tell me that! ☹

He sends me a photo of himself, lying sideways on the couch, a stupid expression on his face.

[Baylee] 😺

I want to tell him I miss him but without it sounding all romantic. I just miss being around him, talking to him, but with the added bonus of having our bodies touch. Is that romantic? I don't know what it is, and I don't care. I just miss him and everything that linked us together.

I miss myself, too.

[Freddie] It's not much fun without you hanging out with me.
[Baylee] 😳

I think that's him saying he misses me, which makes me smile.

Forty-One

Nothing interesting happened today. I'm not sure what day it is anymore. Every day is like a really long Sunday, except there's never any school the next day. There's school every moment of the day, because I can't seem to catch up.

[Alex] Can I tell u something?

[Baylee] Yes, totally.

[Alex] I feel like ur different lately.

[Baylee] I feel like I'm different, too.

[Alex] What does that mean?

[Baylee] I don't know. I'm confused.

[Alex] Is it me?

[Baylee] No. Not at all. It's literally all me.

[Alex] What's wrong?

[Baylee] It's prison life. It's changing me. 🫤

[Alex] . . .

[Baylee] I'll try snapping out of it. Sorry.

[Alex] U don't have to be sorry.

[Baylee] I'm not sure why you're even talking to me, to be honest.

[Alex] 😀

I haven't showered yet today. What's the point when I'm going to bed later?

The red on my right index finger is chipped. Normally, this would grab all my focus, driving me up the wall until I could get home and fix it. Right now, I'm feeling nothing about it. It's just a chip, and it isn't worth the hassle and effort to set my station up. And if I'm going to redo one nail, I might as well do them all— even more effort when there is no point. No one is going to see those nails anyway.

Social, physical, and sexual distancing are still in effect.

There are more than six feet between me and everyone.

There are 180 meters between Freddie and me, according to Google Maps.

That's 590 feet.

FORTY-TWO

It has been eight days of house arrest now. Room arrest, really. I am still alive. A lot of people aren't. So many people are wiped out from the earth, like the virus is a little demon just jumping from person to person. Someone my mom's age from the next town over dies, a man who was just working at the grocery store, putting food on the shelves. They're saying fat people are more likely to die if they get the virus. I've stopped eating chips.

My window is open a crack, letting in some cool mid-April air. It's almost like I'm outside.

"Baylee?" Mom calls from the hallway.

I open the door. Mom is calling from her own bedroom doorway. "Do you need more groceries?"

"No."

"Are you doing your schoolwork?"

"Yes."

These are the kinds of conversations we have. I thought it would've progressed to her letting me out of my room, to us going back to talking to each other normally. During the day, nurses are with Rebecca, and I hear Mom leave for a few hours to go to work. At night, Mom seems to time her trips up the stairs when I'm in the bathroom or otherwise unaware.

The smell of spaghetti makes it up to my room through the vents.

A few hours later, there is a knock, and I find a bowl of spaghetti at my door when I open it. I text a thank-you for the warm dinner.

[Freddie] Today I am very thankful for the fact that we do not live in the United States.

He sends me a link for an article on the US president's latest moves, moves that are described as criminal and led to the deaths of thousands and thousands of people. There are dead bodies loaded in refrigerated trucks outside hospitals because there's no place to put them.

[Baylee] How is this even allowed? How come no one is stepping in to stop this?
[Freddie] When things are just allowed to happen while we all watch is exactly how humanity gets fucked.
[Baylee] This is the apocalypse.
[Freddie] Let's change the subject, OK?

[Baylee] OK.

[Freddie] Pretend you were here right now. What would we be doing?

The next several texts fill me with something I haven't felt in a while.

[Baylee] Wait! I need to go shower real quick. Can you wait for me?

[Freddie] OK but hurry.

I stare at my disgusting, filmy, crusty self in the mirror, ashamed. The shower helps. I throw on a red dress I'd never wear in real life, because the shape of my legs and their pasty whiteness has created a rule that legs must always be covered by a pair of stylish and well-fitting pants. If I'm going to be wearing a dress that is never to see the light of day, the black peep-toe pumps I got from a consignment shop for eight dollars last summer seem like a good match. They fit, so I bought them, but when I got home, it became apparent I couldn't actually walk in them. But that doesn't matter when you're confined to a bedroom at all times.

I head for my closet, making a big cushion out of my pillows, and I settle myself in the dark.

[Baylee] I'm back.

Freddie sends me words that make my cheeks hot. When I go to type back, my phone buzzes with a video-chat request from Alex, right on time, except I totally forgot we planned this call.

Alex is all smiles. I am hoping the surprise on my face registers as excitement. I *am* excited, because talking to her is one of the only things to look forward to. But Freddie . . . my head is in his garage right now.

"Hey, you," she says. "Why are you in the dark?"

"Oh, oops, hang on." I push the closet door with my toe, and my face appears on camera. "I'm in my closet."

"Just hanging out in your closet, in the dark?" Alex says, and I shrug. "How's it going today? Better?"

"Better, but I'm still just stuck in this room."

"I wish I could be stuck in your room with you," she says.

I wonder if this would make everything better, her being here right now. I don't know, if given the chance, who I'd choose to see right now, if the universe allowed me to pick one person to be next to. Freddie . . . Alex. I think I want them both but differently, at different times, for different reasons.

I'm about to respond when there is a loud knock on my bedroom door before it opens. The shock of it makes me drop my phone, hanging up on Alex. I crawl out of my closet, ditching the pumps and tucking my phone in the place between my left boob and bra strap.

"What is this, Baylee?" Mom holds her phone screen up. I

haven't seen my mother up close in over a week. She's wearing a medical mask. I rush to my desk to throw my own on.

"What is it?" I ask.

"Why is there a charge for a hundred and thirteen dollars on my credit card?"

"Oh." I place the palms of my hands against my temples. "Oh my god. I forgot to tell you."

"Forgot to tell me you were going to spend a hundred dollars, just for the hell of it?"

"It was my birthday, and I really wanted the wallet. I forgot to give you my birthday money for it," I say. I fish for the wallet and pull out the bills tucked inside. Then I walk to my piggy bank, grabbing for whatever might be in there. It's not enough, but I hadn't planned on telling my mother about the wallet like this. There's no way she'll just accept covering the remaining forty dollars. "Isn't it nice? It matches the purse I already have, too. It's from a little boutique in Toronto."

"In Toronto? What were you doing in Toronto?"

I lose feeling to my head for a moment. "I wasn't. I ordered it online."

Mom doesn't look impressed. "I might not even have enough this week to buy us toilet paper, and you're buying yourself a new wallet? Really, Boss?"

"It was a while ago. I didn't mean to forget to tell you about it," I say, counting quarters and dimes, hoping to scrounge a couple more dollars.

Mom shakes her head, a heavy sigh puffing out her mask. "It's not the wallet, Boss. It's that I don't really recognize you anymore. You're doing things and saying things that are so unlike you."

"You don't really know what I'm like, Mom."

"What do you mean?"

"It's not like you really know what's going on in my life," I say.

"Look, I know your sister requires most of my attention, but that doesn't mean I won't find the time to be here for you. You know that, right? You can talk to me."

"I don't really want to talk to you about this, though. It's weird."

"Well, you're going to have to, because things have changed. Everything is a lot more serious, more dangerous. I need to be involved in the decisions you make," Mom says. "Your little escapade with Freddie put us all at risk. Has that sunk in yet?"

"I feel bad, okay? I'm glad no one's sick," I say. "But I just . . . I don't know."

How do I tell her that I still don't think what I did was the worst thing ever? That I understand, but at the same time, I don't totally *understand*.

"I don't know what it is you and he were doing, but I hope you used protection. Just because everything is about coronavirus these days doesn't mean there aren't still other viruses to worry about."

"I was careful. I'm always careful, Mom."

I extend my hand, which is filled with all the money I have.

"Can I come out of my room yet?" I ask as Mom grabs the money and puts it into a pocket of her housecoat.

"With a mask," Mom says.

She leaves, and I sigh with full-body relief. This could've turned into a big fight at several points of the conversation, but I managed to steer clear of saying or doing anything stupid.

I grab my phone.

Alex is still on the screen, and I forget how to breathe.

FORTY-THREE

Alex is so still that at first, I think she's frozen. But then her eyes move downward. She's heard everything. She was right below my head, tucked in my bra, right in perfect earshot. There is silence for too long. There are words in my head, but they all sound frantic, guilty, pathetic.

"I shouldn't have stayed on, listening. I thought maybe it was intentional, that you were going to come back or tell me you had to go."

"I, um. This is bad. I'm sorry—I'm so sorry. I should've talked to you before."

"I guess I should've asked if you wanted to be exclusive," she says finally. "I shouldn't have assumed we were both feeling the same."

"We were, though."

"Well, then what happened?"

"It's like a separate thing that happened at the same time."

"That's called being poly—dating more than one person at the same time—and I just . . . I wasn't signing up for that."

"I wasn't either. I'm not poly."

"I knew something was up," she says. "I could tell, but I just wanted to believe it was the pandemic and your quarantine."

"It's all of that. I'm just . . . confused."

"Are you trying to tell me you're just into guys? Because you can go ahead and tell me that. It's not like that would be the first time that's happened to me."

"That's not it at all. I swear that has nothing to do with it."

"So you like him more than me, then."

"No. It's not even that."

I can't explain it to her. There are no words that don't sound wrong. That don't sound like I was secretly committed to two people at the same time, and I chose Freddie over her. When really, I chose myself—or more like, my sex-crazed self chose *for* me.

"I feel like you're far away, and I don't know when I'll get to see you again," I say.

"Well, you shouldn't have been seeing him either."

"I know! But I did. And you didn't end up asking me to be your girlfriend, so I thought . . ."

Her gaze ices over. "Me asking would've stopped you from wanting someone else?"

"No, I just mean . . ."

Her face gets closer to the camera, and I cradle it in both my hands, directly at eye level. "I gave you every opportunity to tell me about him."

"I'm sorry."

"Yeah, well, me too." She lets out a long sigh, then seems to have made her mind up about something. "Okay, well, I'm going to go." She looks up at the screen. "Take care, Baylee."

The chat cuts out.

"Wait," I say to no one.

She's gone.

I send her a message, asking her to DM, because I think the words might come out better this way.

I send apologies.

But I get no reply. I'm left on read.

I bounce up and slip my feet into a different pair of peep-toe heels, ones I won't fall over and crack my skull in. I grab my purse and pleather jacket.

I've done nothing in this room but wait. Now is the time for action.

Mom's in her bathroom upstairs, taking a shower. I stand in the doorway, wearing my mask. The baby monitor sits on the bathroom counter, the volume turned up all the way. Rebecca is swatting at the rails of her crib.

"Mom, can I please go for a little walk?"

"A walk? Outside?"

"Yes," I say. "I haven't left the house in over a week." She doesn't respond, so I add, "I'll wear my mask."

"Don't be long, Boss."

I head down the stairs and stop over to see my sister, who is in her crib, making herself roll back and forth like it's some kind of sport. I place a hand against her chest to give it a little wiggle. She immediately stops rolling, out of breath.

"Hi," I say. "What are you doing?"

She makes this gibberish sound that we assume is her talking back. I give her another little wiggle and she smiles at me. She starts up with the back-and-forth exercise thing, and I head for the door.

Within about eight minutes, the realization sets in about how far of a walk this actually is going to be. Google Maps says thirty-six minutes, and that's regular-person speed—not fat-girl-in-ridiculous-heels speed.

I keep walking.

It's cool and sunny out, perfect walking weather. Even though it's definitely not normal times out there, there are still people outside. There are people standing at the bus stop, no masks on, laughing, standing close. I see a couple of people my age walking down the sidewalk. I see a group of men leaning against their cars as they drink coffee in the parking lot of a coffee place that's closed to indoor seating.

I wonder if the police just drive around, questioning people about who they're with, where they're going. I'm not even sure what's a real law, or bylaw, or guideline. It's all so confusing, so my mom's words are all I have to go by, and she seems a lot more strict about stuff than other people are.

They probably don't think they're doing anything wrong, all those people who are out. Those men, maybe they just drove over to get coffee—because that's essential and totally legal—and they're taking five minutes to talk to their friends, outside, far apart. Alex was doing just that the other day, running into Pen and Blake.

How can you tell who's careless and who is actually a decent person doing something *you* wouldn't decide to do, but that they still took time to consider? Something that isn't as bad as what they could be doing, what *other* people are doing?

My phone buzzes with a text.

[Freddie] Where did you go?
[Baylee] Something bad happened.

He calls immediately.

"What happened?"

"The girl I was seeing—Alex," I start. "She found out about you."

"How? You told her?"

"Not intentionally." Then I tell him about my forgotten video chat with Alex, the reason I disappeared on him. "I thought the video call was done. My mom had just walked into my room to talk to me. It turned into another lecture about my having snuck out to see you. She said pretty revealing things. Alex was there the whole time. The call hadn't ended."

"She heard it all?"

"Everything."

"Oh," he says. "So now what?"

"Now I'm on my way there."

"What?"

"I've been released from custody, and my mom allowed me to go outside for very legal exercise," I say. "So now I'm walking to her house."

"Why?"

"She won't talk to me."

"So you're going to just walk your ass over there. Then what?"

"There are things I should have said."

"Were you her girlfriend or something?"

"No." I check my phone for the tenth time, and still nothing from anyone. "Not officially. She was going to ask me, but it didn't exactly happen."

"What does that mean?"

"She texted me about it, then she told me she wanted to video-chat so she could ask me properly. It was sweet."

"Oh. Then what happened?"

"Well, I didn't answer. I went to see *you* instead."

"Yikes."

"It wasn't technically official. We hadn't even talked about being exclusive!"

"You don't have to defend yourself to me," he says. "I've had plenty of conversations just like this. Usually when I'm leading someone on, though."

"Stop it!"

"I'm just saying . . ."

"Yes, well, I can see where I might have deceived her. I'm not entirely stupid."

"I know," he says. "Where are you right now?"

"I'm at Church Corners," I say, which is this intersection where there is a church on all four corners. "Almost halfway there."

"You think she's going to come out and talk to you?"

"Maybe?" I wait at a red light. "No. Probably not."

"Well, then what the hell are you doing?"

A text comes through.

[Mom] Where are you, Baylee?

"Oh shit—my mom is looking for me. This was such a stupid idea!"

"What were you thinking?"

"I don't know! I've lost my mind," I say. "I have to go."

It has become apparent that all I needed was some fresh air and to cool off. This plan was completely ridiculous. I am standing on the Baptist corner, ignoring the green signal to walk through the intersection to the Catholic corner.

[Baylee] I'm on my way back, Mom. Be there in like, five minutes.

I spin around on my heels and take off down the road, running.

Everything is fine for a couple of minutes, and I almost get into a rhythm. But then my left foot lands on a pebble or something, throwing me off-balance. I recover quickly, but my weight gets displaced from the front of my foot to the back. The heel gives out with a crack, and my body starts tipping over to the left.

I don't fall, but my shoe is ruined.

What do I do now? Take them both off and continue running home? Limp home with the slow hobble of a right foot being four inches higher than the left?

All I wanted was to see Alex. I thought us being near each other would make things clearer. I thought I'd have some kind of realization.

I hobble, carrying the heel of the broken shoe in my hand.

I pass my old elementary school. A car swerves over a little too last minute, pulling into the entrance to the school lot. I turn to see Freddie in the driver's seat.

FORTY-FOUR

I get into the back seat, my mask on. Freddie is also wearing a mask.

"Are you sick?" I ask him.

"No. I just figured you'd feel better if I came like this," he says, locking eyes with me through the rearview mirror. "What happened to your shoe?"

"It gave out," I say, thankful he wasn't close enough to witness me running or nearly wiping out on account of my shoe giving up trying to hold all of me up in the air. "I can't believe you came to get me."

"You told me where you were, and you'll never make it back fast enough," he says. "Plus, any excuse to go for a ride is a good one."

"Your mom still lets you go out to drive?"

He nods. "She knows it's the only way I'll be able to deal with this staying-home-alone thing. If I get pulled over or questioned by the cops, I'm to tell them I'm on my way to the pharmacy to get Tylenol for Shaya."

"That's really cool of your mom."

"Yeah, she's pretty chill."

He rides just above the speed limit, trying to make all the lights before they turn red. We are quiet for the five minutes it takes to get back to my house. I steal glances at him through the mirror, and sometimes our gazes meet. Maybe what I wanted was to see how I felt, being near Alex. It wouldn't have had to break the distancing rule, but just enough to have her in front of me for real, to know—no, to *feel* whether or not I'd been a total idiot.

I must be really warped in the head, just totally damaged or something.

"I'll drop you off here. That way your mom won't see me," he says, stopping near the walkway. "Text me later."

"Thank you."

I'm out and on the sidewalk seconds later, the broken heel still in my hands. This will make a pretty good lie for why I was gone so long, I think.

After making my way up the driveway in a quick hobble, I come to a halt when I see my mother standing on the front steps. Behind her, the front door is wide open, and my sister can be heard babbling happily with her music going.

"Where were *you*?" she asks, sounding curious more than anything.

"I went for a walk that way," I say, pointing to the direction I came from. "I broke my heel, so it took forever to get back."

"How was the walk?"

"It was good."

"So you just went up the road there? How far did you get?"

"Just to the post office, then I turned around."

"Walked all the way home, huh?"

"Well, limped," I say, holding out my broken heel.

She nods, and when I'm about to walk past her, she holds a hand up. "Remember a few years ago, when you got that phone? Remember what the deal was for you getting a phone?"

"Yes," I say. "To keep my room clean and help around the house."

"And?"

"And, um—oh, put away my clean laundry right away," I say, recalling the basket of folded clothes still sitting at the foot of my bed. "I forgot. I'll do it right now."

"And?"

She watches me. I think some more, but no other chores come to mind.

"The deal was that we'd install a tracking app," she says. My heartbeat moves to my ears, and I blink too long. "Forgot about that, huh, Baylee?"

It never mattered, the tracking app. There was never a reason to lie about where I'd been, where I was going. I completely forgot about it.

"I saw you went all the way to Church Corners," Mom says. "Then you were all of a sudden mighty fast at getting home."

"I ran."

"You ran?"

"That's how I broke my heel."

She shakes her head, and the blank expression morphs into something else. She breathes deeply a couple of times and closes her eyes.

"Baylee, I'm done. I've given up trying to understand your stupid reasoning for your inability to follow the rules," my mother says, her tone even.

"I didn't—"

"Did you think you and Freddie were invisible just now, parked in front of Peter's house there?"

"This looks bad, but it wasn't," I say. "I had my mask! And he had one, too. I was—"

"You know what's going on. You've already gotten in trouble for this. I *just* let you out of your room—not even an *hour* ago—and what did you go and do? You ran away to see Freddie."

"No! That's not how it happened," I say.

"You were in the car with Freddie, Baylee! How are you going to try and justify this? You're being reckless. You've snuck out of this house multiple times, and for what? For a boy?"

No use in telling her I snuck out for a girl, actually, and I came to my senses before messing up for real. Freddie was just decent, running over to rescue me, trying to help me avoid what's happening right now.

"I know I've been lenient, letting you come and go as you please, but you should have been able to trust that if I'm suddenly telling you no, it's for a good reason and I mean it."

I open my mouth, ready to counter, but she holds a hand up again.

"Your stuff will be in the garage," she says. "I don't want you in this house anymore."

"What?"

Oh my god. This isn't right.

"I can't take any more risk," Mom says.

"Okay," I say. "I get it."

"No, you don't. You don't get it."

"I can't live in the garage, Mom."

"Then go to Freddie's. It's where you keep trying to go, right?" She's stone-faced. "Just go to Freddie's, Baylee."

"For how long? Should I wear a mask?"

"Do what you want," she says. "Go!"

Mom turns around and heads inside, slamming the door behind her.

I can't go inside my house.

I stare at my house, looking up and down, unable to comprehend this fact.

I can't go home.

FORTY-FIVE

About ten minutes later, the automatic garage door starts to rise. Mom's already gone back inside by the time I get there. I'm too stunned to know what to feel, what my next move should be. This has got to be a joke. A temporary messed-up situation meant to get me to realize how terrible I've been.

The garage is this junk room that's part forgotten sensory room for Rebecca and part garage-sale central. Half of it is a rectangle of fake grass with colorful lights strung from the ceiling, a rubber mat we use for my sister outside in the summer, and this old special custom seat she used to spend hours in before outgrowing it a few years ago. The other side of the garage is boxes of my grandfather's things that my mother keeps around. There are old cobwebs everywhere, and the tiny window is grimy, barely letting any light in.

It's cold out here and there's nowhere clean to sit. The basement is cement floors and unfinished walls, but it would make more sense to put a sleeping bag down there than out here. She must just be trying to make a point. She's probably about to open the door and send me to my room.

At the foot of the steps that lead to the house, there are a couple of large reusable Ikea bags my mom would usually keep for grocery shopping. Inside are some of my clothes, makeup, shower products, different pairs of shoes, my laptop, schoolbooks. Everything is just thrown into the bags, no care for any of the items. I open my favorite Jimmy J eye shadow palette, the one Lara gave me last summer. A couple of the colors are cracked and chunks are displaced, contaminating the other shades.

This is where the urge to cry comes, but I swallow it down.

I switch into different heels, leaving my broken shoes on the garage floor. I drag the bags down the sidewalk, through the walkway.

When I get to Freddie's, he's pulling the garage door open, head gazing around, already looking for me. I stand at the bottom of his driveway, a bag looped over each arm.

"I heard your shoes," he says.

"It could've been anyone."

"I know the way your walk sounds," Freddie says, then he seems to notice the bags. "What happened?"

"I got kicked out."

He waves a hand toward the garage, inviting me in. I sit on my usual spot of the couch, leaving my mask on.

"I think you're safe to take that off," he says.

"How do you know?"

"Well, you've been quarantined in your room alone, and I'm the last person you were around," he says. "It's not like you're going to get the rona over social media."

"That's . . . logical," I say, pulling my mask off and enjoying the feel of air on my face.

In the garage, Freddie and I are quiet for a while. I am convinced this isn't a real thing that is happening. This is my mom being next-level upset, next-level mad, but once she cools off, I'll be able to explain that while this little escapade might've seemed unforgivable, it didn't happen the way she thinks. It wasn't like I was throwing myself at the coronavirus. My plan included a little consideration for safety.

Freddie reads from a stack of pages, a printed version of his script, every once in a while jotting things down in red ink. I scroll through my phone, expecting something to come through from my mom, maybe even from Alex.

"It's going to work out, Bay."

"How do you know?"

He shrugs. "It has no choice but to."

From where I sit on the corner of the couch, I can see down Freddie's street. Sounds call my attention, and I watch two people coming on the sidewalk, walking close. They look a little older than me. If they're not from the same household, then they're definitely using the I-just-happened-to-run-into-my-friend-while-exercising excuse to be out together. I guess it looks bad, unless you know exactly what's going on, what the specific circumstances are that led them to make that choice—it looks like not caring.

Mrs. Morales opens the door to peek into the garage. "Baylee, why don't you come in for a minute? I want to chat with you."

I lock eyes with Freddie before following his mother inside.

Forty-Six

Inside Freddie's house, I go straight for the bathroom and wash my hands. Mrs. Morales is in the living room. Shaya is on the floor, pulling plastic food out of a mesh bag.

"Have a seat," Mrs. Morales says.

"Oh, my mask," I say, and when Shaya spots me, she comes running over. "I forgot it in the garage. Should we all be wearing masks right now?"

"They're saying masks are for those who have symptoms," she says. "Are you coughing or sneezing?"

"No."

"Neither are we. I think we're fine," she says. "But I think it's really responsible that you're thinking about that."

"With my sister, it's not like wearing masks is totally new," I say, taking Shaya's hand and letting her lead me to her pile of food.

"A corn," she says, so I look for it and hand it to her. "Good job, Bayee!"

"Are you okay?" Mrs. Morales asks.

I shrug. "My mom's just very mad."

"I heard you've been having some issues at home."

"Did Freddie tell you that?"

"He told me a little," she says. "But your mother told me a lot."

"When did you talk to her?"

"I talk to her here and there. I know what's going on," she says. "These are weird times, and no one knows what's going to happen. It's scary for everyone, but imagine what it's like for your mother, trying to protect your sister."

"I know that. I wasn't trying to make my sister sick," I say, picking the next food item Shaya asks for. "I would never do that. I'm always careful. But I don't think my mom's being fair."

"How so?" When I shrug, Mrs. Morales nods. "Really, I want to know what you think."

"Well, she talks about risk, and I just don't think out of all the risk I see at my house, being around Freddie is the worst one," I say. "But my mom acts like it's the only risk. Like I'm the only one breaking the rules. And I can't even have a conversation about it to try and make it make sense. My mom is the first person to argue when things don't make sense—I've heard her argue with the nursing agency people enough times about their rules not being fair—but I'm supposed to just be quiet when it's happening to me."

"I don't think you're going to win that argument, Baylee," Mrs.

Morales says. "We have to do what we're told, even though there are probably a hundred examples of it not making sense, of it being totally unrealistic. Ask me how I'm supposed to work from home and watch my toddler alone, yet I'm still supposed to pay the day care right now—what is *that*? I still have to pay them fourteen hundred a month so that I can watch my own kid at home, and I gotta work to be able to be the day care. That's a dumb rule that isn't fair, but there's so much going on right now, and things are changing so fast, and we just can't fight every little thing at the same time and expect it to magically be fixed right away. But it's not fair—you're right."

"I should've been staying away from Freddie," I say. "But I didn't. I didn't want to."

Partly because I felt I made the decision carefully. Partly because I just wanted to see him more than I wanted to do what I was told without question. And, yes—there's a small part of me that just was going to do it no matter what. I can't just accept the fact that what happens to me, what matters to me, isn't important. It's supposed to just be forgotten. It's not fair.

"I know it's tough at your age," Mrs. Morales says. "Believe me, I know. I had a boyfriend I was forbidden to see when I was fifteen. I snuck out to see him so often, my parents nearly threw me out of the house."

"Then what happened?"

"I ended up marrying him." She rolls her eyes. "Anyway. I know what this feels like, and I'm sorry you're stuck going through it during a goddamn pandemic."

"Do pandemics last long?"

She lets out a sigh. "That is a mystery to everyone. We don't know. I heard something on the radio about how closing the country for six months to a year would likely make a big difference in controlling the spread, but it's not realistic."

Six months? Six months in my house without seeing anyone? Without doing anything?

Shaya runs out of toys, so she heads to the big basket of toys in the corner of the living room and comes back with a bag of building blocks.

"So let's talk about what we can do that's realistic. I've got a proposition for you," Mrs. Morales says.

"A proposition?"

"This day care being closed and me working from home thing is not working. Freddie tries to help, but my son is not great with kids, and this little nugget is a handful." She shifts her weight, pausing until I unzip the bag of blocks for Shaya. "So what do you say to being my nanny? You can look after her while I work, and in exchange, I'll let you stay in the guest room."

I'm speechless for a minute, considering the meaning of her proposition.

"Oh my god—thank you. But . . . I think my mom will change her mind," I say. "She'll probably just make me stay barricaded in my room for another couple weeks."

"And if she does," Mrs. Morales says. "You're telling me you and Freddie will cool it for good?"

The version of me who glows pink around Freddie, who can't think clearly and justifies taking off in the night to see him, she warns me to tell the truth. And the truth is that I know better, but I can't promise I will do better. These are things that are only okay to admit in my head and in my journal.

But I have to be honest.

"You'd let me come into your house, in a pandemic?"

"We don't have much of a choice, do we? Your mom's got a lot on her plate," Mrs. Morales says. "We're all tired, and we're doing the best we can in this mess. I prefer to be a little more realistic and find a solution that might actually work for everyone."

"Is Freddie okay with this?"

"He'd be off the hook for Shaya, and you'd be around? I think my son will be thrilled," she says. "I'm thinking of him, too, in all this. He's had a rough year already with everything that happened with his dad. It would be nice to give him something to offset all the loss."

I pick Shaya up, sitting her on my hip, and there's a pang of sadness within when I think of my friend being hurt. Shaya's fingers get tangled in my hair, and she goes for my hoop earrings.

"Now we do blocks," she says. "Down."

I let her wiggle away from me, and she hands me a rectangular red block.

"The rules here are not going to be much better than the ones you had at your house," Mrs. Morales says. "Do you understand that? No going out. No seeing anyone outside this house. Homework gets done on time."

I nod.

"You will clean up after yourself," Mrs. Morales says. "And you will be responsible for all the shitty diapers between the hours of nine to five. And no funny-business stuff with Freddie." As the awkwardness registers on my face, she rolls her eyes. "Just . . . don't be obvious about it, and please be safe and responsible. Got it?"

I grin, glancing at Shaya. So many feelings swirl inside me. "Yes."

Mrs. Morales stands, hands on her hips. "You can start tomorrow."

"Okay."

"Baylee," Mrs. Morales says. "I made myself clear, right? You understand the extreme privilege you've just been granted?"

"Yes, I do."

"You get in a fight with my son, you can't just run on out of here and go home—you get that, right? I'm helping you guys out a little, but you both need to step up and show you can adapt. This is hard for everybody, but I want my family protected," she says. "No one comes in and out of this house. We don't even go out shopping. So you traveling back and forth between your house and mine puts us at risk, too, right?"

"Yes."

"Okay." She nods. "You can go."

"Thank you," I say. "I don't even know what else I can say."

She waves me off, headed for the kitchen. "Come, Boo. Let's get something to eat."

Shaya abandons her blocks and rushes after her mother. I head back out to the garage. Freddie puts his pen down and searches my face, waiting to be filled in.

"Your mother just basically took me on as a live-in nanny," I say.

An eyebrow goes up. "Damn. I guess I should give the universe a bucket of gratitude for giving me *one* awesome parent, at least."

"Next-level awesome."

We fist-bump and settle on the couch. I check my phone for something from my mother, but there are no alerts.

"Are you okay with this?" I ask him.

"As long as you come sneak into my room at night, I'm very okay with it."

I keep the things his mother said about him, about his dad and loss, to myself. This doesn't even need to go in my journal.

"Can we go to your room right now?"

Freddie nods all exaggerated.

"Wait—no. This can't be how I start my new job," I say, sitting up. "I'd really like to bring my stuff up and take a shower."

"I feel like I'm down with this plan. I need a shower, too."

The way he looks at me, it makes me open my mouth in shock. "Oh my god, as if that would ever happen."

"Not even if we keep the lights off?"

I tip my head to the side, like I'm considering it for a moment. "No. God, no."

He fake-punches my upper arm. "You suck."

We each grab one of the Ikea bags filled with my things, and we head inside.

The guest room is right next door to Freddie's bedroom. I spend some time organizing my things in the corner of the room, placing my pillow and duvet on the double bed. There is a little secretary desk and a rickety chair I'd never actually sit on. The bed frame worries me with all the creaking, so I am ever so careful getting on it, as though trying not to wake up someone else who might be sleeping in it. I place my laptop on the desk and put my phone to charge.

[Baylee] I'm at Freddie's.
[Mom] I know. You can thank Sheila for being understanding.
[Baylee] I did.

I take a shower, then throw on my robe and quickly rush back to the guest room. I let my hair air-dry, applying oil to the ends, and slip into fresh underthings. There are so many items I'm going to need, like my nail stuff, some books, more clothes.

[Baylee] Can I come get more of my things tomorrow?
[Mom] Tell me what you need and I'll have it in the garage.
[Baylee] Are you mad at me forever?
[Mom] You broke my heart, Boss. I never thought I'd have to fight you this hard.

Her words make me feel wrong inside, ashamed. They have a way of making me feel so unsure about everything.

For an hour or so, I lie on this bed that isn't mine, reading the news, and I cry, thinking about everything that's happened. I'm at Freddie's house, but now I almost wish I could go home. Except if I went home, I'd just be trying to figure out how to get back here.

This can't be real life.

Through the wall, I hear Freddie talking to someone, and it sounds like Trey and Rav. I can't make out the words, but Freddie's low tones are like vibrations coming through the wall. It lulls me to something that's close to sleep, but then there's a soft knock on the wall.

I knock back.

Freddie comes to the door, opening it a crack and summoning me with a finger. The feeling of homesickness disappears.

Tonight, we're in a bed, in a house. Freddie plays music, leaves only his bedside lamp on, and locks his door. I am drowsy and full of chills and goose bumps.

Freddie hums the slow-rock ballad. I turn my head to catch his gaze. "Freddie? Can you pick a *good* song next?"

He grabs a pillow and smooshes it against my head.

He turns out the lamp, plunging us into darkness. Not total darkness, because the window curtain is open. The glow from the streetlights penetrates the room, allowing us to see a little better. A little bit more. I am full of thrilling feelings and sensations as Freddie and I do things that only get better when you get to really know someone that way.

FORTY-SEVEN

The next few days are odd. Trying to move around a house that isn't mine, acclimating to a routine that I hadn't planned for, all the while thinking of my own house, my room, having no idea when I'll get to go back. The weirdest, most nerve-racking thing of all is the idea of having to use the bathroom for more than just a cute little tinkle while Freddie is right down the hall. I've had to save those moments for when I take a shower, praying my overpowering bodywash camouflages anything else that might be floating in the air. If he only knew I wasn't just having some girly spa night in there. I would die.

[Rianne] Is it time yet? I NEED to hear about this new development.

[Baylee] I'm almost done work.

[Rianne] How do you have a new JOB in a pandemic?!

I am lying on the bed of the guest room, holding my phone up above my face. Rianne's makeup-free face appears on my screen, and her hair is wet from a shower.

"Spill!" she says. "Wait—where are you? That's not your room."

"I know."

"Where are you?"

"Freddie's."

Her mouth hangs. "Whoa. Wait, wait, wait—how?"

Suddenly, I picture myself telling her what's going on, what truly led to this, and it just feels wrong. The avalanche of questions it would lead to. I can picture her asking me if I'm suddenly living with my boyfriend, and the energy it would take to explain that's not what this is, that she'd be looking at this through the wrong lens—I just don't have it in me. Even *I* wouldn't understand what this was if I wasn't living it.

I don't want a boyfriend. I don't want to owe people stories about a relationship or worry about carrying this thing out in public. I want it to be private, for it to include no one else but me and him.

"I am Shaya's nanny now," I say.

"Really? That's pretty cool," she says. "I kind of miss my job. Not my rude-ass supervisor, but just being able to go somewhere else. Thank god my grandpa's here. It's like he's my only friend now. No offense."

"I get it."

"So you get to see Freddie," she says. "You should *not* tell Lara that."

"Why?"

"She's now convinced he might've been the love of her life, and you wrecked it forever," Rianne says. "I think Trey gave up on her for good, and now she's just going a little crazy, home alone with her parents. Talking to Taylor *way* too much."

"Don't tell her I'm here."

Rianne zips her lips.

The next evening, Freddie's new daily chores begin. Since I am watching Shaya during the day, Freddie's responsible for cooking dinners and doing laundry—not mine, of course. He makes spaghetti sauce from scratch, and it is amazing—second only to my mother's sauce.

"You cook?" I ask as he and I clear off after dinner.

He shrugs. "I don't *enjoy* it, but I'm okay at it."

"I am like, next-level impressed. This was *so* good." I would've eaten another bowl if I was at home.

"Wait until I make enchiladas," he says. "They're pretty amazing."

"I literally can't wait," I say. "Can you make them tomorrow?"

"Possibly."

Freddie loads the dishwasher while I wash the big pots. When we're done, we head for the garage. I sit on the couch, scrolling through my phone, enjoying having nothing to do. The garage door is up, and Freddie stands near his car on the driveway, vaping.

[Mom] I get a thousand a year for psychotherapist services. If you're still wondering about that.
[Baylee] Really? Thanks, Mom.

"Would you like to kill some time by reading my screenplay?"

"Finally. You've only asked me five times but never handed it over," I say. He comes back to the couch with a stack of paper he riffles through before finally handing them to me. "Just out of curiosity. Am I doing this out of the goodness of my heart, or am I getting paid for this service?"

"I can definitely think of something to give you in return," he says. "You can even cash in all the favors I owe you."

He gets that look in his eye that I swear, I spend my whole day waiting for. My body erupts in goose bumps. He holds out a hand, and I put the pages down, taking his hand and pushing up to my feet. An observation I've made is that the moments before kissing are sometimes just as exciting as the actual kissing. I trace his jaw with my eyes. Then I focus on his mouth. My own mouth opens. My whole body opens when his face comes toward mine, anticipating that initial contact.

There's something about this thing with Freddie. It's hard to hold it up next to anything else because it can't be compared, and it can't be defined. But I know what the most important part about it is: It's safe. There's no pressure; that's what I love most about it.

I just want to do what I can to preserve the privacy of it all.

"Oh my god. This is sick!"

That voice.

It's Taylor, stopped on the sidewalk that cuts through Freddie's driveway. She straddles the bike she was riding, holding her phone up at us.

FORTY-EIGHT

Taylor is having some kind of revelation while I push Freddie away. This must be a thirty-minute bike ride from her house. I don't know what's happening, how she can even be here, intruding on my secret world. A world not compatible with the one we lived in before. She was supposed to have floated away with the rest of normal life. Or be on hold, at least.

"I was just coming here to drop the thing off for Freddie," Taylor says to her phone. "I can't believe this is what I walk in on! This is so *good*! Well, it's bad. Sorry."

She swipes and types on her phone.

"Don't post that!" I say, trying to keep my voice down.

"I'm not *posting* it," she says, looking at me like I'm crazy. "I'm sending it to Lara."

I glance at Freddie, and he's just shaking his head like he's been confronted with the biggest chore of his life.

"I should probably put a trigger warning for the gross-out factor," she says, making a show of tapping her phone like she's just hit the send button.

"*You're* gross, Taylor," Freddie says. "You're such a loser. Go home."

Freddie moves to the side of the garage door, punching in the code.

"Wait!" Taylor calls. "I have a letter for you!"

"Choke on it," Freddie says, and the door closes fully.

Freddie and I are side by side on the garage couch when the first alerts from Lara start arriving. Question marks flash across my screen. Once, twice, three times.

"Wow," Freddie says while I put my phone on silent.

"What am I supposed to do?"

"I can tell you from experience, she won't stop."

[Lara] Do not ignore me.
[Lara] I saw the video.

"She was trying to have Taylor hand-deliver you a letter?" I say.

"That's kind of sad," he says.

"I bet Taylor talked her into doing that. That's next-level desperate, even for Lara."

I start pacing, more alerts coming through. Freddie's attention is pulled to his own phone, and he swipes through it for a minute, looking thoughtful.

"Is it her?" I ask.

He shakes his head. "Taylor is telling everyone."

"How do you know?"

"Trey just sent me a text about it," he says. "Matt, too."

I cover my face with my hands, the sensation of doom settling over me. People know. *Everyone* will know.

"Baylee, why are you freaking out about this?" Freddie asks.

"I don't want people to know!"

"Why?" he says.

"What if Taylor posted the video?"

"Again, so?"

I let my hands fall at my sides. "People will start thinking all kinds of things. I didn't want that."

"Here's what you do," Freddie says, holding his phone up at me. "You turn it off and look—none of it matters anymore."

I turn my phone off and place it on the workbench. We seem to both be listening to the silence around us, then Freddie's nodding with a grin. "See how easy that was?"

"Freddie," I say. "People are still going to think things."

"Who cares?"

"I do."

"So what if they think you're my girlfriend?"

"I'm not, though."

He stares at me like he's waiting for my reaction to decide where to go with his words. Seriousness is all he must see reflected. "You could be."

"I don't think I want to be anyone's girlfriend," I say, my words slow and cautious. "Especially not just because somehow everyone found out about . . . this."

"So what is this, then? Friends with benefits?"

"Maybe?" I raise a shoulder. "I like having fun with you. Is that okay?"

He nods. "Is it okay that you're the only one I want to have fun with, though?"

I nod, a half smile pulling the right corner of my mouth up. "You're the only one I want to have fun with, too."

"All right, come read this," he says. "And please keep my feelings in mind. If you laugh at me, I'm going to act all tough, but inside, I *will* be crushed."

"I would never laugh at you."

I settle on the couch with Freddie's pages as he hangs around, trying not to look over my shoulder and stress me out with his anticipation. The story is about a college guy who has to drop out when his dad suddenly dies, and the guy has to spend days in this massive old house he doesn't know, clearing memories, feeling super conflicted about his past with his dad. But then he comes across mementos of a girl he went to high school with. So he spends the whole time remembering her. And then . . .

I don't know. I only have the first two acts to read.

"So?" Freddie asks when I put the pages down.

"You're pretty deep," I say. "This is really . . . emotional."

"Was it interesting?"

"Yes. I really like it," I say, and then I think about what Mrs. Morales said, about loss, and it's obvious a lot of his feelings ended up in this story. "Does he find the girl?"

Freddie shrugs. "I don't know."

"Shut up! You haven't even decided?"

He shakes his head and hops up on the workbench. "The end is really hard to write! I don't know what I'm trying to say with this story."

"Well, maybe you should write it different ways? See which one is best?" I suggest.

"That's a pretty decent idea," he says.

"I could read each one and tell you which one people would rather see in a theater."

"Because you're a film critic and an expert on film audiences?"

"No," I say. "But I'm literally almost always right."

"About movie stuff?"

"About all things, in general."

"Ah," he says, winking. "I'm sure that's a fact."

We head inside, and for the next few hours, I lie on Freddie's bed as he sits at his desk, working on his script. Turning on my phone leads to an avalanche of texts and alerts, mostly from Rianne and Lara.

[Lara] I can't believe you would do this to me.
[Baylee] I didn't do anything to you.
[Lara] You knew I liked him.

We could flip this conversation, reverse the roles, and it all sounds very familiar. I give myself a solid five minutes to consider responses. Then I decide to go with:

[Baylee] I'm really sorry. I know that sucks, but he wasn't yours. Maybe you wanted that more than anything, but it wasn't going to happen. That's not my fault.

[Lara] That's so condescending, Baylee.

[Baylee] I know. That's exactly how I felt when you said those exact words to me.

[Lara] You should've told me what was going on.

[Baylee] You should've told me what was going on, too.

[Lara] I have a real reason to be upset.

[Baylee] All I can say is I'm sorry. Sometimes you get caught up in the feelings and you have to follow them.

[Lara] Stop quoting my own words back to me!

[Baylee] Well, do you want to actually talk for real or do you just want to keep talking down at me?

[Lara] I want to talk for real.

[Baylee] OK. Give me 5 minutes.

"I'm going to go to the garage for a bit," I say. Freddie starts gathering his things, meaning to follow me. "I need to talk to Lara, okay?"

He nods and gives me a thumbs-up.

FORTY-NINE

In the garage, the only lights I put on are the Christmas ones hanging above the couch. My hope is that it won't be obvious that I'm in Freddie's garage, which would distract needlessly. There's a part of me that still wants to rub things in her face, but my living here right now isn't one of them.

My phone screen reflects a stone-faced Lara, hair gathered up high on her head, delicate gold earrings shaped like leaves hanging from her earlobes, white silk cami top on. We say hello, then we are silent.

This conversation seems to call for an apology, but there won't be one offered from my end, and I suspect it's the same from hers.

"So Freddie's your boyfriend," she finally says.

My sigh is louder than I meant it to be. "No."

"But you're dating."

"Something like that, I guess?"

"What about the other person you're dating?"

"I . . . messed that up."

"Because of Freddie?"

"No. Just for . . . reasons."

We are quiet again, the very important things that need to be said waiting to be released into the conversation. But I don't know how to start.

"Is all of your family okay?" I ask.

"So far. But Kavith had the nerve to go to a party in Toronto last weekend," she says. "He ended up going to the emergency room the next day, totally freaking out about having the rona. So now my uncle's house is in quarantine because of him."

"Are they sick?"

She shakes her head. "He smoked a ton at the party, so when he woke up with a scratchy throat the next day, he totally lost it and thought he was dying. He's fine, but it was a big party in Toronto— he's an idiot."

"Sounds like it."

"How's your family?"

"They're fine. We're being careful."

"Well, that's good," she says. "I'm still mad at you."

"I'm mad, too."

"Freddie and me—we could've been something," she says. "I can't believe you don't feel bad for getting in the way."

"I'm sorry."

"*Are* you sorry? Because it doesn't seem like you really are."

"I'm sorry for the situation," I say, "and for you being upset."

My words are not acceptable, I can tell by the look on her face.

"I can't believe you were my best friend," Lara says to me. "I honestly sometimes wonder what I was thinking, being best friends with you."

"You don't know what you were thinking?"

"No."

"We've both always known why you picked me as a best friend," I say, letting my gaze drill into her.

"What are you talking about?"

"Do I really need to spell it out?"

"Yes, because I literally don't know what you're going on about."

I watch her a few moments, and the look on her face seems to dare me to tell her the truth.

So I do.

"That's why this is so much worse, this Freddie thing," I say. "That's why it's such a huge deal. I just don't buy that you're suddenly convinced you're in love with him."

"You don't know how I feel."

"I don't, but I still don't buy it. I think that you just never expected something like this to come from me. To lose out on a guy because of *me*, the poor envious fat girl who was never supposed to be a threat. That's what this is really about," I say. "You're insecure, and you kept me close as a reminder that however shitty you feel about yourself, at least you're not me."

Her mouth hangs wide, and I can tell it's a struggle for her to maintain her usual maturity and levelheadedness for difficult conversations. "You are like, literally so wrong."

"I think I'm right. I also think that you really like the feeling of having some sad, desperate girl thinking you're so awesome, wishing she could be you." I say. "Except I don't. Not anymore. And like, why would I continue to be friends with someone who thinks I'm pathetic?"

"I never thought you were pathetic."

I make a face, daring her to be honest, to tell the truth.

"I didn't," she says. "I think it's pathetic that you're picking a guy over our friendship, though."

"That's not what this is about," I say. "But if you really want to go down this road, then should we talk about all the guys *you* picked over our friendship?"

"Not this again," she says. "I already apologized for that, and I'm not the one who ditched this time."

"Lara, this is stupid," I say. "I don't want to argue about the same dumb details. There is a big problem with our friendship, and it's the fact that you think you're better than me. You're up here," I say, holding a hand up, "and I'm down there. That's how it's been. Since day one."

"I'm so confused right now. Here I am, trying to talk to you about a very current problem that I'm upset about, and you're going back in time to tell me our friendship was always bullshit?"

"I guess," I say. "Yes, that's what I'm doing."

"What am I supposed to do with that?"

I shrug. "I don't know. Just think about it, I guess. See if it starts making sense. But for me, I just can't even picture myself talking to you about any of the super-serious, super-important things that have happened to me in the last couple of months. It doesn't work anymore."

"Fine," she says.

"Fine."

I close the chat.

I'm different now, and the version of me that I'm trying to become would never be friends with Lara. At least not the way we have been. The bad things about our friendship are suddenly very noticeable, and carrying on without addressing all the shittery between us feels very fake and like a total waste of energy.

My head spins when I think too hard about all the ways my life is suddenly very different. The last thing I want is to waste time feeling homesick for the way things used to be, deluding myself into thinking everything used to be great when it wasn't. Familiar, that's all it was.

FIFTY

I'm fairly certain that I've broken up with my best friend for good, judging by the total silence from both sides since we had our video chat.

But there are more important things to be dealing with, worse things to be worrying about.

There have been so many deaths of old people that the army has been called in to investigate how this could even have happened in the first place. I've started scrolling through the local obituaries, just to see what some of these people looked like, what kind of lives they had. Yesterday I came across a photo of the lady from the hospital, the one with chin hairs, talking about stocking up on cans and pantry foods. Looking at that website, seeing everyone's faces, the names of the people they left behind—it leads to a terrible feeling inside that wants to linger and come back at night when I try to fall asleep. I want to stop looking at the website, but I don't.

The more the days pass, the less likely it seems that things will just go back to normal.

Within three weeks of having me as her full-time nanny, Shaya can say six more words, and I've taught her to pick up her toys. Sort of. She'll throw all her plastic food to the floor, but now she will put each item carefully back into its bin before throwing it all over the floor again. She's doing it right now, flinging a fake strawberry, ice cream cone, and potato over to the kitchen floor. I sit on the living room rug, laptop on the coffee table and assignments up on the screen.

Rianne, the only person I still have a real relationship with, sends me a link to a video of some designer she loves, where they duetted the vegetable-fruit-salad video of Rianne's.

[Rianne] She legit teared up!!!!! My grandpa gave her the feels! It's got over 5 THOUSAND likes!!!!!!!!!
[Baylee] Your grandpa deserves so much recognition. He is the star of the video.
[Rianne] I know, right?!?! He's letting me dye his hair green later.
[Baylee] Photos, please!
[Rianne] For sure. I'm totally going to film a react video to the duet with my grandpa tomorrow.
[Baylee] Yes!
[Rianne] How's things with Freddie? 🌶🌶🌶🌶🌶😂😂😂😂😂
[Baylee] OMG you're such a loser!

[Rianne] I KNOW! Listen. I started talking to this guy online. I seriously think I'm in love.

[Baylee] What about the guy from the dating app?

[Rianne] That guy was a bag of crap. This new guy is from a different dating app I just got. He's SO sweet.

She sends me screenshots of their messages. Shaya runs over to me for the Goldfish crackers I hold in a cup. Her diaper is starting to look full, so I make a mental note to catch her the next time she runs by me to change her. Mrs. Morales usually comes up from her basement office for lunch right around now, and she gives me time to go have lunch on my own while she feeds Shaya.

I pick up my phone, scrolling until I get to Alex's number.

Since that day—the day she found out, the day I got sent to Freddie's—I haven't heard from her. I haven't tried to text her, either. Whenever I feel the need to send her a desperate text, I go for my journal instead. I scroll through our old DMs and remember the three times I was with her. It just feels like I met her at the wrong time. All the things I was scared about, the nervousness, the total inexperience getting in the way, stopping me from just being there—it feels like I took a test I hadn't studied for, and here I am now, weeks into cramming and prepared to ace it, except the moment's passed. I can't take the test again.

I tap the call icon. It goes nowhere, no voice-mail greeting anymore. She's no longer visible on Instagram either. She erased herself completely.

I'm reading Freddie's latest text when I notice Shaya red in the face, not exactly breathing. Her eyes register confusion, then her arms start flapping with panic.

It happens so fast that I don't even have time to feel anything about it. I'm up and grabbing her, letting myself fall to the floor while I sit her on my knee, leaning her forward, the way I've seen my mother do with my sister so many times, and I give her quick hard smacks with my palm between her shoulder blades.

She coughs and drools the chunk out, already catching her breath.

"Oh my god, you little shit!" I say, and she smiles even though she's got tears in her eyes from the choking and coughing.

"Down!" she says, and she struggles to get out of my grip. I let her go, and she tries to grab the piece of mushy cracker off the ground to eat it again. "Yummy!"

"That's so gross!" I say. "Don't eat that!"

I turn around to see Mrs. Morales watching, standing still with her arms out, maybe frozen with panic? Maybe relieved.

"It's okay. She's fine," I say.

Mrs. Morales scoops up Shaya, who immediately starts trying to get out of her mother's arms. "Baylee, you just took care of that like it was nothing! Oh my god. I need to sit down."

"I had to take CPR a couple of times because of my sister— not real CPR, but my mom and one of the nurses taught me. My mom says gravity is your friend when this happens, to prevent the stuff from being sucked in farther."

Shaya's back to throwing her plastic food around. Mrs. Morales moves to the kitchen to take out the lunch I prepared for Shaya earlier.

"I'm giving you a raise."

I laugh. "You're not paying me, though."

"Well, I'm going to give you a bonus. You have no idea how much of a help you've been. I get to focus on work, knowing Shaya's being well looked after. I clearly don't have to worry. That's a gift for a mother," Mrs. Morales says.

My insides swell with pride. This is the kind of stuff my mother says to the nurses she relies on most, like Dawn, so I know exactly how much Mrs. Morales's words mean. I head to my room for my lunch hour, smiling to myself all the way up the stairs, my laptop tucked under one arm and sandwich clutched in my right hand.

Freddie's bedroom door is open, and he sits at his desk, bent over his keyboard. He looks deep in thought until I notice his eyes are closed.

"Wake up! Get to work!" I call from the hallway.

He shakes the fatigue off and turns. "This is tedious as hell, Bay. I keep falling asleep."

"You could come downstairs and do homework with me," I suggest. "Shaya will keep you up."

"I can watch her, you know," he says.

"What do you mean?"

"If you want to go do something else for a while," he says. "I can deal with her for a bit."

"Really?"

He nods.

"Well, I kind of want to do my nails," I say. "Maybe I can do them at the kitchen counter, and we can study for math?"

He nods. "Math. Gross."

"I know!" I fake a gag.

"Wake me up when it's time," he says, letting himself fall face-first diagonally on his bed.

In the guest room, I lie on the bed, closing my eyes and pretending I'm home, in my own bed. I've barely seen my mother in three weeks, just through the window while picking up some things, or from the lawn while she stands on the porch.

[Baylee] Can I call today?

[Mom] Yep. She's awake.

My sister appears on my screen. The second I say hi, she starts babbling. Long-winded sounds of gibberish that I imagine might be her telling me a story about what's been going on in the last few days. It sounds very serious by her tone, so I match it with my response.

"Wow—really?" I say. "Then what?"

More serious vocalization in a language I don't understand, and she brings her head close to the screen. Then, all of a sudden, she starts yelling and laughing, like she just delivered the punch line to this very ridiculous story.

"That's the craziest thing I've heard!"

"Don't believe a thing she says," Mom says in the background. "She lies."

"Don't worry—I believe *you*," I tell my sister.

Rebecca starts swatting at my mom's phone, and the screen goes wild. Suddenly, I'm looking at the carpet and a leg of the crib.

That night, I sneak into Freddie's room, my mind full of thoughts and considerations after an hour of scribbling in my journal about Lara, about Freddie. And Alex—a lot about Alex. I lie on his bed, in skinny jeans and a black oversized tee, fresh pedicure exposed. I stare at my toes as the shiny black polish catches the light.

[Rianne] So you're like, friends with benefits then?

[Baylee] Something like that. But I don't want anyone else to know. We might just have to pretend we were dating and broke up.

[Rianne] That's actually cool, the friends with benefits thing.

[Baylee] You think so?

[Rianne] It's better than when I had sex with that guy Rod. And the other stuff I did with that guy from St. Peter's.

[Baylee] I know! It sucks to just expect that it'll either be super awkward and cringe or it'll be something to regret.

[Rianne] I'm kind of jealous. The thing with Rod wasn't fun at all. And the guy from St. Peter's . . . 🙁 I definitely realized that I prefer my boys online.

I remember being so jealous of Rianne because the stories she told back then sounded so exciting. She clearly kept the ugly parts to herself.

[Baylee] 🫢 Oh no. What happened with the guy from St. Peter's? Are you OK?
[Rianne] Totally. It wasn't even that bad. He just cut me with his nail or something, but he acted like it was MY fault for making a mess.
[Baylee] That's terrible. That would be so awkward. I'm sorry.
[Rianne] Maybe I'll find myself a Freddie someday. 😄

It's so complicated, the idea of being with other people, but I think what I'm starting to realize is that I can separate the stuff I do with Freddie and the butterflies I felt for Alex. I'm lucky to be able to figure this out, because I've got the opportunity to explore and learn and it feels safe. I get to have fun.

The way Freddie looks at me makes me feel pretty. It makes me feel wanted. The things we do, well, they're fun and I don't really think it's wrong to admit that I just . . . like it. All of it combined—well, it all makes me feel different about what I see in the mirror. I'm not saying I'm going to tuck in my shirt or anything drastic such as that, but it is addicting to feel good, to feel about myself the way I imagine sparkly girls feeling about themselves. It's just about that feeling and getting to hold on to it a little bit longer each day.

"Hey, Freddie? What do you think about the idea that you

can't be loved by someone else until you love yourself?" I ask as he puts away some of the fresh laundry he did earlier.

He turns. "Seriously? Are we going to be this deep right now? It's midnight."

"I'm just curious."

"About what?"

"Do you think it's a valid statement?"

He carries on putting sweaters away. "Kind of but not really."

"Why?"

"I think it's the word. The word 'love' makes it too romantic sounding. I think that takes away from it."

"How do you interpret it, then?"

The basket is empty, so he kicks it toward the door. "I think it means that unless you think you're worthy of it, you won't get someone else's time, or attention."

"Hmm. Interesting."

Freddie takes the space next to me on his bed, fingers interlaced behind his head as he stares up at the ceiling. "It's like—okay, so if you sit there thinking you're a piece of shit, sure someone might find you interesting, they might want to be around you, but if you think all those negative things about yourself, that'll sabotage it. You'll push them away, whether it's intentional or not."

I let his explanation sit in the air. "I literally thought it meant you're supposed to like, love yourself. Like, 'Self, you are so amazing, and I love everything about you!'"

"No one loves everything about themselves. Doesn't mean

they can't also believe they're decent people. Everyone's a work in progress."

"A work in progress," I repeat. "Okay, well, what about the idea that you can't love someone else until you love yourself?"

"Isn't that what you just asked me?"

"No, I asked about being loved by someone. Now I'm asking about loving someone else."

"Okay, well, I think the same thing applies. Like, if you're convinced you're a piece of shit, how are you going to be a decent person to be around? You'd be super self-centered, wallowing in self-pity, always bailing on them, thinking they deserve better," he says. "If you think you're a decent person, and you're always working toward being a better person, then, what's the problem?"

These are words I need to write down.

I guess I never believed Alex could have real feelings for me. I felt like a loser, and why would she have a crush on a loser?

It was doomed to begin with, but that doesn't make me feel any better about it. I completely despise the idea of Alex becoming this person I think back on and feel awkward and cringey about. I know better now, and there's nothing I can do to fix it.

FIFTY-ONE

One Saturday in early May, Freddie and I make our way down the walkway that connects his street to mine. Our hands are full, and once we reach my front lawn, we lay the things we were carrying onto the grass. It's windy out, not very sunny, making for a gloomy Beck Field Trip Day.

Freddie runs to the open garage, plugs in the long power cord, and unrolls it on his way back to me. He plugs the big Bluetooth speaker we borrowed from Rianne's house into the cord, along with this disco party light Rianne also let us borrow for the day. In the large garbage bag I carried, there are six multicolored pool noodles that I, of course, got from Rianne. Freddie and I made a trip yesterday to pick everything up from the bottom of her driveway as she waved at us from her big dining room window.

"I can't believe it's so ugly out today," I say, connecting my phone to the speaker.

"At least we'll be able to see the lights better without so much sun, right?" Freddie says.

Mrs. Morales is next to arrive, pushing Shaya in her stroller. She stays by the curb, ready to walk away should anyone try and call us out on the fact that we're about to be bending the rules a little. We're allowed to gather in groups of five maximum, outside, with plenty of space between us. There are about to be six of us.

Mom pulls the front door open and starts pushing my sister in her chair over the accessible ramp that runs next to the front steps of the house. My sister is in her purple spring jacket, quiet and fidgeting with her hands as she is pushed onto the lawn, her chair angled so she can turn her head one way and see the front of the house, and if she turns her head the other way, she sees me and the speaker.

Right on cue, I press play on the worst playlist of all time, starting with my personal favorite, the song about the teddy bears that go out for a picnic.

Freddie turns on the party light, and multicolored squares project against the house, catching Rebecca's attention, especially with the strobe effect it has to the music coming from the speaker right next to it.

I take a red pool noodle from the garbage bag and throw it across the lawn to my mom. I grab a pink noodle in one hand, a blue in the other.

Mrs. Morales motions for Freddie to take over watching Shaya, and she comes to grab a purple noodle. Freddie stands next to Shaya in her stroller, holding a yellow pool noodle so she can play with it.

The music plays while we wave pool noodles around frantically. My mother gets Rebecca's attention with the red noodle, and once she realizes she can touch it, her arms start waving.

My mom starts singing along with the song while spinning my sister in her chair. Mrs. Morales gets a little closer, waving her pool noodle around and making a show of attracting my sister's attention. Shaya looks ready to bust out of her stroller, so I wander over to pick her up.

"I'm literally going to lose my sense of hearing over this song," I tell Freddie.

"It's kind of catchy," he says, with a laugh. "No, but for real, have you ever considered the fact that she only pretends to like it because she knows you hate it so much?"

My mouth hangs open. "She would totally be sassy enough to do just that."

I bring Shaya closer, and we spin in circles as the lights dance around us.

The whole thing seemed better in my head when I thought of the idea, mostly because it was going to be warm with nothing but a cool breeze. It's still good, though. I'm sure my sister is just as sick of seeing nothing but her bedroom as I was when I was stuck in mine.

Later, Freddie brings the car over to load up Rianne's things and take them back to her. I stay behind to talk to my mom for a bit. From where I stand on the welcome mat, just outside the screen door, I can see my sister on the carpet next to her bed, rolling around on her floor mat. Mom stands on the other side of the door, and the window is down so there's only a screen between us, and we're both wearing masks. Mom is telling me about work, how her main supervisor agreed to take more of an in-person role so Mom can stay home and avoid getting sick.

"How are your midterm grades?"

"There aren't really midterms, Mom. It's all different. But I'm doing okay." I reach into my bag. "I brought something."

I hold up the blue binder, and my mother opens the door to grab it.

She opens it, taking in the cover page I made. A real smile breaks out on her face as she flips over to the next page, no doubt taking in the index.

"I made sure to organize all of Rebecca's information into categories, keeping track of page numbers. It'll be easier to use."

"How long have you been working on this?" Mom asks.

"Three weeks. Dawn helped me with some of the terminology and specifics."

"Oh my god, Boss. You put information about her feeding pump and suction machine in there." Mom looks amazed, running her hands over the pages like they're precious jewelry. "'The battery should last for sixty minutes of continuous suction'—where did you get this information?"

"Dawn sent me photos of the equipment, and I googled the user manuals."

"This thing is seventy pages!"

"There are many details to be aware of," I say. "And I'll email you the digital copy so we can add to it."

Mom shakes her head in disbelief, carrying on flipping through. She looks at the pages where I've included photos of my sister's favorite positions, where we should tuck pillows in to make sure she's comfy and properly supported.

"Dawn took them with her phone and texted them to me," I say.

"This is such amazing work. Such attention to detail. Wow."

Mom's eyes are shiny.

It's complicated, everything that's happened. But just because I did certain things that appeared careless, and just because I picked myself over other people, it doesn't mean that I don't actually care, that I'm nothing besides selfish.

"I guess I'm going to go," I say.

"I miss you, Boss."

"I miss you, too, Mom."

"Rebecca misses you, too."

"Really? Do you think so?"

"I can tell she does. You've seen how wild she gets during your video chats," Mom says. "This was a great idea, the Beck Field Trip Day on the lawn."

"It worked out pretty well," I say.

There is silence for a little while as I look at my sister, thinking it would be nice to walk over and pick her up or wiggle her with a hand on her chest at least. It's so quiet at Freddie's at night, and although sleeping all through the night is really nice, it feels weird and usually leads to a sense of homesickness that's difficult to shake. I'm used to the noises at my house, to the rumbling of the compressor and the mixer, to the crying and hysterical laughter that find their way into my dreams.

"You know the pandemic isn't over, right, Boss?"

"Yes."

"When you make a decision that you think is just about you, it isn't. Do you understand that?" Mom says, and I nod. "Before you make a decision, you need to consider all the things that could result from it."

"But then, what if . . ." I wait, unsure if I want to take the conversation down this path and risk my mother getting mad at me again.

"What if?"

"What if I still want to make the decision?"

"Then you deal with the consequences," Mom says. "There are very serious risks involved with every decision we make. You have to ask yourself if the reason you're taking the risk is worth it, because you're taking on the risk for everyone else who's close to you."

"Does it make sense to know you made a bad decision but also that you wouldn't go back in time to change it?" I ask.

"I think you're only saying that because you have the benefit of knowing that nothing truly awful happened because of it."

Oh.

"Sometimes nothing happens when you take a risk, but other times, something bad happens. I know you're young, and you haven't really learned that lesson yet," Mom continues. "Sometimes risks pay off, and other times, they can ruin everything. A pandemic is not the time to take a chance—that's the point, Boss."

"Okay, okay. That makes sense."

"You were impossible to reason with. Lying and sneaking off."

"I know."

"None of this was easy for anyone involved. Do you think I was glad to lock you in your room for so many days? I barely slept that week."

"Being home in prison upstairs was the worst thing ever."

"I'm sorry, Boss," Mom says. "But I didn't know what else to do. Do you understand?"

"Yes," I say.

Then it suddenly feels a lot colder, the wind making it up my back, and it's not like I can walk right into my house. Part of me wishes I could just open the door and go up to my room right now.

But I can't. I made a deal, and it included no back and forth.

So my mom and I say goodbye, and I head back the way I came.

As I step onto the walkway, I get a text from Freddie confirming that everything was dropped off at Rianne's.

"Hey, B."

Garrett comes up the sidewalk as I head through the walkway. He makes his way over to me, in a pair of black sneakers and a T-shirt. It's May, but the short sleeves are still a little inappropriate, and I have a hard time thinking this is a choice of fashion over comfort. He stops about six feet away from me, but I still keep my hand on my purse, ready to pull my mask any minute.

"Hi," I say.

"How have you been, B?"

"I've been fine."

"You're going to see your boyfriend?"

"He's not my boyfriend. I told you that before," I say.

Garrett leans against the fence, across from me. I stay because I need a couple of minutes to reset myself mentally after just having walked away from my house and returning to Freddie's. Garrett's presence is surprisingly . . . well, I wouldn't say zen, but it's definitely not the total opposite either. For the next few minutes, we are silent. Garrett smokes what I presume to be weed, although the scent isn't making it to me owing to the wind blowing the other way. He exhales O's into the sky.

I check out my Instagram feed, flicking my thumb on the screen as fast as I can. When I stop, it's a sepia-toned selfie of Lara's. I take it as a sign from the universe, and I leave a comment.

[Baylee] Flawless. ☺

"How are you still managing to get weed and cigarettes?" I ask.

"I got my ways."

"I'm sure you do."

He grins and we go back to silence. I pull up my phone to Rianne's latest text when I feel Garrett's eyes on me.

"So, listen. If Freddie's not your boyfriend, and Pen's friend isn't your girlfriend," Garrett starts, offering me his joint, at which I flash a look of total confusion. "Oh, right. My bad—old habit. Anyway, that means you're a free agent, right?"

"What do you mean?"

"It means you got time to focus on someone else now, right? Catch my drift?"

I don't catch drifts very well, not normally, but my body understands something, because there's a spark in my belly. A tiny bit of excitement.

"I just thought maybe you and me—maybe we could hang out," he says.

"Hang out?"

He shrugs, then he's locking eyes with me, and for a second, he's not as ugly as I always thought he was. My mouth wants to pull up into a smile.

But no. Stop.

This isn't right. This isn't real.

This has to do with me, and not with him. I like that feeling, of someone looking at me, but it coming from Garrett? That's not right. I can feel something similar to what I get when Freddie looks at me, except with a big layer of wrong attached.

"I have to go," I say. "Sorry."

"All right, whatever, B."

He hops off the wall, headed back the way he came.

I watch Garrett leave, and I delete my DM conversation with him.

A text from my mother pops through just then.

[Mom] Come home, Boss.

I head back to Freddie's, thinking about my mom's text.

FIFTY-TWO

June is warm and sunny, and my bedroom window is permanently open a crack to let in the summer vibes. I've been home a little over two weeks now, an agreement having been reached between my mother and Freddie's mother that I could continue going over there to nanny Shaya four days a week. There's a paycheck attached now, which means I have a very honest job. Freddie is responsible for Mondays, which he does out of the goodness of his heart. The new thing is social bubbles, a new provincial guideline authorizing one household to carefully mix with another. I went ahead and made the decision for my household when I chose to preemptively mix with Freddie's, but at least now it's officially okay. It's officially acceptable to my mother.

It's Friday evening, almost nine, and my mother is upstairs having a bath and doing whatever else she wants to do on a Friday night. I am in the living room, my sister tucked in safely on the couch next to me. I am cozy on my corner of the couch, eyelids becoming heavy, just as my sister whacks at the child-size keyboard that I'd propped next to her so she could fill the room with truly atrocious sounds. It crashes to the floor, and I roll off the couch to fetch it.

"I swear you're doing this on purpose," I tell her.

Nine p.m. on the dot, I lower the volume of my sister's instrument and sign into the group chat Rianne arranged. Everyone's supposed to be there, including Lara.

Everyone pops up into the meeting around the same time. Squares on my phone show Rianne, Trey, Lara, Rav, and Freddie. The chat turns into a bunch of gossiping about what everyone is up to, who's totally given up on school, who's hooking up with who. We go through the typical questions, asking each other what we think will happen, if we think we'll be going back to real school in September, if the second wave of the pandemic will be worse than the first. No one asks about Freddie and me, which I am grateful for. It's difficult to reel it back in, to try and make it private again, but that's exactly my goal. If we don't talk about it, if we're more careful, then maybe it'll fade back into the darkness.

The whole time, my eyes are on him, but it's easy for me to slip back into my role, becoming the Baylee whose internal tingles and sparks for her friend make no appearance on the outside.

"Ri, get your gramps on camera!" Lara says.

"Are you kidding? This is his bedtime. It's almost eight," Rianne says. "He gets up at four a.m. to eat dry toast and half a grapefruit. He's *very* particular."

We talk about Rianne's semi-viral videos for a while.

"Hey—I have an idea," Lara says. "We should join the drive-bys for hospital workers. What do you guys think?"

"Yeah," Freddie says. "I would."

"I'd be down," Trey says.

"My grandpa would so drive me!" Rianne says.

"I'd be driving by now if I could have taken my damn G2 when I was supposed to," Rav says.

"It's bullshit," Trey says. "I had mine booked for two weeks ago, and it got canceled. Fred's going to be the only driver for a long-ass time."

Freddie shakes his head. "Damn, I got lucky."

Rav groans. "I guess I have to get my mom to drive me. I'm so mad, bro! I could be driving by now!"

"I know, bro," Trey says.

"Okay, so my dad says there's a drive-by planned for Sunday," Lara says.

"I bet my mom would take my sister and me for the ride," I say.

[Freddie] We could go together, you know.

[Baylee] I know. I just don't want to . . . say that out loud.

[Freddie] Oh, OK. I get it.

418

The conversation veers back to all the canceled driving tests for a while.

I get a text from Lara.

[Lara] How are you?
[Baylee] I'm okay. You?
[Lara] Same.
[Baylee] I saw the worst 5-minute Craft ever earlier. Like, so bad that it made me angry.
[Lara] Send it to me. I want to be angry, too.
[Baylee] The drive-by thing was a really good thing to suggest.
[Lara] Thanks. Are we talking again, yet?
[Baylee] I don't know, are we?
[Lara] I think we should. I think there are some broken pieces, but I don't think we should be throwing the whole thing away.
[Baylee] So, you want to recycle it?
[Lara] I think it can be repurposed. I feel like with a glue gun and some twine, it can become good again. Right?
[Baylee] I can't even believe you're suggesting we 5-minute Craft our friendship. 😆 Your cleverity just blew me away.
[Lara] It was good, wasn't it? 😎

Trey insists on making everyone listen to this new song he's obsessed with. I spend some time listening, then I consider Lara's texts.

[Baylee] There's actually something I want to talk to you about.

[Lara] What is it?

[Baylee] It's about that girl I was talking to, Alex. And the letter you wrote Freddie.

[Lara] Oh OK. Well . . . Taylor wrote most of it.

[Baylee] I figured.

[Lara] Can I just say that the whole Freddie thing . . . I guess it wasn't really about Freddie on my end.

[Baylee] I figured that, too.

[Lara] But anyway, do you want to video-chat?

[Baylee] Yes.

I cross my legs on the couch next to my sister, then Lara's face appears on my screen.

The next evening, Freddie and I are side by side on the garage couch.

[Lara] I know it's awkward but you really need to have a conversation with him. You guys need to both be on the same page.

[Baylee] You're right. I know.

I look over at Freddie, ready to start the conversation, but then he shifts his weight and his shirt rides up a little. I give him a sideways glance, starting from the bottom up. Inside, the butterflies start to flutter their wings, and goose bumps travel over my skin. I don't say anything for a while, totally content sitting here with my tingles and sparks.

"What?" Freddie says, noticing.

"Nothing."

I look away. I start typing a message to Lara, intent on telling her this isn't the right time, when a feeling comes over me, pulling my gaze to Freddie's.

We look at each other, and I wait until he makes a move, letting the anticipation build.

So many minutes go by, minutes of me wondering how kissing Freddie continues to be so thrilling.

"Freddie," I say, pulling my face away from his. "What do you think will happen to this when school starts again, when things start going back to normal?"

"I don't know. It doesn't feel like anything will happen to it. We'll just keep it secret, like you want."

"But what if we meet other people?"

He shrugs.

"Would you be jealous?" I ask.

"Would you be jealous if *I* met someone?"

I nod. "I think I would be. A little."

"Same."

I sigh, knowing this warrants being a little more specific.

"I've been thinking about that girl," I say. "Alex."

"Oh. I see," he says. I give him an uncomfortable half smile. He nods, seemingly understanding. "Well, I guess this thing would have to stop."

"Forever?"

"I don't really know," he says. "I guess we'll just have to check in with each other and see?"

"Okay," I say. "I think checking in is a good idea."

There's been so much to learn about in the last months, but I think above all, the lesson is in being careful. Careful physically, but also careful with other people's feelings. Careful with my own.

Freddie and me being together but not really together—friends with benefits—it's a thing I was never supposed to be content with. I know that as a girl, I'm supposed to be very clear about the fact that any connection to another person is supposed to happen with one goal in mind: to find the one, to find true love. All the butterflies, the drama, the dates, the sex—it's all supposed to be in pursuit of a romantic love story. I think a love story would be cool, and I truly hope there's a soul-mate type of person out there for me. But at the same time, I'm totally cool having fun like this. This thing with Freddie has made me realize that's totally okay.

There's always worry, though. Worrying about Freddie's feelings and what would happen if he wasn't okay with this anymore. Worrying about the possibility of him having real boyfriend-girlfriend feelings for me, or me somehow developing those same feelings for him. No matter how unofficial this thing is with him, it could still get complicated and messy.

The truth is, right now, I'm self-centered, a little selfish, and a little too concerned with doing what I want, when I want. But I know there's potential for another version of me to step forward. A version who wants other things, who conjures up Alex in her dreams, who fills with butterflies at the simple, late-night thought of holding her hand.

For now, though, the only love story I can handle is the one with myself.

EPILOGUE

It picks up again months later, with a series of desperate texts that Lara convinced me would be viewed as bold, and not at all as pathetic.

[Baylee] I know this is so random, but do you think there's a chance she might want to hear from me?

[Pen] The balls you have messaging me. Damn.

[Baylee] I know.

[Pen] Why do you even bother? It was months ago.

[Baylee] I'm taking a chance. I don't want to think back and wish I'd tried harder to make it right.

[Pen] You knew Alex for like, ten minutes. Why don't you just move on?

[Baylee] It's not like it's easy to just move on. Alex is really awesome.

[Pen] What do you think I can do about it?

[Baylee] I just want to tell her some things. I can't reach her, and I thought maybe if I earned your respect by manning up, you might be willing to help me out with something.

[Pen] Good point. I am definitely a fan of girls manning up.

And that's how a handwritten letter makes its way by mail to Pen's apartment, and then it gets hand-delivered to Alex. A very vintage way to communicate. Something I hope will mean something to Alex.

Dear Alex,

Remember me?

Oh . . . that was dumb.

Of course you remember me. I'm the stupid girl you wasted all of March and most of April 2020 on.

I could literally fill a whole journal with excuses and justifications for how I ended up wasting your time. But I guess the thing to know about that is that you were never the problem. It was me. And I'm not just being all "it's not you, it's meeeee" about it. It's not supposed to be dismissive. It's just supposed to be the truth.

I really feel like I missed out on the chance to be around you, and not all of it was covid's fault.

I'm totally conscious of the fact that it only lasted two months, and more months have passed between then and now, so maybe I've mostly faded away in your mind. Everything is constantly changing. It all makes so much sense for us to have moved on.

You haven't faded away for me, though. You're still pretty much . . . there.

I guess what I'm saying is . . .

Don't wanna leave you really
I've invested too much time
To give you up that easy
To the doubts that complicate your mind

Anyway . . .

I'm kind of hoping feelings and apologies mean more when they're handwritten. And also when they contain some of Pat Benatar's banging lyrics.

I would just love to talk to you, to hear about what you've been up to. I also hope you and the people around you are safe. I hope you're all okay.

Baylee Marie Kunkel

If this was a book, it would be taking place exactly one year from Chapter 1, on a frigid February Friday night. I'd like to report that the silky black cami I have on is tucked into my jeans right now, but come on, I haven't changed that much in a year. She'll always be there, that mean voice in my head, telling me to suck it in, to sharpen my hearing to be able to hear everyone around me having reactions to my size. I've decided to carry on despite the negativity, cherishing the moment she temporarily shuts the hell up and fades away.

School has been a mess, moving to and away from virtual as they open, close, then reopen the school buildings. Given the unpredictability of it all, and the very real, ongoing concerns with my sister, my mother allowed me to opt for permanently virtual schooling through an official virtual school that's apparently been around for twenty years. Lara convinced her parents to let her do the same, and we enrolled in the same classes. This would 100 percent never have happened in the old world—neither my mother nor Lara's father would've ever allowed such a thing—but this COVID-19 stuff changed nearly every rule there ever was.

Shaya lost her spot at day care when Mrs. Morales hesitated to send her back when day cares opened up in the fall. So I am still the nanny, except now Shaya comes to my house, and we spend our days on the main floor with my sister, who is out of school indefinitely now. Mrs. Morales started worrying about Shaya being deprived socially, the same concerns my mother had about my sister. So now there's a three-year-old nonstop chattering as she plays with blocks on the floor while my sister rolls around next to her, busting Shaya's towers nearly every time with a precise whack of the hand. I do my homework on the coffee table, Lara often up on a tablet screen working on the same assignments as me.

Freddie and I naturally cooled off when more and more time started passing between us getting together. Part of me suspects he might have started talking to someone, but I'd be a hypocrite if I let my pangs of jealousy out in the open.

Crestonvale Square is still fairly well frequented, probably due to our latest provincial lockdown having just been lifted a couple of weeks ago. We came here last weekend for Beck Field Trip Day to watch people skate and enjoy the outdoor light shows, and my sister ended up sleeping the whole time because she just wasn't in the mood for it. That's when I realized what happened to Sweet Little Things. The sign is still up, but it's dark. Inside is empty, tables and chairs stacked and pushed against the wall.

[Lara] Is she there yet?

[Baylee] No. OMG I am so nervous. I feel like I'm going to puke.

[Lara] Take some deep breaths. Watch a couple TikToks. Calm the hell down.

[Baylee] You're making it worse.

[Lara] Should Rianne and I come?

[Baylee] OMG NO. I would literally pretend I don't know you.

"I guess we should start by paying our respects," Alex says.

She stands a few feet away from me, and we both lean against the fence, facing Sweet Little Things. Her hair is all one color now, her natural black-brown, and it's shaggier than I remember. She's wearing a black surgical mask.

"We should," I say.

"Sweet Little Things, the best banana split I've ever had."

"Sweet Little Things, the only time I've ever seen a banana split in real life," I say. "I can't believe this place closed."

"I know."

"Remember when we thought this would only last a couple weeks?"

She snorts. "This has been such a wild ride. And not in a good way. I have maskne."

"Really?" I ask. "Can I see?"

We face each other now, and given that we're outside, we remove our masks. Her cheek piercings are gone, nothing but perfect dimples left behind. There are no zits that I can see.

"Your face looks . . . great," I say.

"As does yours."

I've spent the last month trading DMs with Alex, taking it slow. She wouldn't meet with me until now, which I understand, but it hasn't been easy. I've been completely consumed by her internally, while treading carefully on the outside. There's no guarantee she'll feel anything for me again. But on my end, it's very clear where I stand. I have to steady myself from the rush of feelings and sensations moving through me with her being so close.

"Shall we take a walk?" she asks.

"Yes!"

My stomach rips itself up internally with a fresh somersault of anxiety.

"You want to hear something weird?" I ask, and she nods,

tipping her head sideways to meet my gaze. "My stomach does this thing when I'm nervous, like it's trying to eat itself. Can you hear it? It's so loud!"

She pretends to listen carefully. "I hear nothing."

"Oh, good."

"I pee a lot when I'm nervous."

"Really?"

"I have to pee really bad right now," she says.

"Really?" I flash her one of my coyest smiles, and she nods, that twinkle in her eye making an appearance. "That's really . . . sweet." The look she gives me sends vibrations through me.

"You have hand sanitizer, right?" she asks.

"Of course," I say. "Do you need some?"

She shakes her head and slips her mask back on, so I do the same. Then she walks up to me, reaching for my hand. My eyes rest on our fingers clutched together, totally in awe of the power a simple touch can have. My mask camouflages the over-the-top grin that pulls my lips wide, so I don't even need to reel it in.

All I can do right now is give the universe a bucket of gratitude for allowing this to come back and happen again.

ACKNOWLEDGMENTS

I have to start with my agent who has had my back since way back when, Linda Epstein. Your ongoing support, even during that ridiculous hospital-pandemic-critical-care time when I was convinced I'd never write again, has meant the world to me. The process is just a hell of a lot nicer with a fierce advocate by your side, and I thank you for being the person who protects my interests and gives me much-needed advice.

I am ever so grateful for my editing team. First, to Jill Davis: The relationship we built during the editing of *Girl Mans Up* is something I was really looking forward to continuing with *Then Everything Happens at Once*, but that, alas, wasn't meant to be. I am so grateful to your role championing *TEHAO*, setting everything in motion to ensure it became a real book. To Megan Ilnitzki (and Jenny Ly): I thank you for picking up *TEHAO* upon Jill's departure and for the assistance and insight you (both) provided to tease out the story I was trying to tell during the editing process. Your guidance led to this book that I'm unbelievably proud of—*the* book I wish I would've stumbled upon as a teenager.

A million thanks to HarperCollins for the support. I am so proud to be sending another book out into the world via Harper-Collins. To the entire team responsible for the cover of this book: I just can't say enough about how fabulous this book looks. Thank you to Joel Tippie (designer), Laura Harshberger and Mark Rifkin (managing ed), James Neel (production), Shannon Cox (marketing), Patty Rosati and team (school and library marketing), and Anna Ravenelle (publicity).

There were quite a few years between now and *Girl Mans Up*. Life (+ the pandemic) took me other places, and when I was ready to come back to writing, I found myself in a weird spot: My storytelling and writing skills had gone rusty, I hadn't read anything but emergency and critical care nursing stuff in quite literally years, and my writing community had shrunk tremendously (it was pretty much nonexistent). Having *Girl Mans Up* between my hands was an odd experience because I couldn't really believe that I was the author behind it anymore. I had some anchors, though, and through them, I was able to keep my connection to this world of writing. To my writing bestie Sharon Overend: Thank you for the insightful writing-related chats and for giving a read to an early draft of this story. Your presence and dedication to your own craft kept me tied to the writing world and got me excited about getting back into it. To Mindy McGinnis: I thank you for the amazing conversations and for taking the time to give an early draft a read. Your thoughts and comments grounded me at a time where I literally considered deleting the entire 90,000 words and starting over. To Laura Chandra: Even though we sort of headed on different paths, you were right there, ready and willing to provide me with a quick read and critique, just as you did with *Girl Mans Up*. I am super thankful for your loyalty and follow through.

I would like to acknowledge the readers of *Girl Mans Up* who have reached out to me along the way. I know I told many of you that your words to me sparked motivation as I sat in front of my computer, working on this new book. Hearing how important *Girl Mans Up* was (is) to you fed me creatively, and I cannot emphasize how vital that was (is) because a significant part of me, at that time, had already accepted I'd be a one-book author. Thank you all for taking the time to reach out to the authors of books you love. It is so important for us to hear from you, and your comments are so precious.

Special thanks to Adams Carvalho, the cover artist of *Girl Mans Up* who is now responsible for the cover art of *Then Everything Happens at Once*. It was my wish to go back to you for this cover, and I am completely in awe of Baylee on this cover. I am so grateful for your depiction of my main characters.

Some might wonder about my inclusion of Rebecca in this story, Baylee's little sister. As a pediatric community nurse, I worked many years with medically fragile, special-needs children—fourteen years, to be exact. Although I was nurse to many children over those fourteen years, only one was there from the start and followed me right through to the end (when I chose to change career paths and head for the hospital): Rebecca—or Miss Beckie, as I called her. There were many nights spent working on very early drafts of this story with Miss Beckie next to me, giggling all night and refusing to sleep for school the next day. When I put her in this story, it was with the intent of simply representing someone like her who might not see themselves cast in a literary role just for the sake of being there. The character had a different name and a different personality then. When Rebecca died in 2020, at the age of twenty-two, the Rebecca in my book became a memorial to her, a place where all my memories of her could live. I am every so grateful to her parents, Rick and Karen, for giving me permission to name my character after their daughter and essentially steal every single detail I have in my head about the Miss Beckie I spent fourteen years hanging around with—right down to the dirty looks, the ridiculous giggles, and that god-awful song about teddy bears going out for a picnic. Special thanks to Karen for being my sensitivity reader, because if anyone could read my story with a critical eye and provide me with feedback on Rebecca's portrayal, it was certainly Miss Beckie's mother.